The Crowded Shadows

In the shadows, Wari rolled ⸻⸻⸻⸻⸻⸻ lder as blood flowed out betwee⸻⸻⸻⸻⸻⸻⸻. At his feet, Razi lay pinned to ⸻⸻⸻⸻⸻⸻ him, its jaws clamped around hi⸻⸻⸻⸻⸻⸻ fur, gagged, and Wynter saw th⸻⸻⸻⸻⸻⸻ sure of the hound's teeth.

Across the fire, m⸻⸻⸻⸻⸻ly against stone as Christopher allowed his knife to drop from his hand. A second warhound stood over him, its teeth locked on his straining neck. Wynter lurched to her knees, not knowing which way to turn, and Christopher rolled terrified grey eyes to her, and held out his hand. *Do nothing! Do nothing!* Slowly he lowered his shaking hands to the ground, and he allowed his body to relax under the arch of the big dog's legs. To Wynter's relief, she saw the powerful jaws ease up slightly on Christopher's throat.

Razi gagged again, and a line of blood flowed around the taut curve of his neck as the hound's teeth punctured his skin.

"Brother," cried Wynter, "do not struggle." Razi stilled and Wynter saw him force himself to relax. His hands drifted to the ground. The warhound instantly eased its grip, and Wynter's eyes fluttered shut in momentary relief.

Ashkr edged forward, his sword up, his eyes on Wynter. He glanced at Wari as he passed him by, and asked something in Merron. Wari, still clutching his wounded shoulder, forced a reply through gritted teeth. Ashkr came around to kick Razi's sword into the bushes, and then stood looking down at him, his navy eyes cold.

He flicked a glance at Wynter. "Throw your weapon into bush," he said. Wynter blinked at him. He lifted his chin and the tip of his sword swung purposely to point at Razi's head. Wynter flung her travel-belt into the bushes.

The Crowded Shadows

Celine Kiernan

www.orbitbooks.net

ORBIT

First published in Ireland in 2009 by The O'Brien Press Ltd.
First published in Great Britain in 2010 by Orbit

A CIP catalogue record for this book
is available from the British Library.

ISBN 978-1-84149-822-5

Typeset in Garamond by M Rules
Printed and bound in Great Britain by
Clays Ltd, St Ives plc

Papers used by Orbit are natural, renewable and
recyclable products sourced from well-managed forests and certified
in accordance with the rules of the Forest Stewardship Council.

Mixed Sources
Product group from well-managed
forests and other controlled sources
www.fsc.org Cert no. SGS-COC-004081
© 1996 Forest Stewardship Council
FSC

Orbit
An imprint of
Little, Brown Book Group
100 Victoria Embankment
London EC4Y 0DY

An Hachette UK Company
www.hachette.co.uk

www.orbitbooks.co.uk

For Mam and Dad, I love you.
For Noel, Emmet and Grace, always and with all my heart.
For Fergus, Elaine, Luke and Karl.
Let's never stop lighting camp-fires and setting up tents.

Acknowledgements

With huge thanks to Svetlana Pironko of Author Rights Agency for her protection and guidance. A wonderful agent and friend. Also to my first publishers The O'Brien Press; in particular to Michael O'Brien for his fearlessness.

Many, many thanks to all at Little, Brown who have thrown themselves so enthusiastically into the Moorehawke experience. You guys have been amazing.

Many thanks and much love to Sorcha DeFrancesco (Ni Cuimín) and Phil Ó Cuimín who gifted me their beautiful conversational Irish, and to Gabriel Rosenstock for correcting my spelling and grammar. Any remaining mistakes are all down to my ignorance and are my fault entirely.

Thanks to Pat Mullan, whose kindness and generosity of spirit opened a door I had begun to think was locked for good. And always, thank you, Catherine and Roddy.

Contents

The Crowded Shadows

Wynter sank closer to Ozkar's neck and slowly dipped her head so that the dark brim of her hat hid her eyes. The horse side-stepped nervously under her and tried to back out of their hiding place. He could sense her fear and it was making him anxious. Wynter murmured to him and stroked his shoulder, but he shook his head, snorted and loudly stamped his foot.

The men moving in the trees ahead of her were getting close. Wynter tracked their progress by the noise of their horses, and she shrank further back into cover as the sounds grew louder. She could not believe how easily these men had escaped her attention. The trees here were so thick and dark that Wynter might never have noticed them, only that they had been foolish enough to light a pipe, and its rich tobacco scent had alerted her to their presence. It filled her with fear to realise that they may have been travelling parallel to each other for days and not known it, the sounds of the men's horses cancelling out the noises made by Ozkar and vice versa.

Wynter was just raising her head to peer though the

trees, hoping for a glimpse of them, when a low whistling signal from the road sent her ducking again, her heart racing. There was a moment of silence from the men, then they whistled a melodic reply, and to Wynter's horror, began pushing their horses through the brush towards her.

They came frighteningly close and she was filled with an almost irresistible desire to lift her head and look. But it would take just one careless movement and they would spot her, so she kept her eyes shut and her head down and the men passed slowly by.

They urged their horses down a steeply sloping bank and out of sight. Wynter side-stepped Ozkar so that she could observe their descent to the road.

She found herself looking down on the tops of their heads as they passed from the shade into brutal sunshine, and they came to a halt in the road, looking expectantly into the trees on the opposite side. Wynter followed their gaze, and ducked lower at the sight of four horsemen descending the far slope. As these newcomers reached the road, the original two men shook back their dark hats and uncovered their faces. They were Combermen, their rosined hair and beards glistening in the sun. They squinted warily at the newcomers and one of them called out in stilted Southlandast, the language of Jonathon's kingdom, "So far?"

The newcomers called back, "And not yet there?"

There was a general easing of tension in the men, and Wynter committed these passwords, and the whistles that had preceded them, to memory.

As the newcomers pulled to a halt, the shorter Comberman asked, "I take it we face the same direction?"

"Anything is possible," said one of the newcomers non-committally. They threw back their headgear, and Wynter felt a thrill of fear. They were Haunardii! Warriors, if their abundance of gleaming weaponry was anything to go by. She leant forward in her saddle, trying to get a better view. She had never personally met any Haunardii but they were notoriously savage and wily. Their narrow, slanting eyes were black as night and they regarded the Combermen scornfully, their flat, honey-coloured faces filled with laughing contempt.

"These men humbly suggest that you are not too sharp at keeping yourself hid," sneered the youngest. "What sort of fool needs a pipe of weed *that* much?"

The Combermen glanced at each other. The taller one bit his pipe firmly between his teeth and began to drift back to the trees. "Stick to thy side of the road and my smoke won't bother thee," he said with finality.

The Haunardii looked amused. They smirked at each other and began backing their horses away. It was obvious to Wynter that – like herself – all these men were travelling in secret, eschewing the relative ease of the road for the cover of the thick forest, and it appeared that the Haun's sole purpose in calling the others had been to mock them for their carelessness. As they retreated, the youngest laughingly said, "We pray that it is not your stealth you are offering at the table of the Rebel Prince!"

The Rebel Prince? thought Wynter. *Alberon!* She stared down at the men below. *So you are gathering allies to your table. But, good Christ, Alberon! First Combermen, and now Haunardii? Have you lost your mind?*

Down on the road, the young Haunardii was still

needling the Combermen, his mocking voice drifting up through the heat. "We humbly suggest you may as well dance down the centre of the road yodelling, for all the sly you have exhibited up in the trees."

"Yes, well," growled the shorter Comberman, "thy skills in diplomacy will be a great asset to the future king, I dare say. Sleep well these next twelve nights, Haun, and have no doubt, we'll see *thee* in camp."

The Combermen were ascending the slope even as they spoke and Wynter eased Ozkar back into the deeper shadows, listening as they snarled their goodbyes. The Combermen angled off through the trees, trailing pipe smoke and muttering as they went. The Haunardii must have climbed the opposite slope and melted into the forest there.

Wynter stayed where she was, deep in thought, and Ozkar returned to snoozing beneath her.

Was it possible, she wondered, that the King had been right? Did Alberon actually intend to overthrow the crown? The thought of Alberon in alliance with either the Haunardii or the Combermen made Wynter's blood run cold. Did he really stand against his father now, with greedy expansionists on one hand and bigoted zealots on the other? What would become of the kingdom if this were the case, and what kind of reception could Wynter expect from her old friend if he had truly set his face against the King?

She looked out into the forest and thought about the Haun and the Combermen, and all they symbolised. If it came down to it, and she had to weigh them on one hand, and King Jonathon on the other – Alberon or no Alberon – Wynter had no doubt who she would choose. She shook her head and looked around her helplessly. She did not want to think about the kind of choices she may now have to make. Despair threatened suddenly, out of nowhere, and Wynter sat up straight, forcing it down.

That is enough, she told herself firmly. *There is no point fretting until I have found Alberon and discovered the truth. Then we shall see, all this will be easily resolved.* Grimly, she set her jaw. She had sacrificed her father for this quest, she was risking her own life for it, and she was not about to fail.

The forest was now tranquil and seemingly empty of human traffic, so Wynter gave up her cautious vigil and slid from Ozkar's back. Wearily, she leant against his neck for a moment and let her head settle. They'd been travelling since just before dawn, and it was time for them both to rest. It would be safest to rest further up the hill, but first Wynter had to replenish her water supply. She decided to risk using the stream by the road to fill the waterskins. God only knew when she'd get another chance to restock.

As she undid the ties, Ozkar snuffled at her and lipped her tunic, looking for food. Wynter pushed his head away in exhausted irritation. He was rationed to one loaf of horse-bread morning and night, and it was more than enough for him, even at this hard pace. Mind you, as far as Wynter was concerned, he could *have* it, all of it. After five days' travel she was heartily sick of horse-bread, cheese and dried sausage. Even when soaked, the coarse bean bread was a trial to the teeth, and a torment to the bowels.

What I would not pay for a plate of liver and onions, she thought as she slung the waterskins over both arms and dropped to her hands and knees. *Or, oh God bless us, a strawberry cordial . . . or apple pie and clotted cream.* She began to slither cautiously down the hill on her belly. Her ears and eyes focused on her surroundings, her heart and stomach dreaming of food.

She reached the edge of the undergrowth and peered down at the shallow little stream bubbling its way along the bottom of the ditch. Wynter knew that with her face covered she was just another dark patch in the shifting shadows. Still, she kept her body carefully motionless as she stretched her arm down to the stream and submerged the first waterskin. It began to fill slowly and Wynter laid her cheek on the bank and scanned the road while she waited.

The first waterskin full, she was just about to submerge the second one when the sound of hooves came pounding up through the turf. She jerked back her hand and pressed into the shadows as a horse galloped past.

It was a merchantman, of middling income by the looks of him, leading a fully laden pack-mule. He was travelling much too fast for the animal's bulky load and he kept glancing behind him in a panic. Wynter regarded him with a heavy heart and wondered what the hell he had expected, travelling alone on this road. He had not even had the sense to disguise his expensive tack or the fine quality of his clothes.

There were two pursuers, galloping fast and riding low to their saddles. They quickly caught up with their quarry, flanking the pack-mule like wolves and closing in on the merchant. As he galloped past, the bandit on his left hauled back with a staff and unhorsed the merchant with a wide swing to his head.

The merchant's bright hat sailed through the air and rolled into the ditch across from Wynter. The man himself fell between the horses and was left behind in the dust as the bandits shot forward to corral his goods.

Wynter couldn't take her eyes from the merchant as he lay on his back in the road. He was utterly dazed, his face covered in dust, a thin stream of blood pooling beneath his head. She heard the bandits capture and turn his horses, and she knew for certain what this poor man's fate would be. She dipped her chin and clenched her hands as the bandits trotted into view.

One of them, the fellow with the staff, dropped lightly from the saddle and jogged to where the merchant lay. As the bandit approached him, Wynter saw the merchant raise a gloved hand to the sky, his eyes questing. He seemed to have no grasp of his situation. The bandit raised his staff high and Wynter squeezed her eyes shut as he brought it down onto the merchant's face.

There were not many blows after that and Wynter lay very still and quiet, her face hidden in her hands, while the bandits stripped the body. They chatted amiably as they went about their business, obviously well used to each other and comfortably at ease with their work. There was much talk of the inn, and of Jenny, and of which of them she liked more. There was speculation as to how much they'd get for this haul. They came to the conclusion that they should get quite a bit. Perhaps so much that Jenny might even like them both at once, if they played their cards right. There was a lot of good-natured chuckling, and Wynter pressed her fingers hard into her temples and bit her lips.

Finally, their voices moved back in the direction of the horses and Wynter risked turning her head and looking at the merchant.

The bandits had carried him to the side of the road and laid him neatly at the base of a tree, as though politely disinclined to block traffic. He was curled on his side with his back to her, and once she'd looked at him, Wynter found it impossible to look away. This was somebody's father maybe, somebody's son. Until a few moments ago, he had been alive and breathing, full of thoughts and plans. And now he was nothing but meat, cast aside and abandoned, carrion for the badgers and the foxes, with his family never to know what became of him.

That could be me, thought Wynter, *snuffed out and gone in the blink of an eye.*

Suddenly the bandit with the staff came back into view. He walked to the side of the road, knelt and leant into the ditch across from Wynter, stretching to reach something far in the brambles. He sat back, grinning, and displayed the merchant's hat for his companion to see.

Wynter should have dipped her head, but she was filled with such hatred for him at that moment that she just watched as the bandit knelt there and whacked the hat off his knee to dislodge the dust.

He was about to get to his feet when he lifted his eyes and spotted her in the shelter of the brambles. Wynter saw him blink under the shade of his hat, saw him frown and her heart froze as he rose slowly to his feet, squinting into the shadows where she lay, his face uncertain.

"What is it?" asked his companion, who was already mounted and ready to go.

The man didn't answer. Instead, he crossed the road and hunkered down in front of Wynter's hiding place, gazing across the dancing brightness of the water and staring straight into her eyes.

Everything Wynter had ever been taught, everything she knew she should do in such a situation, fell out of her head. To her absolute horror and dismay, she just lay there, frozen and helpless, as the man took his time looking her up and down.

His eyes travelled the length of her and she saw him register her curves and hollows, her distinctively womanish shape. When his eyes came back up to meet hers, they were calculating and hot. He bared his teeth, and Wynter felt a shrivelling, horrible fear in her belly at the hunger in his grin.

"Oy! Tosh!" called his companion. "What is it?" He had pulled his horse around and Wynter could hear him starting to drift towards them.

The bandit stood and waved him back. "Nothin'," he said, strolling casually back to the horses. "Nothin' but a badger hole! I thought 'twas a person lying there! Sun must a got into my head!"

A wave of nauseating relief washed over her, and Wynter clamped her hand over her mouth, certain that she was going to vomit. As the bandit remounted his horse she heard him say, "Lookit, Peter. Once we settle a price with Silent Murk, you go on ahead and take Jenny to yourself tonight. I got some business of my own to tend to."

"Business?" cried his friend in disbelief. "Instead of Jenny . . . ? What kind of business?"

"Ach, naught interestin'. Just fancy a bit of huntin' is all."

"Huntin'?" echoed the other man, clearly baffled. "Instead of Jenny? Tosh, I ain't complainin', God knows! But are you mad?"

The bandit chuckled. They began to trot away, but before they got out of earshot, Wynter heard his good-natured reply.

"I ain't mad," he said amiably. "I just find myself with a sudden craving for fresh meat. That's all." And he laughed again, a warm laugh that made Wynter tremble and her throat close over with fear.

Travelling Alone

After a while Ozkar began to stumble, but still Wynter drove him mercilessly on and on. She had lost all sense of stealth or caution, and simply shoved forward through the heat and dust, hardly paying heed to her direction, only striving to get away.

Her father had taught her well about travelling alone, and up until this moment Wynter had conscientiously followed all the advice he'd ever given. She had been disciplined, she had been careful and she had been totally in control. Now, panicked beyond reason, Wynter fled through the sweltering heat of midday with nothing on her mind but that man's hot eyes and the fear that he might someday look at her again.

All the things Lorcan had ever taught her about self-defence swam incoherently through her mind. *Your thumbs hard into his eyes. Your knee or your fist to his balls, the heel of your boot to the tops of his feet.* All of his detailed instructions, should a man ever try and assault her, repeated endlessly in her head. *Do not turn your back unless he's incapacitated. If he is incapacitated, then run like hell to the nearest population. If you are alone and with no hope of company, kill him where he lies. Stamp on his head. Gouge out his eyes. Slit his groin or his throat.* Wynter had heard this so many times – Lorcan's unflinching list of ways to keep her alive and her enemies powerless or dead. And most important of all, the one thing he had told her over and over. *Fear will paralyse you, baby-girl. Fear will kill you. You must not let fear win. If it wins, you've lost the fight.*

Well, there was no doubt but that she had lost the fight down by the stream. When that man had looked at her across the glittering light of the water, Wynter had quailed like a cornered rabbit and she had been filled with nothing but fear. Fear had won. That man had won. Had he chosen that time to strike, Wynter would have been useless against him. He and his companion would have taken her as easy as picking berries from a bush.

Ozkar stumbled and Wynter kicked him on, her teeth bared. She would keep going for ever, she would never stop moving. The thought of stopping now, anywhere near that man, and the possibility that he might be able to find her, filled Wynter with terror.

The memory of Christopher rose up suddenly, sharp and clear and unexpected; his quick smiling eyes and his grin, his reckless bravery. *Christopher!* she thought, with genuine grief, *Christopher!* How could she miss him so much when she hardly knew him? But she did. She missed him and she admired him, both for his bravery and for his laughter in the face of all that had been taken from him. *Not like you!* she thought bitterly. *Nothing was even taken from you! Nothing done to you but a look cast your way. And you are destroyed by it! You snivelling coward. You big baby!*

Wynter pulled back with a silent, self-loathing grimace and hauled on the reins. Ozkar came to a relieved halt and stood panting, his head down. The heat pressed around them, and Wynter, crouched in her saddle, listened for sounds of pursuit. Apart from the incessant singing of insects, the forest was silent and still.

Breathing deeply, Wynter straightened and pressed her hand to her chest, urging her heart to calm itself. Razi's note whispered against her palm. Her guild pendant settled against her breast. The forest slumbered placidly around her. She laughed. *All right then*, she thought shakily. *All right. That's over.*

Without wasting any more time, Wynter turned Ozkar and urged him up the hill. She let him carry her far into the high trees, and there she quickly chose a site, slipped from the saddle, and set up camp.

Within half an hour Ozkar was fed and watered, rubbed down and tethered, contentedly snoozing against a tree. Tiredly, Wynter crawled under her bivouac. She lay with her head on her saddle, looking up into the light spattered canvas, and she tried to empty her mind of everything but the calm buzz of the forest. She said a prayer for Lorcan, a prayer for Razi and a heartfelt prayer for Christopher, wherever he might be. Sleep claimed her suddenly, a dark abyss opening soundless and vast, and sucked her under without warning.

Thunder cracked in the sky above the trees and Wynter startled at the sound, trying to get her bearings. She was lying on her back beneath the shelter. It was almost dark. She must have been sleeping for hours. The air was heavy with storm heat, the small space under the canvas steamy and too close, and she was glad that she had made an open-sided shelter. Blinking, she turned her head to stare out into the clearing, waiting for her eyes to adjust.

Lorcan was standing in the forest by her camp, anxiously scanning the dark trees. "Listen," he said.

Wynter swallowed at the sight of him glimmering there in the twilight. "Dad," she whispered. "I'm scared."

Lorcan tutted and shook his head. "I've done all I can about that," he said firmly. "You're on your own now, baby-girl." He glowered out into the darkness. "There are Wolves out there," he said. "They're coming."

"Dad," she pleaded, but Lorcan had drifted away already, his white shirt a pale shape in the lowering gloom. He looked back at her, his features indistinct, and put his finger to his lips.

Wynter cried out as lightning imprinted the trees against the canvas of her tent, and she came fully awake to the sound of thunder booming directly overhead. Ozkar whickered unhappily, and she heard him stamp his foot and shift in fear, pulling against his tether. She turned her head sharply as something moved in the not-quite-dark of the woods.

The bandit was standing just within the circle of trees, hardly fifteen feet from where she lay. He stood sideways on to her, a thick staff balanced in his hand, watching her through the open side of her shelter. He must have seen her eyes gleaming in the dusk because he settled his grip on the staff and grinned at her, his teeth flashing in the shadows.

"Don't worry," he said softly. "It's just me . . . you left me a lovely trail. Very considerate."

Wynter lay still as a mouse and watched as he sidled across the clearing, the staff held out from his side. Lightning flickered briefly again, and Wynter clearly saw a knife in his other hand. There was a moment of blindness after the flash, then Wynter's night vision cleared and the man was standing beside the shelter, looking down at her. His grin had disappeared and his face was wary.

"Now," he said. "I won't hurt you. Understand?" He sank to his knees, his staff held up, the knife held lightly in his other hand. His eyes were locked on Wynter's and his head was tilted back slightly. His voice was low, as if talking to a snarling dog. "You give me what I want, and I won't hurt you. All right?"

Wynter said nothing and did not move.

He knelt there for a moment, assessing her intentions. Then he let his eyes slip down her body, lingering on her breasts, dropping between her legs, running back up to her breasts again. Wynter saw his face become heavy, and his lips parted. He looked her in the eyes again and let her see the knife.

Then he stooped in under the tent.

Wynter waited until he lifted his leg, meaning to straddle her, then she punched *hard* between his legs. The air left him in a soundless wheeze and, as he doubled over, Wynter threw her head forward and butted him between the eyes. Blood gushed from his smashed nose and Wynter drew up her feet and kicked him in the chest, sending him rolling out from under the canvas.

She dived after him, scrabbling for her knife, hoping to kill him while he was still incapacitated. But he must have had the constitution of an ox because he instantly rolled to his feet, his knife raised, his free hand pressed to his groin. Wynter met his eyes, and they told her everything she needed to know about her fate should she allow this man get the better of her. Behind them, Ozkar lunged and heaved and kicked, struggling to free himself from his tether. Lightning seared the sky and thunder roared.

Slowly Wynter rose to face the bandit. His attention dropped to the knife in her hand, and he grinned through the blood that drenched his mouth.

"You drop that potato peeler now, girl, or I'll lose my temper."

Wynter brought the knife up. She crouched in readiness. "Leave now," she said, "and I'll allow you keep your manhood."

The bandit's face darkened with cruel amusement. Knife or no knife, he knew Wynter had little hope against him. He was heavier, taller, stronger than she, and probably well accustomed to fighting men of his own size.

"Come on now," he crooned. "Let's be friends."

Wynter held her ground, and the bandit laughed. Lightning flickered silently again, and Ozkar stamped and threw his head against his tether, backing up as the rope stretched to its limit. The bandit lunged, and Wynter flung herself forward, her knife low and ready to strike.

They collided. The bandit caught her knife hand and mercilessly twisted her wrist. Wynter turned with the pressure, saving herself from a broken arm, but her fingers went instantly numb and her knife tumbled to the leaves. Still, she wouldn't submit, and the bandit had to struggle to keep a hold on her as she thrashed and kicked and bit. Cursing, he shifted his grip. He grabbed her hair, yanking her head back in a flash of blinding pain. Wynter saw his fist raised against the sky. This blow would knock her senseless. *I am lost!* she thought.

A huge shape emerged from the dark and Wynter was jerked from the man's grip. She fell, slamming into the leaves, the breath knocked from her as the great thing loomed above them. The bandit spun, looking up into living darkness, lifting his arms. Then he was catapulted through the air, to land with a loud thud on the other side of the clearing.

Wynter scrambled for her lost knife, ready to defend herself against this new threat. Then the warm smell of horse filled her nose and she realised that it was Ozkar who was looming above her, stamping and pawing in the dark. Wynter fell back onto the cold ground, overcome with relief as the horse stood by, his great, strong body a living shield between her and the man that he had just kicked into unconsciousness. "Good boy!" she rasped. "Oh, good boy, Ozkar. Good boy!"

She dragged herself up by the frayed end of his tether. All the time repeating that he was *A good boy. Such a good boy.* She couldn't seem to stop saying it, and she couldn't seem to let him go.

She packed her camp with one hand knotted in his tangled mane, always keeping him between herself and the crumpled body lying amongst the shadows of the trees. When it came time to leave she couldn't bring herself to take to the saddle. She found herself afraid to raise herself above the level of the horse's neck. She had this horrible fear that if she did, the bandit would leap through the air and tackle her, bringing her finally and irretrievably to the ground. So she walked from the campsite, keeping Ozkar solidly between herself and the bandit. And it was only when the clearing was far from her sight, far from earshot, that she managed to break her death grip on the horse's mane and heave herself into the saddle.

The Mourning Pennant

The trail gradually levelled off as Wynter rode into the long, nameless valley that her map had prepared her for. She expected to reach a river sometime around midday. She planned to follow the river's course for the next six or seven days, until she got to the Orange Cow Inn, and then she would begin to climb again, further into the mountains and up towards the Indirie Valley and, hopefully, Alberon's camp.

Ozkar was much happier on this even ground. He had been finding the steep slope more and more difficult to cope with, and Wynter could sense his relief as her position in the saddle gave him less discomfort and his legs better shared the burden of her weight. Wynter was glad for him, but she did not like the way the trees were thinning out here. The heavy pines of before had been a marvellous cover, but these long-trunked, light-foliaged species were not so dense and it was going to be harder, soon, to stay out of sight.

It had been two and a half days since the bandit had attacked, and she was now thoroughly back in control of her waking hours. During the day, she was disciplined and careful, calmly in command of all she did. Her nights, however, were a different story. Every night the bandit found her again and tormented her in her dreams, and every morning Wynter woke weighed down by fatigue, her thoughts mired in a thick slime of exhaustion.

And then there were thoughts of her father. Sometimes, the rhythm of the horse would lull her into a numb trance and Wynter would find herself with silent tears rolling down her face, thinking of him. She missed Lorcan so badly that it was like a toothache. Her grief for him slithered under her defences at any opportunity, and she could not help, sometimes, but think on how lonely he must be, and how she had not said all the things she had wanted to him on their last day together. Those things would probably never be said now, except as useless whispers over a lovely man's grave, and what comfort was that?

These regrets had once again begun to gnaw at Wynter when the sound of horses intruded on her thoughts. She pulled Ozkar to a wary halt and listened. They were still quite a way off, a large group, travelling fast and hard on the road. Whoever they were, these men had no fear and seemed to feel no need for stealth.

Wynter slid from her saddle and tethered Ozkar to a birch sapling.

"Stay easy," she told him softly, patting his nose. Then she crouched low and ran through the trees, hoping to make the road and get a good look before the men passed by.

She made it just in time, diving under the brush by the side of the road as an impressive body of horsemen came galloping around the bend. It was a squad of Jonathon's marvellous cavalry. At their head, three of the King's own personal guard loomed huge and imposing on their chargers.

All the men were fully armed and wearing their colours. Sitting erect and noble in their saddles, their heads held high, their faces covered against the dust, they were utterly magnificent. They thundered towards her, and Wynter laughed with joy as the vibration bounced her up and down like a pebble in a bucket.

Then she caught sight of the pennants, and the laughter died in her throat. They were flying at half-mast, and all of them were dyed black. Wynter looked from man to man, and noted with despair the fluttering triangle of black cloth that each of them wore on their right shoulder. The plumes that flowed from their nasal helms were also dyed black and bent in two so that they hung down the men's backs like horses' tails.

These men were in mourning, all flying the traditional mourning pennants, all wearing the official trappings of courtly grief. That could mean only one thing. There had been a death in the royal family. Alberon, or Jonathon or Razi: one of them was dead. For no other person, not even her father, would warrant the flying of a black flag or the breaking of the cavalry plume.

Wynter lay on the jouncing ground, pebbles and dust jittering around her, and stared as the streaming banners passed her by. The horses carried on up the road, leaving the air heavy with yellow dust, and Wynter stood up out of hiding. She stepped from the bushes, watching the last of their numbers round the corner and out of sight.

A royal death, she thought. *A royal death. But who? Not Razi! And not Albi either! And, oh God . . . what will become of us if Jonathon is dead?*

What should she do now?

She stood in the blazing sunshine, the dust settling slowly around her, and stared at the empty road. All around her, the forest slowly recovered from the shock of the men's passage. Little birds began to sing in the bushes, while Wynter's thoughts raced around each other like dogs. *Oh Razi*, she thought suddenly, speared with her first real pang of grief since she'd seen the flags. *Oh my brother, oh friend. Do not let it be you!* And she knew at once that this was the truth, she knew, with absolute certainty and guilt that, of all of them, it was Razi she could not bear to lose.

All this ran as a feverish undercurrent to the overwhelming dilemma of what Wynter's next step should be. She was almost exactly halfway to Alberon's camp. In light of the mourning pennants, would it be better for her to continue onward as she was doing now, or would it make more sense for her to return home and find out for whom the pennants flew?

Without taking any conscious decision, Wynter continued her onward progress. And so she found herself at midday gazing across the wide expanse of the river which would lead her through this valley to the Orange Cow Inn and from there to Alberon's camp.

She frowned out across the sluggish green water, then laughed. So! While her mind had run itself in knots, her heart had led her here. Alberon it was then. She turned Ozkar's head east and kicked him forward. Another hour, that was all, she'd travel one more hour and then they would rest. She fished a handful of nuts from the pouch on her travel-belt and chewed thoughtfully as she drove Ozkar on.

Not So Easy
When There's Two

I t was, in fact, five hours later when Wynter slipped from her horse. And even then, it was only because she could hear activity in the trees ahead. The day was sinking into its lazy, golden decline, and the woods were full of dusty beams of light. Wynter stood quietly, her hand on Ozkar's neck, and listened.

She recognised the unmistakable sound of a camp being set up. Across the still evening air she could hear the hammering of stakes, the sawing and chopping of firewood and the occasional whinny of horses. The smell of camp-fire came drifting through the trees. This was quite a large group, at least ten men, maybe more. *Good Christ*, she thought, *I've been in less crowded fairgrounds than this forest. Alberon must be sending engraved invitations.*

She patted Ozkar's shoulder and scrubbed absently between his ears while she pondered her options. It was more than likely that this was the cavalry settling down for the night. If that were the case, she wondered if she might not just ride straight into camp and ask what their business was. She had no fear of the cavalry themselves – her father commanded a lot of respect with that fine body of men – but Jonathon's three guards gave her pause for thought. If Jonathon were dead, where would their allegiance lie? If they were loyal to some faction or another unknown to Wynter, how might they react to the King's Protector Lady riding into camp and demanding information? On the other hand, if it were Albi who was dead, and they were here to search for his supporters, how would it look? The Protector Lady, wandering about in a forest swarming with suspected rebels.

And then again, what if this was not the cavalry at all, but some group of as yet unknown protagonists in Alberon's complex dealings.

Wynter sighed and ran her hand over her face. Could nothing be simple? *All right*, she decided. *I'll go have a look, then make my decision.*

She regretted having to leave Ozkar saddled up, but she promised him that as soon as she had satisfied her curiosity they would camp for the night. With a last fond scrub between his eyes, she tethered him to a long line and ran in the direction of the sounds.

It rapidly became clear that this site had been very well chosen. It would be next to impossible to get close without being seen. Wynter came to a frustrated halt, her back against a broad oak. The sounds from the camp were much clearer now, and she could occasionally hear men calling to each other in what sounded very much like Hadrish. This was not the cavalry.

She listened for a while, but was still too far away to make out anything of use. The ground sloped up to the south of camp, and Wynter skirted around behind this small rise to see if she could get a vantage point.

Once behind the hill, she dropped to the ground and scurried under cover. The camp was just over the rise, and she could clearly hear the men talking as they set up their tents. Peering up through the branches of her hiding place, Wynter took her time, looking for sentries. She would have to be very sly breasting that hill. There was little vegetation up there and she would be easily seen if she wasn't careful.

A good four or five minutes passed with no sign of a lookout, so Wynter took a deep breath, covered her face to blend into the shadows, and eased out from hiding. Slowly belly-crawling up the leaf strewn slope, she thanked God for the recent rain. Without it, this hill would have been a noisy crackling hell of dry leaf litter. As it was, it was still just damp enough to make no noise as she slithered upwards.

Halfway up the hill, a small sound froze her in place. Dropping her head, Wynter lay motionless for a moment, then turned her cheek into the ground and glanced in the direction of the noise. It took her a moment to find him, and when she did he was so close that she had to bite back a cry of shock. A darkly clad man, less than ten feet from her, quietly crawling through the vegetation to her right. His attention was focused upwards and he had not yet seen her.

Swallowing dryly, she began to ease herself backwards. With any luck, the man would just keep going and she would be able to sneak away through the woods before he knew she was there.

A sharp hiss from above stilled Wynter, and she snapped her head up to see another man, almost at the brow of the hill. He pointed Wynter out, and there was a flurry of movement beside her as the first man rolled and drew his knife. She didn't even bother to look at him. She just scurried backwards until she got to the bottom of the hill, then got her legs under her and ran as fast as possible towards Ozkar.

It was obvious that these men couldn't afford to make any noise, and the silent, wolfish way they rolled to their feet at the base of the hill and took off after her through the trees caused the hair to rise on the back of Wynter's neck. She made no attempt to stay low, only ran at full tilt, her arms and legs pumping, trying to get as much distance between herself and the camp before turning and facing her pursuers.

Her mind was screaming at her. *Don't turn your back! Don't turn your back! Turn and fight! If they get you on the ground, you're dead!* But she couldn't seem to stop her arms and legs from churning and she felt her eyes beginning to start from their sockets. *Oh Christ!* she thought. *There's two of them. What am I going to do?*

She could hear them dashing through the bushes behind her. They had split and were attempting to flank her, one of them coming up very fast in a wide encompassing circle, while his companion gained on her from behind. They were hoping to cut her off and bring her down together.

She was beginning to lose her breath and she realised with a stab of despair that she wasn't going to make it back to Ozkar. As she ran, she unsheathed her knife and zigged left to put more space between herself and the fast-paced man who was trying to cut off her escape. She dodged around a thick patch of bramble and lost sight of him. The fellow behind her was very close. She could hear him smashing through a bush, only yards away now.

She dodged again, leaping a deadfall, and cut left once more, putting even more space between herself and the man to her right. For the moment, it was just herself and the fellow behind her. She might have a chance if she could stop this desperate forward run and turn to face him, get him while he was alone, and slit him quickly, before she grew too tired to fight.

Still her pursuers maintained their silence. The only thing audible was the whisper of their feet in the leaf litter and the brief shushing rustle when one or the other of them leapt through a bush.

Up ahead, the ground rose sharply into a steep bank topped with the long body of a fallen tree. Wynter sped towards this slope, hoping to give herself an advantage over the man behind her. She could taste blood on her breath. She was running out of energy; it was now or never.

Lorcan's voice spoke loud and calm in her head, *Keep your knife low, darling, and strike upwards, just like I taught you. Remember?* As she skidded to a sudden halt she pressed her arm straight down, holding her knife against her thigh, exactly as Lorcan had said. Wynter spun to face her attacker, just as he launched himself through the air to tackle her.

She was on the ground before she knew it, slamming backwards, all the air driven from her, and the man's considerable weight bore down on top of her as he tried to press her into submission. She was stunned for a moment, and he had the chance to straddle her and bring his arm down hard across her windpipe. He was hot and panting, incredibly strong and smelling of sharp sweat and horse. Fear clenched Wynter's heart as all the nightmares of the previous three nights flooded her mind.

She jerked her knife upwards, turning her head as she did so. As the blade came slicing up between the man's legs, Wynter found herself glaring triumphantly into a pair of brown eyes shot through with gold flecks.

Razi jerked and made a sharp little *guh* as her knife came up into his groin. Wynter froze with a cry. She had no idea whether or not she'd cut him. Before she could do anything, there was a *thud* above her and a wild scattering of leaves as the second man leapt the dead tree and slithered down the hill.

Razi lifted his eyes to the new arrival and grated out a hoarse, "*Don't!*"

Wynter hardly dared to hope. She turned her head to look up into the masked face of the man sliding into place beside her, and whispered, "Christopher?"

Christopher's knife was already pressed to her throat. As he registered her voice, his fury changed to shock and he jerked the blade away from her neck. He lay still for a moment, as though not trusting his eyes. Then he gently pulled the scarf from her face. Wynter couldn't help but smile as his clear grey eyes creased up in joy.

"Razi," he said. "You've finally apprehended the scoundrel who stole my coat."

Razi, still frozen in place, huffed dryly. "Oh aye," he said, "though I think the scoundrel may well have apprehended *me*. Wynter? Could you perhaps . . .?"

Wynter laughed as Christopher leant forward to look between herself and Razi. He squinted theatrically, as though peering down a rabbit hole, and raised an eyebrow at the position of her knife. "Oh my . . ." he breathed. "Tell you what, Razi, swap places, will you? I do so love a woman who knows what to do with her hands."

Company

"*G*ood God . . ." Razi's stunned voice trailed off into muttered Arabic.

Wynter put her hand over her mouth, torn between laughter and apology. Her friend was sitting on the leafy slope, his long legs splayed, his body hunched as he examined the slit her knife had left in the crotch of his trousers. Christopher was kneeling by his side. Wary of the nearby camp, they spoke in hushed tones.

"Good *God*." Razi held the torn fabric apart and gaped at the long shallow cut high on the inside of his thigh. "Wynter! You almost gelded me!"

Christopher chortled. Razi turned to him in wounded dismay, and Christopher turned his palms up in apology, trying to swallow his laughter. "Sorry, friend! I don't know what's wrong with me. I can't . . ." He started laughing again and had to turn his head so that Razi's hurt look wouldn't push him over the edge entirely. "After all," he chuckled, getting himself under some control. "It ain't like we were playing patty-cakes. We were fully intent on slitting the poor woman's throat."

This bald truth stunned them all into silence and stole the smile that had begun to creep into Razi's face. They'd all come so close. One small slip of blade or hand and any one of them could have inflicted real harm on someone they loved.

Wynter swallowed hard. "Chance would have been a fine thing, Christopher Garron," she said softly. "You being such clay-footed creatures, and so timid in battle. Be grateful I decided to take mercy on you, and thank your gods that I do not demand your eternal obsequience as tribute."

Christopher gave her a shaky smile. "What are you doing here, girly?" he asked, his eyes grave.

Razi pressed his hand against his thigh and stared at Wynter for a moment, then he rose abruptly to his feet. "Let's save all that," he said. "We need to get some distance between us and them." He began to pick his way down the slope, grousing as he did. "Good God, Wynter Moorehawke, if this cut rubs against my saddle, I shall tan your hide."

"Don't you want to see who they are, Razi?" she said, leaping to her feet. She had to restrain herself from taking his arm as though he had lost the leg entirely and needed her support. Truth be told, she wanted to fling her arms around the two men and squeeze them both until their heads popped off. Razi was already limping away and Christopher was gazing anxiously in the direction of the camp, his posture tight.

Razi gestured for her to catch up. "Come on," he grunted. "We can check on them tomorrow. Let's get some distance."

Wynter realised that he was trying to take her away from

the men in camp and get her to safety, and she was instantly filled with impatience. This struck her as so utterly funny that she grinned. Would they ever, *ever* change?

"Razi!" she said, laughing.

"*What?*" He turned to look at her, flinging his hands out in exasperation, still backing resolutely away from the camp.

"My horse is this way!"

Razi gritted his teeth, turned sharply without pause and stalked away in the direction she had pointed. Christopher chuckled and she heard his light footsteps as he jogged to catch up.

They gathered up the horses and put a good thirty minutes' ride behind them before setting up their camp. It was falling rapidly to dusk, and they set about their work with maximum efficiency and minimum talk.

The men didn't seem to be bothered with bivouacs so Wynter didn't unpack hers. It would be a hot night; a groundsheet and cloak would do. Like Wynter, they were camping cold, so there was no fire. Instead, Christopher combined their supplies and set about soaking some horse-bread in a small pot. He added spices and dried fish and shaved an apple into it as Wynter and Razi tended to the horses.

Razi kept looking at her as they were working. She smiled at him, but he just tightened his jaw and turned his face back to the horses. Wynter felt a knot of tension tighten in her chest and she tried not to get angry before she had any good reason to.

By the time they were done, Christopher was finished

laying out their bedrolls. He had arranged them in a loose triangle in the small clearing, with the pot at its centre where a fire would normally be.

"Wash yourself first," he said, pointing to a copper bowl full of water that he'd set aside for them.

Wynter stood back to allow Razi first go, but he gestured that she go ahead while he undressed. It was so delicious to wash herself with water that she longed to strip and plunge headfirst into the bowl, but she satisfied herself with scrubbing her face and neck and arms to the shoulder, then stood aside to dry herself while Razi gave himself a good wash.

Once dry, Wynter stood for a moment, her tunic dangling from her hand, and closed her eyes. For the first time in six days she felt safe enough just to stand and breathe, to let the world drift off while she took her ease. Her body was utterly spent, her head stuffed with thistledown, and she was certain she would sleep like the dead tonight.

She opened her eyes to find both men staring at her. Razi, drying his neck, glared at her from angry eyes. Christopher crouched expressionless by the pot. Wynter lifted her chin. "It would appear that you two got lost on your journeys to Italy and the Moroccos," she said. "How fortunate that you happened to meet up. What a tremendous coincidence that you both ended up here."

Christopher lowered his eyes and went back to stirring the food.

Razi continued to glare. "Did you leave your father alone?" he asked flatly.

Wynter's heart dropped, and her eyes flew to Christopher, whose head shot up at the question. He stared at her, his spoon poised over the bean mush.

For one shameful moment, looking into Christopher's wide eyes, Wynter was tempted to lie. She was sorely, *sorely* tempted to say that she had stayed with Lorcan to the end, and only left him when it was too late to do more. But instead, she just nodded. Christopher dropped his eyes in sorrow and disbelief.

"You . . .? After all that man has *done?*" Razi's voice was low and cold, and Wynter burned under his terrible disappointment in her. "How could you, Wynter? How could you abandon him like that?"

"Leave her be, Razi," commanded Christopher softly. "We *all* abandoned Lorcan." He lifted his eyes to meet those of his friend. "And all for the same bloody reason. So leave her alone, and come sit for your meal."

Razi deflated at the quiet bitterness in his friend's voice. Wynter smiled gently at him. He looked away, nodded and crossed to hunch down by the food pot.

They ate their fill in silence, then Christopher covered the remaining food and put it aside for breakfast. "Bloody beans," he grumbled. "My gas could fill a swamp."

Razi went to scour their bowls while Christopher carefully split an apple in three. "Here," he said, holding Wynter's segment out to her. She reached for it and their eyes met. "Are you all right?" he asked.

She nodded gratefully. "Aye."

He looked her up and down uncertainly, released her portion of the apple and looked away. Razi returned and sat cross-legged on his bedroll, his sewing kit in his hand. Christopher tossed him his third of the apple and Razi caught it neatly.

"It's the last one," said Christopher, lying back against

his saddle and looking up into the trees. The horses shifted quietly in the gathering gloom. Wynter sighed and bit into her apple; it was good – juicy and sharp.

"What are you doing here, Wynter?" Razi's deep voice was grudging, and he did not look up from sewing the hole in his britches.

"Same as you, Razi. I'm heading for Alberon's camp to see what he is up to."

Christopher snorted. "Good luck finding it. We've seen neither hide nor hair of aught since we set off. We've been chasing our bloody tails this last week. Those buggers over there were the first sign we'd found since we trotted into this forest. You know something, Razi," he mused, picking apple skin from his teeth. "I think that Comberman spy back at the palace was pulling your tail. Your brother's nowhere near here."

Wynter sat up straight. "Don't you know where he is?" she exclaimed, a little seed of excitement growing in her chest.

"No, Wynter, we do not," said Razi, snapping off his thread. He grimaced sarcastically at her as he put his needle away. "Do you?"

Wynter grinned at him and Razi's eyes widened. Christopher propped himself on his elbow.

"Good God!" said Razi, and he actually started to grin. "Wynter, are you serious?"

Wynter told her friends about Isaac's ghost and the Indirie Valley. She told them about her encounter with the Combermen and the Haun, and their remarks about the Rebel Prince. By the time she was finished it had come on to night. An almost full moon filtered down through the trees, and it gave the silently listening men the air of watchful spectres in the gloom.

"The Indirie Valley," murmured Christopher. "We'll have to ponder our maps tomorrow, friend."

"But *I* know the route," said Wynter. "There's another ten days journey left."

The pale smudge that was Christopher's face bobbed as he nodded his understanding.

"Haunardii," whispered Razi. With his dark skin and clothes, he was almost completely invisible, but Wynter could see his eyes flashing as he lifted them to look at her. "Oh sis, what is he thinking?"

"I know," she said softly. "Bad enough the Combermen, after everything our fathers have done to rid this place of intolerance . . . but the Haunardii? What does Alberon expect will happen if he tries to wrest the throne from Jonathon with those allies? The people will revolt against him. There's still too much bitterness left after the Haun Invasion. Also . . ." she paused. "Also, Razi, there is the matter of my father's invention. This machine of his. This Bloody Machine."

Wynter barely made out the movement as Razi lifted his hand and ran it across his eyes. Christopher shifted quietly against his bedroll.

"Do you know anything about it?" she asked.

"No," he said. "Only that my father seems to fear it. And my brother seems in some way to have gained control of it."

"Dad . . . Dad was brought to his knees at the thoughts of its use, Razi. Whatever it is, the mere mention of it tore him apart. It seems as though our fathers had used it before, at the end of the Haun Invasion."

"Aye," whispered Razi. "Just before the Lost Hundred were expelled from the kingdom." He glanced at Christopher. "You recall my telling you of the Lost Hundred, Chris? The Haun nobles and business-men, expelled with the rest of their race at the end of the war?"

Christopher shrugged in the dim light as if he had for-gotten, or hadn't paid much attention at the time.

"From what I could make out, our fathers agreed to suppress the machine after its first use," said Wynter. "I don't know why."

"And now your brother is using it to threaten the crown," said Christopher. "Looks like your father weren't quite as lunatic as he seemed, Razi."

"Good God," sighed Razi. There was a rustle as he lay back against his saddle and put his hands to his face. "My bloody family."

Wynter looked down at her hands, ghostly starfish against the darkness of her crossed legs. She debated for a moment and then said quietly, "Did you see the cavalry, Razi? Did you see their pennants?"

There was a heavy silence.

"Razi?" she said.

"Aye," he said, "I saw them."

"What do you think . . .?"

"Wynter?" His voice was utterly weary. "Could we . . . could we leave that until tomorrow?"

There was another moment of heavy silence.

"I'll take first watch," said Christopher, slapping his hand lightly against his thigh. He gathered his cloak around him and sat back against his saddle.

"Aye," sighed Razi. "Thank you, Christopher. Call me when the moon is at its zenith and I'll take the next watch."

"Call him when the moon reaches its first third, Christopher. I'll take the watch after him."

Razi snorted in impatience. "You'll do no such—"

"All right, girly," said Christopher. "Razi will go after me, you go after Razi. It'll do us good to get more sleep."

Razi lifted his head and gave them both what Wynter took to be a glare. "Good *God*," he growled. "I should have you both flogged for insubordination!" He turned his back on them, settling grouchily against his saddle.

Wynter grinned at Christopher. He was watching her, his face unreadable in the poor light.

"Go to sleep," he said quietly.

She was suddenly so grateful to him that it almost turned to tears. "Good night, Christopher. I'm glad we all found each other again."

She heard him swallow. "Aye," he said. "Now go to sleep, girly. I'll see you in the morning."

The bandit found her again, his laughter filling the darkness. This time she tore his throat, ripping his flesh with fangs she hadn't known she possessed. As she sank her teeth into his neck and his blood filled her mouth – hot, sweet and delicious – something inside her screamed in despair. But she no longer cared. She had given in at last, and there was nothing left in her now but hate.

"Girly . . ." A gentle hand on her forehead brushed lightly at her hair. "Come on, sweetheart. It's all right." Wynter opened her eyes, and Christopher smiled, his face hovering over her in the dark. "You were whimpering in your sleep," he said. "Were you in a bad place?"

Despite his smiling face, the dream would not leave her, and Wynter had to cover her mouth with her hands to keep the horror and the fear inside. Christopher's gentle smile fled as he read her expression. Snatching her to him suddenly, he held her against his chest, his scarred hand covering her eyes as though he wanted to hide her. Wynter knotted her fists into his undershirt and tried to bury herself in him.

"Oh God," he moaned. "Who hurt you? Who *hurt* you? I'll kill them! I swear it."

Wynter shook her head. She would not tell him. She could not, and despite the comfort she found in him, she pushed away. Christopher kept his hands on her shoulders, his eyes searching her face and she shrugged him off.

"It was just a dream, Christopher. Do not worry."

He took her hand, but she would not look at him.

He tilted his head and ducked to catch her eye. "Wyn," he said softly.

"It was just a dream!" she insisted. "It's just a *dream*," and she buried her face in her hands and curled her head onto her knees.

Wynter hoped Christopher would just go, but when he put his arm across her shoulders and pulled her to him again, she surprised herself by not pulling away. And when he continued just to sit beside her, his chin resting on her hair, rocking her gently in the quiet night, she felt overwhelmingly grateful for his presence.

Somehow she found herself holding his hand again.

"Christopher," she whispered, "please don't tell anyone . . ."

Christopher said nothing when she told him about the poor merchant. He did nothing but continue to rock her gently as she spoke about that man's hot look across the bright water of the stream, and about how he had followed her and attacked her and haunted her dreams afterwards. He didn't draw away or show any anger, or make any comment at all. At the end, when he was certain that she was finished, he tilted his head against her hair and looked down at her.

"Are you all right now, sweetheart?"

She nodded against his chest. "Aye."

"Will you be able to sleep?"

She nodded again and Christopher tilted his face up to the moonlit canopy and sighed. "This bloody world," he said softly. Then he kissed her hair, pressed his forehead to her shoulder, and got up to rouse Razi for his watch.

It took quite an effort to wake the poor man.

Wynter wrapped herself tightly in her cloak and listened to them moving about in the dark. Razi coughed and stretched, and went behind a tree to piss. He pottered around the edges of camp, checking the horses and stretching his legs. She heard Christopher yawn; there were soft sounds as he settled down for the night. Eventually, he was lost in silence for a while. Wynter could just see his pale face glowing in the corner of her eye.

"Christopher?" she whispered.

"Aye?"

She lay quietly for a moment, uncertain. Then she got to her feet, her cloak wrapped around her. She saw

Christopher's eyes follow her as she crossed the camp.

Razi called softly from the dark. "Are you all right, sis?"

She smiled at him, though she knew he wouldn't see it in this light. "I'm fine, Razi. Thank you." She shuffled around behind Christopher, and he turned his head to look up into her face. "Is it all right?" she asked, gesturing to his bedroll.

He nodded wordlessly, still gazing up at her. Wynter hesitated, then lay down beside him. Christopher tensed for a moment, as if unsure of what to do, then he turned his back to her, as he had on their last night together. Wynter pulled herself in close, looped her arm across his waist, and rested her forehead against his back. Behind them, Razi was motionless in the shadows.

Wynter closed her eyes. Christopher took her hand. Razi went back to checking on the horses.

The Box of Hay

"You have no right to ask that of us." Christopher's lilting voice, speaking quietly nearby.

Wynter opened her eyes to pale pre-dawn light. She blinked slowly into the dimness, orientating herself. She was lying with her back to the camp, facing out into the trees, and it took a moment to remember that she had come across in the night to share Christopher's bedroll. She felt her cheeks grow hot at the memory and at the same time she realised that Razi hadn't woken her for her watch. She was just about to turn and give him a piece of her mind when his deep voice stilled her.

"It is what I want," he said.

"Oh, I have no doubt," countered Christopher mildly. "But that's beside the point. Don't ask it again."

"Chris . . ."

"She will not leave, and I will not attempt to persuade her. She is a full-grown woman, Razi. She has her own mind."

"She is *fifteen* years old," exclaimed Razi, his voice pitched low so as not to wake her.

"You were negotiating your father's business in Algiers at fourteen." Christopher was stirring a pot, or scouring a bowl, and though his voice was still mild, the grating sound of his activity grew louder in agitation.

"I am different!"

The sound of stirring paused. "How are you different? Because you have that pudding between your legs, is it?"

"Christopher! Do not be crude!"

"She is a *full-grown woman . . .*"

"So you seem determined to point out."

Wynter thought she heard amusement in Razi's voice now, and Christopher resumed his activity, his voice muffled as if he'd ducked his head. "She is strong and brave and quick."

"Yes, but—"

"She would have gelded you on that hill had her reflexes not been so fast."

"Chris—"

"She was already heading straight as an arrow for your brother's camp while we were still sniffing our own arses here in these woods!"

"All right, Chris." There was a definite smile beginning to creep into Razi's voice. Wynter could not help but smile herself. Christopher sounded so earnest.

"You cannot always treat her like a baby, she is—"

"A full-grown woman. Aye. You've said. She is strong and brave and clever. The equivalent of ten strong men. *How* have I not seen this before? Why, with Wynter by our side we shall overthrow the Haun in a day, and convert the rabid Combermen to Islam." Razi was laughing now, but there was no sting in it.

Christopher muttered an amiable "Oh, shut up," under his breath.

There was a long moment's pause. Then Razi murmured softly, "I want you both safe, Chris. This fight is not of your making. I want—"

"Do not insult me," interrupted Christopher flatly. There was more silence, then Christopher said, "Stop shirking and go fill those waterskins. Your little sister is going to murder you when she realises that you took her watch, and I want your chores done before you're too crippled to walk."

"You had better run, Razi Kingsson," growled Wynter from her bed, "for as soon as I get these covers off me, I'm going to kick your arse." She rolled and glared across the clearing at him.

Razi was already walking off, the waterskins slung across both shoulders. He backed away, spreading his arms in challenge. "Catch me then, warrior woman! Come on!"

Wynter settled back, folding her arms, and Razi grinned. "I thought not!" he said, and strode away towards the river.

Wynter watched Christopher's slim back as he served out three bowls of mush. Like herself, he had his hair bound tightly against his head to protect it from the dust and parasites, and she thought the nape of his neck had a very strong, pleasing look to it. He had left off his tunic and she could see the closely muscled contours of his back and shoulders under the thin cloth of his undershirt. She swallowed hard at the feelings these things awoke in her.

"Christopher," she said. "I am sorry that I intruded on your kindness last night."

Christopher was perfectly still for a moment. Then he tilted his head towards her slightly, so that she could see a portion of cheekbone and the black shadow of his eyelashes. "Do you regret it?" he asked softly.

"No, I do not."

She saw his shoulders relax, and he went back to dishing out the breakfast. "Would you mind packing away the bedrolls?" he asked. "There's much to discuss before we leave, and it's best to get everything done now."

"All right."

He sat still and quiet while she began her task, but she'd only knotted the ties on the first ground sheet when he spoke again. "Razi has asked us to leave him," he said. She stopped in her work and they turned to look at each other. "I told him you'd be no more willing to leave him than I, but it has just occurred to me . . . I have no right to speak for you, girly. I don't know your mind."

Wynter smiled. *Oh, I think you do, Christopher Garron. I think we are of one mind in this. But thank you for asking my opinion.* "I will be staying," she said.

Christopher regarded her closely, those clear grey eyes searching her face.

"Girly?" he asked.

"Aye?"

"Do you think this Alberon fellow sent those assassins to kill Razi? I have this fear that we are allowing our friend walk to his execution here, and it haunts me that I may be aiding him in his own destruction."

Wynter thought of Albi, of his generous, loving nature, of his adoration of Razi, and she tried to dovetail it with the images of the assassins – the knife thrown across the banquet hall, the murderous arrow through the poor guard's head. How could her sunny, laughing friend have been behind them? Then she thought of Razi, standing by while that poor man was tortured so awfully, and she realised that time and circumstance could change anyone.

"Girly?" insisted Christopher. "I am in the dark here."

She sighed. Razi would be back from the river soon. In the short time left, how could she let Christopher know what Razi meant to Alberon and herself? How much he had done for them, and how unthinkable it was that Albi would ever want to hurt him. "Did you know that Albi and I were born on the same day, Christopher?"

He shook his head, puzzled by the direction the conversation had taken.

"We were not meant to be, but Albi came very late and I came much too early." Wynter glanced in the direction of the river. Marni had been the one to tell her this, and she was never too sure that Razi would want her to know it.

She looked back to Christopher. "Princess Sophia . . . Albi's mother? . . . had the most appalling labour. My mother and Sophia had been in their confinement together . . . you know about my father, of course?" Christopher shook his head, and Wynter spread her hands in frustration and glanced towards the river again. "Father was still on the run with Rory at the time, Jonathon's father being determined to see them both dead."

She held her hand up to deflect Christopher's shocked questions. "Another time," she said. "It is irrelevant to this story. Anyway, my mother was under Jonathon's most steadfast protection, and so she had been sharing the Princess's quarters. But the sounds of Sophia's awful torment terrified my poor mother, who was already mortally afraid of the prospect of labour, so Mamma fled the palace, seeking the tranquillity of the home she had shared with . . . with my dad."

Wynter faltered; somehow putting everything into words like this was very difficult. It brought everything sharply into focus for her. Most awfully, the fact that she, squirming and kicking in her mother's womb, had been the reason for that good woman's death and for the barrenness of her father's remaining years. She stared at her hands for a moment, then blinked and carried on.

"Razi was most devoted to my mother. He must have followed her from the palace. Marni thinks that he must have found her very soon after she fell. It had been raining, the ground must have been . . ." Wynter paused again, the image of her seventeen-year-old mother, giving birth alone and frightened in a wet field, was much too vivid in her mind. "Razi turned up in the kitchens hours later, covered in blood and carrying me wrapped in his tunic. I was tiny, apparently, and blue with cold. Marni swaddled me and put me in a box of hay like a kitten. By the time they found my mother, she had already bled to death."

Christopher shifted slightly, but did not speak or reach for her. She rubbed her forehead and continued.

"Albi was born that night. Princess Sophia lingered till morning, and then she too died. No one really knows why, though Razi has his suspicions." Wynter raised her eyes to Christopher. "He blames her death on the same thing that kept Jonathon's next two wives from carrying children, the same thing that led to *their* deaths. Poison . . ."

Christopher sat up a little straighter. "Oh," he said.

"Two days later, Razi turned up in the kitchens again. This time he was carrying the royal prince under his arm, a weighty, great dumpling of a baby, apparently. It's amazing that a four-year-old could have carried him so far."

"Why did he do it?" asked Christopher quietly.

Wynter glanced towards the river again. "Have you met Razi's mother, Christopher?"

"Aye."

"What think you of her?"

Christopher gave it some thought. "I think . . ." he said carefully, "that she is a woman who has managed to make her way in a world dominated by men. There is much to be admired in her."

This so stunned Wynter that she was speechless for a moment. Christopher was the first person she had ever met with anything positive to say about Umm-Razi Hadil bint-Omar. "My father calls Hadil 'the Hidden Dagger'," she said.

Christopher's amused dimples blossomed into a grin. "That is also apt. Why was it that Razi brought his brother to the kitchens, girly?"

Wynter flicked a glance towards the river. Razi's curly head was just coming into sight as he made his way up the slope towards them, and she continued in a whispered rush, "According to Marni, Razi would say nothing but '*my mother is looking at him*'. No matter how many times they returned Albi to his chambers, he would eventually be found in the kitchen, sleeping in the box of hay by my side, Razi sitting on the floor at our feet."

Christopher turned his head at the sound of Razi's footsteps approaching through the dry leaves.

"Razi has protected us our whole lives, Christopher. He has been our rock. Albi would never hurt him. I can't *believe* that Albi would ever hurt him."

Razi came trudging into camp, his long body curling forward with the weight of the waterskins and his own heavy thoughts. He sighed and glanced up as he began to make his way down the slope, then paused to see the two of them sitting cross-legged and deep in conversation.

"You God-cursed laggards!" he exclaimed. "You've done naught since the time I left!"

"Hmm . . . ten days," mused Razi. They were packed and ready to go, the three of them hunched over Wynter's map. The sun was just up, the heat already a curse and flies had already begun to swarm. Wynter blinked sweat from her eyes as Razi traced the journey from the Indirie Valley all the way down the map to the spot where they were camped. "Ten days," he said again, and tapped the parchment thoughtfully.

"It's a long way to go without knowing the situation at home," said Wynter. "We need to know for whom the black pennants fly, Razi."

He lifted his eyes to meet hers and they both looked away almost immediately. There was a moment of strained silence in which they stared blindly at the map.

"We could stop at an inn," suggested Christopher quietly. "No better place for news and gossip."

Wynter raised her eyebrows. Not a bad idea. "The closest inn is . . . here," she indicated the Wherry Tavern, a ferry house and traveller's rest located at the ferry ford. "It is only five days from here, and on our route."

Razi leant forward to see.

"No, there's another one," said Christopher.

"Do you mean the Orange Cow?" Wynter traced her finger up the river to show the crossroads inn. "That's seven days from here. Better to—"

"No," he insisted, gently brushing her hand aside and turning the map to face him. "I'm certain I saw . . ."

"Christopher," she said patiently, "I've been over this map many times, there are only two inns."

"Wait, wait," he held his hand up, scanning the page. "What kind of map is this?"

"It's a merchant map, a silver guild's merchant map."

"Ahh!" Christopher raised his eyes in excitement and traded a grin with Razi. "Ours ain't so refined, lass!" He went and fetched the map case from his horse. "Look!" he said, spreading another map out to cover Wynter's. "Here." He jabbed his finger down to show Wynter a tiny dot in the heart of the deep forest, less than a day's ride away. He tapped the map for emphasis and Wynter tore her eyes from his awful scars and forced herself to concentrate on the area he indicated. "See, this is a tarman's map, girly. Details all the local places merchants wouldn't be caught dead in."

"That will take us less than two days out of our way," murmured Razi. "I think it is well worth it."

"Aye," said Wynter, eyeing the nondescript spot. "I wonder if they'll have a bathhouse. After seven days without a proper wash, I'm starting to stink like a Northlander." She blushed immediately, appalled at herself. "Oh, Chris! I am so sorry!"

The dimples flashed wryly as he continued to study the

map. "No offence taken, girly," he said. "You Southlanders are insane about your soap and water. You're almost as bad as his lot." He jerked his thumb at Razi.

"I *am* a Southlander," said Razi mildly, and it was Christopher's turn to redden and mutter an apology. Razi just glanced affectionately at him, and went back to chewing the beanstalk he'd found in his breakfast. "A bath does sound good," he mused, scrubbing his jaw. There was a good seven days of growth on it, the beginnings of an admirably thick and curly beard. "Yes," he said softly. "I wouldn't mind that at all."

"It *is* fierce habit-forming," admitted Christopher grudgingly. He squirmed and tried to scratch his back. "Once you've got the routine of it, you can't seem to do without."

"All right," said Razi, reaching over and scratching Christopher between the shoulderblades. "Put the map away, friend, and we will go have our baths."

Christopher crossed to tie the map cases to his saddle and Wynter began folding away her own map. She was so sunk into her thoughts that she jumped when Razi gripped her wrist.

"Wynter," he said, his deep voice quiet. "I want you to ask Christopher to take you home." At her frown, he bore down hard with his hand. "He cares for you, sis. He will go if you ask."

She held his eye and purposely removed his hand from her wrist. "Do not insult us again," she said. "We will not tolerate it." He crumbled before her, his desperation palpable, and she couldn't help but love him for his concern. "Razi," she said gently, "I am staying, and that is an end to it."

"Oh, Wyn," he said.

Affectionately, she scrubbed her hand through his beard. It was surprisingly soft. "I like this," she murmured, smiling. "It suits you."

He rolled his eyes. "I'm sure! I probably look like a crusty old imam."

Wynter traced the white scar where his father's punch had split his lip, then pressed her finger to the tip of his nose. "I *like* it. It makes you look piratical!"

Then she patted his knee and left him sitting looking at his hands, while she joined Christopher in his final check of the horses.

The Tarman's Inn

"*J*esu help us, but this is remote."

"I cannot imagine," sighed Razi, "that we shall be seeing our bathhouse, sis. It's more likely that this 'inn' will be a tent with a barrel and a couple of tree stumps for stools."

"I cannot imagine we shall get any *information*!" Wynter exclaimed. "What kind of custom could a place this isolated get? Bears? Foxes maybe? Badgers?"

They had been following a rutted donkey track through the deep and cavernous pines for most of the day. There wasn't room to ride three abreast, so Christopher was slightly ahead of Wynter on the trail, Razi bringing up the rear.

Christopher was very quiet, perhaps feeling guilty for having suggested this in the first place. Wynter watched him forge doggedly ahead, slouched in the saddle, a haze of black insects all around him. Flies swarmed on his shoulders and knapsack, crawled drowsily across his back. His horse's tail swatted the bedroll on its rump and thwacked irritably against the saddlebags. Wynter knew she was probably in the same state and her shoulderblades twitched at the thought. Christopher shifted slightly in the saddle, his travel-belt settling around his hips, and he adjusted his knife to a more comfortable position.

Wynter tilted her head. *Huh*, she thought, *I didn't notice that before.*

"It just struck me, gentlemen," she said aloud, "you're both travelling very light compared to when you left the palace. Where are all your possessions?"

Christopher squinted back at her. "I left all my things with that al-Attar fellow from town," he said. "He met me in the forest and took them from me. Razi? He *will* take care of them, won't he? He won't leave my father's trunk in the damp or aught?" Razi must have gestured reassuringly because Christopher lifted his chin in an unconvinced response, and turned forward again.

"What Attar fellow?" asked Wynter. "Jahm? Does he mean Jahm al-Attar?" She twisted back to look at Razi who nodded and swiped at the flies that swarmed his half-covered face.

"Aye," he said.

Wynter frowned uncertainly. Jahm al-Attar was the palace apothecary. He had been a great friend to Razi's mentor, St James, and both Lorcan and Razi considered him a noble fellow. Still, she was surprised that Razi had trusted anyone enough to let them in on his plan.

"Meanwhile," continued Razi, a mischievous gleam in his eye. "Shuqayr ibn-Jahm is making sure that my blue robes get to Padua without too many rips or stains."

It took a moment for Wynter to understand, then she jerked her horse to a halt and turned to stare her friend in the face. Grinning, Razi brought his horse to a dancing stop. Wynter heard Christopher sigh as he halted on the track ahead.

Shuqayr! The apothecary's eldest son! Now that Wynter came to think of it, Razi's age, Razi's equal in height, Razi's lanky build.

"Oh, Razi," she said, appalled at the risks everyone was taking. "You were not even on your horse that day, were you? It was Shuqayr, wearing your clothes."

Razi nodded his head, laughing. "I walked out the palace gates on my own two feet with Umm-Shuqayr Muhayya, her daughters and other sons. I used Shuqayr's papers, then just strolled into the forest without a care in the world." Razi's eyes lost their joy, his delight stolen from him by worry. "I hope that Simon keeps him safe," he said quietly. "It is a long journey. What if . . .?"

"Razi, how in God's holy name do you expect Shuqayr to fool Simon all the way to—? Oh," she said, as cold understanding dawned. "Simon knows."

Razi nodded again and Wynter was suddenly irritated at how many people he had trusted with this plan, while leaving herself and Lorcan in the dark. "*Simon*, Razi?" she exclaimed. "You trusted Simon De Rochelle, yet you did not trust . . .?"

She bit her lip and looked up into the sky for a moment. No. She would not begin that argument. There were far too many fingers that could be pointed at her in return. She took a deep breath and counted slowly backwards from ten. Razi's deep voice cut across her attempts at self-restraint, and he at least had the decency to sound ashamed of himself.

"I *know* he seems an unlikely ally, sis. But I assure you,

Simon no more wants the kingdom in chaos than you or I." Razi wryly spread his hands. "After all, it is not to his economic or political advantage."

Wynter tutted bitterly, but she had to admit, it was a brilliant ruse. Once outside the palace environs, any tall, brown man could easily pass for Razi, particularly with a cadre of knights bowing and calling him *my Lord*. As far as anyone was now concerned, his Highness, the Royal Prince Razi – poisoner, usurper and black-hearted pretender to the throne – was wending his way to Padua and safely out of the picture for the next month or more. Palace life had at least a chance of getting back to normal, and Razi himself was free to slip around behind the scenes and try to find out the truth about the terrible rift between his father and the real heir to his throne.

Christopher chuckled. "He's a devious fellow, our Raz, ain't he? No wonder I can't beat him in a game of chess." Wynter turned to him and they traded a smile through the cloud of flies that danced between them.

Razi's horse neighed suddenly and the man himself gave a loud growl of frustration. "Oh good *God*!" he yelled. "Let us get away from these God-cursed insects before they suck us dry!"

They worked their way up through the trees, the donkey track getting rougher and the flies more invasive with each mile. Wynter was just wondering if they'd ever get there, when Christopher came to a crest in the hill and pulled his horse to a halt.

Dwarfed by the massive pines on either side of the road, he was silhouetted sharply against the open sky at the curve of the road, and Wynter saw him look down as though into a valley.

"Good Frith," he said, pulling the scarf from his face. "That is unexpected."

Wynter and Razi brought their horses crowding up to join him. As soon as they crested the hill, they felt the refreshing effects of a breeze that swept up from the valley, and the flies disappeared like a conjurer's trick. They removed their scarves and wiped the sweat from their faces as they took in the landscape. Wynter whistled in surprise.

A wide area of cleared land spread out before them, at least forty acres, neatly divided into paddocks and fields, a bright ribbon of stream running straight through the middle. At the very heart of the farm land, nestled into a couple of acres of mixed orchard, sat a large, neatly maintained complex of outhouses and stables, fronted by a handsome log building that must be the inn.

The smell of wood smoke and cooking came up to them on the breeze, and Wynter heard the men's stomachs growl just before hers did.

"Hot mutton and gravy," groaned Christopher.

"A bath," sighed Wynter.

There was a moment's silence from Razi as he surveyed the complex of buildings. "Stay sharp, you two," he said finally. "And keep your knives handy. This place is mighty rich looking for a peasants' haunt." Then he clucked his horse forward and led the way down the steep slope into the heart of the valley.

"Shall we unsaddle the horses?" Wynter asked as they approached the inn. They were still elevated and could see down into the yard. A long line of mules stood patiently at the hitch, all weighed down with full barrels of tar. Two saddled horses were also at the hitch, and a small goods-cart, fully laden, stood against the yard wall. Dogs were getting to their feet and padding to the gate, looking up the hill towards them.

Razi scanned the area uncertainly. "Not at first," he said, "we'll carry everything of value in with us; get the lay of the land inside. If we feel comfortable, we can order a lad to tend the horses."

The dogs began to bark, advancing and retreating and milling around each other in their excitement. A man came to the front porch, wiping his hands on a cloth. He yelled at the dogs to *settle down*, then looked up the hill and raised his hand in casual greeting. Christopher raised his in return, and the man went back into the inn, leaving the door open. Two more men came to the door, peered curiously up at them and went back in.

Wynter shifted nervously in the saddle and wondered what the three of them would do if this turned out to be a nest of bandits.

A man and a boy came out from what looked like the stables, and stood watching them as they rode into the yard. They were Arabs, unmistakably father and son, but when the man spoke, it was with a broad local accent. "Would ye like us ter take the horses?"

"Not yet, thank you," said Christopher, dismounting and stretching his saddle-weary body as he looked around him.

Wynter dismounted and bent to rub the cramp vigorously from her calves.

"Perhaps you could supply them with water and a feed-bag each?" suggested Razi. "And we can call on you to rub them down should we decide to stay."

The man nodded suspiciously, thrown by Razi's well-bred accent. His eyes swept to take in the abundance of well-made weaponry, the saddlebags, the heavily loaded travel-belts. He turned to appraise Wynter, realised that she was a woman, and respectfully averted his gaze, but not before he checked her finger for a wedding band.

"Perhaps," said Christopher, tucking his hands casually behind his back. "I could examine the feed?"

The man nodded and Christopher followed him into the stables while Wynter and Razi took the saddlebags and weaponry from the horses. Christopher soon returned, apparently satisfied with the quality of oats and grain on offer. He took his saddlebag from Razi, slung his crossbow over the rucksack on his back and the three of them headed into the unknown territory of the inn.

It was a dim room, low ceilinged, smelling of wood-smoke, roasted meat and tobacco. A big fireplace dominated the wall to their right, and the wall directly ahead of them was entirely given over to a rough serving counter. Two greasy looking women were eyeing them from the kitchen, which was visible through an arched doorway behind the serving counter. All the occupants of the room seemed to have been waiting for their entrance and they were silently taken stock of as they crossed the threshold.

The long table under the window was occupied by three middle-aged men and a youth. They were obviously tarmen, grimy and pickled with smoke, their hands and faces black from work. The older men were thoroughly occupied in eating their dinner, and they raised their eyes to take in the strangers without ceasing shovelling their food. The youth, however, stopped eating and leant artlessly from his seat to watch Wynter's arse as she passed by. She gave him a cold stare and he made a shockingly lewd gesture at her with his tongue.

Thankfully, Razi's attention was on a trio of rough looking men sitting at a centre table, so he did not react. Christopher, however, put his hand protectively on the small of Wynter's back and sucked his teeth in a sharp and unmistakably aggressive manner. Wynter was surprised to see his hand fall to his knife.

"Keep your eyes to yerseln', lad," growled the older of the boy's companions, and the young man dropped his gaze back to his bowl.

The men at the centre table had turned from their conversation and were openly staring at the new arrivals. They were grimy and patched looking, well-armed and sly-eyed. The skin on Wynter's back did a slow crawl as the men watched the three of them get settled. As she set her saddlebags down on the floor behind her, she glanced at the only other customer. He sat by the cold fireplace, seemingly absorbed in mending a harness. There was a tankard of cider by his elbow and an unfinished game of chess sat on a stool between him and the empty chair on the other side of the fireplace. Another tankard sat in the ashes of the hearthstone, with a half-eaten trencher-bread of stewed meat going soggy by its side. Wynter scanned the room for the man's missing companion, but there was no sign of him.

She had just finished divesting herself of her rucksack

when the landlord, his cloth still in hand, came trotting from a back hall. Unsmiling, he approached their table. He took them in very quickly, their pile of belongings, their weighty travel-belts, their weapons. He made the usual check of Wynter's finger for a ring, before dismissing her as unimportant.

"How do, travellers?" he said. "Not seen your faces afore. You lost?"

"We know where we're headed, thanks," said Christopher amiably, settling his crossbow against the wall.

"We were hoping for some hot food, and perhaps . . ." Razi stalled at the expression on the landlord's face.

Christopher turned back from securing his weapon and his eyes shuttered as he caught the landlord staring at his mutilated hands. The landlord slowly raised his gaze and they locked eyes for a moment. Then Christopher's mouth curved, his dimples flashed and he tilted his head in what Wynter recognised as the precursor to a joke. The landlord spoke first.

"Well, lad," he said softly. "Some greasy magistrate had a field day with you, didn't he?" Christopher opened his mouth to deny that he was a criminal, but the landlord turned and called into the kitchen. "Minnie! Some cider fer our friends." He looked back down at them, still not smiling. "First one's free. After that ye pay fer everythin' according to the table of charges." He jerked a meaty thumb to the chalked slate leaning against the counter. "Can ye read that?"

They nodded, a little dazed. As soon as the landlord had called for the free cider, the tarmen all pointedly concentrated on their food. The three men at the centre table craned to see Christopher's hands, then turned back to their conversation. The man at the fireplace settled back in his chair, the tension gone from his posture.

It was obvious, now, what kind of trade was normal in this establishment. This was a bandits' haunt all right, perhaps not exclusively so, considering the tarmen, but criminals were welcome; they were made to feel safe, and the three of them were now accepted as being part of that dubious brotherhood.

The landlord nodded at Christopher's hands. "I hope yer kin went back to burn the courthouse down," he said gravely. "I hope they put the Wig's eyes out. Outrage like that shouldn't go unavenged."

Christopher remained expressionless, but Wynter felt Razi jerk beside her, his hands splaying compulsively on the tabletop. The man obviously approved of their continued silence and he let the subject die. "Minnie'll be over fer yer order, nigh," he said, and ambled off to occupy himself behind the counter.

They sat in silence for a moment. The landlord's comment about vengeance seemed to have unbalanced Razi and Christopher, and they sat like stone lions on either side of Wynter, completely absorbed in their own thoughts. Wynter found herself watching the man at the fireplace; he was doing a skilful job on the harness. Now and again he would take a sip from his cider. His companion's trencher-bread was going to collapse soon if it was not eaten.

The girl came with the cider. She placed it carefully in front of them, a tankard each, then leant her hip against the table. Her eyes roamed from Razi to Christopher and back.

Wynter might as well have been an oily patch on the floor for all the attention she paid her.

"We sell company, if you fancy," said the girl, smiling.

Christopher, still a little distant, cleared his throat and politely shook his head. Wynter took a sip of her cider and looked away. The girl's eyes drifted to Razi who didn't seem to have heard her at all.

"We got nothin' against dark men," she assured him.

Christopher chuckled. "We're all right for company, thanks," he said.

The girl's eyes turned to Wynter in misplaced comprehension. "Ah!" she said.

"He doesn't mean me!" cried Wynter.

"We just want some food, lass. If that suits?" grinned Christopher. His dimples were back in full force and Wynter saw the girl melt under his unrelenting charm. "Tell me," he cried, slapping his hands together. "What's the mutton like and does it come with gravy?"

Get What's Coming

The mutton was delicious, if Christopher's quiet sighs and groans of pleasure were anything to go by. Had Wynter not been so absorbed with her own food she would have teased him mercilessly. Even Razi seemed transported, and he ate with silent relish until, mopping the last of his fried onions with the last of his rye bread, he sighed, and pushed his empty plate away. "Magnificent," he proclaimed.

Wynter peered hopelessly into her now empty trencher, wondering if it would be ill-bred to break it up and suck the gravy from it. Before she could decide, the landlord ambled over to gather their empty plates and tankards, so she pushed it reluctantly towards him and sat back instead.

"What news of the world?" he asked, stacking dishes on his arm. "Now ye have full bellies like, and aren't so peaked looking."

Razi leant back in his seat, removed a toothpick from his purse and began cleaning his teeth. Since their having been mistaken for thieves, he had deliberately kept his well-bred voice to the background, letting Christopher's more likely accent do the talking. As a woman, Wynter was either an object of lascivious attention or disregarded completely. The landlord didn't expect anything like a reply from her.

"We ain't too up on current affairs," said Christopher. "Having been out of the path of men for a little while." There was a smile in everything but his eyes, and it somehow gave dangerous significance to his words. The landlord nodded slyly, as if fully aware of his meaning.

"Though we did see cavalry on the road yesterday," said Wynter.

Every eye in the room looked up at that and one of the men at the centre table said sharply, "Wot road? Where headed?"

Christopher glanced at him. "North road," he said. "Headed to the crossroads, I reckon."

There was some relaxing amongst the rougher men, but the tension didn't fully leave their faces. The yard dogs began to bark and one of the tarmen turned and looked out the window. "More tars heading in," he said. "Still off up the valley."

The landlord shouted into the kitchen. "Tars are 'ere. Get hot water on. Tell the other bints to open up the extra rooms." He turned back to Christopher and raised his eyebrows for him to continue.

"The cavalry were flying black flags," said Christopher. "And the plumes were broken on their hats."

"That's on account o' the dead prince," explained one of the men.

Wynter felt the colour drain from her face, and Razi sat forward slowly. He reached for her and she took his hand under cover of the table.

"Which prince?" asked Christopher hoarsely.

"The . . ." began the man by the fireplace.

"What will that Moorehawke bint do now, I wonder?" interrupted one of the tarmen, picking his teeth, and Wynter felt Razi's grip tighten on her hand.

"She'll have ter go back to the palace and throw 'erself on the mercy of the King."

"He'll bloody kill 'er. She's better off to run, after what she done."

"I'd say she's dead already."

"They didn't find 'er body!"

"Don't signify. After what they done to the Arab, who knows what they'd do to 'er. That were bloody savage, so it were."

Wynter blinked. Her eyes felt gritty and hot. *After what they did to the Arab.*

"He deserved it. Poisonous devil, got what was coming to 'im."

Razi sat rigid and unmoving, his hand crushing hers with tremendous force.

Then Christopher's voice, dry and halting, scratched through the haze of her shock. "What . . ." he said reluctantly, "what did they *do* to the Arab?"

But the conversation had taken its own course and Christopher went unheeded.

"Was it the King you reckon?" asked the young tarman. "In revenge for Lorcan Moorehawke's death?"

Wynter jumped. "What?" she cried. "When?" They all turned to look at her, shocked into silence. She banged her fist on the table and all the men jerked. "*When?*" she shouted.

"When did Lorcan Moorehawke die?" asked Razi, his deep voice surprisingly calm.

All the men went *ahhh* and looked at Wynter sympathetically. Lorcan had been a most popular man, and they nodded their heads in understanding. Poor tender female, at the mercy of her emotions.

"He succumbed four days ago," said one of the tarmen sadly. "The Arab's poison finally ate away his heart."

Wynter made a small noise of despair, and Razi curled in on himself, as if with bellyache. "Oh, no," he whispered. "Don't . . ."

"They say the King flung hisseln' on the corpse and wouldn't allow no one touch it for two whole days. Then he laid it out hisseln'. They say the priests came to anoint the body and the King near threw them down the stairs."

Wynter looked up at the ceiling, her eyes swimming. That much, she figured might actually be true. Considering Lorcan's hatred of the church, maybe Jonathon had spared him at least that hypocrisy. She gasped at the sheer black depth of her grief and tried to hang on to her self-control as the conversation spiralled around her.

"I still can't get over the girl, aiding the Arab in her father's murder."

"Women is always drawn to power," observed one of them sagely. "Reckon she thought he'd make it to the throne and wanted a nice soft cushion for her arse."

"Well, she bet her cunny on the wrong bloody horn, didn't she?"

The room chuckled grimly. Wynter felt sure she was going to lose her dinner, she could actually feel it pressing up against her throat.

"I don't figure it were the King though," mused someone

else. "I figure it were the Royal Prince Alberon what done the Arab in."

Everyone looked up at that and the man spread his hands. "What other choice did he have? At least now the King might snap out of whatever witchcraft he's been under and take home his rightful heir!"

"What *became* of him?" demanded Christopher. "What became of the Arab?"

Outside, the yard was chaotic suddenly, with the arrival of many horses and the barking of dogs. There were shouts and catcalls, and the landlord moved to open the door. Sunlight and sound streamed in.

The man at the centre table raised his voice over the din. "His men were caught unawares after they'd set up camp!" he yelled. "Someone managed to slip poison into their waterskins, and while all the knights lay round about, screaming and holding their bellies, a group o' men walked among them and slit their throats, easy as killing chickens."

"What of the prince?" asked Razi quietly. "What became of him?"

"Oh, *him*," the man looked at Razi, his eyes sly. "*He* weren't so lucky. They strung him up and dragged him behind his own horse till there weren't an inch of flesh on his body, then they cut off his head and played a game of football with it. It's said he went home to the King in a hessian bag, so mushed up that his own snake of a mother wouldn't recognise him."

Wynter gripped the table, overcome with horror at the brutal satisfaction in the man's voice. Poor Shuqayr! That poor man. She turned to Razi without thinking and tried to put her arms around him. He shrugged her off with a violent upward swing of his elbow and pulled away. "Let me go!" he cried and surged to his feet, pushing the table forward with a mighty shove.

The room had begun to fill with blackened, smoke-pickled men and Razi elbowed his way through them and stumbled out into the yard. Wynter knew she should follow him, but she buried her face in her hands instead, and tried not to look at the pictures that filled her head. Christopher sat tightly beside her, his hands clenched into useless knots on the table.

Chaos and disorder flowed around them and all threads of conversation were lost in the arrival of the sooty tarmen.

Someone knocked on the table top. "Oy," they said.

Wynter recognised Minnie's voice and she pressed her fingers harder into her eyes and willed her to go away. Christopher put his hand on the small of Wynter's back as he looked up at the serving girl.

"What is it?" he snapped.

"That dark fella paid me earlier to heat a bath. It's ready now. Which of you wants to use it first?"

Wynter felt Christopher lean in close. "Sweetheart?" His low murmur, warm in her ear, made her want to curl into him and go to sleep. "Would you still like to take your bath?" He slipped his arm around her waist, and Wynter realised that, more than anything, she wanted to stay here, in the comfort of his presence.

"Let Ra . . . let my brother go first," she said, raising her head and wiping her face all in one motion.

"All right. I'll be back in a moment." And to her disappointment, Christopher slipped out from behind the table and left her alone while he went to find Razi.

The room was full of men now. Laughing and hurling themselves into chairs, calling out orders and inquiring after news. Wynter watched them as though they were a badly written play, unreal, distant and of no interest to her. She was filled with smoky numbness and empty of thought. She found herself staring at the man beside the fireplace again, not really seeing him. He was looking up. His missing friend had returned. The new man sat down. He swigged at his cider and fished a morsel of meat from his trencher-bread.

His face was so badly bruised that Wynter didn't recognise him at first. But then his companion laughed and said loudly, "I'm amazed she still gives you the time of day, looking the way you do, Tosh."

Wynter's stomach went cold. Tosh. She turned her eyes to the new man, *really* looking at him now, really *listening* to him.

"What's my looks got to do with it?" he sneered. "'T'aint like she's doing me no favours."

The first man grinned and said something, his words lost in the surrounding noise. The bandit wasn't really listening and his eyes roamed the crowd as his friend spoke. He found Wynter quick enough and she stared at him, unable to move. At first he grinned, showing the gaps where Ozkar had kicked his teeth out – just a man greeting the sight of a new woman in a world of all too familiar women. Then he faltered, frowned, and Wynter saw murder rise up in his eyes as he realised who she was.

Christopher chose that moment to sidle through the crowd and lean across the table to speak to her. He saw her expression and turned immediately to follow her gaze.

Wynter did not look up at him. She was utterly incapable of tearing her eyes from the bandit. It was as though her whole body had been dipped into a winter river and taken out again, a frozen statue of her former self.

The bandit ran his tongue across his broken teeth, his eyes hard. He knew Christopher was there, but he took his time looking up at him. When he did finally raise his eyes, he held Christopher's glare insolently with his own. Then he sneered, dropped his eyes once more to Wynter and winked.

Then Wynter couldn't see him anymore because someone was blocking her view. The someone sat down opposite her and it was Christopher. He positioned himself so that she could no longer see the fireplace.

"Hey," he said.

He reached across the table and took both Wynter's clenched fists in his. Wynter looked down at their joined hands. She might as well have been a hawk flying high above the inn for all the contact she felt between them. Then Christopher tightened his grip. On his left hand, the twisted stump of his middle finger was bent to the side, folding in slightly beneath his ring finger, and as he squeezed, Wynter felt it push itself into the back of her hand. At this unique pressure, she suddenly came to the surface of her shock and broke through it. Everything snapped into focus. The noise of the crowd intruded.

She blinked, took a deep breath, concentrated on Christopher's narrow face. He was paler than she'd ever seen him, his eyes intent.

"Is that him?" he asked softly.

He seemed no more angry now than he had been the

night she had told him, and that calmed her. She nodded. Christopher straightened his back. She expected him to turn and look at the bandit, but instead, he slid his eyes to the left, his eyelashes casting long shadows on his cheek, and tilted his head, as if listening to something over his shoulder. He ran his thumb along the back of her hand, then lifted his eyes to her again.

"Let's get all our stuff out of here, girly. We can carry it to the bathhouse and sit outside, eh? Talk to Raz through the wall while we wait our turn? I'll get that girl to bring us some cold cider and some apple pie. We'll sit in the sun and make a bloody picnic of it before we head out again. What do you think?"

Wynter nodded, and together they gathered their things and went outside. She did not look back at the man.

Naught But A Ghost

The bathhouse was in the orchard. Dappled in the lacy shade of the fruit trees, it was a little, dirt-floored, one-tub hut, and whether by accident or by virtue of Razi's purse, they were the only ones waiting to use it. It felt miles from anywhere. Safe and at peace.

Wynter sat beside their pile of belongings, leaning against the wall of the bathhouse, her face turned to the sun. There was a blackbird trilling in the apple tree above her. She closed her eyes and listened, while Christopher, a plate in one hand, a tankard in the other, elbowed his way in through the bathhouse door and let it swing shut behind him.

"How do," he said. "Brought you some cider and a pie."

"I don't want it." Razi's voice was quiet and flat.

"Aye. I know. It's just an excuse to come in without you throwing things at me. I'll leave them here." There was a soft clink and a rustle as Christopher set the food down on the other side of the wall from Wynter. "You'll be wanting it later, you know. You can't have much left in your belly, after what you coughed up behind the barn."

There was an abrupt splash, as if Razi had sat forward suddenly, or lifted his arms, and then a long moment of silence.

"Are we heading home now?" asked Christopher, eventually. "You and me and Wynter?"

"No, Christopher. We are not." Razi's voice was muffled and Wynter suspected that he had lifted his hands to cover his face.

There was another brief silence, then Christopher's quiet voice pressed tentatively on. "At home, you could resume your practice. Wynter can build that hospital for you. I can . . . I can roll bandages or something. Open the stables again, go back to breeding horses."

Wynter opened her eyes. She knew that Christopher wasn't talking about the palace; he would never refer to the palace as home. He was talking about the Moroccos. About Algiers. He was talking about starting a new life. She turned her head, waiting for Razi's answer, not sure what she wanted it to be. Razi stayed silent.

"Razi," insisted Christopher. "Come *home*. Before these people see you dead."

This was met with more silence. Wynter could picture Razi lying in the tub, his elbows on the rim, his head tilted against the back. She imagined him, his hands pressed to his eyes, waiting for Christopher to let him be. The silence stretched on and Wynter heard Christopher sigh and shuffle his feet.

"I'm sorry about Lorcan, Razi," he said softly. "I'm sorry about that poor Arab boy."

Wynter closed her eyes again and rested her head against the wall. Razi still did not speak.

"When your father finds out that it wasn't you . . ."

"He will not. Jahm will be too frightened to let him know." There was a gentle *splash* as Razi dropped his hands. "Those poor people," he said, his voice cracking. "Those poor . . . I sent that poor man . . ."

"If your father thinks you are dead, he will try to avenge you. There will be chaos unless—"

Christopher was silenced by Razi's quiet laugh. "Vengeance often comes amazingly slow in our circles, Christopher, and then only if politically expedient. You of all . . ." There was no sound for a moment. Then Razi spoke again, his voice very broken. "You of all people should know *that*. Oh God! Simon and his men . . . and poor Shuqayr! How can . . .? Chris, I can never make up for this."

Wynter wanted Christopher to come outside. She wanted to tell him to leave Razi be, to let the poor man suffer in private. She opened her mouth to call him, but Christopher obviously knew Razi just as well as she did because he said, "Wynter and I are just outside, all right? Call through if you want us."

The door of the bathhouse creaked. Wynter could see Christopher's hand on the latch. He began to pull the door open, but then hesitated and turned back. "I know I don't have to say it to you, Razi. You're no bloody fool; but it weren't you that killed Shuqayr, and you didn't cut De Rochelle's throat or kill his men, neither. And, Raz, I know we don't ever talk about it, but what that landlord said? It doesn't signify between us. You didn't steal my hands from me, Razi, and it weren't your place to sacrifice a kingdom for the sake of revenge. I ain't never held it against you, and you shouldn't go trotting down tired old roads now, just because you're heartsick and weary."

Wynter listened for Razi's response, but there was utter silence from the bathhouse.

"Take as long as you want in there now," said Christopher. "They can always heat more water if it gets cold." He stepped out and closed the door. He stood for a moment, gazing unseeingly at the rough wood planking, then he came across and sat on the grass beside Wynter.

He slouched back against the wall. Wynter leaned against him. She slipped her arm through his and took his hand. They gazed out into the orchard.

"I'm so sorry about your dad," he said at last.

She nodded.

"He was . . ."

She tightened her grip on his hand. "Please, Christopher. I can't."

Christopher shook his head suddenly and his face drew down as though he were about to cry. Wynter tilted her head against his shoulder, turning her cheek into the fabric of his tunic. After a moment he kissed her hair.

"I'm just sorry, lass," he said hoarsely. "I want you to know."

She put her free hand on his chest and they sat like that, comforting each other in silence. Gradually the sound of gentle splashing from the bathhouse told them that Razi had decided to wash himself.

"They played football with that boy's head," whispered Christopher. "They thought he was Razi. They thought he was *Razi* and they did *that* to him."

Wynter continued to stare out into the golden hazy

afternoon, willing Christopher not to say any more. She suspected where this conversation was going and had no desire to follow it to its natural conclusion.

"It wasn't the King that did this, was it, girly? He *wants* Razi on the throne."

"It could have been anyone," she whispered quickly. "The people hate Razi. They *hate* him, and now they think he killed my father. Any peasant could have done this."

"A peasant wily enough to poison the water supply of a group of knights? To get the better of a man like Simon De Rochelle?"

"They think Razi murdered my *dad*," she insisted. "The people loved my—"

Christopher cut across her, his voice flat and certain. "I will *kill* Alberon, if it turns out to have been him." Wynter groaned and tried to pull her hand from his, but Christopher tightened his grip and turned to look her in the face. His eyes shocked her, how bright and hard they were. "If it turns out that Alberon ordered his brother dragged to his death, and had a football made of his head, *I will kill him.* Whether Razi wants me to or not."

Wynter took a breath and clenched her free hand over their joined fists. "You will not have to do that, Christopher. I know Alberon would never hurt Razi. I *know* it. So you will never have to do that."

"But if I do?"

Wynter blinked. He was asking her would she still love him? Would they still be friends? "You will never have to," she said desperately.

Christopher's face went blank, and Wynter felt him begin to draw away, but he stopped almost immediately and all his brutal determination melted to tenderness. He leaned forward and pressed his forehead to hers. "Of course I won't," he whispered. "I'd never have to do that."

Wynter closed her eyes, suddenly too close to tears.

They drew back and leant against the wall, their shoulders touching. Sunlight settled down around them in a dusty haze. The birds continued their joyous trilling in the trees. How life went on. How it all went on around them, in the midst of such darkness.

Wynter began to doze, had actually begun to dream, when she felt Christopher startle beside her. She took a sharp breath, snapping awake abruptly, and looked around for the source of his anxiety.

The bandit was leaning against one of the apple trees at the edge of the orchard, chewing on a toothpick and grinning. His eyes crawled over their entwined arms, slid slyly to the hand that Wynter had resting on Christopher's thigh. His expression made something scurrilous of their affection, and when he looked back up, he held Wynter's eyes with a knowing, scornful leer. Immediately her heart began to skitter about in her chest and she felt a rush of shameful panic that no one in her life had ever instilled in her before.

Christopher rose to his feet, and the bandit shifted the toothpick from one side of his mouth to the other, looking him up and down with confident disdain. He was a good bit taller than Christopher and a great deal bulkier, and Wynter knew that this was all he saw. She could tell that he did not consider her friend a threat.

This careless dismissal of Christopher re-awoke something in her. The real Wynter seemed to step up, and the trembling child this man threatened to make of her slipped quietly away. She rose smoothly to her feet and moved to Christopher's side. Neither of them reached for their knives, but Christopher's hands hung loose and ready. His face was blank and watchful. Wynter had her court mask on, looking up slightly from under her eyes, and she balanced lightly on the soles of her feet.

The bandit's expression sharpened. He spat his tooth-pick to the ground, his eyes flicking from Christopher to Wynter. Behind them, the bathhouse door swung open, and Razi came out into the sunlight, shirtless and rubbing his hair with a cloth. He paused as he took in the situation. At the sight of the bandit, he instantly dropped the cloth and stepped forward.

The bandit's eyes opened just a touch wider. All of Razi's sinewy power seemed to be burning within him suddenly, and though only half a head taller than the bandit, his rage seemed to tower him over the other man. The bandit's eyes slid to the long, ugly crescent of scar on Razi's right shoulder and that seemed to make his decision for him. He shot one more sneer at Christopher and Wynter, tipped his head as if bidding them a fond adieu, and sauntered casually away through the trees.

"Who in God's name was that?" snapped Razi.

Wynter opened her mouth but couldn't find the words to explain.

Christopher watched as the bandit disappeared behind the wall of the inn. "That was no one," he said. "No one. Naught but a ghost." He turned and looked around him. "Right," he said, not meeting anyone's eyes. "Right. I'm taking these dirty plates back to the inn. Our girl can have her bath, then I can have mine, and then we'll all head off, clean and happy and—"

"Christopher?" Razi interrupted suspiciously. "Who was that man?"

"Why don't you eat that pie now, Raz?" suggested Christopher, gathering the dirty dishes. "Let the sun dry you off. Drink a bit of cider. I'll only be a moment down at the kitchens. I'll settle our bill, see that the horses are ready to go, restock our provisions. You stay here and protect Wynter from any more sly-eyed dicks. What say you?"

Razi's face cleared in comprehension. "Ahhhh!" he said and gave Wynter a sympathetic look. He obviously now thought the bandit was just some slithering peeping Tom. "It's all right, sis," he said gently. "He wouldn't come back now; he probably didn't expect you to have company. Go on ahead." He stood aside and held the door open for her. "I'll be just here, all right?" His voice was so kind and his eyes so tired that Wynter wanted to grab him and hug him. Instead, she passed him out his pie and his drink, and he closed the door behind her.

She heard Christopher murmur and Razi rumble a short reply. His long silhouette moved against the sun raddled gaps in the planks, and he sat himself down against the wall as she unbound her hair and let it fall in a lank mess down her back.

"I am still here, Wyn," he called suddenly. "Everything is all right."

She smiled. "I know, Razi. Thank you. Eat your pie, won't you?"

She heard him sigh again; there was a clink as he picked up the plate. *Don't just look at it*, she thought, *eat*. Finally she climbed the steps and slipped thankfully into the still-hot water, closed her eyes and floated away.

She was drying her hair in the sun when Christopher hurried back up through the orchard and came jogging up the path. He had been gone so long that they were seriously beginning to fret. He stripped off his tunic as he approached and bundled it in his hand, then reached back and pulled the tie on his undershirt. He unpinned his hair as he elbowed his way in the bathhouse door, and it fell in a heavy coil past his shoulders.

"Won't be long," he said.

In barely any time at all he came stalking from the bathhouse, his hair soaking, his clothes damp from having been pulled over wet skin. He moved immediately to gather up his things.

"Come on," he said. "It's getting late." He shrugged on his knapsack, slung his crossbow and quiver across his back and shouldered his saddle bags. "Come *on*!" he demanded, and Wynter and Razi froze, alerted by the unaccustomed sharpness in his voice.

He looked up to find them staring. His eyes slid to the side. "We need to go," he said. "It's getting late." Wynter slowly met Razi's eyes. He shrugged and the two of them hurried to pack their things. Whatever it was, they weren't going to dawdle. If Christopher wanted to leave that badly, they'd leave.

The yard was quiet when they went to fetch their horses, all the tarmen drowsy after their dinners. There was a line of men snoozing and smoking pipes on the benches in the yard, their tankards at their feet, but they barely raised their heads as the three travellers rode from the stables, heading for the exit.

They had almost made it out the gate when a woman began shouting and screaming from the complex of buildings at the back of the inn. Wynter looked back to see the sleepy men beginning to rise to their feet. The woman's cries became more coherent as she neared the yard, and Razi brought his horse to a halt and looked back as her words became clear.

". . . needs help! Someone help him! Someone get help!"

Razi immediately went to turn back. He opened his mouth to call that he was a doctor, but Christopher reached across and gripped his wrist, silencing him and staying the dancing turn of his horse.

"Ain't naught you can do," he said quietly. "Fellow was careless, got himself crushed beneath a barrel. He's naught but a ghost now." He looked at Wynter. "All right, sweetheart?" he said. "He's naught but a ghost."

He let go of Razi's wrist and reined his horse back a few steps, awaiting his decision. Wynter and Razi stared at him for a moment, their eyes wide. Then, as if someone had dropped a starter's flag, or given a secret command, the three of them turned their horses and trotted out of the yard and off up the road.

Distant Storms

It was late at night and the moon was shining brightly by the time they finally slid from their saddles. They had just enough energy to tend their horses, then they didn't so much set up camp as sprawl, exhausted, on their randomly scattered bedrolls and gawp up at the milky stars. They were still deep in the monstrous pines, but they had made excellent progress. By noon the next day they would be back at the river and ten days after that they would be in Alberon's camp and the truth would at last be within their grasp.

After a while, Razi hauled himself up and settled himself on a tree trunk, preparing to take first watch, but Wynter and Christopher had secretly agreed to split the first two shifts, and they were determined he would not win out. Christopher silently took the cloak from Razi's shoulders and threw it onto his friend's bedroll, while Wynter folded her arms and glared her support.

"Go to sleep," he commanded. "You're taking *third* watch."

Razi groused and bitched, and generally stamped about for a few minutes as he tried to bully them into submission.

But within moments of grudgingly laying down, he was unconscious. Wynter smiled at Christopher across Razi's sleeping back. Christopher winked at her. She wrapped herself in her cloak, lay back and was gone as soon as she shut her eyes.

Seconds later, Christopher was insistently shaking her awake.

She rose to the surface of consciousness as if struggling her way through tar. Christopher mumbled something incoherent. He stumbled his way to his bedroll and was out cold before she'd even wiped the sleep crumbs from her eyes.

Wynter blinked around in bewilderment. The clearing was swimming in moonlight. The horses were softly breathing spectres against the trees. At her feet, Razi's dark silhouette sighed and muttered in his sleep.

Slowly, Wynter's confusion drained from her, and she cursed and bowed her head. It was time for her watch. She forced herself to get to her feet and staggered about for a while to get her blood flowing. When she was fairly certain that she wouldn't drop off as soon as she stopped moving, she pulled her cloak around her and sat on the tree trunk, listening to the quiet movements of the night.

Time passed. The stars wheeled overhead, and the moon made its steady progress across the sky. Over the horizon, far, far away, thunder rolled dryly. Wynter thought about her father. In her mind, Lorcan stood in a meadow at sunrise, looking over the river by their home. The sun was in his hair and he lifted his hand and whispered, *Look, darling. There, on the far bank. A deer!*

She did not think that anything short of a scream would wake the men; still, when the tears came, she buried her face in her cloak and muffled her sobs.

"Razi," she whispered, reaching to shake him awake. He opened his eyes before she even touched him, and she withdrew her hand, smiling. He gazed back in curious, wide-eyed detachment and she realised that he was still asleep, with his eyes open. "It's time for your watch," she said, patting his chest.

Razi blinked vacantly a few times. Then the childlike roundness left his eyes and he winced, rolled over and pushed himself up with a groan. "Oh, bloody hell," he hissed. "I miss my bed."

He heaved himself to his feet and shambled about to get the kinks out of his legs. Then he wandered over for his habitual check of the horses.

Christopher was fast asleep, flat on his back, his covers pooled around his ankles. He was as lax and as sprawling as a puppy, his mouth open slightly, his breath sighing out into the still air. Wynter watched his chest rise and fall, his pale undershirt glowing softly in the waning moonlight. She hitched her cloak and shuffled to his side.

"*Wynter!*" Razi's sharp call startled her, and she glanced over at him, nervous suddenly that he might object to their sharing a bedroll. To her surprise he gestured to Christopher and whispered, "Check for his knives!"

His knives! Wynter peered down at their sleeping friend. She didn't see any knives, but she hesitated now, wary. She had forgotten Christopher's tendency to leap from his sleep with a blade in his fist.

"Christopher?" she whispered. "Chris?"

He startled, his hands jumping slightly as he opened his eyes. "*Sea? Táim anseo . . .*" He cleared his throat and looked up at her, frowning. "Girly?"

Shy now under his blinking, grey-eyed confusion, Wynter nodded tentatively to Christopher's bedroll. "Is . . . is it all right?" she whispered.

Christopher gazed at her, not quite awake. His eyes wandered for a moment as if he was about to fall back asleep. Then he lifted his arm in bleary invitation and Wynter lay down into his embrace. She put her head on his chest and looped her arm across his warm stomach. He snaked his arm around her waist, pulled her in close and sighed. She felt his breathing deepen and his body relaxed beside hers.

She lay with her eyes open, looking out into the clearing. She could hear Razi taking the aired clothes down from the trees and folding them away into their bags. He did not seem bothered in the least by their intimacy.

This is strange, she thought, *this lying here together*. And it *was* strange. But somehow it was also fine. It was comfortable, and good, and right. She closed her eyes and settled her cheek against Christopher's chest, listening to his heart pump steadily beneath her ear.

"I didn't think you'd come back to me," he said, surprising her that he was still awake. She opened her eyes again and felt his voice vibrate inside him as he said, "I thought you'd think me too wicked, after what I did to that man."

She turned her cheek against his shirt again, taking comfort in the soft fabric against her skin, and she inhaled his smell, that lovely spicy odour. She tightened her arm around his waist. For a moment she hesitated, then she whispered, "Do you think it wicked that I'm glad he's dead?"

Christopher didn't answer. He was blinking up at the stars, just as she was blinking out into the moon-washed trees, both afraid of what the other must think of them. "I was afraid that he would follow us," he said. "I was frightened of what he might do. If he found you alone again."

She nodded against his chest. *Me too*, she thought. *Me too*.

"I couldn't stand the thought of it," he said, tightening his arm around her.

"My God," said Razi softly, his voice heavy with dread. "Did that man hurt you? Did . . .? What did that man do to you, Wynter?"

Wynter shut her eyes and turned her face into Christopher's chest. She did not answer. Christopher brought his hand up to rest against the thick coil of hair at the back of her head. He took a breath to tell Razi about the bandit and she immediately pressed her fingers to his lips to make him stop. But Christopher gently pulled her hand away and clasped it to his chest. Then he went ahead and told Razi everything, just as she had told it to him.

Razi was still and silent for a long time after Christopher stopped talking. Eventually Wynter couldn't stand it any longer and she turned her head to see him. He was standing looking at them, his face lost in shadows.

"Why did you not tell me?" he said, his voice thick and disbelieving. "Why did you not ask for my help? I would have protected you!"

Wynter stared at him, not knowing how to explain.

Christopher lay very still beneath her, his hand on her

hair, her palm still pressed to his chest. "She was ashamed, Razi," he said quietly. "She didn't know what to say."

"But what if that man had *killed* you, Chris? What if his friend had come and . . ." Razi cut himself off. He pulled his hands across his face, and then stood looking up at the stars, gathering his patience. "Next time, tell me," he said at last. "Next time you are in trouble, *tell me.* Together we'll find a better way."

Wynter jerked awake, images of fire in her head, drums beating. "Embla," she whispered, but the dream fled before she could catch hold of it, and even that name left her, lost as soon as it passed her lips.

The moon had sunk behind the trees, and the clearing was very dark and still. Wynter's eyes slid shut again, sleep pulling her like an undertow. Christopher had rolled onto his side and she lay pressed to his back, her forehead resting against his shoulderblades, her arm looped across his waist. As she began to spiral downwards into the dark, she stroked his stomach lightly, the way a drowsing child might stroke a blanket or a doll. At her touch, Christopher mumbled and stretched a little.

Wynter felt herself floating off the edge of consciousness. She slid her hand beneath Christopher's shirt, enjoying the softness of his skin against her fingertips. He sighed, and she continued to stroke his stomach, almost asleep.

Suddenly Christopher gripped her hand in his, pulling her fingers up and away. Sleep retreated a fraction and she half-opened her eyes. "You 'right, Chris?"

He seemed very tense, holding his breath, Wynter's hand squashed tightly in his. She went to speak again, but her eyes slid shut of their own accord and she stumbled completely into the dark, losing her grip on the world for a while.

When she drifted back up, he was gone. She put her hand out to feel for him but his side of the bedroll was empty. She closed her fingers in his abandoned cloak and sleep claimed her again.

She woke one more time that night to find Christopher slipping back into their bed. He pulled their cloaks over him and settled down with his back to her. She scooted over and looped her arm across his waist again, snuggling her head in against his back. He hesitated, then took her hand in his, kissed her fingers with his cold lips and settled down with a sigh.

Over the horizon thunder boomed again, dry and lightless, the uneasy promise of storms.

Silver Bells

"This is quite a travel party," said Christopher. He ground his toe into a post-hole and looked anxiously around the deserted camp. "Must have been at least three big tents here. Ten men, perhaps, maybe even more."

Wynter stooped and lifted a handful of cinders from the remains of the camp-fire. It had been almost two days since they had tried to spy on the inhabitants of this camp, but warmth still lurked under the surface of these carefully damped down ashes. "These fires haven't been doused long," she said. "They only struck camp this morning." She cleaned her hands on the grass and got to her feet. "I wish we'd managed to get a good look at them, instead of chasing each other through the woods like idiots."

Christopher strolled over to the large area of poached ground where the travellers had kept their horses. "They've made no effort to hide their presence. They seem to have no fear of being discovered."

"They were speaking Hadrish," commented Wynter. "Perhaps they're fur merchants?"

Razi stood on the other side of the clearing. He was

staring at something on the ground, absently running his thumb across the scar on his lip. His expression disturbed Wynter, and as Christopher wandered off to follow the tracks of the horses, she drifted over to Razi and looked down at what was so absorbing him.

"Oh!" she said softly, "a rein bell! You used to love those! I notice you don't use them anymore; don't the Arab horses like them?" She crouched, intending to pick the little silver globe from the leaf litter, but Razi startled her by putting his foot on it and grinding it into the dirt. She glanced up at him. He was glaring at the ground under his foot, his eyes hooded, his expression cold. Wynter had the feeling that he would like to crush that little bell until it was nothing but dust under his heel.

"What is it?" she whispered, still crouched at his feet. He lifted his eyes to meet hers, then snapped them to Christopher.

The young man had followed the trail of heavy hoofprints away from the camp and down towards the water. Unaware of their scrutiny, he called back over his shoulder as he examined the trail. "I think they're heading towards the ferry. We might run into them yet, if they're following the river."

Wynter looked back to Razi. She gestured questioningly to the bell. Razi shook his head and spoke softly, "Don't mention it to him. It may just be a rein bell; it probably *is* just a rein bell. But don't mention it to him. Not till I know for certain."

"Why?" She jogged after him as he went to fetch the horses. "Razi?"

Christopher had given up on the spoor and was strolling

back towards them, his eyebrows raised expectantly at their tense expressions. "What are the shifty eyes for?" he called. "Found something interesting?"

Razi leant close as he handed Wynter her reins. "I'm afraid it may be a slave bell, Wyn." Wynter's eyes widened and she looked anxiously at Christopher. He was eyeing them very dubiously now as he approached the clearing.

"The Loups-Garous use them," whispered Razi, bringing his horse between them and their advancing friend. "They put them on the poor creatures they consider their . . . their private property." He stepped into the stirrup. "Do not mention it to him." He rose smoothly into the saddle as Christopher came within earshot. "Come on, Christopher," he said. "Let us go see who these fellows are, shall we?"

Christopher watched as Razi kicked his horse forward and headed off down the trail, then he met Wynter's eyes. "What is it?" he said. "What did he find?"

Wynter blinked. She turned away, hopped and rose in the stirrup. "He didn't tell me," she said, settling into the saddle. "You know what he's like."

Christopher stood for a moment, his hand on his horse's neck, gazing up at her, and Wynter's heart twisted. She couldn't stand that look on his face. She didn't want to keep things from him. But maybe Razi was right, maybe it *was* just a rein bell. Until they knew for certain, was there any point upsetting Christopher, and perhaps stirring unwanted memories for him?

"Come on, love," she said softly. "He'll be angry."

Christopher's eyes sparkled at that, and he tilted his head back with a wicked grin.

"What?" she said, surprised.

"Oh, nothing." He swung up into his saddle, still grinning, and turned his horse to follow Razi out of the clearing.

"What?" she shouted, irritated at the pleased twinkle in his eye.

Christopher just waved his hand over his shoulder and kicked into a trot so that she had to hurry to catch up.

The day took on a breathless, pre-storm swelter and, once again, thunder grumbled beyond the horizon. They rode for hours and didn't take their break until late that afternoon, so they decided to make a meal of it, unsaddling the horses and settling down on a large flat rock by the river to eat and rest.

Even this close to the water, it was unbearably sultry, and they lolled about, listless and silent in the heat. Wynter lay far up the rock, deep in the shade of an overhanging tree, tiredly chewing a piece of cheese. Christopher sat at the water's edge, dangling his bare feet in the river and staring up at the sky.

Razi was his usual quiet self, sprawled in the sun, gnawing on an apple and brooding. Wynter knew he was worried about that little silver bell, but she thought he was overreacting. The Loups-Garous would never ride so blatantly through Jonathon's kingdom, particularly not with slaves in tow. They knew what would happen should Jonathon's troops find them. No, the Loups-Garous would have been slinking quietly around the edges of things, slipping through the shadows and getting away fast, not traipsing through the woods leaving their spoor like a bunch of frilly-headed court ladies on a picnic.

Relax, brother, she thought, *it is Northlander fur traders, that is all. Or Musulman pilgrims on their way home from the Moroccos. Plenty of people use rein bells. There does not have to be a dark reason for everything.*

"Just a small rest now," Razi warned. "We move on soon."

"Bloody monarch," muttered Christopher, leaning back on his elbows and looking across the vast expanse of slow moving water. "Always giving orders . . ."

The small rest turned into a deep sleep and it was about twenty minutes later when Wynter jerked awake. Someone was rustling about at the tree line and she snapped to attention, her hand on her knife, but it was only Razi walking up the rock towards the trees. He smiled at her and whispered, "It's all right, we're not leaving yet."

"Where are you going?" she asked.

He rolled his eyes, holding up his short-spade and grinning. "Never question a man heading into the trees with a spade in his hand, Lady!"

She grinned and waved him off. He strolled away into the dappled shade, "I may be a while," he called back lightly.

Wynter reclined on her elbows, enjoying the quiet. The water was peaceful and chuckling against the round stones of the shore, the river gleaming like polished soapstone. Wynter felt like a fox peering from its den into the heat of the day. It struck her then that Christopher was not by the water's edge and she scanned the sun-baked rocks and the gently buzzing reed-beds with a small frown.

She turned to call after Razi and realised that Christopher was right beside her. He must have come up into the shade after she'd fallen sleep, and he sat facing her, his back against the rocks, his hands folded peacefully on the flat plane of his stomach. His hat was low over his eyes, and as her vision adjusted to the shade Wynter realised that he was watching her with a soft kind of intensity.

"Hello," she whispered.

The sun chose that moment to step from behind the clouds, and Christopher's face was flooded with reflected light, all his fine-boned features abruptly jumping into sharp relief. Something amused him and he grinned at her. Wynter had to grin back, his delight was so contagious.

"What?" she laughed.

"The sun just lit your eyes up, green as fairy-fire," he said softly. "You look like a bewitched cat. Any self-respecting Midlands biddy would be crossing herself and strapping you to a ducking stool if she saw you."

Wynter chuckled. "Oh, shush," she said, turning to look out at the water again.

The peaceful sounds lulled gently around her. In the brambles above them a robin began to sing.

"What is your name, girly?"

Wynter sighed. It was a question that had been asked more than once in her life. As usual she didn't answer; she just treated Christopher to *that* smile and *that* look, the combination of which would let any courtier know that the question should never be asked again. But Christopher was no courtier, and the subtleties of such body language were completely lost on him. He waited a polite moment, and then when she still didn't reply he pressed on.

"Wynter, well it ain't a *real* name is it? It's the same here as in the North, ain't it? Wynter-baby. It's a foundling title. Or it's what they temporarily call babies when their mothers die before naming them, ain't it?" Wynter continued to gaze at the water and didn't answer. "Well . . ." Christopher sounded uncertain now, as if finally aware that he was trespassing on unwelcome territory. "Um . . ." he said. "Did . . . did your dad not name you, then? When he got back from—"

"Jonathon named me," she said abruptly, "while Dad was still on the run. He thought it would please my father to call me after my . . . he named me after my dead mother." She felt her face harden with the bitterness she now harboured towards the King. Until recently she had always considered this as nothing worse than a sad mistake, but now it had come to symbolise what she saw as the man's unrelenting thoughtlessness. "Marni knew it would devastate my dad," she said, "to have to hear my mother's name day after day, but never again see her. She knew that he would never be able to bear it. She refused to call me anything but Wynter. By the time my dad had been fetched home and recovered from his wounds, I must have been five months old. I was almost a year old before the poor man could bear even to look at me. No one called me anything but Wynter by then. Wynter is the only name I ever answered to, Christopher. It is my name."

She glanced at him. He was watching her uncertainly, as though he had something to say, but wasn't sure how she'd take it.

"What?" she said. "What is it?"

"It's a *baby's* name," he said.

She didn't answer, not certain where he was heading.

Christopher blushed, his eyes sliding away. "Well," he said. "Well, it's just . . . you're a *woman*!" He waved his hand at her body, not looking at her. "Don't you . . .? Ain't it . . .? Gah!" he exclaimed, suddenly irritated. "How can a man be expected to call you by a *baby's* name? It's ridiculous! What if some fellow wants to wed you? How could he walk you under the bower with a *baby's* name hanging over you?"

Wynter laughed, convinced he was jesting. "Is that what you'd like for me, Christopher Garron?" she asked, not quite teasing. "After all my years training and getting my guild approval? You want me to wed myself to some lad and become a slave to my belly for the rest of my life?"

"You . . . That surely ain't your only opinion of marriage?"

Wynter snorted sarcastically. *Easy for a man to say*, she thought. *What risk to him, baby after baby for the rest of his days? No man ever died in labour and that's for certain.*

"No wife of mine would have a child till she wanted one," said Christopher softly, and Wynter glanced at him in scorn.

"Oh aye," she said. "Like any man would deny himself the pleasure of his bed for the sake of his woman's belly. How long would that last? A few weeks? A month? What about years? Could you hold yourself for years, Christopher?"

"For God's sake," he shouted, his sudden anger taking her by surprise. "Does no one tell their women *anything* in this place? Don't you know the pleasure is for the man *and* the woman to enjoy? And there's no need to deny yourself

aught! There are ways . . . there are . . . good Frith!"
Christopher suddenly leapt to his feet and ducked out from
under the bower. He was flushed red with rage and embarrassment, and poor Razi chose that unfortunate time to
present himself in his path.

"You!" yelled Christopher, poking a finger in the
shocked young man's chest. "You ought to be ashamed of
yourself! You call yourself a doctor? She's your sister, for
Frith's sake! And Lorcan! Of all men I'm surprised at him!
What's wrong with you people? Leaving your women
floundering around in the dark at the spurious mercies of
their men folk! Shame! Shame on you, Razi Kingsson! You
should be bloody whipped! Give me that!" He snatched the
spade from Razi's hand. "*Tá orm cac a dhéanamh!*" he said,
and stormed off into the brush, disappearing quickly into
the shadows.

Razi stood with his hand out, his mouth open.
"Whu . . .?" he said. He turned to look at Wynter. "Huh?"
he said.

Wynter felt herself flush scarlet. It began at her breastbone and rose like a tide to the roots of her hair. Razi's eyes
widened. His voice deepened, and this time he said
"What?" with real command.

Struggling to get a hold of her tangled conversation with
Christopher, Wynter took a deep breath and did her best to
explain. As she spoke, Razi's expression changed from wary
to tender and by the time she was finished, he had his hand
over his mouth, and he chuckled in a kind of mortified
amusement.

"Oh, Wyn," he said, shaking his head. "Oh." He
laughed again and looked back into the woods as if sharing

a smile with Christopher. "Oh, Chris," he murmured. "How wonderful."

Wynter was utterly confused and very unhappy now at what seemed to be a shared secret that was totally over her head. "Why is he so angry, Razi?"

Razi looked kindly at her. "Because he's a good man, sis." He looked back into the trees again, grimaced and crossed to sit down by Wynter's side.

"All right," he said. "I certainly don't know as much about the female side of things as the Merron women do – contraceptive infusions and such, but I'll tell you what I can, if I may?"

Wynter looked steadfastly out at the river while Razi told her everything he knew. When he finally stopped talking and ran his hands over his heated face, she felt like she might never be able to meet his eye again. But she also felt tremendously powerful and liberated and strong. It was as though Razi had opened a door and shown her an immensity of possible futures, where once she had believed there was only one.

Christopher came back to find them saddling up the horses. He was embarrassed and hangdog, and Razi fought a grin as he took back the spade.

"Sorry," said Christopher, his eyes downcast.

Razi clunked him gently on the top of his head with the spade. "Oh, you are *not!*" he said slyly and carried it over to tie it to his horse.

Christopher rubbed his head, looking confused. Wynter came and gazed up at him until he met her eyes. When he finally turned to her, she shocked him by stretching up

and kissing him softly on the lips. He kept perfectly still for
a fraction of a second, then he pressed his mouth down on
hers so that their lips parted delicately against each other.
They didn't touch, except for that singular exquisite contact. But, just before they parted, the tip of Christopher's
tongue brushed gently against Wynter's and it felt like he
had run his hand all the way from the top of her head to
the soles of her feet.

She pulled away with a small sigh and the two of them
stood for a moment, their eyes shut, their heads still tilted
at the angle with which they had ended their kiss. Then
Razi coughed softly behind them, and they turned away
from each other, blinking. When they hit the trail again,
Wynter was smiling and Christopher hummed quietly to
himself as they got underway.

The storms moved in by dusk, and they hurried to set up
camp in the rapidly encroaching twilight. They had just
enough time to get their belongings under canvas and lay
out their bedrolls before the sky opened in a tremendous,
bruising downpour.

They dived into the tent and lay in the dark, listening to
the rain batter itself into the unresisting forest. At Wynter's
feet, Razi drew up his cloak and curled against the pillow of
his saddle. Christopher tightened his arms briefly around
her and she felt him kiss her neck before settling down to
sleep.

There had been no more sign of the other travellers. As
she fell asleep, Wynter thought about them out there somewhere, no more aware of her presence in the world than all
the little animals of the night. She imagined their two

camps as seen by God, minuscule and insignificant, their paths little threads laid on the map of the world, intersecting once and then never again. Overhead, the thunder finally made its appearance and she jumped as it bellowed its anger to the sky. Christopher took her hand and settled his forehead against her back. Razi snored softly in the gloom. Wynter settled deeper into the warmth of her cloak. After that, sleep pulled her swiftly down, and the world bled away into darkness and muffled sound.

Sons of Wolves

Around mid-morning the next day, the sun finally came out. The joy it brought was short-lived, however, as midges descended in a vicious cloud, and everyone sighed and pulled their scarves up around their faces. Wynter was swatting at the flies and grumbling miserably to herself when Razi jerked his horse to a sudden halt, blocking the path. Warily, she pulled Ozkar neck and neck with his big dark mare. Christopher pulled up behind them, silently watchful.

Razi was staring intently ahead.

"What is it?" hissed Wynter, peering into the forest and seeing nothing.

"Shhhh," Razi held up his hand. "Listen."

They sat for a moment, their horses blowing and stamping beneath them. Then Wynter heard it, quite a distance away – hammering and the sporadic shouts of men. Somewhere up ahead, a large camp was being set up or, more likely, it was being struck, the travellers getting ready to leave after having waited out the rain.

Wynter glanced at Razi. Perhaps they had found the owners of that little silver bell.

The three of them slid from their saddles, secured their mounts and took off on foot through the trees. They came to a halt at the base of a small hill, where they crouched, pausing to catch their breath. The camp was on the other side, out of sight, the men shouting to each other as they did their work.

Christopher went to crawl forward, and Razi snagged him by the sleeve, tugging him back into hiding "I want you to stay here, Chris. Keep an eye out for guards, while I go take a look."

Christopher sank back into the leaves. "What?" he said, puzzled.

"I mean it; I want you to stay here. I want you to warn us if anyone comes."

Christopher tilted his head back and looked Razi in the eye. Then he turned to Wynter, searching her face. She looked away, letting her attention slip up to the brow of the hill. Christopher's eyes narrowed. He knew they were keeping something from him. "Let Wynter keep watch," he said flatly. He broke free of Razi with an upward swing of his arm and began a determined crawl to the top.

"Shit," spat Razi.

Wynter sighed and they began to crawl after him.

Neither of them could match Christopher's stealthy speed, and he gained the brow of the hill while they were still only three quarters of the way up. Wynter glanced up to see him pause at the skyline and then cautiously raise his head to look down into the camp. She turned to see if Razi was watching, then jumped, startled, as something dark and low rushed past her down the slope.

She pressed herself into the leaf cover, convinced that

some big animal had launched itself over the hill. But it was Christopher, crawling frantically backwards through the leaves, heading for the base of the hill at tremendous speed. He shot past so quickly that Wynter was looking down on him before she knew it. His face shocked her, it was so terrified. His teeth were bared, his eyes staring as he propelled himself away from whatever it was he'd seen.

Razi reached for him and missed, and Wynter understood at once that Christopher had forgotten that they were there. He was possessed only with the desire to get away, and as she watched, he hit the bottom of the hill, gained his feet and fled.

Razi paused for only a moment and then he, too, scurried backwards to the bottom of the hill. Wynter hurried after him. They hit the ground running and took off after their friend, speeding through the trees in silence, trying to keep up with Christopher's terrified pace.

They arrived at the horses to find Christopher clumsily pulling his mare's tether from the highline. Even as Wynter ran towards him, he was flinging himself into the saddle, so she veered for Ozkar, expecting them all to mount up and ride as far and as fast as they could. Razi, however, ran straight across the clearing, wrapped his powerful arms around Christopher and snatched him bodily from his mount.

Christopher released a sharp cry as Razi heaved him backwards, then he lapsed into an eerily silent frenzy. Razi had grabbed Christopher's right wrist as he snatched him from his horse and he pinned Christopher's left arm against his body as he pulled him down. But even with both arms restrained, Christopher writhed like an eel, and it took all of Razi's immense strength just to stop him from slipping free.

"Wait now," Razi murmured. "Wait . . ."

With a growl, Christopher shoved back with his heels, and Razi staggered backwards to keep from falling.

Wynter watched helplessly, overwhelmed by Christopher's soundless, blind panic. He seemed to have lost all track of who they were and what they wanted with him. She had no doubt that, had Christopher been able to reach for his knives, Razi would have suffered for it.

Christopher threw his head back, attempting to butt Razi between the eyes. The blow would surely have broken Razi's nose had it connected, but he seemed to be expecting it, and had already twisted so that Christopher's head struck his shoulder and not his face. Wynter was amazed at how calm Razi was. His deep voice remained soothing and quiet, and his face was almost expressionless as he continued to ask their friend, "Wait . . . wait, Christopher . . . wait . . ."

Then, without breaking his strange composure, Razi suddenly lifted Christopher off his feet and shook him, quick and hard, as if trying to rattle his fear from him. "*Wait*," he said loudly.

Christopher stilled instantly, his head pressed back against Razi's shoulder, his face blank. His breathing was rapid and terrified against Razi's straining arms, and Wynter was appalled by how white he was, at how wide his eyes were.

Razi lowered Christopher to his feet without releasing him. "Chris," he murmured. "Can you understand me?"

Christopher's eyelids fluttered and he nodded.

"Just wait a little moment. Just a moment and then we can go. All right?" Christopher didn't reply. Razi, his arms still wrapped tightly around him, turned his head against his friend's hair, trying to see his face. "I just need to know a few things, then we can go, all right?"

Wynter did not like the way Razi was holding Christopher's mutilated fist captive against his chest. He was so much bigger than Christopher, and it seemed brutal, somehow, and cruel. She opened her mouth to tell Razi to release him. Then Christopher's clenched hand relaxed suddenly against the fabric of his tunic. His eyes slid towards Razi's voice, and something made Wynter lower her hand, and stay silent.

"Was it the Loups-Garous?" murmured Razi.

Christopher nodded stiffly.

"Was it André's sons?" Christopher jerked his head in another nod and Razi tightened his arms, drawing Christopher's hand even further across his chest. "Was it *that* pack? *David's* pack?"

"Aye," whispered Christopher. "David's pack." The sound of his own voice seemed to wake him, and Christopher became aware of Razi's arms around him, and of where they were. He flushed and his face creased up with embarrassment. He shifted miserably, shrugging his shoulder, and then his arm. He twisted his wrist against his friend's grip, and Razi slowly released him. Razi tried to keep a comforting hand on his shoulder, but Christopher shrugged him off with a little wincing movement and stepped away, rubbing his wrist.

"Sorry," he whispered, avoiding Razi's eyes. "Sorry . . . it was the shock. That's all. Just the shock." He lifted his eyes to Wynter and looked away immediately. "Sorry," he said again. He looked at his hands, snarling in disgust at the way they were trembling.

"*Look* at me!" he hissed. "*Look* at what they still reduce me to. I'm . . . I'm bloody *palsied*." He broke off with a little cry of self-loathing, staggered towards the horses, seemed to change his mind and veered away again. He ended up just stumbling in a circle. "Shit," he said, finding himself back where he'd started. "Shit." He lifted his hands to Razi in a helpless gesture. Razi just stood watching, his arms hanging impotently by his sides. Wynter reached for Christopher's hand. His fingers closed briefly on hers, but then he broke free of her grip.

His sturdy little mare was strolling free, her reins trailing perilously on the ground between her hooves. Reflexively, Christopher crossed to her and fixed the tack. He did not come back to his friends when he was done, but stood with his hand on his horse's neck, staring blankly into the trees.

Wynter tore her gaze from him. "What are Wolves doing *here*, Razi?" she cried. "I thought Jonathon drove them *out*."

Razi turned burning eyes on her, and she stepped back at the unexpected rage in his face. In a sudden flash of understanding, Wynter realised that Razi had been handling Christopher as he would a bolting horse. He had been dominating him, using his own strength and will to quell Christopher's panic and calm his fear, and now that he had succeeded, all Razi's self-possession had deserted him, leaving him seething and furious.

"Why are they here, Razi?" she asked gently.

Razi just pushed past without answering and crossed

the clearing with his head down like an angry bull. Swinging into the saddle, he pulled his mare around, yanking the reins with uncharacteristic brutality so that the big animal tossed her head and snorted in protest. He jerked to an aggravated halt at the tree line.

"Come on!" he snapped. "We're heading out." Then he pushed his horse through the undergrowth and into the trees without waiting for the others to mount up.

The heavy foliage made it difficult to ride close and they kept splitting up and coming together, drifting into single file and then separating again. Wynter watched the others come and go through the screen of leaves and the intermittent trunks of the trees. Christopher slouched in the saddle, clucking his horse around obstacles and through patches of light brush; Razi, deep in glowering thought, was thoroughly unapproachable. He stayed well ahead of them, setting a ruthless pace that neither Wynter nor Christopher chose to question.

Eventually, the undergrowth thinned a little, and Wynter took the opportunity to pull up beside Christopher's horse so they rode two abreast for a while. He did not look at her, though she kept glancing his way, and after a while she leaned over and touched his arm.

"Christopher," she said quietly. "Are you all right?"

"Oh, aye!" he said. "I told you, it was just the shock." He steered his horse one-handed around a stump, and forgot to look at Wynter again when they got back on course. "I hadn't expected them here, you see. Razi had told me they wouldn't . . . if I had known, I could have . . . I would certainly have . . . you see . . ." He seemed to realise that he was talking in fragments and shut up, snapping his spine straight and taking a deep, aggravated breath through his nose.

Razi rode on in silence, his back rigid.

"I ain't usually such a coward," Christopher said suddenly. Wynter frowned and reached for him in protest, but he sidestepped his horse away from her and kept looking steadily ahead. "It was the shock," he said firmly, as if she had disputed the fact. "I just didn't expect to see them here, so I weren't ready. At home, I *know* they'll be there, I *expect* to see them and I can steel myself. That's the . . . it was just the shock."

"At home?" she said. "In the Moroccos, you mean? You see the Wolves *there?*"

He glanced at her and away again. "Sometimes. When they're in town. Their estates are very close to Razi's. They are our neighbours."

Wynter turned to look at Razi, but if he felt her eyes boring into him he didn't show it. *Their estates?* she thought. *The Wolves have estates in the Moroccos?* She had always thought that they lived feral, like wild animals. She had always imagined them crouched in filthy dens, or lurking in caves, swaddled in dirty furs.

She looked at Christopher's ruined hands. His left hand was resting on his thigh, his right loosely holding the reins, guiding his little mare on her way. Wynter had assumed the Wolves had done that to him, but surely – she glanced again at Razi. Surely whoever had done that to Christopher didn't just wander about Algiers day after day? Dear God! Surely Razi would have made them pay? *It weren't your place*, Christopher had said, *to sacrifice a kingdom for the sake of revenge.*

Wynter's face flushed with building anger.

"Razi said they wouldn't be here," said Christopher softly, as if talking to himself.

"Chris?"

At the sound of Razi's voice, Christopher's head snapped up. "Aye?" he said.

Razi brought his horse to a halt and half-turned his head towards them. They pulled up beside him.

"You travelled for how long with the Wolves?" he asked. "Nine months? Ten?"

Jesu, thought Wynter.

"Over ten months, counting the boat and the trek through the muh . . . the markets." Apart from the stumble, Christopher's voice was perfectly even and calm. Razi turned to him, his face well-schooled. Christopher met his eyes without hesitation.

"This is how they always travel?" asked Razi. "This obvious? With the pack all together?"

Christopher nodded. "I never once saw them try to hide," he said. "They set up their tents every night, nice and comfortable. If they have guh . . . *captives* with them, they give them bivouacs and sometimes fires, but the Wolves sleep in the big tents with their . . . with the . . . the ones . . ."

"Aye," said Razi, holding up his hand, and Christopher ground to a grateful halt. "Do they stay close to camp? Can we expect them to wander? Go hunting?"

Christopher shook his head. "Unless they are raiding, no. They like their comfort, the Wolves." He drifted off for a moment, his face blank. Wynter looked at his uncharacteristically dull eyes and felt a solid block of rage rising in her throat; it was like a lump of unchewed meat. "If they're raiding, or moving in for a . . . for what they call a *visit*, then the camp is set and most of the brothers go . . . visit . . . while the others stay and watch the goods." Christopher made no attempt to correct the word this time, his mind far away. Then his eyes snapped into focus and he looked sharply at Razi. "But they don't *raid* here, do they, Razi? They don't *visit*, do they?" Christopher's voice was hard suddenly and bitter. "You said they wouldn't be here at *all*."

Razi winced and almost looked away. "So," he said tightly, ignoring Christopher's comment, "do they tend to travel fast, Christopher? Once they've struck camp? Will they cover much ground?"

"They ain't got any *goods* with them," said Christopher holding Razi's eye. He was almost belligerent now, daring his friend to look away. "Just *property*, so, yes, Razi, they'll travel fast. Where are they going?"

Razi shook his head; he looked away into the trees. He seemed to be deep in thought. Then he half-turned his head to speak over his shoulder again. "Christopher," he said, his voice soft, "were I to get to my knees now and beg of you to return home, would you misinterpret it as an attack on your courage?"

Christopher blinked and looked up into the leaves above them. His eyes were bright, the broken sunlight making them glitter. For a moment he seemed very young, and Wynter wanted to put her arms around him. She wanted to tell him that it was all right. If he needed to leave, it was all right. She would not judge him for it.

"You'd come too, of course," said Christopher, but Razi just smiled and shook his head. He glanced at Wynter.

She shook her head. *No, Razi. I will not leave.*

"You can get on your knees if you wish, Razi," said Christopher hoarsely. "It would be amusing to see. But it would avail you naught but muddy britches." He tried a watery grin on for size. It slipped away a little too soon to be effective and his eyes never lost their tightness, but Razi obliged with a snort.

He pulled his horse around and moved on without comment.

"What are we going to do, Razi?" called Wynter, unable to keep the dry anger from her voice.

Razi kept his horse moving forward. "We're heading for the Indirie Valley, sis. Remember? We're looking for Alberon."

She willed him to turn around so that he could see how enraged she was. When he didn't, she called after him. "What are we going to do about the *Wolves*?"

Razi didn't answer. He let the distance grow between them, so that Wynter was left seething and glaring impotently at his retreating back.

"Chris," she asked. "What do we do about the Wolves?"

He shrugged wearily. "Avoid them," he said. He kicked his horse forward. Wynter pulled Ozkar into place behind him, and they followed Razi as he made his way through the ever thickening brush.

André Le Garou

To Wynter's surprise, Razi headed back to the river. He brought them all the way to the water and followed the shore for a half mile or so until they came to a wide and sandy beach, circled by big round boulders and shaded by cooling trees. He trotted to the middle of the soft, clean sand, brought his horse to a halt and looked around him.

"Here," he said quietly and slid from his saddle.

Christopher and Wynter sat looking expectantly at him, thinking maybe he needed to relieve himself, or that his horse had a problem. But he just led his mare to the tree line and began to unsaddle her. Christopher shrugged wearily and slid from his horse without comment.

"What are we doing?" asked Wynter, and she swore to herself that if Razi Kingsson gave her another sarcastic reply she'd trot Ozkar to him and kick him in the head.

Razi paused in the middle of lifting the saddle from his horse. He looked across at her with a tiny smile and said, "I think we'll set up camp here, wait out the night."

She spread her hands in disbelief. There were *hours* of daylight left – what was he talking about?

Razi nodded in understanding. "We'll let them get ahead of us. Just let them go wherever the hell it is that they are going. Let them just bloody . . . let them just bloody well *go*. And then we won't have to worry about them any more. All right?"

Christopher paused at that, just for a moment, his face uncertain, then he continued tending to his horse.

Razi carried his saddle to the rocks and laid it down, then returned to pull the blanket and saddle-pad from the mare's broad back. "They can go to hell for all that I care," he muttered. Then he lifted his eyes to Christopher. "But when this is settled, Christopher, between my brother and I, when all this is settled . . . you and I will take my knights and we will hunt the Wolves." His face grew hard suddenly, his handsome features drawing down into dark intent. "We shall drive them from my father's kingdom once again, and they shall pay the price for ever thinking that they could take advantage of the temporary chaos here."

Christopher stared at Razi, his hands spread against the dusty chestnut hide of his horse's shoulder, his eyes questioning. "I mean it this time, Chris," said Razi quietly.

Christopher's eyes narrowed and his mouth curled into a sudden, brutal smile. His pale face was like a sharpened blade then, his mouth, his eyes, the set of his jaw all lethal. He nodded and Razi smiled grimly at him and they went back to their work.

Wynter looked behind her at the trees. They fluttered in the hot breeze, peaceful, serene and lovely. She shivered, watching the shadows, the hair on the back of her neck rising in prickly spider-legs of fear. What if the Wolves didn't move on? What if they were not just passing through? Razi's squad of knights wasn't with them here, and all the violent intentions in the world wouldn't protect the three of them if the Loups-Garous took against them.

The darkness under the trees moved, and Wynter abruptly kicked her horse over to the others. She kept a watchful eye on the shadows and stayed close to her friends as they tended to the horses.

"What in God's name are you doing, Razi?"

Razi paused at the tree line and looked back to where Wynter was laying the rain-dampened ground sheets out to dry. He had an axe in his hand and a coil of thin rope looped over his shoulder, and it was quite obvious he was going to collect firewood. But it was inconceivable in these circumstances that he would actually want to light a fire.

"Have you lost your reason?" she said. "You will draw them down on us!"

Razi glanced briefly at Christopher. He was down at the water's edge in the full sunshine, shaking damp cloaks out over the bushes and draping socks across a highline. "I am going to cook us a good meal tonight, sis," Razi said. "We are going to eat properly, and sit around a fire like human beings. I will not cower in the dark tonight. I will not have . . ." His eyes flickered to the river's edge again and he lapsed into silence.

"Oh," whispered Wynter. "All right."

"Ask Christopher to tickle us up some trout," he said, then he glanced at her uncertainly. "Would you like that? Would you like some fish?"

"Aye," she said softly. "I would."

"All right." He went to turn away from her, and then hesitated and looked back. "I will try and find some garlics if you like?"

"I would like that very much, Razi."

He nodded and they traded a smile. Then he disappeared into the undergrowth.

Wynter finished laying out the equipment, then she jogged down to the water's edge to help Christopher with the rest of their things. She rounded the bushes and came to an awkward halt. "Oh," she said, "I'm sorry."

Christopher was sitting deep in the shade, his back against a tree, and as she appeared he scrubbed his face in a furious attempt to hide the fact that he had been crying. "Oh, curse it," he said desperately.

Wynter half-turned to go, paused, swung back to him and trotted up the rock. "Razi wants us to tickle up some trout," she said. "He seems to think it a great idea to light a fire. I think he's lost his God-cursed mind!" She stepped over Christopher's sprawled legs and dropped lightly to sit beside him, looking out at the river.

"The . . ." he started hoarsely, then cleared his throat. "As long as the breeze stays blowing upriver we'll be all right." There was a moment's tense silence. "I quite fancy some fish," he said, turning to look at her. "Do you?"

Wynter knocked her shoulder against his in an affectionate, teasing gesture, and smiled. "Aye," she said. "I do. I can catch it if you like."

Christopher sniffed. "Oh aye?" he said doubtfully, wiping his hand under his eyes again. "You tickle trout do you, lass?"

"Christopher Garron," she admonished with another

nudge to his shoulder. "Do you doubt me on foot of my sex?"

He gave her a sideways smile, and looked out at the river again. "Nay, lass," he said softly. "I just didn't think court life would afford much time for dangling your arms in rivers."

"My dad taught me. He was very good at it."

He sighed. "So was mine."

They sat in gentle silence for a little while, watching the sun glitter on the water.

"My dad were a lovely man," whispered Christopher suddenly. "Lorcan would have loved him. And my dad would have loved Lorcan. They were very alike." He breathed out a little laugh. "Though I think my dad's language may well have shocked yours. He were a mite foul-tongued."

Wynter chuckled. It was true, her father had detested foul language. Though in Christopher's case, he hadn't seemed to mind too much. She glanced fondly at him. *Dad loved you*, she thought.

"What was your father's name, Christopher?"

"Aidan," he said, then repeated it quietly to himself. "Aidan Garron.

She nodded. Aidan Garron and Lorcan Moorehawke. Gone.

All of a sudden the light glittering off the water became a little hard to focus on. Wynter looked down at her hands. They too were blurred. She swiped her eyes angrily.

"It hurts me, girly, that my memories of him are all caught up with those curs." Christopher whispered this, as though he was telling her a shameful secret. "It shames me that every time I think of my dad, I end up thinking of *them*. It's like I'm letting them steal him twice . . ."

"Oh, Christopher. Don't."

They sat rigidly side by side for a moment, both perilously close to tears. Then Christopher shook himself and ran his hands over his face. "Augh!" he snarled. "Good Frith! Pull yourself together, Garron!" He knocked his head back against the tree. "Stupid baby!" he said, and dropped his hands heavily onto his knee.

Without thinking about it, Wynter reached across and pressed gently on Christopher's left hand, splaying the fingers out against his thigh. His hand would not quite flatten, the fingers being clawed slightly and incapable of straightening.

At this contact Christopher grunted and jerked forward, as though to get up. It was the first time he'd ever reacted badly to her touching his scars, but Wynter looked beseechingly at him and kept her hand firmly on top of his. Gradually, he leaned back against the tree, and watched, tense but unprotesting, as Wynter pushed his sleeve back and ran her fingers along the neat white ribbon of scar tissue that ran all the way from his missing finger to the crook of his arm. It must have been a massive infection indeed to have needed so long an incision to drain it.

"I almost lost it," he said quietly. "If it weren't for Razi . . ." Christopher bunched his hand into a fist and straightened it again. Wynter felt his muscles move under his skin. She slid her hand along his sinewy forearm and settled her palm against the warm hollow of his elbow. "After I got better, I lay in bed for weeks, just wishing I would die. Marcello thought I'd never recover."

"But you did."

"Aye. I did."

Wynter tried to imagine that. Wondered what kind of strength it took to pick yourself up after something like that. She found it beyond the realms of her imagination.

"One day," he said, "I just got up. I made my way down to the stables and I burnt everything."

She clenched down hard on his arm. "What do you mean? Everything?"

"Everything. My guitars. My violins. All the music we'd collected over the years. My dad's recorders, his mandolin, all our other little bits and pieces. I burnt them all because they'd never be aught but pain to me. Thankfully, Marcello caught me before I could burn my father's trunk. I'm eternally grateful for that; it's all I have left of him." He looked at her. "It weren't originally a dressing case, you see. It was an instrument case. All our gear fitted in it. In neat little compartments. Nice and safe. My dad had it made specially, he designed it." Christopher's voice became very quiet. "They sold it with me," he said. "We were a job lot. Me and the case."

"Christopher," she whispered. His eyes were wide and bright. He was looking right at her, but she was not sure what it was he saw.

"It was desire for revenge that got me out of that bed, girly. I were a black seething pit of it. I worked daily to get my strength back, so that one day I'd be able to go and kill the bastards that had stolen my family, and stole my hands and . . ." He scrubbed his mouth, his eyes wide over the top of his hand. "They still had my girls, you see. My girls – the rest of my troupe." He absently touched his cheek, just under his eye. "They had gone on ahead of me. To our new master. Already branded. Already out of my grasp. Beyond even Razi's considerable power to save." His eyes grew impossibly wide. "They might still be there for all I know, in that bloody place."

"What place, Christopher?"

"The compound. André Le Garou's compound."

"André Le Garou?" asked Wynter. "The man that these Wolves call their father?" Christopher did not answer. He was very far away now, seeing things she could not. She persisted with her question, squeezing his arm gently.

"That is what they call their leaders . . . Father? And they are all considered his sons? Christopher?" She moved her head into his direct line of sight. "Chris?"

"They say that André's compound is filled with music," he said distantly. "All day and all night, musicians play there. Because André Le Garou, he *loves* his music." He sneered at that. "Aye, he loves his music and he loves his . . . he loves his women." He swallowed, his anger falling away to despair. "Women and music," he repeated softly. "His harem . . . his bloody *brothel* . . . is just crammed full of artists, captured from all around the world."

Christopher looked out blindly into the daylight. He was so very, very far away that Wynter wanted to grab him and hold him very tightly and say, *stop. Stop now. Come back. This is too much*. But he went on talking in his flat, dull voice and she went on listening, her hand on his arm.

"We were a gift for him, you see, the famous Garron troupe. As soon as the Wolves set eyes on us, they knew that their father would want us. And so they took us to him, or what were left of us after that bloody journey. More little monkeys for André's zoo."

He looked at Wynter then, really focused on her, really *seeing* her face instead of the memory pictures that had been there before. "Razi explained to me later how André has no right to call it a harem, how it's nothing *like* a harem. He told me the very word *harem* implies protection and respect. André's palace is nothing like that. The poor women . . . bullied and abused and shared amongst the Wolves. My poor girls," he whispered desperately. "My poor . . ."

"Why did they sell you, Christopher? And not your girls? Were you not—?"

"I weren't ever meant to be sold, girly. I should have gone straight in with them. Only for I'm a *man*, you see, a *male* slave. There was no way that André would have allowed me to mingle with his women."

He looked at her closely, hoping he wouldn't have to spell it out. But he must have seen that Wynter didn't really understand. "They would have to . . . I would have to be gelded first, you see." He ignored her gasp of shock and went on, "André insists on doing *that* job himself. He don't trust no one else to do it, for fear they damage the *goods*. He's very good at it, apparently. No matter how old the slave, they very rarely die, very rarely even catch an infection." Christopher smiled a bitter twisted smile at that. Wynter reached for his hands and squeezed them hard, but he couldn't seem to feel her touch.

"No doubt he would have done a very neat job," he murmured. "Had he ever got the chance. But Le Garou was away in Fez, and his sons had urgent business outside of town, so I was left in the care of Sadaqah al-'Abbas, one of their brokers. He agreed to hold me in his pens till Le Garou returned." Christopher went very quiet. He seemed to have lost the energy to tell any more and just sat with his hands clasped in Wynter's, his chin almost on his chest.

When nothing more was forthcoming, Wynter gently shook his hands and Christopher went on talking as if he were a clockwork toy. "Sadaqah decided to make a little money on the side," he said. "So he rented me out to Hadil for the length of the wedding celebrations, strictly on the sly, of course. And that's how I met Razi. That's how Razi saved my life."

Good God, thought Wynter, *the randomness of it all.* She could not get past the tenuous circumstances that had brought her two friends together. Had even one small thing been different, some element of time, or of place, then they would never have met. Razi would never have been able to help him, and she would never have found this man who had come to mean so much to her. She tightened her grip on him, as if afraid he'd slip away.

"I wouldn't have been able to live like that, girly," he whispered. "I'd never have *let* myself live, not like that." Christopher lifted one of his hands and made a delicate pressing motion in the air, as if lightly touching something only he could see. His lips curved into a smile. "In my father's trunk there's a secret drawer. It hides all my knives. I had a plan, you see. Once Le Garou had . . . had cut me, and once they'd brought me inside the compound, I planned to take those knives and kill my girls. Then I would have killed myself. It would have been our only chance of release. It would have . . ."

Christopher lifted his eyes to the horizon, his hand still poised in the air, his expression wondering. "I couldn't believe it when he came and bought me. I still don't know how he persuaded Sadaqah to fall in with it. Razi must have threatened him something wicked, or bribed him something wicked. Either way, the broker took a huge risk, backing al-Sayyid against André Le Garou. They faked a clerical error, made it look as though I'd been auctioned by mistake. Razi came and bid for me. I couldn't . . . I couldn't believe that he'd kept his promise. It was just too incredible. This brand new life." Christopher's eyes widened in sudden horror and he curled in on himself, his wonder swallowed by darkness. "Oh, but my poor girls," he moaned. "I left them. *I left them there.*" He released a groan of physical pain, and bent double, clutching his stomach.

"Christopher!" Wynter tried to put her arms around him, but he slipped forward and crawled out of her embrace.

He held his hand out to stop her approaching, and knelt there for a moment, his hand hard on his stomach, trying to push everything back down into the place it had been before. "It's all right!" he gasped. "It's all . . . just . . ." He glanced at her, nearly lost himself at the expression on her face, and looked quickly away again. "You know," he said. "I think I'll take you up on that offer to catch the fish. Would you mind?"

"No," she whispered. "I wouldn't mind."

"I think," he said, rising swiftly to his feet and pulling off his tunic, "I'll go for a swim." He kicked off his boots halfway down the rock and discarded his undershirt at the river's edge. He dived headfirst into the water without removing his britches and disappeared from her sight for an alarming amount of time.

Wynter shot to her feet, then saw him break the surface about forty feet out, his dark head, sleek as an otter, almost invisible against the glittering reflection of the sun. He did not look back and she watched him swim steadily away from her, until the dancing water-glare had so blinded her that she saw nothing but white.

"Ahhh, Raz! I swear you could take a handful of mud and a pocketful of stones and make a meal to bring back the dead." Christopher stretched and wriggled his toes and arched his back with a happy sigh.

Razi smiled at him across the flames of their little fire and returned his attention to cleaning his fingernails. Christopher settled lower against the stones, and Wynter smiled at his cat-like contentment.

The three of them were damp, sandy and tingling, dressed only in their britches and undershirts, their water-chilled bodies soaking the heat from the sun-warmed stones. The sky was a scarlet blaze above them, the river a crumpled copper ribbon, edged in purple shadows. Razi had done incredible things with half a dozen fish, a hatful of lingon berries and a pocket of wild garlics. They were full and warm, and serene.

Earlier in the day, Christopher had padded his way from the river, smiling and easy. He had sneaked up behind Razi who had been hunched over, preparing the fish, and had shoved his freezing hand down the back of his tunic. Razi had roared with shock and Christopher had skittered away, cackling wickedly and shaking drops of water from his hair like a dog.

Razi had flung a stick at him and called him a *bloody menace*. Then had watched in tolerant forbearance as Christopher grabbed Wynter, treated her to a lingering, icy kiss, and threw her into the river.

It had been easy, after that, to pretend that everything was all right.

Now they lay together around the fire and looked up at the purple twilight as it blotted the sunset from the sky. One after another the stars began to shine, and little black bats appeared, flittering about in the branches above their heads.

Razi lay back against his saddle, his hands behind his head, his dark eyes roaming the sky. Wynter watched him through the dancing flames and thought about the Wolves and what they might be doing here. It made no sense. Why would they travel through Jonathon's kingdom, when they could simply hop across the Spanish Rock and trot up through the Castilian provinces? The lawlessness and banditry there would be of no consequence to them. Unlike the merchants and diplomats who courted the use of Jonathon's Port Road, Wolves had no need for an orderly, well-policed route to and from the Moroccos.

Why did you let them go? she thought. *After what they did to him? What possible reason caused you to let them go?* As she watched him, Razi frowned in puzzlement as though something had just occurred to him.

"Wynter," he murmured in amazement, still looking at the stars.

"Aye?"

"What date is it?"

"Summer," answered Christopher sleepily, as if that were as accurate as anyone need ever be.

Razi chuckled, and Wynter twisted her mind around the puzzle. "Let me see," she mused. "'Twas Angel's Sunday when Father and I came down through Lindenston. That was two days before . . ." she bit her lip and counted backwards and forwards for a moment, her forehead creased. Then her face cleared and she leapt a little at the realisation of what day it was. "Oh, Razi!" she said and he turned his head to grin at her through the flames. "Happy birthday!"

"Thank you! I am twenty years old today!"

Christopher huffed in amusement. "I can just hear your mother now!" Suddenly his voice was very soft and very proper, an uncanny imitation of Hadil's unswervingly quiet, unrelentingly disapproving tone. "One would think now, that al-Sayyid Razi ibn-Jon Malik al-fadl would take it in his mind to acquire himself a wife. It's not for me, his humble mother, to suggest that al-Sayyid does not know his own mind . . ." (here Wynter pictured the usual raising of the graceful hands, the meek tipping of the darkly elegant head) "but it does seem a little undignified that Omar ibn-Omar, seventeen years old and just a lowly spice merchant, would already have two wives and a son and two daughters to honour the family's name." Across the flames Razi's handsome face creased into a wide grin, his teeth gleaming white in the dancing light. "After all, my precious son," Christopher's voice perfectly took on that sly cutting edge that Hadil always managed to make sound so utterly feminine, "You are getting *soooooo* old. So very, *veeeerrrrrrryyy* old."

"Shut up, Mother," grinned Razi.

Christopher tutted. "Ungrateful viper-child," he sighed.

Wynter tipped her head back to look up at his face. His eyes were closed and he was half asleep. She stretched her arm comfortably over her head and laid the backs of her fingers against his cheek. He put his hand lightly on her collarbone. The flames blurred and softened and filled her mind as she slipped into a doze.

Something woke Wynter, some strange rhythmic sound, and she opened her eyes in bleary confusion. She still lay facing the fire, but she had slid down to lie on her belly, one hand under her cheek, her other arm thrown loosely across Christopher's chest. The flames had died down to hotly glowing coals, and across the fire she saw Razi staring fixedly at her, his face unhappy and tense.

There seemed to be a big dog prowling the camp. Wynter could hear it panting, its breath coming hard and fast, as if it had run a long way or was very hot. It was hard to listen to because the poor animal was in such obvious distress. *It's such a warm night*, she thought absently. *Someone should give that poor creature a bowl of water*.

Razi's face came into focus as Wynter woke completely, and his misery increased as she lifted her head to look at him. "Razi?" she asked softly.

His eyes lifted to look behind her and Wynter turned to see.

"Do not wake him," Razi whispered and Wynter got to her knees, carefully lifting her arm from Christopher's heaving chest. He was the source of the ragged animal panting that had woken her.

"It's so much worse if you wake him," said Razi.

"Oh, Razi," she said. "We must! It's too cruel!"

Anyone who looked at him would want to wake him. Christopher lay on his back, his hands clenched at his waist, his chest rising and falling in rapid, terrified breaths. His eyes were wide open, staring blindly at God knew what.

Wynter moved to touch him.

"Sis!" She looked around at Razi's insistent face. "*Believe* me!" he hissed. "It's better to leave him. It will be over in a few minutes, then he will sleep peacefully. If you try to wake him, the dream will cling; he won't be able to wake up and he won't be able to fall back asleep. It will be very bad. He will end up frightened and embarrassed." Razi blinked at her, his eyes bright. "Just leave him, Wyn," he begged. "Please."

Christopher's eyes were moving slightly from side to side, but apart from that and the rapid, shallow movement of his chest, he was perfectly still. He looked like a fox caught in a snare. Wynter gently placed her hand over his heart. It was beating wildly, dangerous and fevered, frightening. She turned horrified eyes to Razi and he pleaded with her silently not to do anything more.

But it wasn't in her to let Christopher suffer. She had no doubt that Razi's experience of these nightmares was as awful as he implied, but Wynter just couldn't stand by and wait for this to pass. "Christopher?" she murmured, leaning over him, her hand still on his chest. "Will you wake up?"

Christopher's breathing sped up and his eyes began to roll.

"Sweetheart?" she said, hovering over him.

His heart hammered frantically beneath her palm and he bared his teeth. Wynter brought her face close to his. A long tendril of her hair fell down between them, flaring red in the firelight. She looked into his eyes.

"Christopher," she said firmly. "It is over! Wake up!"

His breathing hitched. His hand flew to hers. He looked into her face.

Wynter smiled. "How do," she said.

Christopher held her gaze intently for a moment, then he relaxed and his eyes slid to the side. He lifted his hand to touch her hair and sighed. "Polished chestnut," he said.

"Aye." She pushed her fingers through the fine black locks at his temple. "Go to sleep." His eyes drifted shut and his hand floated down to lie against his chest.

His breathing evened out and he slid under into peaceful sleep.

Wynter turned glittering eyes to Razi and they looked at each other, Razi shaken and dazed, Wynter drained. Then she lay back down, her arm thrown protectively across Christopher's calmly breathing chest, her eyes fixed on the dying embers of the fire. She curled her fist under her cheek and fell into a deep and dreamless sleep.

On the Wolves' Tail

*R*azi unsheathed his falchion sword and held the long blade down by his left thigh. The shadows of the forest dappled his dark clothes and swaddled face, blending him into the background of the trees. Behind him, Christopher, his right hand encased in the ornate metal cup of his belt-knife, gazed intently through the foliage. He was calm and sharp, despite the incessant tinkling of little silver bells that floated across the evening air. He glanced back at Wynter. She nodded gravely and adjusted her grip on her knife.

The Loups-Garous were just to their right, very close. They were mostly hidden by the undergrowth, but Wynter caught random details through the shifting foliage: a portion of one rider here, a section of another there. She saw scarlet leather gauntlets and a moss green tunic. She saw an emerald green sleeve and strong black hands, ornate with rings. Further back in the trees, the sun flashed on a head of gleaming yellow curls as a huge man ducked under an overhanging branch. There were four men, all exceptionally well-armed. They made no attempt at silence or stealth, and the sounds of their progress through the heavy undergrowth was underscored by the continuous and melodic tinkling of slave bells.

Suddenly, a horse crashed into the bushes by Wynter's side, sending Ozkar shying to the left. Wynter sat down hard in the saddle and tightened her legs to keep him in place. The Wolf's horse wheeled about, stamping and snorting. Much too close. Wynter saw gold fringes on a red leather saddle, a tall, dark-clad rider, glossy black boots. Then the Loup-Garou hauled on the reins and kicked his mount back into line. Before he passed from sight, Wynter got a good look at the grey wolfskin that covered his horse's back. Its head snarled at her from just above the horse's tail, its onyx and amber eyes glinting, its gold-tipped teeth bared.

Three heavy-laden pack-mules trailed clumsily after the Wolves, their pack-saddles piled high with camping equipment. Behind them, two horsemen brought up the rear. At the sight of these men, Wynter's hands clenched on the pommel of her saddle, her fear turning to anger in the blink of an eye.

They were dressed in tunics and britches of a simple cut but excellent fabric, and their horses' tack was plain but very well-made. From what Wynter could make out, they were Christopher's age, eighteen or so, both with his kind of lithe, close-muscled strength. They were both Arabs.

One of them ducked and lifted his arm to get past an overhanging branch, and just for a moment, Wynter saw his face. A brand had been burnt into the flesh just below his left eye. It was about the size of a gold coin and depicted a wolf's head enclosed in a curling G. The young man kicked his horse on, hurrying to catch up with his masters, and his companion did the same. At the increase in pace, the silver bells that decorated their riding boots added a gentle, tinkling melody to the circlets of bells at their wrists.

Razi, Christopher and Wynter stared at the slaves' retreating backs, their eyes hard and glittering through the gaps in their scarves.

When all sound of the travellers had gone, Razi jerked the scarf from his face and turned to speak, but Christopher held up his hand and put a finger to his lips. The hairs rose on the back of Wynter's neck and she immediately unsheathed her knife again. Christopher raised two fingers to his eyes and then swept his hand out to indicate that they should continue to be on guard. With his mutilated hand it looked as though he had just made the sign of the devil, and Wynter impatiently quelled the urge to bless herself against evil, a relic of Marni's superstition that she'd never been quite able to shake off.

Christopher went back to scanning their surroundings, and Razi and Wynter followed suit. A long moment passed and Wynter was just starting to wonder what Christopher was up to, when a discreet movement to their right drew her attention. She lifted her hand slightly, not certain. The two men snapped their attention to her and she pointed to the suspect area. They all squinted into the trees and . . . yes! There.

This time the riders were completely silent, slipping through the forest with low, dark skill. Again Wynter only got a fleeting impression of each, but again they were big, finely dressed men, well-armed and in excellent command of their mounts. There were four of them, and they passed by like dappled shadows, obviously on the hunt for anyone who was inexperienced enough to think that the Wolves had already gone by.

Wynter and Razi straightened and moved to sheath their weapons. But Christopher raised his hand again and shook his head, and the two of them sank back into wary vigilance. One or two minutes passed in buzzing silence, then four more riders went past, slipping quietly along behind the others, the eyes of their wolves' heads gleaming, the shifting light winking on the dull silver of their sword hilts and the fine engraving on their matchlocks.

It was only when these four were safely out of earshot that Christopher relaxed. He sheathed his knife and pulled back his scarf, gasping at the heat, and wiped his sweating face. Wynter did likewise, greedily accepting Razi's offered waterskin.

As they sat, silently quenching their thirst, Wynter couldn't help but glance sideways at Christopher. In the three days since they'd first encountered the Wolves, he seemed to have completely regained his equilibrium, but Wynter was not certain how fragile this self-control might be. She looked away, not wanting to make him self-conscious, then glanced back again, worry eating her. Christopher was staring straight at her, his eyes grave, his mouth tight.

"I'm fine, lass," he said. "Stop burning holes in the back of my bonnet."

Wynter blushed and dropped her eyes.

"We must find out where they are going," said Razi. "I'm tired of running into them by chance. I want to follow them for a while. Just to see what way they are heading."

"I still think they're making for the ferry," said Christopher evenly.

"That's on our route," said Wynter. "We could easily follow them that far without losing time, and then, if they do not cross the river and remove themselves from our path, we can decide what it is we want to do about them."

Razi stared at Christopher until the young man met his eye.

"What?" growled Christopher, his voice hard and challenging.

Razi dipped his head, exasperated. "Nothing," he said. "Not a thing." He turned in the saddle and kicked his horse on. "Come on then," he said. "And, for God's sake, be quiet."

Hours later, when the light was sliding to dusty twilight, a sharp whistle up ahead brought them to a wary halt. Razi lifted his fist and sank low in his saddle, peering ahead. There was nothing to be seen. He lowered his fist, still glaring into the trees. Then he pushed slowly onwards.

Moments later he raised his fist again and sat, peering intently ahead once more. Then he slid from his saddle, secured his horse to a tree and took off at a low, fast run. Wynter and Christopher exchanged a look and followed suit. Razi sprinted forward for several minutes and then flung himself into the cover of a thicket and wriggled forward on his belly. Wynter and Christopher dived after him. The three of them lay flat, peering from their hiding place and trying to catch their breath.

They seemed to be close to the edge of a bluff. From their current position it was impossible to tell how high it was or what lay below it, but they had an excellent view of the Loups-Garous, who were, just that moment, trotting their horses to the edge. The sun was low, blazing its dying light through the storm clouds that were piled on the horizon and the riders were sharply defined against the vivid sky as they brought their mounts to a stop and looked down at the view.

As soon as the four Wolves came to a halt, the slaves slid from their horses and ran forward to stand beside what Wynter assumed to be the Wolf leaders. One ran quickly to the horse of the big blond and the other dashed to the side of a broad-shouldered dark-skinned man. Neither Wolf seemed to pay any heed to the young men at their sides, but, as one, the two slaves lifted their right arms and put their hands on the neck of their master's horse. It was the automatic and expected action of a dog that has been trained to run forwards and lie at his master's feet.

A movement to Wynter's right drew her attention. It was the next set of Wolves emerging from the trees. They hung back until the blond signalled them forward, then they ranged themselves behind the others, seemingly content not to see down the bluff. The blond murmured something and the young man at his side ran to fetch a waterskin. He offered it first to his master, and then passed amongst the others with it, waiting patiently as each rider drank their fill. When all the Wolves were satisfied, the slave stowed the skin and resumed his position at his master's side, his hand on the horse's neck once more.

The two leaders turned to converse with each other, murmuring low in Hadrish. As they spoke, the blond reached absently to stroke his slave's head, running his fingers through the young man's silky curls the way one would pet a dog. The slave accepted his caress without any apparent reaction. The leaders traded a few sentences and gave each other a significant look. Then the dark-skinned man turned to speak to the others behind him.

"They are below us," he said in Hadrish, "moving through the trees. We will let them be for now. They will no doubt be joining others at the ferry house, but I think we can let it go and move on."

"We're *bored*," growled one of the men behind him. The dark-skinned leader turned to glare at him. "Don't look at me like that, Gérard!" snapped the man. "We've been on the trail for months. I'm sick of lying low."

Another of the shadow riders spoke up. "It *is* wearing thin. "'T'ain't natural to be so restrained on the trail. We should be free here, to be Wolves. It's galling to pass the sheep and leave 'em quiet."

Gérard shook his head, but there was a touch of amusement in the look he gave his blond companion, and the two of them turned back to their men with brotherly forbearance. "This ain't a Wolf trip we're on, brother, you know that. This is business."

There was general grumbling and shifting about from the others. A tall, Arab-looking man mumbled, "We get enough of *business* in Algiers!"

Gérard held up his hand. "Hold on, hold on," he laughed. He raised his head and released a low whistle. Within moments the last four riders slunk silently from the trees and the circle of horsemen expanded to include them. Gérard kicked his slave gently between the shoulderblades, and the young man ran forward with a waterskin. Everyone waited while the newcomers quenched their thirst and the slave resumed his position.

"We'll set camp," said the blond. He pulled his horse around, and the slave moved expertly beside him, barely losing his place by the horse's shoulder. "And we'll draw lots for four, all right? Just four."

There were mingled noises of excitement and discontent amongst the Wolves.

"Take it or leave it, you ungrateful curs!" snapped Gérard. "We're being damned generous! We'll all answer to Father if your unruly nature pulls this down around our ears." His irritability seemed to cow them, and the objections died.

The blond gestured in dismissal and the eight shadow-riders bowed their heads and slipped back into the trees.

"Are we included in the draw?" asked one of the other lead Wolves. It was the man with the red saddle and black riding boots, a broad, square-shaped fellow, with narrow, cruel eyes.

"Don't be ridiculous, Jean," said the fourth man. He had a soft voice and long brown hair, and had, until now, been sitting silently looking out at the sunset, his back turned to the others. Wynter noted that this was the man with the scarlet leather gauntlets. "You ain't a cub no more," he said. "You need to remember that."

The other man grimaced but ducked his head in obeisance.

"Sorry, David," he said.

David! thought Wynter.

David half-turned his head and said quietly, "You may drink." The two slaves leapt for the waterskins and drank as if they had just crossed a desert. Wynter was surprised by how thirsty they seemed to be, and how frantic their movements were in contrast with their previous calm. "Enough," murmured David. They ceased at once, gasping and reluctant, and Wynter realised that they had been trying to drink as much as possible before he spoke again. They obediently corked the skins and replaced them. "Mount up," he ordered, and the two young men returned immediately to their horses.

Wynter stared as the Wolf pulled his horse around. So this was David, the leader of this particular pack of André's Wolves. The pack that Razi had referred to with gritted teeth as "*that* pack".

David Le Garou was lithe and tall and had a weary set to his shoulders. As he turned towards her, his face was blotted into shadow by the sunset. He kicked his horse on and the others fell into place around him. Wynter watched as he ducked beneath the trees and led his men into the forest. The pack-mules followed closely behind. Silently, the two slaves sat waiting their turn, then they too trotted forward and were swallowed by the darkness beneath the trees.

There was a long moment of silence. Then Christopher began to slither forward from their hiding place, and Razi and Wynter followed suit.

They stood at the edge of the cliff and looked down. Below them, there was more forest and the slow, wide river gleaming in the stormy light of the sunset. Wynter scanned the trees, but there were no signs of life. Whoever it was that the Wolves had seen, they had now disappeared. Christopher turned away from the view and stared after the departed Wolves.

"I'm starving," he said softly, still staring out into the trees.

Wynter squeezed his arm. "So am I," she whispered.

"It's about twenty minutes' ride to the river," murmured Razi. "Can you last that long?"

They nodded. "All right," he said, already heading for the horses. "We'll set up camp there. Settle for the night." He turned back at the tree line. "I'd like to stop off in the Wherry Tavern tomorrow. See who's there."

Christopher sighed and Wynter blinked at Razi with burning eyes.

"All right," she said numbly.

Christopher said nothing, just waited patiently for Razi to get going and then fell into step behind. Wynter put her hand on his back as she followed on. She kept it there for as long as she could, but eventually the dense foliage broke them apart.

Hunger

They set up camp in grim silence, sticking close together and anxiously scanning their surroundings. Dinner was rye bread, hard cheese and dried sausage, and they consumed it without the comfort of a fire.

"It's madness to have promoted Jean to Second," whispered Christopher.

His soft voice looped a thread out into the night that bound the three of them together, breaking the silence that Wynter had begun to think would consume them. She sat, the last of her dinner in her hand, and gazed thankfully at him in the gloom.

Razi peered at his friend, his face uncertain, then sighed as if giving in to an unwanted conversation. "He will make a poor leader," he agreed softly. "I doubt that he was David's first choice. I suspect that André would have foisted the decision upon him."

"Jean is a mindless, unruly whoreson cur," said Christopher without much emotion. "David will have him dead within a nine-month, if he knows what's good for him. He'll kill him as soon as he can."

"I hope they kill *each other*," spat Razi suddenly. "Every one of them. I hope they all poison each other, and die screaming in a pool of their own *shit*."

Jesu, thought Wynter, shocked.

Razi blinked and his eyes widened as though he had surprised even himself. Christopher had drawn the collar of his cloak up around his face and was peering at Razi over the top of it. He did not seem shocked in the least.

"Wh . . . why are they drawing lots, Christopher?" asked Wynter uncertainly, her voice low.

Christopher briefly met her eye and then laid his head back and looked up at the stars. "Don't know," he said.

"But why might they do that? From what you know of them?" She was wondering if it had anything to do with the business they claimed to be on. Razi shifted beside her, but did not try to silence her. Christopher didn't reply.

"Christopher?" she persisted. "Have they—?"

"I *don't know*," hissed Christopher. "I ain't one of *them*. How would I know why they do what—?" his angry voice cracked, and he shut his mouth tight for a moment. "It could be any of a dozen dreadful things," he said.

Wynter shuddered and drew her knees up; she no longer wanted to know. The silence threatened to envelope them again. Wynter spoke quickly, just to stop it in its tracks. "How come the slaves don't run to David?" she asked. "Surely as their leader, he should—"

Christopher laughed, a dull, unpleasant croak, and he put his hand over his face. "David don't need no bloody slaves, lass. David owns the pack. He owns *everyone*. They're all his, to command as he will."

"I would have thought," said Razi, "that André would

have allowed David to settle by now. It's over four years since they enslaved your troupe, Chris, and I had thought that would be David's last trip. I expected André to have made him a Father by now, to grant him an estate in the Russias, or in Fez. But he persists in sending him out year after year, like any other son. It puzzles me."

"I think André fears David," murmured Christopher. "He needs him, but he fears him. I think he resists giving him his freedom, for fear it will split the packs."

Wynter watched her friend as he watched the stars, and the question she had chewed upon for days just slipped from her without warning. "Are these the men who hurt your hands?" she whispered.

"I don't remember," said Christopher immediately, his voice flat.

Wynter frowned, "How—?"

"He doesn't *remember*, Wynter!" snapped Razi. "Leave him be!"

Wynter bowed her head, but Christopher sighed softly and relented.

"Razi thinks they probably paid someone to do it for them, lass," he said. "The Wolves don't get their hands dirty in Algiers, you see." Wynter saw his teeth flash in a sneer. "In Algiers they just do *business*."

This last sentence came out hard, with a bitter emphasis on the final word, and Razi shifted uncomfortably. "Chris . . ." he whispered. There was a long silence.

"I could have won that race," murmured Christopher inexplicably, his eyes still on the sky.

"I know you could," Razi said, "I never once beat you in a race." He stared steadily into the gathering dark, his face blank. "That is how I knew," he said. "That is how we got back to you so soon. When you were not at the house, I turned around straight away and we went looking for you. God help us, Chris! What were we thinking? Leaving my knights behind like that? God help me! Such idiots!"

"Ah," Christopher gestured soothingly. "We were just wee lads," he said. "We needed to kick loose."

"I should have known better!" cried Razi. "People like me aren't *lads*, people like me don't *kick loose* . . ." he clamped down hard on his bitterness, and finished softly, "we should never kick loose."

"Aye, well," murmured Christopher. "I'm a bad influence, ain't I?"

"How did you find him?" asked Wynter quietly. "When you turned back? How did you find him?"

Razi just shook his head, and looked away without answering.

"I was screaming." Christopher rolled slightly to face her, his cloak bundled around him as if for protection. "Marcello tells me I was still screaming. That's how they found me. Razi thinks they saw him coming, he thinks that's why . . ." he gestured stiffly with his left hand, "why they were so very brutal at the end. He thinks they were trying to finish quickly before they ran."

"You were right in the middle of the road," whispered Razi. "They didn't even try to hide you."

"Aye, well. They wanted you to find me, didn't they? I was their little present to al-Sayyid. No doubt they had a grand old chuckle over how you'd get your money's worth from a fingerless musician."

There was a long, awkward silence. Razi was lost to his

memories, and Wynter found herself staring at Christopher, her mind filled with terrible pictures. She did not know what expression was on her face but, whatever it was, Christopher's eyes slid from hers and he swallowed. It was obvious that he didn't want this to go any further; that he wanted to break this downward slide, but had no idea how to change it. He glanced at Razi, then back again, his face pleading, but Wynter didn't know how to rescue him. She could not free her mind of the terrible image of Razi and Christopher, screaming and frantic, and covered in blood beneath the African sun.

"You know what?" Christopher said suddenly.

She shook her head.

"I'm hungry . . ."

Razi snorted. Wynter laughed harshly. And the spell was broken.

"You can't be hungry," she croaked. "You just ate a horse-weight of bread and cheese."

"You're like a God-cursed tapeworm," grated Razi.

Christopher put his hand to his eyes and coughed dryly. "Well," he said, "'T'aint so much as how I'm *hungry*. I just fancy a *taste*, you know?" He rolled onto his back, dropping his hand to his chest and gazed up at the sky.

Wynter looked at his pale, narrow face, all bundled around with his cloak and she realised that, yes, she did know. She knew *exactly*. She looked at Christopher and she became aware of a hollowness inside her, a longing that she had never noticed before. An empty, scooped out space beside her heart.

"You know what I'd fancy?" he said.

"No, love," she said, "what would you fancy?"

"An orange." He lifted his hand and made a gesture, as if he were plucking an orange from the tree. "I'd quite like an orange, just for the taste."

It felt like she spent the next few hours curled beneath the canvas peering out at Christopher, but she must actually have dozed off because she couldn't remember him coming over to shake Razi awake. The first thing she knew of it was his voice, hissing low in the darkness.

"Razi . . . *Raz* . . . good Frith, man! Come on, you sluggard, wake *up*. It's your watch."

Razi startled and banged his head off Wynter's feet. He cursed blearily and fumbled free of his covers, rolling out from under the bivouac. He left the bedroll in a terrible disorder and Wynter kicked at it in irritation. She was instantly filled with the itchy, sand-eyed restlessness that had plagued her all night. Her body was exhausted, almost painfully worn out, but at the same time she could not seem to settle. Every time she shut her eyes she saw the same thing. She saw blood, she imagined screams, and she felt the proximity of Wolves. She moaned in exasperation and shoved her covers down to her feet. It was too damned hot.

"Aren't you going to bed, Chris?" asked Razi softly.

Wynter stared up at the canvas and tensed, listening for Christopher's reply. She was suddenly aware of the fact that she had been waiting for Christopher. She had been longing for him to come in and lay down beside her. She could just about see his boots, loitering hesitantly by the tent. There was a moment's silence, then he turned away.

"I'm too restless," he said. "I'm going to have a swim."

"Be careful. Stay close."

Christopher tutted in exasperation and walked away.

Wynter took a deep breath, pressed the heels of her hands into her eyes and told herself to go to sleep.

Moments later she rolled from beneath the canvas and got stiffly to her feet. The night was much brighter now, the clouds having clotted along the horizon, leaving room for stars and the naked half-moon above them.

Razi peered at her in concern. "Wyn," he said. "Are you all right?" She glanced furtively at the river. Razi's eyes widened, then he looked away, his face tight with embarrassment. "It's a warm night," he said.

"Aye."

"Much cooler by the river," he said.

Wynter nodded. Razi kept looking fixedly into the trees and eventually she turned and made her way down to the water. She thought fleetingly how lonely he might be and glanced back once, but she didn't stop walking.

At the water's edge, Christopher's boots and socks and tunic were lying in a tidy pile at his feet. He was just reaching back to loosen the tie on his undershirt when Wynter rounded the bushes. His hair was unbound and it swung heavily around his shoulders as he turned to look at her. He left his shirt tied and pushed his hair behind his ears in a gesture Wynter hadn't seen for a long while.

"How do, girly," he whispered. "I was just going for a swim."

Wynter nodded.

He stood with his arms hanging loose by his sides and tilted his head questioningly. The moon gleamed off his cheekbones and outlined his lips in pale light. "Can't you sleep?" he asked softly.

She shook her head.

"Me neither," he said.

Christopher looked at her with that familiar gentle intensity, and Wynter knew with absolute certainty that she'd never love anyone as much as she loved this man.

She took the last few steps and stood very close to him, gazing up into his face.

He hesitated for a moment and then he lifted his hand and stroked her cheek. "Girly," he whispered, and Wynter pressed herself against him and stopped his words with her mouth on his.

His reaction was powerful and immediate. He pulled her close and bent himself to her kiss with a hunger that should have been frightening. But instead of fear, Wynter felt her own hunger rise up, so she wrapped her arms around him and responded with an intensity that made him groan. Christopher pulled her closer and she ran her hands up his back, feeling all the strong, flat planes of his slim body. He opened his mouth against hers. She pushed her fingers into his hair. He tasted wonderful, he smelled so incredibly good, and Wynter felt a powerful desire blaze to life between them.

For a moment Christopher pressed tightly against her, and Wynter abandoned herself to the need to get closer and closer. But then she felt him bare his teeth and he brought his hands to her waist, pushing her away until she had to loosen her grip, and they were separated.

They stood for a moment, panting, their foreheads pressed together, their hands resting lightly on each other's hips.

"Christopher . . ." she moaned, her body aching to be near him.

He gasped and held her firmly away. "You're a sore trial to my self-control at the best of times, lass. Please . . . I ain't too certain of restraint at the moment. You need to give me a bit of space."

Wynter opened her eyes and looked up at him, her forehead still pressed to his. He did the same so that they were watching each other within the swinging black curtain of his hair.

"I feel very strongly for you, Christopher," she whispered.

"You ain't sport to me, lass. I couldn't make sport with you."

She frowned, not understanding.

"I couldn't . . . if we lay down. I couldn't just . . ." Christopher paused. The moonlit river sent dappled currents of light across his face as he searched miserably for the right words. "You'd be for ever to me, lass," he said. "If I lay down with you, it wouldn't be sport. It would be for ever with me."

Wynter smiled. He looked terrified. "For ever would be just fine by me, Christopher."

He shook his head uncertainly. "Now, you think what you're saying, Protector Lady. You think careful about who you're saying this to – a fingerless musician, a foul-mouthed tape-worm . . . and a dubious Merron at that." There was a smile in his voice when he finished this and they grinned at each other in the rippling light.

"I know what I'm saying, Christopher Garron. Do not be wheedling out of things by implying that I don't know my own mind."

She slowly ran her hand up his ribs and across his chest,

and Christopher closed his eyes for a moment, his heart thudding beneath her palm.

"Aren't you . . . provisioned?" she asked shyly.

Christopher chuckled and his grin got a lopsided wickedness to it that weakened Wynter's knees. "Sweetheart," he whispered. "I'm *always* provisioned." He opened his eyes suddenly, grave and sincere. "But I will not have your first time a heated fumble against a tree, with the two of us looking over our shoulders for fear of Wolves." He brought his hand to the side of her face and stepped away from her. "I'd like to wait till we can put some joy in it, girly. If that's all right?"

Wynter turned her cheek into the palm of his hand, looking at him from the corner of her eye. She kissed his wrist. Christopher turned abruptly, ran, and dived into the river. He broke the surface of the water a yard or two from shore and began to swim away from her.

"Christopher!" she called softly.

He flipped onto his back, still pulling steadily from the shore. "Aye?"

"My name is Iseult."

He grinned at her, his face surrounded by sparkling moonlight and slivers of dark. "Oh, lass," he said happily. "That's a bloody lovely name!" Then he rolled backwards and disappeared beneath the surface like a fish.

The Wherry Tavern

It rained all day, a gentle, unending drizzle that softened the edges of everything and cooled the air. Every now and again the sun would step briefly from the clouds and the green surface of the river would explode into a multitude of rainbows. It had been breathtaking the first time Wynter saw it, but after five hours lurking in the cover of the trees and looking down on the Wherry Tavern, the glory of nature was palling.

"We've been here for *hours*," she complained.

"Is that so?" whispered Razi with mock surprise. "I had not noticed!"

Wynter grimaced at him. *Sarcastic old coot*, she thought.

Christopher poked her in the back and she glanced around to find him holding out the bag of walnuts he'd bought at the Tarman's Inn. She took one, discovered that they were candied and immediately took two more. Razi went to help himself, and Christopher squeezed the bag shut on his hand.

"Hey!" he whispered. "No one offered *you* any, you bloody pirate!" Razi gave him a narrow look. He had taken exception to the nickname, and so of course, Wynter and Christopher delighted in using it. Christopher grinned and offered the bag again. Razi took a handful of nuts with a tolerant sigh and returned to looking down the hill. He popped a walnut into his mouth and chewed thoughtfully.

"Who are they after?" he mused. "It seems as though they're waiting, rather than just making a random check."

"Perhaps they're hunting the Wolves?" suggested Wynter.

"Perhaps. Certainly Father would have the curs hunted, if he knew they were here."

"Either way it don't have much to do with us," said Christopher quietly. "We can move on."

Razi watched the cavalry move about in the valley below them. All the evidence suggested that the men had been there at least two days. They had set up camp on the green beside the inn, and the ground was well-trodden by men and horses, and scarred with the evidence of many cook-fires.

"Whatever it is that they were hoping to discover, I wager they've not found it," mused Wynter. "They're about to head out."

As if on cue, the cavalry began to dismantle their tents.

Razi ran his thumb along his scarred lip. "My father's men . . ." His dark eyes followed the members of his father's personal guard as they walked amongst the cavalry. He glanced at the small knot of watchful civilians standing in the doorway of the inn and then turned his attention to the other side of the water. "Who do you seek?" he said softly under his breath.

In all the time that the three of them had been hidden here, the ferry-raft had made only one journey across the

river. Its cargo had been a single man with two lightly bur-
dened pack-mules. The cavalry had questioned him and
examined his cargo and his papers closely, then allowed
him on his way. The empty ferry had made its way back to
the other side and, since then, no one else had come across
the wide swell of water.

Every now and again during the day, the captain of
Jonathon's personal guard would stalk up and down the
pier in the rain, tapping his riding crop against his thigh,
and it was obvious to Wynter that his patience was wearing
thin. Now he stood, glaring across the water, as his men
packed away their equipment. Suddenly, he turned on his
heel and bellowed to the inn. There was a long moment of
inactivity and then a small, broad-shouldered man in an
apron came out into the yard – the landlord. He stood, as
if waiting for the officer to come to him. The captain
snarled and gestured him over. The landlord took his own
sweet time coming up the pier, and Razi and Wynter
frowned; this was no way for a civilian to treat representatives of his Majesty the King.

"He should be cuffed around the ear," said Wynter.
"Who in God's name does he think he is?"

The landlord came to a halt, brazenly holding the captain's gaze. Wynter was amazed at the captain's forbearance
in the face of such blatant disrespect. In his place she would
have kicked this fellow's insolent arse.

The captain coolly stared the landlord down, and
Wynter felt a spark of admiration for the man. During the
chaos and fear at the palace, it had been easy to forget what
a disciplined body of soldiers the King's personal guard
were. In the old days – the days before Jonathon's reign –

the landlord's behaviour would have seen him horse-whipped and his business burned to the ground. She wondered if he had forgotten that. Watching Jonathon's man resist the temptation to strike out in rage, Wynter felt a tiny flame of hope that the King's former, even-handed method of rule may yet prevail.

The captain snapped a few curt instructions to the landlord. Then, apparently satisfied, he turned on his heel and stalked back to his men. The officers took to the saddle, their men followed suit, and within moments the cavalry had pulled into formation and trotted off up the track, heading towards the main road. The landlord watched them leave, his face grim, then he made his way back into the inn and slammed the door on the sight of them.

"He has no love of my father's men, does he?" murmured Razi, his eyes on the firmly shut door. "You know, I do believe this man may be a sympathiser to my brother's cause. This may be a rebel den . . ."

"Oh, marvellous," exclaimed Christopher dryly. "No doubt you are now itching to pop in and make yourself known." Razi's lips curved and he continued to watch the inn. "No doubt," continued Christopher. "You are now simply *choked* with the desire to trot on down and wave your arms about, hoping that some miscreant will recognise you, and knock you about and drag you off to your brother's camp. No bloody doubt you—"

"Christopher," smiled Wynter. "Shush."

"Oh, *you* shush!" he said.

"Just because they sympathise with Alberon does not mean they would know me from any other brown man,

Christopher. I have no intention of 'trotting on down and waving my arms about'."

"Good!"

"I would, however—"

"Oh, here we have it!"

"I *would*, however, like to go down and see who it is the cavalry are seeking."

Christopher flung his hands up in despair.

"I suggest we hold off a while, brother," said Wynter. "Now that the cavalry have gone, maybe we should wait and see what might crawl from the trees?"

Razi smiled. "Aside from us, you mean?"

"Aye," she said, grinning. "Quite apart from us."

Christopher startled suddenly and sank to his haunches, pulling Wynter with him. He pointed to the trees across from them and hissed, "There!"

A man stepped warily from the forest. He was as tall as Razi, but broad built and heavy boned. He wore a long dun coloured cloak, beaded with rain, and had a longbow and a quiver of arrows slung across his back. His hood was pulled up over his head and face, and he stood just within the tree line, observing the trail. Carefully, he scanned the trees on their side of the clearing. Then he turned to look across the river, peering in the direction of the ferry. After a moment, he tipped his head to the trees behind him and Wynter realised with a start that he was listening to someone speaking to him from the cover of the shadows.

"He's not alone," hissed Razi.

The man looked out across the water and shook his head. He spent another long moment watching the river, and then melted back into the forest.

Wynter, Razi and Christopher spent the next few minutes anxiously dividing their attention between the river and the trees. The rain continued to whisper its way through the foliage and sigh across the valley, but this and their own quiet breathing were the only sounds. The inn remained silent, its doors and windows firmly shut. After a while, Razi rose cautiously to his feet, wrapped his cloak around him and once more leaned against his tree. Wynter sat herself on the sodden moss of a fallen log, and Christopher returned to slouching quietly in the shadows behind her.

It was over an hour later when the ferry-house bell sounded from across the water, its distant toll startling them out of their daze. There was the crack of a horsewhip and the heavy, creaking turn of the pulley-wheels as someone out of sight behind the inn got the mules moving on their treadmill. Slowly the pull-ropes tightened and rose from the water as they began the long haul necessary to bring the raft from one side of the river to the other.

As the ferry raft came into view through the mist, the rain stopped as if a sluicegate had been sealed and a blackbird trilled suddenly, its sweet song falling down to them through the luminous silence. Low evening sun broke the clouds, and Wynter had to slit her eyes against its reflected brilliance.

Gradually, details began to show through the shimmering glare. The ferry was full, at least fifteen people, standing side by side with their horses. They were tall and dressed in long cloaks, their hoods covering their faces. All were quiet and watchful, scanning the shore with careful attention. As they came closer, the sounds of the polemen's chant became audible, and the sun began to raise steam from the water.

Suddenly Christopher jumped and cried out softly, and Razi had to grab the back of his tunic to stop him leaping impulsively to his feet. "*Féach!*" he whispered. "*Na cúnna!*" He seemed quite unaware that he had spoken Merron, but Wynter realised that he was addressing her when he turned to her and grinned. "Look at the dogs!" he said, pointing.

She leaned forward and gazed at the raft. Once she had diverted her attention from the human passengers, Wynter saw the dogs immediately and her heart leapt in recognition of their distinctive size and shape. They were huge, fearsome-looking creatures, their great shaggy heads easily as tall as Wynter's shoulder. All six stood at the prow of the ferry and looked around them with proud intelligence and nobility.

"*Jesu,*" breathed Wynter. "They cannot be . . ."

"They are!" murmured Christopher. "They are!"

Razi shook his head in wonder. "I have never seen their like. You two know these creatures?"

Christopher answered without taking his eyes from the raft. "They are *na Cúnna Faoil,* Razi. *Na Cúnna Cogaidh.* It's beyond belief." He laughed softly under his breath. "It's beyond belief," he said again, lapsing into dazed silence.

"They are the wolfhounds, Razi," said Wynter. "The warhounds. Their breed is exclusively the property of the Merron. No other people are allowed ownership of them."

"Then these people are *Merron*?"

Christopher laughed again and ran his hand over his face. "Good Frith," he said, grinning.

Razi's brow creased in concern and he turned troubled

eyes to the river. The ferry had lowered its gate against the pier and the Merron were making their way onto shore. "What are Merron doing in my father's kingdom?" he said tightly.

Wynter glanced at Christopher, expecting him to prickle at Razi's wary tone, but their friend just shook his head, his eyes wide. "I have no idea. I have never heard of our people coming this far south."

"Might they be in alliance with Alberon?"

Christopher grimaced, spreading his hands apologetically. "I'm afraid that my father was the least political of men, Razi, despite his having been a *filid* born and bred. He kept me well out of such matters and I have no understanding or love of politics. I cannot help you with this." He flicked his eyes to Wynter. "Can you, sweetheart? It seems more within your field of experience."

Wynter shrugged. "We did encounter Bear and Panther Merron in Shirken's kingdom. They were suffering badly under Shirken's repression of the old religions and Father was trying to get them some leeway for freedom of practice and retention of rights of way. But," she shook her head, "I cannot say that I understand the Merron, Razi. I cannot comment on what they might be doing here."

"What tribes are these, Christopher?" asked Razi, gesturing to the inn and looking searchingly at his friend.

"How can I tell from this distance? Grow some sense, man!"

"Look," Wynter pointed to the trees across from them and they all sank a little lower again as a long line of men and women began to descend from the forest. There were nine in all, their horses following beside them, and as they

advanced upon the ferry party they raised their hands and
called out in Merron.

There was some exchange of formal greetings, and much
deference was given to the masters of the six wolfhounds.
The great dogs flanked their owners like watchful soldiers,
eyeing each person who advanced and lowering their
snarling lips only at the light touch of their masters' hands.
The gentle evening light rebounded softly from rings and
torques and brooches and gleamed on the fine metalwork
that detailed the dogs' collars and the horses' tack. Such rich
clothing, such fine animals – this was a diplomatic party,
there could be no doubt of it.

So, Albi, thought Wynter. *You have invited the Merron to
your table.* She shook her head, she could think of no purpose to this. The Merron swore allegiance to no king,
bowed their knee to no nobility but their own. What was
more, they were exclusively a Northern people, never ven-
turing south. Why were they here?

She glanced at Christopher. He was watching closely as
the Merron led their horses from the pier. He seemed just
as puzzled as herself, and his face was dark with thought as
he watched his people pass out of sight and into the stable
yard of the inn.

Merron

"Now listen close and pay attention," Christopher stripped off his tunic as he came around from the barn and rolled the sleeves of his undershirt to the shoulder, exposing his snake bracelets. "These are Bear Merron. Set, devoted and mad wed to the old ways. Very high and mighty when it comes to etiquette. If you were *coimhthíoch* they wouldn't pay no mind to you, and you could act as you pleased, but you're not foreigners, you're with me, and they'll expect some decorum from you."

Wynter and Razi exchanged worried glances. Christopher was busy unbinding his hair and he kept up his rapid instructions as he shook it from its tight coil and let it fall down around his shoulders.

"You cannot wear any concealed weapons," he said, bending to take his dagger from his boot and slipping it into his belt. "If you have any jewellery – rings, pendants, bracelets, you'll have to wear them where they can be seen; otherwise it implies you do not trust the company." He reached behind Wynter's head and undid her hair, running his hands through it and shaking it out around her shoulders. She looked up at him while he was doing so and he glanced into her eyes, giving her a brief, fond smile.

"Lovely!" he whispered.

He stepped back and looked expectantly at herself and Razi. He was buzzing like a hive of bees, glowing with excitement. They stared blankly at him and he spread his hands. "Jewellery?" he prompted, "hidden weapons?"

Wynter pulled her guild pendant from the neck of her undershirt, allowing it to lie openly against her tunic. Razi looked down at himself as if concerned something about his apparel might take him by surprise. "Um," he said anxiously.

Christopher rolled his eyes in amusement. Then he slapped his hands together and thought for a moment. "Let me see, let me see," he said.

They had decided to approach the inn openly, and to try and establish some rapport with the Merron. While Wynter and Razi had distracted the stable lad with instructions for the care of their mounts, Christopher had strolled up and down the stalls, looking at the tribe markings on the Merron horses. Now they huddled in the stable yard by the back door of the inn, while the noise inside began to swell into what sounded suspiciously like a party.

Christopher grinned, distracted, as someone inside began to tune up a fiddle.

"All right, Garron!" he said, shaking himself. "What do these folk need to know? Yes! Now. Look, I'm not too certain of a welcome here myself, so it may be that we'll get short shrift, but should we be allowed stay—"

Suddenly, the interior of the inn exploded into a roaring

cheer and a wild tune was struck up on fiddle, flute and drum. There were whoops and roars, and Christopher's fragile solemnity shattered into another grin. Wynter smiled fondly and Razi grinned at their friend's obvious happiness. Christopher bent his head, ran his hands over his face and looked up at them, his eyes serious.

"Don't go near those dogs," he cautioned. "They'll take the head off your shoulders if they think you're going to harm their owners. That's no story! They will decapitate a man as easy as eat their supper. Wait for an invitation to the masters' table, and if an invitation don't come, *stay clear*! If anyone does this to you . . ." He lowered his eyelids slightly and bit the tip of his tongue between his teeth. It was a gesture of such obvious sexual invitation that Wynter blazed red in embarrassment. Christopher chuckled. "Just smile politely," he said, "and look away." He glanced at Razi, his face stern. "I don't want any of your foolishness in there, Razi. If a *man* makes the gesture to you, just treat it as the compliment it is and react with good grace."

Razi grimaced miserably. Christopher turned to Wynter. "Girly," he began, "if anyone . . ." He paused and something stilled in him, as if he had been spinning somehow, without her noticing, and had only now come to a halt. "Actually," he said, gazing into her face. "Actually . . ."

He reached out and snagged a long strand of wool from Wynter's tunic, then pulled one from the hem of his own. He quickly twisted the threads together, entwining the dark green wool of hers and the black wool of his own to make a single cord. This he tied around Wynter's wrist. Then he repeated the process, holding out the second bracelet for her to tie around his arm.

Wynter looked up at him as her fingers brushed the delicate flesh of his wrist.

"Are we wed now, Christopher?" she teased.

Christopher blushed, not certain what she wanted to hear. "Just pretending. So that . . . to make things easier for you."

Wynter paused and tilted her head back, looking him in the eye. "Just pretending?" She smiled wickedly and held his eyes as she finished knotting the cord around his wrist, then kept her hand on his arm. They stood gazing at each other, while within the tavern the music swung into a jig. Christopher's lips curved gently.

"Lass," he whispered.

Razi coughed and they glanced at him, startled. "I am not so certain that I am happy with that," he said.

Wynter's heart sank, and Christopher's expression drew down into a sudden, fierce resentment. He took firm hold of her hand, and stepped forward. "Not happy with what, Razi?" he said. "What *exactly* is it that you are not happy with?"

Razi met his furious grey eyes and pouted in a most un-Razi-like manner.

"Well, how come Wynter gets to wed you?" he said. "When surely it is I who most needs your protection?" He held out his wrist in mock supplication. "Wed me, Chris! Wed me and save me from those wicked Merron men."

Wynter laughed in relief, and Christopher punched Razi hard in the arm. "You bloody menace!" he growled, "I'll feed you to them!"

There was another roar from the inn and the three of them turned their faces to the door. Christopher squeezed

Wynter's hand and glanced at Razi. "Are you ready?" he said. They nodded and without any more hesitation made their way inside.

The heat was tremendous, and the small room seemed thronged with giants. They slunk around the edges of the crowd and claimed a table that had been shoved up against the wall. Wynter and Razi sat themselves down, tensely facing the room, while Christopher remained standing.

The entire company of Merron had their backs turned, their attention seemingly focused on the music, but Wynter had no doubt that every living person had noted their entrance. Christopher bounced up and down on the balls of his feet, his grin uncontrollable as he surveyed the room.

Wynter turned to Razi, a question poised on her lips, and the look on his face stilled her. Razi was staring across the room, his brown eyes unusually wide, his lips parted. It was the same expression he sometimes had on first awakening – an innocent, round-eyed kind of wonder that Wynter had sometimes caught in him before the world inevitably rushed in and stole it. It plucked her heart, this expression; it was so rare in him. She turned to follow his gaze.

He was looking at four people seated on the opposite side of the room. The indisputable leaders of this rowdy throng of men and women, they sat with their backs to the wall, looking out at their people. The six warhounds lay on the floor, their huge heads resting on their paws, their intelligent brown eyes following the movement of the crowd, an immutable barrier between their masters' table and the rest of the room.

Wynter regarded this group with interest. *Yes,* she thought, *these are the ones we should try and get to know. Of all here they would have the information we seek.*

But there was no political interest in Razi's appraising look, and she was amused to find his attention solely focused on the female member of the party. Wynter dug her elbow into his side and he jumped.

"Pardon?" he said, startled.

Wynter held his eyes and grinned. "Interesting people," she said dryly.

Razi blushed and made a show of looking to where Christopher stood, tapping his foot to the music, his way blocked by a solid wall of Merron backs. Just then, Christopher, apparently tired of the view, reached out and poked the man in front of him. The man, a great hairy bruiser, ignored him, but Christopher was not so easily dismissed, and to Wynter's alarm, he tugged sharply at the man's long red hair.

The man spun with a snarl, his fist pulling back, and Razi and Wynter lurched forward in dismay. But something in Christopher's grin seemed to hit home, and the man paused in mid-swing, his face questioning. Wynter saw him take in Christopher's fine, pale skin and his long hair. His eyes slid to the tops of Christopher's arms and his eyebrows rose at the unlikely sight of the snake bracelets. The man lowered his meaty fist. Smiling, Christopher waved a hand in the direction of the unseen musicians and asked a question in polite, respectful Merron.

"*Le meas, a dhuine uasail. Ach cé hiad na ceoltoirí?*"

The big Merron tilted his head uncertainly and growled, "*Cé thú féin, a luch?*"

Christopher smiled. "*Gabh mo leithscéal, ach b'fhéidir go n-inseofa dóibh go bhfuil Coinín Garron, mac Aidan an Filid, anseo.*" He bowed. "*Mura mhiste leat.*"

The huge man looked at him uncertainly, then pushed away through the crowd. Christopher bounced happily up and down, waiting.

"Christopher!" hissed Razi tensely. "Chris!" but Christopher had barely time to fling a placating gesture at him before a roar interrupted the music.

As one, the Merron turned to stare at the slim, pale man standing at the edge of their circle. Wynter swallowed at how incredibly slight Christopher looked beside them. He gazed up into their wild, bearded, frowning faces and grinned.

"*Scéal?*" he said impudently.

Wynter leapt as two huge men suddenly grabbed Christopher around the waist and flung him into the air. Christopher howled. Within the blink of an eye Razi had his sword in his hand and was on his feet, shoving the table out of his way. Wynter leapt to his side. At their sudden movement, the four noble-folk startled, their hands dropping to their weapons. The great dogs rose and silently bared their teeth.

It only took a moment for Razi and Wynter to see that Christopher's howl had been one of joy. Slowly, they lowered their weapons and gaped in disbelief as their friend was hoisted over the Merron's heads. Christopher whooped, the Merron laughed and he was passed from hand to hand across the crowd.

Wynter looked around for a better vantage point, then hopped onto the table so she could witness her friend's progress across the room. Razi, his sword still in his hand, leapt onto the bench at her side and the two of them watched, round-eyed, as a delighted Christopher bobbed away from them like a leaf on water. He was eventually deposited, feet first, onto a raised platform where a man and two women were standing, waiting for him.

Christopher landed with a little bounce and stood smiling at the musicians, suddenly shy. The man and younger woman regarded him with glittering eyes, saying nothing, but the older woman launched herself at him with a little shriek and dragged him into a violent hug. She was a good head taller than Christopher and quite overcome with emotion. She squeezed so tightly that Wynter feared for her friend's ribcage.

Christopher laughed against the woman's bony chest, murmuring something soothing and he lifted his arm to pat her on the back, unintentionally revealing his hands to the man. At the sight of the dreadful scars, the man roared in horror and grabbed Christopher by the wrists, dragging him around to face him. He pulled Christopher's hands up to his eyes, as if doubting what he saw, then gave a great cry of devastation. The women wailed.

Christopher leant back, tugging at the horrified man's grip, his face desperate. He said something and made an awful attempt at a grin, but the man held on, staring at Christopher's ruined hands. The crowd fell silent and Wynter's heart dropped. Razi moaned quietly. This would be so far from what Christopher would want.

There was a long emptiness of silence, and for a terrible moment, Wynter thought the evening was lost to her friend. Then Christopher broke free of the man's grip, leapt to the side and snatched up one of those wide, flat drums the Merron so loved. He swung to the crowd, and with a desperate yell commenced beating out an intricate, driving rhythm.

Everyone stared at him.

Come on! thought Wynter, willing the crowd to respond. *Come on!*

Christopher yelled again and began to stamp his foot. Wynter started to clap in time with the drum.

Suddenly, a man in the crowd whooped in counterpoint to Christopher's driving tattoo. Someone else began to clap in time, and gradually the sound of stamping began to vibrate up through the floor.

"*Yes,*" hissed Razi.

The younger musician rose abruptly to her feet. She grabbed her fiddle and shoved it beneath her chin. She stood for a moment, eyes closed, bow poised, waiting as her body caught the cadence of the drum. Then she was away, the rhythm overtaking her, her hands flying, and music joyous as sunshine spun out from her bow. Christopher whirled towards her, his hair flying, his face lit with joy.

The older woman bent to retrieve something from the table. When she turned she had a recorder held to her lips. She nodded in time to the music, and then she too was away, carried forward and up with the sheer joy, the sheer *exuberance* of the drum. The crowd roared and stamped, and Christopher whooped. The man jammed his fiddle under his cheek and let fly.

Wynter and Razi stood for a long moment, watching as Christopher lost himself to what he used to be. Then the landlord came over and rapped his knuckles on the table at

Wynter's feet, pointedly looking up at herself and Razi. Wynter blushed, wiped her eyes, and stepped primly from the tabletop to take her seat.

Razi, however, took his own sweet time in getting down from his perch. As he descended from on high, Wynter glanced at the table of Merron nobles, and to her delight she caught the woman giving her tall, long-legged pirate a very appreciative look. Razi adjusted his sword and folded his hands on the table, all the time staring coolly at the landlord.

The Merron woman laughed in amusement and leant to murmur to her neighbour. He turned with a fond smile and Wynter realised that they were twins. There could be no doubt of it; they were the same height, both tall and slim with high sloping cheekbones and clear, dark blue eyes. The man's face was slightly heavier boned than the woman's and dressed with a neat beard, but they shared a similar cool beauty that made Wynter think of tapestries and fairytales.

The man pushed his hair back behind his ear and listened to his sister's murmured comment. His mouth curved into a smile and he looked Razi up and down with amusement as his sister glanced back their way. They both had luminous waterfalls of blond hair. The woman's fell around her shoulders and down her back like lemon fire.

No wonder Razi noticed you, thought Wynter. *You are like sunshine on ice.* The woman dipped her head and smiled another comment to her brother. She looked older than Razi, well into her late twenties, but Wynter decided that they would make a handsome couple. *The pirate and his pale lady,* she thought. *That would be lovely to see.* Then she thought slyly, *perhaps this will be our way to their table.*

Caoirigh Beo

"You are being watched, Razi," murmured Wynter, as she took a sip of her cordial.

Razi lifted his eyes and discreetly took in the room. "Where?" he asked. He had been pointedly ignoring the noblemen ever since Wynter had caught him eyeing the woman, and so had not noticed the amount of attention he was getting from that quarter.

Wynter chuckled. "Your pale lady seems quite taken with you. It must be the beard."

Razi tutted irritably, but he glanced across the room nonetheless, and then looked quickly away. The lady must still have been watching. He immediately began fiddling with the hem of his sleeve and Wynter felt a great rush of tenderness for him as the colour rose in his cheeks. She pucked him in the arm, and his teeth flashed in a quick grin.

Wynter found it very tempting to fall into their old tease and rattle. But she cleared her throat and forced herself to concentrate on their surroundings. She reminded herself that Razi was one of the most hated men in this kingdom.

At every turn of his back there were daggers and Wolves, and an entire way of life depended on his actions. It would not do to forget their precarious position.

She glanced sideways at him, and saw him cast another fleeting glance at the blonde lady. Wynter smiled. *What harm?* she thought. *To see him so charmed for a little while, and so distracted. Can't Christopher and I watch his back?*

She glanced around the room as she took another sip of her drink. The Merron were starting to dance, and she regarded them with interest. Her father had described Merron dancing to her wild, swinging set-pieces, complex and fast. Lorcan said he had never seen dancers leap so high. Wynter wondered if Christopher could dance like that. Maybe he would show her how? Razi tapped the table in time to the music. Somewhere across the crowd Christopher was still working the drum, adding his own thread to the sound, happy and wilsd. They had ordered him a meal, but Wynter did not think they would be seeing him for quite some time.

Despite her best intentions, she did not notice the two men crossing the room until Razi got warily to his feet, his hand on his sword. Wynter rose to join him, and met the men's eyes as they approached.

One of them she recognised as having come from the noblemen's table. He had been seated at the left hand of the male twin and had been much amused by the pale lady's interest in Razi. Sandy-haired, wiry and slightly stooped, Wynter guessed this man was in his early thirties, though it was hard to tell because his pale face was so very weathered. He wore the symbolic bracelets of the Bear Merron at the tops of his bare arms and a plaited band of copper and silver on his wrist. He had an air of slouching good-humour, and as he came to the table, he pushed his curling hair behind his ears and smiled with open curiosity. Wynter saw that he was missing two top teeth and his neck and wrists were ringed with old scars. His companion, a broad-shouldered brown-haired giant, looked down at herself and Razi with similar openness and curiosity.

The sandy-haired man offered his hand, and Razi shook it. Then, without deferring to Razi, the man turned and offered his hand to Wynter as if she too were a man. She accepted this as if it were normal, nodding as he met her eye. His hand was very strong, callused and tough as if his palms were made of polished wood, and his slim arms were like corded iron. He began to introduce himself in Merron, saw that they did not understand him, and paused, his forehead creased.

"I am terribly sorry for our ignorance," said Razi. "We have no understanding of your language."

The two Merron looked at each other.

The sandy-haired man cast a glance at the noblemen's table, and the male twin raised his eyebrows in query. The man waved the twin's attention away, as if to say *give me a moment* and, with a determined roll of his shoulders, turned and addressed Wynter and Razi in Garmain. Wynter could speak this Northland tongue quite well, but she knew that Razi could not, so she stayed silent. Razi tried French and then Italian, but to no avail.

The Merron men sighed in frustration.

"Forgive me," said Wynter in Hadrish, "but do we perhaps share this language?"

The sandy-haired man gave a cry of delight and flashed his gap-toothed grin. He bowed slightly to Wynter and

Razi and said, "With respect, honoured people, the Lords talk with Hadran tongue; it would be our pleasure for you would join us at our table for visit?" His hoarse voice and the drawling burr of his accent were warm and somehow reassuring. He indicated his companion, who had already turned away and was craning to see over the crowd. "Wari will get your small friend," he said.

Wynter felt a pang of regret that Christopher's fun would be cut short so soon, but neither herself nor Razi moved to prevent the man named Wari from whistling for attention and waving towards the stage. It was time to play politics and they would need Christopher's knowledge of the Merron to guide them. They went to gather their stuff, but the sandy-haired man waved them off with a frown. "All safe," he said, impatiently. "All good."

Wynter and Razi glanced at each other and recalled Christopher's warning about implied lack of trust. Razi dipped his head amiably and they turned away from their travel-belts and belongings with concealed misgivings. They had just eased from behind the table when Christopher was handed across the crowd and deposited lightly onto the ground by their side. He shoved his clinging hair back off his face and Wynter saw wariness creep into his smile as he eyed the two grinning Merron.

"What's the story?" he said in cautious Southlandast.

"We've been invited to the nobles' table," answered Razi, through a smooth smile. "We'll be speaking Hadrish, as apparently it's the only language we all share."

The Merron men nodded politely to Christopher. He smiled at them, still speaking quietly to Razi and Wynter in Southlandast.

"Have you tried to introduce yourselves? Because that wouldn't do at all."

"No," said Wynter. "They approached us."

"Good, good. Now let them lead the way."

Wynter and Razi followed Christopher's lead by bowing once more and letting the two men go ahead of them. The music continued unabated, but the crowd paid discreet attention to the strangers as they approached the noblemen's table.

Wari slipped easily between the warhounds and moved to stand by the wall. Wynter suspected that he was some kind of guard or personal assistant to the silent, black-haired fellow who sprawled in the chair on the pale lady's right.

"*Tá teanga na Hadran acu,*" said Wari. The twins raised their eyebrows and said, "Ahh, Hadrish."

The black-haired man watched the three of them, his dark eyes expressionless. His fingers were ornate with silver rings, the tops of his bare arms enclosed in the ubiquitous heavy silver bracelets. Wynter was surprised to see that these bracelets did not symbolise any of the four tribes of Merron. Instead of the usual hawk, panther, bear or snake, the tops of the open spirals depicted a human head, in its mouth a lamb or a small dog. Christopher eyed this man warily and the man eyed him back.

The sandy-haired fellow did not reclaim his seat, but instead stayed close to Razi, Wynter and Christopher, keeping himself between them and the warhounds. Wynter was glad of this, as the big dogs had risen to their feet and were growling low, their teeth bared. She knew you should not show fear to a snarling dog, but she suspected that her entire head would fit inside one of these creatures' mouths, and the image did not inspire courage. She moved closer to Razi, and he protectively took her hand.

The sandy-haired fellow spoke to the dogs.

"*Tóggo bogé,*" he said quietly, "*is cairde iad.*"

Christopher translated softly, "He said, '*relax, they are friends*'."

The female twin leant forward and looked across the heads of the dogs, blatantly staring at Razi and Wynter's joined hands. She frowned when she spotted Wynter's twisted woollen bracelet, and Wynter saw her search Razi's wrists for its match. Then she flicked a glance at Christopher, found the matching bracelet and grinned. She lifted her eyes to Razi and gave him a private smile.

Sitting back, she said "*Tarraingígí siar!*" and immediately two of the great hounds flopped to the floor and laid their heads on their paws

Her twin sprawled in his chair, his eyes switching from Wynter to Razi to Christopher with great amusement. He rapped his fingers on the table. "*Tarraingígí siar!*" he said, and two more of the great hounds lowered themselves to the floor. When they continued to growl, the man rapped the table again. "*Tarraingígí siar,*" he insisted sharply, "*Anois!*" and the two hounds laid their heads on their paws, whining.

The male twin smiled crookedly and spread his hands with apologetic good humour.

"They have temper," he said in drawling Hadrish.

His sister grinned. "Just like their master!" she said, her eyes sparkling.

Her brother elbowed her none-too-gently in the ribs, and the sandy-haired man snorted in amusement.

Wynter was astonished. When Christopher had told her that the Merron would expect "decorum" this was not the behaviour she had expected. She had been prepared for haughty disdain, a willingness to be offended, not this easy, teasing good humour. She began to fret about what "decorum" might entail.

In counterpoint to the warm amusement of the others, the black-haired man continued to lean back in his chair, his face shuttered, his fingers tapping in time to the music. His dogs still growled out their warnings and stood as a barrier between the strangers and their master's table.

As one, the twins turned to look at him. The man, leaning forward to see past his sister, raised his eyebrows expectantly. When the black-haired man did not respond, the male twin rapped the table and said something impatient in Merron. The black-haired man ignored him.

"Úlfnaor," admonished the lady.

At her gentle disapproval the man rolled his dark eyes in defeat. He waved his hand at his hounds and snarled, "*Tarraingígí siar!*" looking away into the crowd as he did so.

The last two dogs flopped submissively to the floor and the male twin gestured that the guests come forward. Wynter felt Razi's hand tighten on hers as they passed between the hounds, but once they were within the dogs' protective inner circle he let go.

The sandy-haired man slid behind the table and stood by the male twin's chair, his arms folded, his smile gone. Wynter noticed that Wari was regarding them solemnly, and the twins, too, had lost their smiles. Everyone was waiting with the same grave expectancy on their faces. Úlfnaor leaned further back in his chair, his expression challenging.

Ah, thought Wynter, *now comes the decorum*. She waited for Christopher to speak. There was a long moment of silence, during which Wynter resisted the urge to prompt her friend. She could hear Razi breathing softly beside her. He shifted his feet. Still no word from Christopher. Wynter wondered if they had misjudged his grasp of the situation.

After a long, tense wait, Úlfnaor lifted his eyebrows in what looked like pleased surprise and straightened in his chair. He nodded to Christopher.

Immediately, Christopher stepped forward and bowed his head, bringing his fist to his chest. He spoke directly to Úlfnaor.

"With respect, Aoire," he said in Hadrish, meeting the man's dark eyes. "Would you grant us the honour of hearing our names?"

The rest of the company grinned and Wynter felt a knot between her shoulderblades untie itself. He had got it right. Christopher kept his fist to his chest and gazed expectantly at the black-haired man. The silence stretched on and slowly the grins faded and a small frown grew between Christopher's dark eyebrows.

When the black-haired man finally spoke, it was coldly and in Merron. "*Cén fáth an teanga coimhthíoch? Nach Merron thú?*"

"With respect, Aoire," said Christopher quietly. "My company does not speak the Merron tongue. I will not speak above them."

The corner of the man's mouth twitched, and he waved his hand, as if to say, *go ahead then, if you must.*

Christopher nodded formal thanks. "With respect,

Aoire. Allow me to say to you that I am Coinín Garron, *mac Aidan an Filid.*"

"You are Aidan Garron's foundling?"

Christopher lifted his chin and Wynter saw that dangerous spark of pride show in his face. "With respect, Aoire," he said warningly, "I am Aidan Garron's *son.*"

"And so," asked the man, "you call yourself *filid*?"

The company watched Christopher carefully. They seemed very interested in his reply. He held the man's gaze for a moment, then dropped his eyes. "I am not of the blood, Aoire," he said. "I have no right or desire to claim what is not mine."

This must have been a very respectful answer, because the twins smiled and the sandy-haired man raised his chin in warm approval. The corners of Christopher's mouth lifted in a sad smile. The Aoire nodded, and Wynter was surprised to see kindness in his face now, and acceptance. "Very well then, Coinín Garron mac Aidan," he said softly, indicating Wynter and Razi, "introduce your company."

Christopher's dimples blossomed in renewed delight and he turned to Razi. "This," he said, laying his hand on Razi's chest and beaming like a proud father with his firstborn, "is my great friend and the brother of my heart, al-Sayyid al-Tabiyb." Razi smiled crookedly at that, and Wynter couldn't help but grin. Christopher had just introduced Razi as "my Lord the Doctor." "You can call him Tabiyb, for short," said Christopher happily, patting Razi's chest.

The male twin got to his feet and reached a hand to Razi. "Welcome to our table, Tabiyb," he said. "My sister is pleased to meet you."

The pale lady's hand dropped beneath the table and her

brother leapt slightly as if he had been pinched. The sandy-haired man snickered and even the black-haired man seemed amused. Razi shook hands up and down the table.

All eyes turned to Wynter, and she bowed formally from the hip as if she were a boy at court. Christopher reached for her and drew her to his side. "This," he said, "is Iseult uí Garron, *iníon* Lorcan." Razi startled at Christopher's use of Wynter's proper name, and Wynter gave him a reassuring look. "She is my *croí-eile*," said Christopher softly, putting his arm around Wynter's waist.

The lady sighed and murmured something in the manner of someone saying *how sweet*.

The sandy-haired man grinned. "*Dhá luch beaga,*" he said, his eyes sparkling. "*Rua 'gus dubh!*"

The male twin tilted his head to him, his eyes still on Wynter and added, "*A gcuid páistí chomh beag bídeach go gcodlaíonn siad i ndearcán.*"

All the Merron chuckled and clucked like a chorus of hens, their eyes slipping slyly to Christopher. He waved his hand as if to say, *Yes, yes. I've heard it all before.* But his face was flushed and the Merron crowed.

Wynter regarded their smirking faces, smiling uncertainly.

"What?" she said.

"Oh, they're just being silly. Because they think we're small."

"*Tell* me," she insisted.

Christopher muttered. "They said we're like two little mice and . . ." his colour deepened. "Our children will be so tiny they will sleep in an acorn."

Wynter felt her cheeks flare red.

The pale lady took pity on the mortified couple. She stood and extended her arm. "Welcome to our table, Iseult," she said, shaking Wynter's hand.

At the lady's touch, Wynter started. This was a tribal woman of at least twenty-five years of age, but her hand was as soft and as clean as a newborn babe's. Wynter could not believe it. Even the sheltered ladies of court had fingers roughened by a lifetime of sewing, their nails often black from soot. In comparison to them, this woman's fingers were as blemish-free as fresh snow. It was so extraordinary that Wynter forgot herself entirely and stood staring like a halfwit, turning the lady's hand over and over in her own.

Razi murmured, "*Sister*" in dismay, and Wynter looked up, suddenly aware of herself again. "Oh, my goodness!" she exclaimed, mortified. "I am so sorry! Your hands are just so beautiful! I've never . . ."

The lady smiled tightly and extricated herself from Wynter's grip. All around the table, the Merron were wary suddenly, and grave, and Wynter saw that they were looking to Christopher. He was staring at the lady with wide-eyed comprehension and a kind of frozen disbelief. She stood very straight and still, her eyes locked on his. Christopher looked to her twin, and reluctantly lowered his eyes to take in the man's hands. Wynter followed suit and saw, that he, too, had impossibly clean, unblemished skin and beautifully tended nails. Slowly, Christopher raised his eyes. The man gave him a knowing, wistful kind of smile, and nodded.

"*Caoirigh Beo*," whispered Christopher. He turned to stare at Úlfnaor, who met his eyes without expression.

There was a general air of suspense amongst the Merron lords, and their eyes darted between their three guests.

Razi cleared his throat. "Forgive me," he asked, his deep voice uncertain. "But . . .?"

"They are the *Caoirigh Beo*," said Christopher flatly. "They are treasured. They are . . . they are protected." His tone brooked no more questions and Razi lifted his chin in feigned understanding and let it go.

There was an uneasy silence, and then the male twin held out his hand and looked Christopher in the eyes. "With respect, honoured person," he said, "would you grant us the honour of hearing our names?"

Christopher frowned, his grey eyes uncertain. Razi and Wynter looked at him in concern. They needed him to go on, surely he knew that? Whatever his differences here, he must not refuse. Christopher took a deep breath and held it for a moment as if gathering something inside himself. Then his body relaxed, his face softened, and he took the twin's offered hand. "With respect, *a dhuine uasail*," he said. "The honour would be ours."

Smoke

The sandy-haired man bowed slightly and touched his chest, flashing his charming, gap-toothed grin. "Allow me to say to you that I am Sólmundr an Fada, *mac* Angus an Fada, *fear saor*."

Christopher glanced sharply at him, his eyes widening. "*Fear saor*," he whispered. Sólmundr offered him his hand and Christopher shook it vigorously, a stunned smile on his face. "Well met, Sólmundr."

Sólmundr faltered at Christopher's intense look, then moved on to offer his hand to Wynter and to Razi. He turned and introduced them to the male twin. "This," he said fondly, "is my Lord, Ashkr *an Domhain*."

Ashkr leant forward, his bracelets flashing. Despite his soft skin, his handshake was firm and strong.

"Well met, Ashkr," said Razi.

Ashkr's sister smiled expectantly and Sólmundr introduced her as the Lady Embla. She nodded at Christopher and Wynter, then turned all her attention to Razi. "Tabiyb," she said, her voice rich and low. "At last, we know each other's name."

She leant across the table, her pale hair swinging forward like a veil of flax and Razi shook her proffered hand, staring without speaking. Wynter cast a smiling glance at Christopher, expecting him to be amused, but his attention was still, inexplicably, on Sólmundr.

Embla clasped Razi's tough, dark hand between her own soft ones and tilted her head. A slow smile spread across Razi's face. He held Embla's gaze and ran his thumb against the soft white flesh of her wrist. There was a moment between them that seemed to suspend the room.

After a long silence, when it seemed that neither Razi nor Embla were inclined to separate, Ashkr snorted and poked his sister in the side. She broke away with a secret smile and Razi rubbed his palm dreamily, as if feeling the memory of her touch. Embla drifted slowly down into her chair.

Sólmundr cleared his throat and raised his arm to introduce the black-haired man formally. "Respected people," he said, "allow me give you the honour of naming our *Aoire* – our Shepherd – Úlfnaor, *Aoire an Domhain.*"

Unlike the others, Úlfnaor did not offer his hand, but no one seemed to take exception to this. Instead, Christopher bowed with grave formality, a proper bow, deep and lingering, his tangled hair swinging forward to hide his face. Razi and Wynter quickly followed suit.

"We are honoured," they said.

"The honour is mine," rumbled Úlfnaor.

With that, the Merron relaxed into such a sudden and unexpected informality that Wynter was left reeling.

"Sit! Sit!" urged Sólmundr. He leant across, gesturing to the stools that dotted Wynter's side of the table, then pushed at Razi's shoulder and pressed Christopher down. Embla offered a bowl of olives to whet their appetites, and Ashkr called to the landlord to bring more tankards and a pitcher of wine. Úlfnaor leant back and murmured to Wari, who quickly left and returned with the meals that Razi and Wynter had ordered.

Wynter took her seat, still dazed by the sudden turn in atmosphere, and all the Merron laughed at their guests' confusion. Sólmundr, having ensured that everyone was sitting comfortably, went to take his own seat. He was lowering himself into his chair and turning to Ashkr to make a smiling comment when Wynter saw him blanch, and he froze, half-in, half-out of his seat. He bent over with a grunt and gripped the table, gritting his teeth against what looked like sudden pain.

Ashkr clutched his friend's arm and bent to get a good look at the other man's face. "Sól!" he said in concern, "*an bhfuil drochghoile ort arís?*"

Sólmundr bowed his head, nodding, and his knuckles whitened against the table.

Razi half-rose from his stool. "What is it?" he said.

"Sól has . . ." Ashkr spun to Embla and asked her something in Merron.

She ran her hand over her belly. "In his guts," she said. "He is bad. Only this three day." She stood and looked into the crowd. "I will to get Hallvor."

"My friend is a doctor," exclaimed Christopher. "He can help."

"We have own healer!" snapped Úlfnaor.

"And a wonderful one, no doubt! But my friend is a *physician*! Of the blue robe!" Christopher held up his hands to demonstrate, the long, clean scar of his left arm a testimony to Razi's skill.

Sólmundr bent lower, his eyes widening.

"Get Hallvor!" cried Ashkr, rubbing the small of Sólmundr's back.

Wari and Úlfnaor began to scan the crowd, but Sólmundr relaxed suddenly and straightened from his pained crouch. He stood for a moment, his hand pressed against the base of his stomach, and then he grinned.

"It gone again," he said, blushing in sudden embarrassment.

Ashkr continued to gaze up at him, his face drawn, his hand on Sólmundr's arm, and Sólmundr tutted. "It is good, Ash." He grinned around at the company. "I tells you, it this rotten Southlander food. It not suit my gut."

Ashkr nodded reluctantly, watching his friend as he took his seat.

Razi sat back down, studying the man's face for further signs of pain. "Where is the discomfort, Sólmundr?" he asked, "when it comes."

Sólmundr tsked impatiently and waved his hand to divert all attention from his stomach. He leant across and tapped the table in front of Christopher. "Coinín," he said. "You stare at me all the time. Why for?"

My God, thought Wynter. *These Merron! They are so direct!* Now she knew where Christopher got it from. Sólmundr rapped the table again, insistently.

Christopher hesitated, then he said, "I, too, am a free man."

Sólmundr frowned, not understanding, and Christopher reached over and pressed his fingers to the scars on the man's wrist. He repeated himself in Merron. "*Is fear saor mise freisin*, Sólmundr."

Sólmundr's frown deepened and Ashkr grew solemn. To Wynter's surprise, he reached for Sólmundr's hand. Their fingers entwined for a moment on the table top, Ashkr's smooth hand squeezing Sólmundr's roughened one, and then Ashkr released his grip and sat back, looking at Christopher.

"Who took you?" he asked quietly.

"The Loups-Garous."

The Merron winced at the dreaded name.

Christopher lifted his chin to Sólmundr. "You?" he asked.

"Barbary Corsairs."

Razi groaned, and Christopher nodded.

"They sell me for . . . um . . ." Sólmundr murmured something to Embla. She thought for a moment, then shrugged apologetically.

Úlfnaor, reaching for an olive, glanced up and said, "Galley slave."

Sólmundr nodded his thanks. "They sell me for galley slave," he said. "I galley slave for . . ." he held up two fingers.

"Two years?" asked Wynter, aghast, and he nodded again. Two years chained in the dark, in his own filth, toiling day and night without respite. Wynter looked at his good-natured face and couldn't imagine it.

"Then, one day . . ." Sólmundr made a whistling noise, his hand flying through the air to represent a cannon ball or some such thing, and then he hit the table with a loud *bam*! The hounds jerked, growling at the noise, and

Sólmundr grinned at them. "Oh, shush," he said, "Stupid fellows!"

"Sól swim," continued Ashkr gravely. "He swim many distance and then he come to shore. He walk home many distance, after many year." He looked at his friend and shook his head. "Many year."

Sólmundr sucked his teeth in dismissal and tossed Ashkr's hair. "Yes, yes," he said. "I wonderful. Strong and beautiful. Rising from sea like a god."

Ashkr snorted. "Like dead fish!" he said, fixing his hair.

"There is no slaves here. In this kingdom. This is what I heard." Úlfnaor gazed earnestly at Christopher when he said this, and Wynter realised that he was asking a question.

"That's what I've been told," said Christopher quietly. "That the King here is opposed to slavery."

"And you," Úlfnaor asked Razi. "You of colour." He tapped his face, in case he wasn't making himself clear. "You too are accepted?"

The irony of that had Wynter ducking her head to hide a bitter smile.

Razi nodded. "For the most part," he said carefully.

Úlfnaor sat back. "And faith?" he asked.

Razi frowned questioningly. Úlfnaor looked to Embla for help; she creased up her face in an attempt to find words. "People of religion," she said, glancing warily at Christopher, "of *different* religion. They are accepted?"

"It depends," snarled Christopher.

Razi frowned at him. "No, it *doesn't*," he snapped. "Yes," he said to Úlfnaor. "Yes, my fa . . . the King is very clear on it. Yes. All faiths are accepted."

Christopher shook his head angrily and looked away.

Úlfnaor leant back in his chair, looking very thoughtful, and Sólmundr and Ashkr went quiet. Embla just watched Razi's mouth, her finger tracing a languid figure of eight on the table top.

Wynter looked at Úlfnaor's pensive face and it dawned on her. *They are thinking of relocating*, she thought. *They want to move their people South!* Her heart sank for them. It was unlikely that the highly structured society in the kingdom would suit a large tribe of nomads. *You have been misled, I think, as to the likelihood of being accepted here. Someone has made you promises they are unlikely to fulfil.*

Wynter glanced at Christopher. He was glaring out into the crowd, his lips tight, but the disapproval rapidly drained from his narrow face, and his mouth curved into a wistful smile as he watched the Merron dance. The music had whipped up into a mighty frenzy. The crowd spilt into groups of four and began to weave in and out, forming and reforming intricate knots and patterns. Suddenly, someone in the centre of the group leapt like a fish and Wynter gasped as his hand slapped the smoky beams of the high ceiling. The crowd whooped. Christopher and Wari yelled and clapped their hands, once, in a formal expression of praise.

Embla reached across the table and tugged Razi's sleeve. "You dance, Tabiyb?"

Wynter snorted at the thought, but Razi's mouth hooked up at the corner and he gave her a very smug look. "Actually," he said, "I do!" He leapt to his feet, holding his hand out to Embla with a flourish. "Coinín taught me!" he yelled.

Wynter looked on, amazed, as her pirate swung his pale lady out onto the floor.

"Christopher Garron!" she yelled, thumping the quietly grinning young man on the shoulder. "What have you done to my brother?"

"It's a rajput katar," said Christopher as Ashkr examined his unusual belt-knife, admiring the etchings in the steel. "Tabiyb bought it for me when he got the matchlock. He thought it would be easier to use for . . ." Christopher held up his brutalised hand and stiffly waggled his fingers. "He felt it would be much easier to keep a grip."

"And is it?" asked Sólmundr, glancing at Wynter who gestured that he pass the knife across the table to her. She slid her hand into the metal brace, closing her fingers around the grip inside. It was very stable, like replacing her fist with a sword, but there was no fluidity to her wrist.

As if reading her thoughts, Christopher said, "I still prefer my dagger. Better freedom." He made some swift, lethal movements with his arm as if striking quickly with a blade, and Wynter saw the Merron eyeing him thoughtfully. She smiled to herself. She would not like to face Christopher in an even match – mutilated hands or not, he would be a sly opponent, and quick. She was pleased to see this realisation dawn in the big men around her.

Wynter passed the katar to Úlfnaor just as Razi and Embla returned once again from the dance floor. Razi pulled a stool to the head of the table and Embla tugged Sólmundr's hair and gestured that he move. Sólmundr and Ashkr moved up a seat so that Embla could take the chair beside Razi. As they shifted about, the men clucked softly under their breath in that suggestive, teasing way of theirs, and Embla *tsk*ed and hid a grin.

As he took his seat, Razi watched Christopher pass the falchion sword to Ashkr. The tall blond man turned the sword over and ran his hand down the blade, his navy eyes grave with admiration.

"It is Indian steel," said Razi, "just like the matchlock and the katar." He paused to drink from a beaker of cordial. His hair was so damp that he looked as though he'd been swimming. "When I bought it," he gasped, passing the beaker to Embla, "the smith demonstrated cutting through a pig's leg. It sliced through the bone in one blow. It keeps an edge on it like nothing I've ever seen."

"They are tremendous weapons," said Wynter.

"Aye," sighed Razi, watching as Úlfnaor took the falchion and balanced it on his hand. "Aye. But in the end, they are just weapons. I'd rather . . ." he cleared his throat and shook himself. "Aye," he said firmly. "They are marvellous. The men who made them were wonderful craftsmen."

Úlfnaor glanced at Razi. He swung the blade around his shoulders, swiping it through the air with great skill and control. He grunted in approval and ran his thumb carefully across the edge.

"The Southlands is very strong in weapons," he said. "This what I hear. There much powerful weapon here."

Wynter glanced at Razi. He too had sharpened in response to this. "We are indeed a strong country," he said carefully. "Despite our recent troubles, our King is much loved. His armies armies well-trained."

"And well-armed?" asked Úlfnaor. "His son is great warrior, I hear. He have weapon of great power."

"That's a good story," murmured Christopher with a casual lack of interest. "Who told it to you?"

"Someone," drawled Úlfnaor. "Up North. It not true? He not warrior, this prince? He not have weapon?"

"Do the Merron spend a lot of their time discussing our royal family around their camp fires up north?" asked Wynter, smiling despite the tightness in her chest.

"I not say *Merron* say this," said Úlfnaor, "I just say *someone.*" He dismissed the topic with a wave of his hand. "It not matter. I may be wrong. It can to be hard, sometimes, to understand when someone talk."

Sólmundr snorted a little laugh through his nose. "Aye," he said, "special when they not know you listening at the time."

Úlfnaor shrugged. "I not help it that some people think Merron have no more intelligence than dog. It people's own trouble, the things they say, thinking we not understand." He grinned at Sól. A surprising expression in the Aoire's usually grave face, at once charming and dark, filled with an unexpected depth of wicked humour.

"Who was it told you this?" asked Wynter. "What exactly did they say?"

But Úlfnaor just tutted and waved her off. "Just talk," he said. "Half talk, half understood. It not worth the breath."

Wynter met Razi's eye. A great weapon, in the possession of the Prince. Had this rumour reached even to the Northlands? He shook his head. Later.

"You pass drink, Coinín?" Sólmundr gestured at the cordial.

Christopher went to pass the pitcher and grimaced when he realised it was empty. He looked around for the landlord. Wynter spotted the small man at a table across the room, gathering up empty pitchers. As he did his work, she saw him cast about to find his daughters and watch with anxious attention as they wandered the room.

Shy, soft-eyed little things, the girls were refilling the bowls of olives and gathering up stray dishes. Neither of them could have been older than thirteen and the Merron paid no heed to them, but Wynter could understand their father's concern. In the last few sets the atmosphere had taken rather a heated turn. These dances were blatantly suggestive of desire, their movements a good deal more lusty than would have been normally accepted, and Wynter had to admit, were these her daughters, she'd have packed them off to their rooms and locked their bedroom doors.

A handful of men by the door roared suddenly and laughed very loudly. The smallest girl flinched, though she was nowhere near them, and the landlord, his arms full of empty pitchers, gave his guests a suspicious look. He whistled for his daughters and they finished what they were doing. The landlord elbowed his way through the door to the kitchen and the girls followed close behind.

"Wyn?" Razi startled her by crouching down beside her and slipping an arm around her chair. He gazed hopefully up at her, his cheeks heated, his eyes wide.

Wynter laughed at his expression and pressed a finger to his nose. "You, my dear brother, look as though you are about to wheedle me for money!"

Razi blushed. "Well," he said, glancing off into the crowd. "The Merron . . . the Merron are staying the night and I . . ." A smile wriggled around on his face for a moment, too embarrassed to become a grin. "Would you . . .?" he said. He looked back up at her, his face saying *please.* "Would you fancy sleeping in a bed tonight, sis? Would you like us to rent a room?"

Razi glanced at Embla. The lady was watching him with heavy lids, her chin propped on her hand, her blonde hair tangled around her flushed cheeks. The expression on her face made even Wynter's heart go thud.

Oh! she thought.

Razi forced his eyes back to her. He bit his lip. Should they decide to rent a room, Wynter doubted that Razi would ever see the inside of it. She glanced at Christopher and he met her eye, his face contained. He was leaning back in a chair at the end of the table, his arms tightly crossed, his legs stretched out before him, taking his ease after so much dancing. His shirt was patched with sweat, his narrow face shining with the heat. His hair was in complete disorder. Wynter sat looking at him – her black-haired Hadrish boy – and she thought with great clarity, *I love you.*

Whatever expression this put on her face, Christopher's mouth curved at the sight of it and he tilted his head, his clear, grey eyes questioning. Razi followed her gaze. He looked quizzically at his friend.

Wynter bent forward and whispered in Razi's ear. "Would you let Christopher and I share a bed, Razi?"

His big brown eyes widened and he turned to stare at her, his expression shocked suddenly and uncertain. He looked so troubled that Wynter laid her hand on his neck and pressed her forehead to his, their old gesture of affection.

"Do you not love him, Razi?" she whispered, searching his face.

He swallowed and nodded. "I do," he said, "very much."

"Then, do you not think that he will do his best by me?"

He looked up into her eyes. "I do, Wyn. I think there could be no better man for you."

Wynter raised her eyebrows. *Well then?* her look said, *why the uncertainty?* "We have made our promises to each other, Razi. I am certain that I love him, and I trust him to mean what he has said to me."

Razi's eyes slid away and he seemed to think very deeply. Then he shook himself and nodded once. Quickly he grabbed the sides of Wynter's face and kissed her forehead. "Make each other happy, Wyn," he whispered fervently. "There's little enough joy in this world as it is." He leapt to his feet then and clapped his hands. "We stay!" he exclaimed and flung his arm out to a smiling Embla.

"Lady!" he said. "Dance with me!"

Embla slipped from behind the table and the two of them spun out into the crowd. Christopher watched, his eyes hardening briefly as Razi swung Embla into the air.

"What was all that whispering about?" he asked.

"We're staying the night," said Wynter, expecting him to look amused.

Instead, he grimaced and glanced around at Úlfnaor who was quietly discussing Razi's matchlock with Ashkr. "Huh," he grunted. "Well, it's only one night." He took a deep breath and let go whatever it was that was bothering him. "Girly," he said, leaning over to Wynter and taking her hand. "They want me to play the last set with them. Do you mind?" His dimples made a sly appearance as he smiled a crooked smile. "I won't be gone long," he promised.

Wynter pushed his tangled hair back from his face. "I'll

be here," she said softly. "I'm just going to get some more cordial from the landlord." She leant forward and whispered confidentially, "I think you dubious Merron have frightened him away." Their eyes met in amusement and she kissed Christopher briefly on the mouth before shoving him away from her. "Go on!" she said, "Go play with your drum!"

He slipped off into the crowd, and Wynter gathered up the empty pitchers and shouldered her way through the kitchen door. Something made her glance back, just in time to see Christopher mount the stage. As he reached for his drum, he turned his head briefly and looked at her. He grinned and raised his hand to push his hair behind his ear, then the door swung shut and he was gone.

Fire

"Hello?" Wynter stepped into the fragrant dimness of the kitchen and frowned at how still and silent it was. The big central table was filled with pitchers and beakers in various states of cleanliness, and the shelves by the wash tub were stacked with dripping dishes. There was no sign of the landlord, his daughters, or his cook.

A charcoal-grey cat sidled through the shadows by the dying cooking fire and Wynter caught its eye as she put her pitchers on the table. "All respect to you, mouse-bane," she whispered, wary these days of being overheard speaking to a cat. "Where are the humans as live here?"

The cat blinked at her in disdain, then rolled its eyes and jerked its head to the partially opened back door. Wynter craned her neck to see through the gap. The door led almost directly into the woods. Surely the landlord hadn't taken his daughters outside? She glanced back at the cat, but it had already slunk away.

I suppose I could help myself to a drink, Wynter thought, licking her dry lips and eyeing the barrels of cider and cordial. She was sorely tempted, but how mortifying would it be if the landlord came in and found her pilfering from his supplies? She swallowed against her thirst and moved deeper into the quiet, dripping gloom.

"Hello?" she called again, her hand falling automatically to the hilt of her knife. She came around the side of a locked cupboard and another door was revealed. Golden lamplight spilled a dim wedge on the dirt floor, and she smelled horse and straw. This door undoubtedly opened into the stables.

As she came level with the square of light, Wynter heard voices, low and urgent, speaking in Merron. She drew back into the darkness and moved to get a better view.

Sólmundr and Wari were standing in the barn, caught in a wavering circle of lantern light. Wari had a tight hold of Sólmundr's wrist and he was speaking quickly and persuasively, stooped to look into the other man's face. Sólmundr frowned and shook his head. Wynter made out the name Tabiyb, and she froze, listening carefully. Wari gestured desperately to Sólmundr's stomach and once again said something about Tabiyb. Sólmundr shook his head and twisted his wrist from the other man's grasp. Suddenly the two men paused with a start, and turned to look behind them, their faces wary.

"*Cé hé sin?*" growled Wari, glaring into the depths of the barn.

A small noise outside the back door distracted Wynter and she stepped backward to take a look out into the night. When she glanced back, Wari and Sólmundr were gone. The noise came again from outside, clearer now, and the hair on the back of Wynter's neck did a slow rise as she recognised a human whimper. She drew her knife from her belt and, staying in the shadows, pushed the edge of the back door so that it swung fully open.

At the tree line, twenty or so feet away from Wynter, stood the landlord's youngest daughter. The little girl was white-faced and dazed, staring into the kitchen, her eyes dark with shock. Her bodice was torn from her shoulder, hanging down in front, exposing her shift. Her cap was gone and one of her shoes.

What is this child's name? thought Wynter, her heart racing. *I know I heard her father call her something.* She eased closer to the door, scanning the trees behind the girl. *Laura?* she thought, *Linnet? Lorraine? Elaine! That's it! Elaine!*

"Elaine," she whispered, edging into the square of moonlight cast by the opened door, her eyes still on the motionless trees. The little girl didn't respond and Wynter glanced at her. "Elaine," she hissed. She held out her hand. "Come here, darling. Come on inside."

The girl's eyes slid left and welled up; her small hands started to shake. Wynter moved closer to the door, searching the shadows behind the child. Then she popped her head around the doorframe. There was nothing there, just the moon-washed wall of the stables and a path leading around to the yard. Wynter once more offered her hand to the little girl.

"Elaine!" she said sharply. "Come here!"

The little girl put her hands to her mouth, her eyes glued to the shadows at the base of the wall by the door, and to Wynter's horror, she took a step backward and into the trees.

"No!" said Wynter. "*Come here!*" Elaine raised her eyes to

meet Wynter's and suddenly a shadow detached itself from the forest and swallowed her whole.

Wynter cried out in shock and fear, then cursed herself for a fool as she made out a big man running through the shadows with the poor girl in his arms. She caught a brief glimpse of the child's eyes, wide and terrified over the hand that was clasped across her mouth, and all Wynter's common sense was swallowed in a blast of outrage. She turned briefly and yelled in Hadrish, hoping that the men in the barn would hear her. Then she ran like a fool into the darkness of the trees.

She could see the man up ahead, flitting through the shadows. He had flung the child over his shoulder and was dashing easily through the trees. The little girl, silent with shock, was looking back at Wynter, her pale face bobbing in the dark. The man glanced back. Wynter saw him grin and to her horror realised that she had been drawn alone into the forest. Oh God! She glanced behind her. Already there was nothing but trees. She looked ahead and there was no sign of the man or his captive.

Wynter stopped dead, listening. All around her there was shushing and sighing, and then the yip and call of animals communicating to each other. She crouched, her knife up, and the night flowed about her like a living thing.

Move! she thought, and turned to run.

The first blow came from nowhere, a fierce punch, striking her cheek. Her head rocked sideways. Her body spun. She brought her knife blindly upwards, and felt a bright spark of satisfaction as something yelped. Then a second blow hit her in the kidneys, and pain bloomed like paralysis up through her body. Something slammed hard between her shoulders, hurling her forward, and her head smacked against a tree with stunning brutality. Her eyes filled with sparks, her ears buzzed, and she fell. The world rolled over on her as leaves filled her mouth and eyes and nose.

Something grabbed the back of her tunic and Wynter gagged, her collar choking her as she was hauled up from the ground. Unbreakably strong arms clamped around her and someone chuckled as she was pulled tightly in against a strong body. There was a furnace rush of breath in her ear, and the feel of sharp teeth and fur against her cheek. Then a shape flew through the air towards them, long and high and fast. Everything fell backwards and the ground drove the air from her as she went down again. Sparks exploded in her head once more and then darkness closed over her.

There was only sound for a moment, grunting and scuffling. Then a solid, painful *thump* as something rolled over her, and the sound of heavy footsteps running away.

"Come on, lass! Come on!" That voice. His voice. His lilting Northland accent urgently hissing in her ear. The trees swooped and swung around her as she was pulled up from the darkness and she felt his hard arms close around her waist as he tried to get her to her feet. "Oh God!" he murmured. "Come on, girly! Stand up! They're all around us!"

Her legs were wild. They'd gone off on their own and she had nothing left to stand on. Every time he pulled her up, empty space opened beneath her and she was sucked back down into the leaves. Where had all her bones gone? She felt herself dribble through his arms, flopping to the ground again as soon as he tried to get her moving forward. *I'm terribly sorry*, she thought, *I don't seem to be working properly.*

"Oh God, oh God!" he moaned, and there were tears in his voice now.

It's all right, she thought, *don't worry, love. Razi will fix me.*

He made a desperate noise in his throat and clutched her in against his chest, crouching low. Wynter tried to lift her arm to pat him reassuringly, but he made that desperate noise again and put his hand over her mouth.

They seemed to be huddled against a tree. Wynter laid her head back against the pale fabric of his undershirt and looked up at the clean slope of his jaw. He was staring out into the darkness. His hair was falling into her eyes.

He looked down at her suddenly and said, "Shhhhhhh."

Animals howled somewhere in the trees, and he jumped and moaned. Darkness moved over her like a buzzing cloud and the world swung again, rolling. Her stomach rose up and she clenched her jaw against a mouthful of heat. She was lying on her side and he was kneeling in front of her, anxiously gazing into her face.

I'm going to be sick, she thought. She shut her eyes.

" . . . long coming to find you," he whispered and she rose up from the buzzing dark to find him pressing something into her hand. He peered into her face again. His lips were moving. His lovely pale face, glowing. " . . . so just don't make a sound, sweetheart."

She frowned. *What?*

He put his hand on the side of her face. "Don't worry," he whispered. "I can run like a bloody rabbit." She looked down at her hand and found she was clutching his black knife. *What?* Something yipped and shushed through the trees, very close by. Then darkness again. Like a long, held breath.

She gasped and opened her eyes. His boots were striding away from her. His pale shirt. Too pale, too obvious.

Darkness again.

A whistle. Her eyes floated open. He was standing a short distance away. Blatantly standing there in the moonlight. Waiting.

Then footsteps, moving fast, ran towards him. Still he waited. Then he turned and dove into the trees, haring away from her, his pale shirt glowing in the shadows like a beacon, his dark hair flying. Blackness exploded from the bushes and chased him – one, two, three shadows running low, yipping. Then they were gone.

Wynter pushed her useless arm into the leaves, trying to roll, and darkness took her eyes from her again. It dragged her down into sparks and noise and sucked his knife from her hand.

A fizz and whistle of bright shapes and glitter filled her head as she was pulled from the leaves again and turned. She opened her eyes and the world groaned and twisted, spinning. Arms closed around her, and she gasped as she was heaved upwards. *I'm going to be sick.*

She flopped, useless and loose-limbed, as someone gathered her to them like a doll. Her head lolled against a warm neck. Then she felt soft beard against her face and was looking up into Razi's curls as he stared out into the trees. He held her to him, unbearably tight, and she opened her mouth to say, *Christopher is gone.*

Razi glanced at her, his eyes enormous. "Shhhhhhh!" he hissed.

But Christopher, Razi! Christopher is gone! She tried to

reach for Christopher's knife, to show Razi. But her stomach lurched and she flung out an arm as her mouth filled with bile.

He released her just in time to let her roll, and her dinner finally escaped in a scalding flood onto the forest floor. She scrabbled in the leaves as lightning went off against her eyes and in her stomach. Then the trees did a lazy circle around her and the forest turned on its head for a moment. The ground bounced alarmingly under her, bumping her up and down as if she were in a cart on a rutted road. *What's happening?* she thought in panic. *What's going on?* But it was only Razi, running with her through the trees, his breath coming in panicked little moans. The light and shadow of the moonlit forest flashed against his desperate face like fireworks.

It was bright then. Orange light everywhere, blurred and too hot. There was a smell of smoke, and men were shouting and scuffling. They passed into dim coolness and then out again into that hot orange light. The world fell sideways. Straw pressed against her cheek, and she was watching through a warped mirror as Razi's tall shape ran from her into the orange light. Black shapes moved. Horses screamed and stamped. Smoke burned her throat. She felt her stomach rise again and she closed her eyes against the fury of the fire.

Something cool pressed to her mouth and she opened her lips to strawberry cordial. *Oh bless you*, she thought. *Bless you, whoever you are.* She swallowed and opened her eyes to find Razi, smoke-blackened and grim, holding the beaker to her mouth. He smelled of wet ashes and sweat, and his hands were shaking.

Dim light pressed into Wynter's brain like a rusty needle, and she squinted stiffly against the nauseating pain in her head. She groaned and lifted a heavy hand to her forehead.

"All right," murmured Razi. He stared anxiously into her face, pulling her eyelid up so that she winced. "All right," he said again. His hands were shaking so badly that Wynter could see the tremors in his arms. People were scuffling behind him. She looked over Razi's shoulder at them — they were nothing but shapes in the painful light.

Razi rose to his feet and walked towards the sound. Wynter tried to get her eyes to focus. The barn was a reeking, sodden mess of smoky darkness. Near the centre, a tight knot of Merron was standing in flaring lantern light, their swords drawn, their faces hard. The landlord, the cook, the ostler and his two stable boys were facing them down with pitchforks and cudgels.

"Where are they?" screamed the landlord. "Where are they, you bastards? Give them back!" The Merron regarded him in silence, their eyes skipping from man to man.

Outside, the warhounds were baying. Wynter looked blearily towards the sound and was shocked to see the sky showing grey through the big barn doors. Horses moved and stamped in the yard. There seemed to be many people out there, milling about. Someone called out in Merron, and the small knot of warriors at the centre of the barn began to edge warily around the landlord and his frantic, staring men.

"No!" screamed the landlord, leaping forward. "No! You come back here!" He raised his cudgel at the departing Merron and they jerked their swords up, their faces threatening. The landlord howled in impotent fury and slammed his cudgel down onto the swiftly raised shield of one of the men. The knot of Merron surged forward, and the poorly armed tavern staff fell back, their faces desperate.

Razi ran up behind the little group and snagged the tunic of one of the Merron. "Please," he said in Hadrish, "my friend is missing. Please! Help us find him."

The man whirled, his sword raised, and Wynter saw that it was Wari, dishevelled and black with smoke. He stared blankly at Razi.

"Please!" cried Razi again. "He's one of your *own*! Won't you help me find him?" Wari just continued to back away, his eyes wide, his sword raised.

Wynter pushed herself forward on shaky arms and slid to the floor. Her legs buckled and she held herself up against the feedbags, watching as Razi's hand fell to his side.

The Merron circled around the fuming tavern staff, their weapons up, then they backed towards the door. The landlord followed them all the way, begging now for the Merron to please, *please* give his daughters back. Razi watched helplessly as the Merron backed out into the yard. Wynter took a few tottering steps towards him and grabbed his arm.

There was a flurry of violent movement outside. Then a large body of horses clattered into sudden action, their hooves ringing out in the quiet morning. The sounds diminished quickly into the distance and silence descended on the smoky barn as the Merron left them.

Ashes

*R*azi led the way through the dim and misty trees. In the distance, the men from the tavern called for the little girls. They had taken the opposite direction to Wynter and Razi, following some other trail through the forest, leaving the Arab and his girl to make their own way.

Razi was looking for the place where he had found Wynter hidden against the base of the tree. He was looking for the tell-tale patch where she had thrown up, hoping that, from there, he might find signs that would lead him to Christopher. Wynter staggered along behind him, her stomach rolling, her head thumping in time to her heartbeat. She squinted at the dark ground, looking for anything that might help, hoping against hope that Christopher would just pop out of the bushes, grinning and safe.

Razi shot forward to crouch in the misty gloom, his fingers resting lightly on a little patch of leaves. Wynter shivered, looking down at the dark patch of ground under his hand. She smelled vomit, faint but definite. She shuffled her foot in the leaves by Razi's boot and Christopher's black dagger rose to the surface like a body exhumed. Razi stared at it expressionlessly. Then he shoved it into his belt and got to his feet, wiping his hand on his britches. He stalked into the forest, scanning the ground.

For a while the tracks were easy to follow. Heavy and rucked, they told of three or four big men, running fast. But then they petered out, and Wynter and Razi were left wandering, clueless and desperate in the shadows. It seemed as though Christopher had outrun the men. There was certainly no sign that he had been caught.

Razi kept going, pushing his way deeper into the trees, searching the ground for clues. *Perhaps we should call out*, thought Wynter as the distant shouts of the tavern men drifted to them across the brightening air. But Razi just kept walking, slowly scanning the ground, and she stumbled after him, her head buzzing with pain.

About fifteen minutes later, Razi came to an abrupt halt, staring at the ground. Wynter shuffled to his side. She followed his eyes, gaping blankly for a moment before realising that she was looking down at one of Christopher's boots. It had been flung under a bush. A moment's searching found its companion at the base of a tree on the opposite side of the trail. Wynter took the boots and clutched them to her chest, watching as Razi examined a wide, violent scattering of leaves in the centre of the trail. It seemed to have been kicked up in the course of a fierce struggle. He bent and retrieved one of Christopher's socks from the leaf litter, balling it in his hand as he looked off into the trees.

Christopher's trousers lay buried in the leaf mould on the far side of a clearing and his underthings were a few yards further on, next to another, smaller area of disturbed leaves. Razi gathered these up and continued into the trees, following a line of deep, skidding footprints that spoke of further pursuit.

These tracks did not tell of many people – two men, perhaps, and Christopher – but they ended in another big, ragged circle of disturbance, the golden surface of the leaves kicked aside to expose the dark rot beneath. Christopher's undershirt was cast to the side here, all the laces broken. Razi picked it up and held it with the others against his chest.

Wynter looked at the bundle of clothes in Razi's arms and tried not to picture what they signified. She tried not to imagine Christopher struggling and being held down while his clothes were pulled from him. Christopher being chased, naked, through the dark. She tried not to imagine the fear and the humiliation this would have brought.

There were more prints – long, desperate tracks in the soft leaves – and they led to a wide clearing.

It was a much bigger disturbance this time, a massive, sprawling explosion of leaves, the ground flung about and rucked up from one side of the clearing to the other. Razi stood looking over this devastation, his breath coming fast, shallow and misty on the damp air. Wynter pressed close to him, not sure what they were looking at. She began to shiver again.

A pale flicker of movement to their right made them jump, and they reached for their daggers. It was Christopher, ghost-white in the gloom, drifting towards them through the trees. His slim body was covered in scrapes and painted with mud. His long hair was a tangled mess of leaves. He wandered towards them with an aimless sort of vacancy, his face dazed.

Wynter slumped with relief at the sight of him. *Thank God!* she thought. *Oh thank God!* There were purple bruises on his neck, and a long, deep trio of scratches running down his left arm. He was limping and his beloved bracelets were gone, but apart from that, he seemed fine. Wynter had seen worse injuries at a stick and ball match. She began to stagger forward, meaning to put her arms around him, but Razi stepped between them, holding her back.

"Christopher," he said, "are you with us?" His wary tone stopped Wynter in her tracks, and she looked between them, cold creeping into her stomach, wondering what she had missed.

"I got away," said Christopher. He stopped drifting towards them and stood looking about in puzzled confusion. *He's in a dream*, thought Wynter. *He thinks he's in a dream.*

Christopher blinked. "They took my bracelets," he said.

Wynter hung back while Razi dressed Christopher. She watched for a moment as he helped their friend into his clothes, but in the end she had to turn away. There was something terrible about the numb way Christopher just stood there and let Razi pull his filthy clothes onto him. Even with her eyes averted, it was difficult to bear. She could hear Razi say, "Lift your leg, Chris. Good man. Now the other one. Good fellow. I'm just going to tie this now, all right? Chris? Is it all right? Straighten your arm, Chris . . ."

She stood looking off into the brightening trees as Razi's voice went on. The light began to rise, slanting through the fluttering leaves, and the pain in her head grew with it. She slit her eyes against the sun and fought not to get sick.

To her amazement, Razi never once asked to examine Christopher, didn't once try and ascertain the extent of his injuries. He just dressed him and then straightened, wordlessly drew his sword and began to stalk back to the tavern. She watched his retreating back in shock, and then turned to Christopher. He stood for a moment, looking at his feet, and then he fell into stumbling step behind Razi.

Razi's deep voice snapped at her from the trees, "Wynter! Come on!" And she had no choice but to stagger along behind as he led the way back through the trees.

At the tavern, Razi paused at the tree line, tensely scanning the silent buildings. Smoke dribbled from the open barn doors and the kitchen was firmly shut. There was no sign of life. Christopher and Wynter stood gaping mindlessly at Razi's back, waiting for him to tell them what to do next.

"Take out your knife, sis," he said quietly. "Keep it in your hand where it can be seen." He looked anxiously into her face. Wynter tried to keep eye contact. "Try and look as though you know what you're doing, all right?" She nodded and instantly regretted it, pressing her hand to her temple and clamping down on the nausea that rolled up into her throat.

"Chris," said Razi softly. "There's going to be trouble in here. I need you."

Christopher's eyes wandered to his.

"Can you understand me, Chris?"

He didn't answer and his expression didn't change. Razi reached to the small of his back and slipped Christopher's black dagger from his belt. "*Here,*" he said. Christopher looked at his hand. "Here," insisted Razi. He tucked his falchion sword under his arm, took Christopher's hand and pressed the handle of the black dagger into Christopher's palm. Christopher blinked for a moment, then his hand closed around the knife. Razi nodded, patted his shoulder and led the way into the tavern.

He took them through the smouldering barn and into the kitchen. The landlord's men were all there, pressed silently around the walls. The landlord sat at the head of the big table, all the pitchers flung to the ground and shattered in pieces under his feet. No one looked up when Razi's long shadow fell across the room. All their eyes were on the table and the pale body of the little girl that lay, motionless and broken, on the damp wood.

"Oh no," said Wynter. At her voice, the landlord raised dull eyes and finally registered their presence.

The eldest daughter was crouched by the fireplace, a blanket pulled around her naked shoulders. She was dazed and staring, swollen with bruises, her hair a wild nest around her chalky face. She rocked gently and gazed into the ashy grate.

Wynter expected Razi to stalk to the girl's side, expected him to insist on treating her. Instead, he kept his eyes on the men and settled his sword in his hand. The landlord's eyes dropped to Razi's weapon, then lifted with a dangerous glint.

"We just want to get our things and leave," said Razi softly.

"You were with them," said the landlord, rising to his feet.

"We did not do this."

"You were *with* them!" The landlord's men stood away from the walls, their cudgels in hand.

"We tried to save her," croaked Wynter. "Look!"

She lifted her hand to indicate Christopher. *Look at my friend*, she meant to say, *see how they hurt him.* But Christopher was hunched and lethal looking, his lip curled, his face a feral mask within its tangled mess of hair. He shifted his knife and the light glinted in his eyes.

"We . . ." Wynter said desperately, tearing her eyes from him. She could not understand how things had gone so wrong. "We . . ." Unexpected tears rolled down her face and she rubbed them away with her wrist, her knife flashing in the slanting light. "Tried to save her."

Razi stepped forward. "Let us get our things," he commanded, "I have no wish to inflict any further hurt on you." He balanced the sword in his hand and looked around the group of glowering men.

Anyone seeing him would wonder what he had hidden up his sleeve to make him so certain that he would win. The men looked to the landlord, then backed off.

Razi kept guard as Christopher and Wynter slipped into the tavern and gathered up their things. He never once lowered his sword and he edged carefully around things, his eyes on the men, while Christopher and Wynter collected everything together. He sent them ahead of him into the yard, where they found the horses wandering loose, their tack a reeking, smoke-darkened tangle on the ground. Christopher and Wynter did a slow and clumsy job of getting the horses ready, while Razi stood between them and the prowling men.

When the horses were finally set and Christopher and Wynter had heaved themselves into the saddle, Razi turned his head, his eyes still on the men, and spoke softly over his shoulder. "Christopher, load your crossbow and keep them at bay for me, will you?"

Christopher numbly loaded the weapon, pulling the specially designed lever and cocking it easily, despite his hands. He leaned back in the saddle and aimed at the loose circle of men, his face utterly devoid of emotion. Wynter did not doubt that he would let fly an arrow as soon as draw breath. The men seemed to share her conviction and they stepped back.

Razi spun to his horse. He hopped the stirrup, launched himself into the saddle and swung to face the men again.

"Please," he said, lifting his sword. "Please, do not allow some misguided attempt at revenge to cost you your lives. We had nothing to do with this, and I have no wish to kill you in the defence of my friends."

The men stared at him. Slowly, and one handed, Razi began to back his horse from the stable yard. Christopher did the same, his crossbow still aimed at their chests. Wynter could not manage the co-ordination necessary to dance Ozkar backwards from the yard. She slumped instead in the saddle, the pain in her head completely overtaking her, and allowed him to follow the other horses as they made their cautious and wary exit from the ill-fated tavern.

Once on the road they turned and galloped. No one followed.

Bruised

As they journeyed on, the pain in the small of Wynter's back quite overpowered the pain in her head. It was as though someone had reached a knotted fist inside her and was twisting her kidney slowly in place. The men rode ahead, Razi leading the way, Christopher lagging behind him, both lost within themselves, and Wynter watched them through a mindless haze. Everything seemed very far away somehow and the world had taken on a curious reddish hue. After a while she found herself leaning forward in the saddle, her hands clenched on the pommel, tears of silent agony rolling down her face.

Then Ozkar stumbled, and the pain in Wynter's back spiked to a new level of unbearable. She listed sideways with a gasp, and gritted her teeth against the urge to scream. Oh, that was bad. That was *very bad*. She heard herself sob, and realised that she couldn't go on.

Scrubbing her face in her sleeve, Wynter quietly cleared her throat. "Razi," she said. It was nothing but a pathetic little croak, and neither of the men seemed to hear it. "Razi," she said again. "I need to stop."

Razi glanced around at her. His eyes widened in horror and he dragged his horse to a panicked halt. The frantic way he scrambled from the saddle told Wynter a multitude about how she must look. As he ran, he flung his arms up to her, causing Ozkar to shy, and Wynter cried out as bolts of agony flared through her back.

Christopher wearily turned his head to see what the fuss was, and his face did a slow crumble at the sight of her. Razi was holding his arms out for her to slide into, but Wynter knew that it would only bring agony, and she clung to her saddle.

"I can't, Razi," she gasped. "Don't make me."

"Oh, Wyn," he said, his face creased in sympathy. He put his hands on her waist. "You must. Come on. I'll lift you. Come on, it's all right."

He pulled gently, and Wynter cried out at the unbearable agony of it. She gripped the pommel.

"Don't make me," she cried, "don't make me." But Razi was reaching his strong arms around her waist and pulling, even as she begged him not to. A massive spike of pain lanced her lower back and she couldn't help it, she screamed.

The last coherent thing she remembered before sliding from the horse and into breathless agony was Christopher's hand, prying her fingers from the pommel and clutching her sleeve as he lowered her into Razi's arms.

She did not lose consciousness, but for a while everything came and went through shifting clouds of pain. When, finally, she was capable of focusing her wits, she became aware of a little fire burning. The men's small cauldron was suspended over it, hanging from a split branch tripod, its contents steaming gently.

Wynter concentrated on that for a while, before looking past the flames to find Christopher. He was staring at her, his crossbow cocked and ready, lying across his knees. She squinted uncertainly at him. She could remember Razi carrying her and laying her on the ground, then lifting her again so that Christopher could spread a cloak for her. She remembered clutching Razi's arm and weeping when he had tried to sit her up. She recalled Razi stripping her of her tunic and her undershirt, and his horrified yell at the sight of her back.

How long ago had that been? It could have been hours, it could have been only moments.

She was lying on her side now and the pain had subsided to a dull kind of toothache, gnawing into her kidneys. She shifted and moaned, and Christopher suddenly focused on her, as though he had been asleep with his eyes open. He lifted his gaze to look past her and someone laid a big callused hand on her shoulder. Razi. She was briefly embarrassed by the fact that she was wearing nothing above the waist but her breast cloth. Then Razi scooped his arm under her shoulders and the pain drove everything from her as he lifted her into a sitting position.

"I am very sorry, sis. I am so sorry." Wynter had never heard that tone in Razi's voice before and she was suddenly very frightened at what might be wrong with her. She was terrified to see fear in Christopher's glittering eyes and she looked away. She wanted to say *what's wrong with me, Razi?* but was only capable of gritting her teeth for a long moment.

Gradually the sharp pain faded, leaving only a dull, gnawing agony, and Wynter let herself relax against Razi's chest. He ran his hand over her hair and she leaned her head back onto his shoulder.

"Better?" he asked.

She nodded.

"I need to look at your back."

She cursed and squeezed her eyes shut, then bent slowly forward to rest her chest on her drawn-up knees. Pain squealed high again and she bit her lip with vicious force, tears leaking from beneath her eyelids. There was a rustling as Christopher knelt in front of her. She was afraid to look into his face and see that expression again, but when he took her hands, she squeezed his fingers in gratitude.

"What . . . what is it, Razi?" she gasped. *I've been stabbed*, she thought, *I've been shot in the spine.*

"Some whoreson kicked you in the back." Razi had his calm, professional voice on now, and Wynter was amazed at how soothing it was. It made her feel safe and protected. It made the sharp pain of his gently pressing fingers endurable. "You are deeply bruised," he said. "And I am worried that they might have hurt one of your kidneys." Christopher's hands tightened on hers, and she opened her eyes to look up at him through the fringe of her hair. He was gazing at Razi in despair. Wynter tugged his hands and he looked down at her, his eyes drowning.

"It's all right," she whispered. "Razi will fix me." She smiled at him, but he seemed incapable of changing his expression from that bleakly staring mask.

Razi sat back then, and gently patted her on the shoulder. "I will help you lie down now, sis. If I may?"

Christopher's face creased up at the distress this brought to her eyes, and he gripped her hands tightly while Razi eased her down onto the reeking, smoke-dirtied cloak. He let go then, so that Razi could roll her onto her stomach.

Wynter rested her head on her folded arms, waiting for the pain to subside. The sounds of boots crunching in leaves told her that the men were moving about. Sure enough, Christopher came into view and resumed his vigil on the other side of the fire. *That fire is such a bad idea*, she thought as he laid his crossbow across his knee, and scanned the trees with restless, red-rimmed eyes.

Razi took a hot cloth from the cauldron and wrung it almost dry, hissing at the heat. He came back to sit cross-legged at Wynter's side, curling his long body forward so that they were almost eye to eye.

"The fire is a bad idea, Razi," she whispered.

He nodded. "Do not fret about it, sis. Just . . ." he cut himself short with an impatient grimace, and leaned across her with the cloth. She flinched as he laid it on her back. Then there was blessed relief as the heat of it seeped into her bruises. Slowly she relaxed, and Razi pulled another, equally rancid cloak up to cover her. She slid her eyes to look at him, and he ran his hand across her hair.

"Listen to me," he said. "You have a cramped muscle in your back."

She closed her eyes in shame. *Just a cramp?* she thought. *Oh, I'm such a God-cursed girl.* Razi's soothing, rich voice went on, as did the gentle movement of his hand on her hair.

"They have not broken your ribs, thank God, nor mis-aligned your spine. But I need you to pass water before I know whether or not your injuries are severe."

Wynter's face blazed, and Razi sighed. "Do not feel bad, darling," he said. "There is no need for shame; just let me take care of you. Will you do that for me? Let me take care of you?" She nodded without looking at him, and he patted her shoulder. "I am brewing some willow-bark tea for you, it will not be long in coming. And when you need to pass water you *will* tell me?" She nodded again. Then Razi pushed himself to his feet, and she heard him make his way to Christopher.

She cracked her eyes open and watched him hunker down by their friend, his elbows on his knees, his eyes averted. The two men stayed like that for a moment, not looking at each other. Finally she heard Razi ask, "Have you pain?"

Christopher said nothing. His knuckles whitened against the grip of his bow.

Razi kept staring at the ground. "Sometimes, after the nightmares, you suffered a lot of pain." Christopher's eyes flickered from tree to tree. He looked besieged, ready to run. Razi slid his eyes up to his face. "I could give you something if—?"

"There ain't no pain," whispered Christopher. "Not when you do it on purpose. It feels good." He glanced down at Razi, saw the shock that his friend couldn't hide, and immediately looked away.

Razi scrubbed a filthy wrist under his wide eyes, stunned. "Um . . ." he said. Then, as if finding something he could deal with, he abruptly straightened and said, "I should clean those scratches, Christopher. You are in danger of infection. Come along."

Razi put his hand on Christopher's shoulder, and to

Wynter's shock, their friend snarled and shoved him violently away. Razi fell into the leaves and Christopher shrank back, appalled at himself. "Razi! I'm sorry! Just . . . Razi, you mustn't startle me. I'm too . . ." He tilted his head and helplessly spread his hands. "Don't startle me, Razi," he whispered.

Razi just sat, staring, and after a moment Christopher's shoulders slumped, his eyes wandered, and a numb, distant expression crept into his face. "Have we soap?" he asked dully. Razi nodded, and Christopher pushed to his feet and stood swaying for a moment with Razi still sitting at his feet. "Give it to me," he said. "I'll go wash myself."

To Wynter's surprise, Razi did not argue. Instead, he got to his feet, fetched his wash kit from his saddlebag and handed it wordlessly to his friend. Christopher laid his crossbow down on his saddle, helped himself to hot water from the cauldron and carried the copper bowl and the wash kit off into the trees.

"Christopher!" called Razi. "Won't you stay in camp?"

Christopher didn't turn around or reply and they watched him limp away. Wynter was unnerved and confused by the defeat she saw in Razi's posture.

"Razi," she said. He glanced sideways at her, like he always did when he did not want to discuss something. "Perhaps he just needs some time alone." Razi watched her from the corner of his eyes and she turned her cheek against the vile grit of the cloak, wishing he would look at her properly. "Perhaps he feels ashamed, Razi." Razi caught his breath at that and looked helplessly into the sky, his eyes glittering.

"Perhaps," she said, "he is ashamed because those men

took his bracelets. They meant so much to him, Razi, and it would hurt Christopher terribly that he could not stop them being stolen again. Perhaps it is because they stripped him and hunted him in the dark. Christopher has always seemed so very proud, he might imagine that you think him less of a man for allowing these things to happen."

Razi was looking at her with utter misery. He shook his head, then he pressed his hand to his eyes suddenly.

"What?" she said, completely lost, swimming with confusion and despair. "What is it, Razi?" The cloth was cooling on her back, and she clenched her teeth and her fist against the slow increase of pain. She pressed her forehead into her arms to stop from groaning.

There was a rustling as Razi came and sat beside her. His hand resumed its soothing movement through her hair. "How is your head, darling?" he murmured. "Your wits seemed thoroughly scrambled last night. You must have a powerful headache."

She laughed. "It is quite overpowered by the agony in my back."

"You have a sizeable bruise on your forehead."

"How lovely," she mumbled, her eyes closing at the sleepy comfort of his caress. "I must look simply divine, like a princess from a painting. It is no wonder Christopher has fallen for my charms." He continued to stroke her hair, the fire crackling in the background, and Wynter knew he was looking out into the trees, fretting that Christopher was out of sight. "The fire is a bad idea, Razi," she said again. "It will draw them down upon us."

"No," he said quietly. "They will not come again today.

They will be sleeping now, and sated. Heavy from the change that always happens before . . . beforehand."

Wynter's eyes flew open, pieces dropping into place. "It was the Loups-Garous?" she said, startled that she had not made the connection before, horrified that it had been them. Had they recognised Christopher, then? Had they done those things to him, purposely to shame him, knowing who he was? "Oh, Razi," she said, "did they know it was him?"

It took him a moment to gather the threads of her meaning, then he shook his head. "No, Wyn, in that state they barely know their own names. They know only what it is they want and . . ." he shuddered and shook his head, his eyes full again. He looked away, swallowing back his despair.

"Those poor girls," said Wynter. Razi's hand tightened on her neck for a moment, then resumed its steady motion through her hair. She turned her forehead into her arms again, trying not to see that little girl's face, bobbing away from her in the dark.

"Life was so much simpler when you and Albi were babies," whispered Razi, his voice far away.

Wynter snorted. "Oh aye?" she said bitterly. "In whose happy dream?"

"Oh, but it was, Wynter. It was so much simpler." She opened her eyes, but Razi's voice was full of tears and she could not look up at him. "Wyn?" he whispered. "I do not think that I am strong enough to finish this. What kind of a man would that make me?" he said. "To carry the two of you forward after this? After . . . this?"

Wynter turned her cheek and gazed up at him. With his

big brown eyes and his transparent hurt, Razi looked like a little child. Despite the beard, despite the scar, he looked as Wynter imagined he might have looked as a four-year-old, solemnly carrying the weight of the world through the doorway of a kitchen and laying it in a box of hay. She reached for his hand and kissed it, pressing his fingers to her cheek and wearily closing her eyes. "It will be all right, Razi," she promised. "You are not alone. You and me and Christopher. Together we can fix everything."

What Kind of Man

"Wynter? Wyn? Come along now . . ."

She drifted up to the smell of food, and Razi's deep voice whispering.

"Huh?" she said none too intelligently, and squinted up into his sooty face.

"Here you go," he said, offering her a bowl of the spicy soup he'd made from their supplies.

She took it from him, yawning and bleary, and pulled herself up from her cramped slouch. Her back screeched dully, but the pain was nowhere near as bad as before. She was shocked to see evening light slanting low and golden through the trees.

"*J . . . Jesu*," she croaked. "Was I asleep?"

"If your snoring was anything to go by, then I would wager that yes, you were." He turned to Christopher, another bowl in his hand. The young man was limp and motionless, his hands folded on his chest, his head laid back into the crooked embrace of tree roots. Even so utterly relaxed, Christopher had a sleepless look to him, the skin under his eyes swollen, his face drawn, as if exhaustion were a permanent resident in his face. Razi hesitated, then he bent to lay the bowl of food by the fire.

A twig snapped in the trees and Razi jerked his eyes up, his hand dropping to his sword. There was a huge man silhouetted at the tree line. Razi crouched and unhooked his sword, and the man turned, yelling into the trees behind him. Whatever it was that he shouted was lost in Razi's furious bellow. Wynter barely had time to push to her hands and knees, her back screaming in protest, before Razi drew his weapon and leapt across the flames. He kicked the man hard in the stomach and brought his sword flashing down onto his head. With a cry, the big man fell onto his back, bringing his shield up just in time to absorb Razi's ferocious blow.

The falchion sword sliced through the shield with ease, biting into the man's collarbone in a blow that would have taken the head from his shoulders had it not been deflected. The man screamed and his blood shot up in a fine spray to redden Razi's hands and stipple his snarling face.

Wynter scurried forward, scrambling for her travel-belt and the knife it contained. Christopher surged silently to his feet, his katar already in hand, his grasp of the situation uncertain.

Razi planted his foot firmly on the man's shield, holding him in place. He pulled his sword free with a cracking splinter of wood and raised it over his head, ready for the fatal blow.

Something low and grey shot from the trees. It hit Razi full in the chest, bearing him backwards and away from the man, carrying him to the ground. Christopher screamed and rushed across the clearing, the katar flashing. Another murderous shape launched itself from the shadows and Christopher was carried backwards, missing the camp-fire by inches and landing in an explosion of leaves at the base of a tree.

Wynter screamed and struggled with the tangle of her belt, trying to release her knife. There was the sound of yelling and someone ran into the clearing. A panicked voice shouted in Hadrish, "Drop the weapons! *Frith an Domhain*, drop! Coinín! *Abair leo a gcuid airm a chaith-camh uathu!*"

Wynter froze and crouched, glaring through the tangled mess of her fringe. Ashkr, wild-eyed and frantic, stood at the edge of the trees, his sword drawn.

In the shadows, Wari rolled to his side, clutching his shoulder as blood flowed out between his fingers. He was white-faced with pain. At his feet, Razi lay pinned to the ground, a huge warhound standing over him, its jaws clamped around his throat. Razi, his hands knotted in the dog's fur, gagged, and Wynter saw the flesh of his neck dimple under the pressure of the hound's teeth.

Across the fire, metal clinked softly against stone as Christopher allowed his knife to drop from his hand. A second warhound stood over him, its teeth locked on his straining neck. Wynter lurched to her knees, not knowing which way to turn, and Christopher rolled terrified grey eyes to her, and held out his hand. *Do nothing! Do nothing!* Slowly he lowered his shaking hands to the ground, and he allowed his body to relax under the arch of the big dog's legs. To Wynter's relief, she saw the powerful jaws ease up slightly on Christopher's throat.

Razi gagged again, and a line of blood flowed around the taut curve of his neck as the hound's teeth punctured his skin.

"Brother," cried Wynter, "do not struggle." Razi stilled and Wynter saw him force himself to relax. His hands drifted to the ground. The warhound instantly eased its grip, and Wynter's eyes fluttered shut in momentary relief.

Ashkr edged forward, his sword up, his eyes on Wynter. He glanced at Wari as he passed him by, and asked something in Merron. Wari, still clutching his wounded shoulder, forced a reply through gritted teeth. Ashkr came around to kick Razi's sword into the bushes, and then stood looking down at him, his navy eyes cold.

He flicked a glance at Wynter. "Throw your weapon into bush," he said. Wynter blinked at him. He lifted his chin and the tip of his sword swung purposely to point at Razi's head. Wynter flung her travel-belt into the bushes. The warhounds jerked at the sudden movement, their growls intensifying, their eyes turning to her. Christopher made an unconscious moan of fear, and Razi's hands flew upwards as the great jaws tightened on their throats.

Ashkr hissed and snapped something to the dogs. Razi's hands drifted down into the leaves again as the hounds relaxed their grip once more. He glared up at the tall blond, his face full of hate. Ashkr balanced his sword in his gloved hand and spoke to Wynter. "Iseult," he said. "Bring to me all your weapons." She looked to Razi, and Ashkr yelled at her. "*Now!*"

Wynter scrambled stiffly to her feet and limped around the camp, picking up Christopher's katar, his crossbow, her short sword and Razi's matchlock. "Now, the knife in

Coinín's boot and on the leg of Tabiyb." Fuming, Wynter
stooped to slip Razi's knife from the sheath on his thigh.
She looked up into his face as she did so, but he was glaring at Ashkr with trembling fury.

She crossed to disarm Christopher, and he shifted to try
and see her as she slid the dagger from his boot. She looked
into his eyes, and his face creased in agonised apology.
Wynter grabbed his hand, holding his gaze. *It's all right,
love. It's not your fault.* Christopher closed his eyes and swallowed against the constricting teeth of the warhound.
Wynter squeezed his fingers. Then she rose to her feet and
dumped their weapons into the bushes before returning to
Ashkr.

He levelled his sword at her, and his eyes flicked to Wari,
who was groaning and trying to pull himself into a sitting
position. Ashkr said something. At Wari's strained reply,
Ashkr's eyes went hard with fury and he suddenly pressed
his sword to Wynter's neck.

There was such rage in his handsome face that Wynter
thought he was going to slit her throat right there, but he
just kept the blade on her neck, and ordered, "Kneel! Now!
Hands in legs!"

She wasn't sure what he meant but she sank to her knees,
her hands up, looking him in the eye all the time. "Hands
in legs, Iseult! Hands in legs!" He tapped her raised hands
with the flat of his sword and, in a flash of understanding,
she tucked them in behind her knees and knelt down on
them.

She glanced at Razi. He was straining against the awkward angle of his head, his eyes wide with fear for her. He
watched as the tall blond brought his blade to Wynter's

throat again. Wynter felt the sharp metal grate against her pulse, and she drew her head back, locking eyes with Razi, trying not to look frightened.

"Tabiyb," snarled Ashkr, his voice tight with fury. "Why you put fight to Wari? What for you harm?"

Razi's eyes widened in disbelief, and Wynter glanced across at the wounded man. He was slumped against the base of a tree, his eyes screwed shut in pain, his blood-soaked hand pressed to his shoulder. Wynter dropped her eyes to his sword and moaned.

"Oh Christ, Razi," she whispered. "He had not even unhooked the keep on his scabbard. I do not think he ever intended to attack."

Razi stared up at her. *No, no . . . you are wrong.*

She met his eyes and shook her head regretfully. *I am not.* Razi groaned and pressed his head back into the leaves, appalled. The dog's saliva mingled with the blood from Razi's neck, trailing to the ground in revolting strings, and Razi looked beseechingly at Ashkr, raising his hands from the ground, palms up. Ashkr frowned at him for a moment before realising that Razi was too frightened to speak with the dog's teeth still puncturing his throat.

He clicked his fingers. " *Tarraing siar, Boro.*"

At once the huge hound released its grip on Razi's neck and stood over him, snarling, its long teeth only inches from his terrified face. Razi held its eyes, too frightened to look away. "I am sorry, Ashkr," he grated. "I thought he meant us harm. I thought—"

Ashkr clicked his fingers again and said, "*Anseo,* Boro. *Anois!*" The dog turned away at once and trotted across to flop placidly at its master's feet.

Razi rolled to his side, his hands flying to his throat, then lurched to his knees. His eyes flicked from Wynter, still kneeling with Ashkr's sword at her throat, to Christopher, splayed beneath the legs of the other growling warhound.

"Let them go!" he rasped. "Let . . ." He coughed and wiped his neck free of slime and blood. "Ashkr, let them go."

Ashkr stood tall, his face rigid with anger, his blond hair drifting around him in the evening light. "You fix Wari, Tabiyb!" he said coldly. "Now! You make Wari good, and not do more harm." Razi, his hands to his throat, looked up into Ashkr's furious eyes and nodded.

"I have broken your collarbone," said Razi, indicating the bandages that held Wari's huge arm to his chest. "I'm afraid you must keep your arm like this for at least two months, so that the soft ends of the bone may harden against each other. It is vital that . . ." As Razi proceeded with a stream of instructions, Wari continued to glare at him. Ashkr, who insisted on communicating through his sparse Hadrish, stood over them both and translated as best he could.

At the fire, Wynter placed her empty soup howl on the ground and wiped her mouth with her sleeve. The hounds followed her every movement with their eyes. "Christopher," she whispered. "Why doesn't Ashkr just speak Merron and have you translate?"

"If Ashkr starts to speak Merron, girly, you'll know he thinks yourself and Razi below respect and we will be in real trouble." He looked down at his untouched soup and held the bowl out to one of the hounds. It glanced guiltily towards Ashkr and slunk forward. Christopher put the bowl on the ground, and watched as the huge creature ate the meal he seemed to have no stomach for. Then he addressed Ashkr in cold Hadrish.

"What do you want with us, *Caora*? Why are you here?"

Ashkr glanced at him. Then he turned back to Razi who was looking up at him, wiping his bloody hands on a cloth. Ashkr still had his sword in his hand, levelled at Razi's head. "Can Wari be safe on horse now, Tabiyb? Can we go on?"

Razi nodded. "It will cause him pain, and he must be careful that—"

Before Razi could finish, Wari had pushed himself to his feet and turned for his horse.

Ashkr gestured with his sword, motioning Razi to his horse. "Come," he snapped. "Get things. Get doctor things. We go."

Razi rose slowly to his feet, Wynter and Christopher did the same.

"Are you asking for my *help*?" asked Razi. "After your people ran off and *left* us? After they left *Christopher*?"

"Safety of my peoples come before that of strangers. We needed move quick."

"But now you need my help? Is that it? Now you need me, so you—"

"What has happened?" interrupted Christopher, his eyes on Ashkr.

Ashkr snapped his attention to him. "Sólmundr bad," he said. "He near . . . near to . . . Sól bad. Need help."

"Oh," said Christopher softly, "Sólmundr."

Ashkr looked back to Razi, deep distress evident in his

face. "Sól not want you help him, Tabiyb. He think . . ." He dropped his eyes. Whatever it was that Sólmundr thought, Ashkr decided not to share, instead he rambled on in broken Hadrish, his expression more and more desperate. "Úlfnaor not want you help, he say that Hallvor do all. *Ach Hallvor, duairt sí* . . . Hallvor, she say that nothing left she do can to help." Ashkr shook his head at that, his face crumbling. "But *I* want you help, Tabiyb. *I* want you save Sól, like Coinín say you able." He looked pleadingly at Razi. "Please, Tabiyb, to you I am begging. Fix Sól."

To Wynter's utter shock, Razi's face grew stiff as ice and he shook his head coldly.

"Go to hell," he snarled.

Ashkr gaped. Wari stood with his hand on his horse's neck and froze in absolute horror. He perhaps did not fully understand the words, but he couldn't possibly have missed the sentiment. "*Cad é?*" he said, his tone one of disbelief.

"Go to *hell,*" repeated Razi. "How *dare* you? After—?"

"*Tabhair nóiméad dúinn,*" said Christopher, stepping forward with a strained smile, holding his hand up to the stunned Merron.

Razi rounded on him. "What did you just *say?*" he growled in Southlandast. "What did you just say, Christopher? Because I am not helping them! I'm *not!* Why should I?"

"Because that's who you *are!* You're a man who fixes; you're a man who *heals.* Or have the Wolves stolen that from us too?"

Razi blinked, and his eyes slid away.

"Besides," said Christopher, nodding reassuringly to Ashkr, and moving to pick up their things. There was a trace of his old sly humour in his voice and he glanced at Wynter and gave her a weary half-smile as he said, "I have a feeling the Merron might know the way to your brother's camp a lot better than we do."

The Will of the World

*A*shkr set a gruelling pace, forging relentlessly onwards, his face set, his posture taut. Wynter could tell that he was trying hard to make allowances for their ragged state, but if anyone lagged behind for too long, the desperate man would eventually heave his mount in a tight circle, gallop around to the straggler and ride alongside them, urging, "Hurry! Hurry! Please, to you I am begging, can you hurry?"

Over an hour later, when they finally crested a hill and found themselves looking down on the Merron camp, Wynter almost fell from her horse with pain and relief. Beside her, Wari moaned what sounded like a prayer of thanksgiving, and Christopher relaxed his white-knuckled grip on the pommel of his saddle. Razi, silent for the whole journey, sat rigid and wary, looking down at the tents below.

Ashkr spurred his horse down the hill and between the tents, heading for the rear of the camp. His hounds accompanied him, baying and howling, and the other dogs flowed from the shadows to greet them. It was very late in the evening, dusk settling in a rosy haze over the tops of the trees, and glowing cook-fires scented the misty air. All around the camp, men and women exited tents and rose from camp-fires, looking up at the little knot of travellers that straggled behind their returning lord.

"Wari!" shouted a woman, panic evident in her voice. "Wari!" She began to run forward, and Wari, hearing her voice, straightened from his agonised slump. He lifted his good arm in weary greeting as he trotted from the trees, and several men and women advanced on him in concern. There were noises of outrage over his injury. Razi began to walk his horse through the crowding Merron, and Wynter and Christopher fell into place behind him.

Up ahead, Ashkr brought his horse to a sliding halt. He leapt from the saddle and ran the last few yards to where Embla was emerging from the depths of a tent. Anxiously, Ashkr grabbed his sister's shoulders and questioned her. She put her hand on his chest and her reply caused Ashkr to cry out in despair. He pushed his way past her, the tent-flap closing behind him with a snap. Embla stood looking after him for a moment, then she turned to watch as Razi, Wynter and Christopher made their way towards her. There was no welcome in her beautiful face, only strain, and a distressed sorrow that was on the edge of tears.

Wynter glanced around them as they made their way towards the waiting lady. The camp consisted of eight or nine of the Merron's famous conical tents, most of them lit from within, most with small cook-fires out front. Wynter squinted to see into the gathering dusk beyond the fires. There were a score or more of horses, side-hobbled and set loose to graze on the grassy plain that sloped down to the river. Behind the tents a series of washing lines fluttered in the breeze, and there were large piles of firewood dotted about. This was no hastily erected sick-stop; this was a well-established, well-selected, semi-permanent camp. Perhaps a base from which the Merron intended to operate.

Wynter began to suspect that the men and women who had been waiting in the trees at the Wherry Tavern had been an advance party, sent ahead to prepare for the arrival of their lords and lady. She saw Razi studying the environs, no doubt coming to similar conclusions. Christopher was slouched in his saddle, guiding his mount one-handed through the wary crowd. He only had eyes for Embla, and he seemed to be reading her face, judging her intent.

Embla cast a brief glance at Wynter and Christopher, then turned all her attention to Razi. He brought his horse to a stop and sat looking coldly down at her, waiting.

"Sól will not let you to treat him," Embla said softly. "It not matters what Ash says."

Razi eyed her without replying, grunted and slid from his saddle. Wynter saw him hide a stagger as he hit the ground, and for the first time it occurred to her how exhausted he must be. "Wyn—" he said, then cleared his throat. "Iseult," he amended, lifting his arms. "Come along." He took Wynter by the waist, and Embla frowned in concern as she saw the wince that Wynter couldn't hide. Her navy eyes darted between Wynter and Christopher, and she seemed genuinely shocked at their battered appearance.

Razi gazed up into Wynter's face. "Are you ready?" he whispered. She nodded, biting her lip, and Razi used all his strength to swing her from her horse. Pain exploded and everything threatened to fade out for a moment, but her senses returned almost immediately, and she was able to push from his grip and support her own weight before her weakness became too obvious. Razi turned to look questioningly at Christopher. The young man hesitated, then he set his jaw and slid from the saddle unaided. Razi placed a discreet hand on his back to steady him, and then turned to Embla.

"Step aside," he said. "I wish to hear for myself what Sólmundr has to say."

Embla gestured to Christopher and Wynter. "They must stay out," she said.

Razi froze her with a look. "I think not," he said, and made his way around her and into the tent. Wynter and Christopher followed, ducking past Embla without meeting her eye, and passed into flickering torchlight.

The tent was hot and airless. It smelled of sweat and vomit and seemed crowded with people despite its roomy interior. Sólmundr lay curled on a pallet of furs. His torso was bare, his covers pushed to his hips, and Wynter was appalled at the multitude of old lashmarks and scars that latticed his wiry body. Ashkr was hunched by his side, clutching his hand. He glared up at Úlfnaor, who was arguing with him in low and angry Merron. Behind the pallet crouched a sinewy, dark-eyed woman of about forty. She watched the two men with calm detachment, her hand on Sólmundr's trembling back.

That must be Hallvor, thought Wynter, eyeing the copper fire-basin and the herb pouches and vials at the woman's side. *The healer.*

At their entrance, Úlfnaor threw them an aggravated

glare and turned away. He stalked to the rear of the tent and stood in the shadows, his arms folded defensively across his chest. Hallvor looked them up and down with no discernible emotion.

Christopher and Wynter slunk around the edge of the tent, and stood side by side in the shadows. Razi paused by the door, gazing down on Sólmundr, his face unreadable. Wynter could not believe the difference in the poor man since the last time she had seen him. His good-natured face was transformed with agony, and he was curled into a tight ball, his fist pressed against his stomach. He was panting, and seemed incapable of containing the small sounds of pain that escaped him with every breath. Ashkr gestured Razi to his side.

"Come!" he said. "Here, Tabiyb, come. Look at Sól."

Embla ducked into the tent and crossed to kneel beside Hallvor. She murmured a question, and the dark-haired woman shook her head hopelessly.

"Tabiyb!" cried Ashkr. "Come *here*!" He slammed his fist into the ground by Sólmundr's bed, and his friend leapt in shock. Ashkr turned back to him immediately. "*Gabh mo leithscéal, a chroí!* Shhhhh!" He placed his hand tenderly on Sólmundr's head. Then he snarled over his shoulder. "*Frith an Domhain,* Tabiyb. Come here! Fix Sól, or I will take sword to your *head*!"

Christopher pushed himself forward and Wynter saw his hand drop to his katar, just as she reached for her knife. She stepped from the shadows, her face hard. Ashkr should not have returned their weapons if he intended making threats.

Ashkr saw them advance and held up a placating hand.

"I speak from fear," he rasped. "Fear make me stupid. I not hurt your friend." He tried to swallow down his distress, and patted the furs. "Tabiyb," he said. "You come help, yes? Come help, as good man you are."

Razi put out a hand and, without looking at them, pushed Wynter and Christopher back into the shadows. He glanced at Hallvor, then crossed to kneel by Sólmundr's side. "Sólmundr," he said. Sólmundr opened his eyes with a gasp and focused on Razi's face. "Embla tells me that you do not want my assistance."

Sólmundr looked up at Ashkr. "*Tá m'uain tagtha, a Ash. Tá an Domhan do m'iarraidh . . . tá . . . ugh . . .*" he squeezed up in agony again.

Razi looked around for Christopher. "What did he say? Christopher! Get over here; tell me what this man is saying."

Christopher limped across to kneel stiffly at the foot of Sólmundr's bed. "He says it is his time. That *An Domhan*, the World, our . . . my people's version of God, wants him." Christopher sighed and ran a shaking hand over his white face. "He wants to die, Razi. There's nothing you can do about that; it is Sólmundr's right to choose."

Razi and Wynter both turned to gape at Christopher. He shrugged wearily at them. "They believe it is his right to choose," he explained softly.

Sólmundr whispered something in Merron. He pulled Ashkr's clenched fist in against his chest, and for the first time Wynter noticed the slave mark branded into his upper arm. "I not need your help, Tabiyb," he rasped, slitting his eyes to look at Razi. "I ready. It good that *An Domhan* call me. Now . . . of all times."

Ashkr crouched over Sólmundr, his hand moving lovingly through the poor man's sweat-soaked hair. He murmured with persuasive intensity and bent to gaze into Sólmundr's eyes. Sólmundr gazed back at him, his body trembling with pain, and Ashkr leant his forehead against his friend's temple and whispered something pleading and heartbroken.

Wynter looked at the men's fiercely interlocked hands. She took in the grinding depth of Ashkr's despair. She looked at the matching bracelets of plaited silver and copper that the men wore around their wrists, and with a spark of insight she touched the woollen bracelet on her own wrist. The nature of the men's love for each other leapt into focus. *Oh*, she thought, *oh, I see.* She frowned uncertainly, utterly thrown for a moment by the kind of men Ashkr and Sólmundr had turned out to be. But as Ashkr continued to whisper desperately to his friend, Wynter filled with sympathy for him and she found herself longing to take Christopher's hand.

"Chris?" she asked softly. "What is Ashkr saying?"

Christopher translated in a low murmur. "You promised me, remember? You made a promise. Won't you keep it for me? Now, of all times, could you leave me here to do this alone?"

Suddenly Sólmundr's eyes opened impossibly wide and he cried out, hunching over as if trying to roll to his knees. Ashkr turned to Razi, silently pleading with him to intervene.

Razi leaned forward. "Sólmundr!" he said. "Will you not allow me to look at you? I swear to you, I shall do nothing without your permission, but please, at least allow me to look at you!"

"Sólmundr!" Christopher clutched at the man's foot through the furs. "If it is the will of *An Domhan* that you die, why would it have sent Tabiyb? Why would it have sent you a man who can do this?" he shoved his left sleeve up and thrust his arm forward, displaying his long scar. "It makes no *sense*, Sól," he cried. "It makes no sense! Think for just a moment and you will see it."

Hallvor looked at Christopher's arm and then at Razi, her dark eyes assessing. She leant forward and said something into Sólmundr's ear, caressing his back with long soothing strokes. Sólmundr hid his face in the crook of Ashkr's arm. Wynter was sure he would continue to refuse Razi's help, but then he groaned something in Merron and nodded. Hallvor, Ashkr and Christopher looked to Razi, their faces full of hope.

Immediately, Razi pushed the furs away from Sólmundr's body. "Ashkr," he said. "Get behind him, pull him up slightly and lean him back against you. Hallvor!" He looked the woman in the eye, tapped the fist that Sólmundr had clenched against his stomach and made a motion that Hallvor pull the man's arm to one side. She did this. Sólmundr made a high, keening noise and tried to pull his knees up tight to his stomach. Razi glanced at Wynter. "Sis!" he said and she leapt forward to crouch by Christopher's side. "Help Christopher. Pull gently to straighten Sólmundr's legs. Embla, push down on his knees. Gently . . . gently now! That's enough!"

It took Razi only moments to finish his examination. Then he nodded at everyone to release the poor man's arms and legs, and Sólmundr curled back up, rolling to his side. Hallvor pulled the furs back up to Sólmundr's waist, and

Ashkr sat and stroked his damp hair, gazing at Razi as if he held the world in his hands.

Razi sat back on his heels and looked from face to expectant face. Wynter knew by his expression that the news was not good. She had very little Arabic, but she understood perfectly when Razi turned to Christopher with soft regret and murmured, "I cannot save this man."

Christopher tore his eyes from Sólmundr's suffering. "This is what killed my father, Razi."

Wynter put her hand on his arm. "Oh Chris," she whispered.

Razi nodded miserably. "Aye," he said, "I suspect it is."

"You told me that you knew what caused this," said Christopher. "You said you had cut into the human body and seen the canker that makes this happen."

Razi's eyes widened in horror. "Aye, Chris, but in cadavers! Not in—"

"You *told* me you had witnessed St James treat a man with this. You said he opened his belly and pulled out the canker."

"Chris!" pleaded Razi. "I also told you that man *died*. Victor could not save him, the shock was too great, the infection—"

Christopher leant across and gripped Razi by the wrist. "You can try!" he insisted. "You can at least try."

Razi's covered his friend's hand with his own, clamping down hard. "Christopher," he whispered. "I will not have these people take vengeance on us for a death that will occur anyway. If this man dies under my knife—"

"Good Frith! We ain't bloody animals! They ain't going to kill you for an honest failure!" Christopher pulled his hand free and gestured to Sólmundr. "Don't leave him like that, Razi. Don't let him go out like . . . don't let him go out like that."

Wynter rubbed her hand up and down Christopher's arm and turned sympathetic eyes to Razi. Unable to comprehend the Southlandast, the Merron were quiet, their eyes hopping from man to man as they tried to interpret the tone of their conversation.

"Chris," said Razi softly. "Look at me." He held his hands up. His fingers were trembling, his hands not just shaking, but weaving to and fro. "I will kill the poor fellow, Chris. I will kill him as sure as if I plunged my sword into his neck."

Christopher stared at Razi's unsteady hands, then back to Razi's soot-stained face. "I'll tell them that," he said. "I'll tell them that you need to get some sleep. You take a draught, go to bed, forget everything till tomorrow. If *An Domhan* spares Sólmundr till then, you can save him when you wake up."

My God, thought Wynter, gazing at Razi. *My God, what a burden.*

Razi blinked. "You will explain to them what it is I will need? You must translate everything precisely. I cannot afford misunderstandings."

All the tension flowed from Christopher's body, and he squeezed Razi's shoulder. Then he turned back to the expectant Merron and began to translate Razi's instructions for the next day.

A few hours later, with everything settled for the morning, Wynter ducked outside and breathed deep to clear the sick tent air from her lungs. Shivering and drawing her cloak around her, she gazed up at the stars. To her surprise, she felt the first sharp promise of autumn in the night air. Where would this winter find them, she wondered.

Razi stumbled from the tent, knocking her shoulder as he followed Embla to their quarters. He was barely capable of putting one foot ahead of the other and didn't seem to notice Wynter standing there.

Christopher came up behind her and laid his hand on her back.

"Come on, lass," he said softly. "The lady has given up her tent to us." Wynter leant her head back against his shoulder and closed her eyes. After the briefest of moments, Christopher kissed her hair, then broke away and the two of them trudged wearily after the others.

The Healing Cut

"*Níl sé réidh.*"

Christopher? thought Wynter, rising to the surface of a black sleep.

Ashkr's voice came through the darkness, insisting something in desperate Merron. "*Tá sé beagnach ina mhaidin!*"

Christopher hissed some reply, his voice fierce and brittle. Wynter blinked away her tiredness and rolled to her side, peering through the tent flap to see the two men outlined against the flames of a huge fire. Christopher appeared to be wrapped in a cloak, or a fur, his shape obscured by its bulk. He stepped close to Ashkr and snarled up at the tall man, his pose belligerent.

Whatever he said, Ashkr made a compulsive move towards him, his fist clenched and Christopher lifted his chin in defiance. Ashkr groaned and abruptly swung away, stalking off into the dark, his pale hair swinging behind him.

Wynter sighed with relief and rolled onto her back. She still felt utterly drained, despite her deep sleep. "*Jesu,*" she whispered and pressed her fingers into her eyes. Sighing again, she stretched her limbs and revelled in the soft fur that swaddled her naked body. Her bed consisted of a base of fragrant pine boughs covered with hides and blanketed in fur. Wynter thought it the most comfortable and sweet-smelling nest she had ever slept in.

The night before, she had mindlessly shed her filthy clothes and slipped beneath the covers before remembering that Christopher would be sharing her bed. She remembered staring into the dark, acutely aware of her own nakedness, both terrified and excited. She remembered thinking, *I can imagine no better marriage bed than this.* She had lain with her face to the wall of the tent, her heart hammering in her chest, waiting and waiting, and eventually she had fallen asleep. Now it was morning and, with a pang of regret, Wynter realised that Christopher had never joined her beneath the furs.

On the far side of the tent, Razi gasped suddenly and sat bolt upright. He was silent for a moment, an indistinct shape in the dark, then he sighed and pushed the covers from his legs, sitting forward with his head in his hands. Wynter turned to squint at him. The night before, he, too, had stumbled into the tent and stripped himself naked, crawling wordlessly beneath the furs of Embla's bed. In the end the poor man had not needed a draught to put him to sleep; he had been unconscious long before he'd even pulled his tunic over his head. Wynter did not think it possible that such a short sleep would have refreshed him enough for the task that lay before him.

"Wynter?" he whispered hoarsely.

"I am awake," she said, watching his dark silhouette bend and stretch, as he gathered up his clothes.

"Get ready," he said. "It is time."

With a sigh, she reached for her things and began to dress under the cover of her blankets.

"Where is Christopher?" whispered Razi, pulling on his trousers.

"I'm here," answered the young man, ducking into the tent. "It's very early; are you sure you're ready?"

Razi glanced at him, the firelight catching his profile for a moment before the tent-flap dropped in place and cast its partial shadow. "How is Sólmundr?" he asked.

"Hallvor has been giving him the tincture of opium all night, just as asked. He's much calmer."

Razi sighed and shook his head as he laced his boot. "It will not be enough to dull the pain of what is to come. I wish we could use those herbs she spoke of, and let him sleep through this ordeal."

"Aye, well. Hallvor is right, Razi, they would kill the poor fellow. Those herbs are too strong for someone as weakened as Sól."

Wynter looked at Christopher's profile, outlined against the illuminated side of the tent, and saw a deep weariness in his posture. "You did not come to bed," she said softly, trying to see his face.

Razi paused in dressing himself and peered at his friend. "Have you slept at all, Christopher?"

"I had a rest."

"I need you sharp, Chris. You know that."

"I'm sharp enough," he said quietly. He put his wrap down on Wynter's bed and she saw that it was one of the fur blankets that they would have shared. He must have taken it from their bed while she slept. "Everything you asked for has been done," he said. "Are you ready?"

Razi sat for a moment, looking at Christopher's indistinct outline. Then he bent to pull on his other boot. "Is it morning?"

"Very near to. You will have plenty of light by the time you are ready to start. They have moved Sólmundr to a narrow pallet, like you said, and opened the top of the tent to let in the light and the air."

"Very well," said Razi. He got to his feet and took a deep breath, running his hands over his face and pushing his heavy curls back from his eyes. "Let us go," he said and stalked out into the camp.

As Razi had requested, Wynter and Christopher bound their hair tightly to their skulls and left off their tops. Wynter felt strange walking through the crowd of silent Merron wearing nothing but her britches and her breast cloth, but when she saw Hallvor waiting by the wash table, similarly attired, she breathed deeply, let it go and concentrated on the daunting task ahead.

Razi immediately began scrubbing himself clean, soaping and rinsing his arms and chest many times before he was satisfied, cleaning his hands and nails with great care. Wynter and Christopher did the same, as did a bemused Hallvor. The Merron stood just outside the ring of bright firelight, watching every move as if it were a magic trick. Above the black shapes of the trees, the sky began to fill with rosy light.

Wynter glanced up as Christopher bent his head to soap the back of his neck. She continued scrubbing her nails, but kept her eyes on him as he worked the soap across his shoulders and down his arms. He was covered in bruises and scrapes, every movement stiff. Wynter knew she must look very similar. Even now her body groaned in protest at every turn. Christopher began to soap his chest and under his arms. As he did so, he lifted his sleepless eyes and inadvertently looked into Wynter's face. She dropped her gaze, and concentrated on scrubbing her hands. The loose ends of her woollen bracelet came untucked and they waved like seaweed in the soapy water.

When she finally glanced back up, Christopher had turned away from her and was standing looking off into the trees, his dripping hands hanging loosely by his sides. The claw-marks on his back and shoulders were a savage contrast to his pale skin. Wynter stepped to his side, shaking her arms free of water. For a moment the two of them stood looking into the darkness beyond the firelight, saying nothing. Then dawn burst in sudden glory across the tops of the trees, spilling liquid gold against their wet bodies and cancelling the firelight in a mythical flood. Both Christopher and Wynter inhaled as one and closed their eyes, turning their faces instinctively to the sun.

"Are we ready?" asked Razi. Everyone nodded and he jerked his chin at two men who were standing by the fire. At his signal they lifted the cauldron of boiling water that held his instruments and carried it after him into the tent where Sólmundr lay waiting.

Razi knelt down beside Sólmundr's bed, speaking softly in Hadrish and smiling. "Hello Sól." Blearily, the poor man opened his eyes and gazed up at him. "I am going to prepare you now, if I may?"

Ashkr released Sólmundr's hand and gently took the covers from his body, leaving him naked and exposed. Sól was lying on a narrow pallet of pine boughs and hide, his body still curled around his fist, as he had been the night before. He was sweating and shaking, though the opium seemed to have dulled much of his pain.

Razi spoke to him again, leaning forward so that he could easily make eye contact. "You understand now, Sól, what we are about to do? You remember all we spoke about last night?" Christopher translated all this into Merron, as he, Wynter and Hallvor took their appointed places around the pallet.

Sólmundr nodded once, his eyes full of fear and pain. The men set the cauldron of instruments down by Razi's side, and Sólmundr's eyes drifted to it, his breath quickening. "Do not look there, Sól," said Razi, gently turning Sólmundr's head. "Just look at Ashkr. That is it. You keep looking at him." Razi's soothing voice went on, as another bowl was laid beside him, this one filled with hot water and soap. Christopher went on translating, his voice just as calm, just as soothing as Razi's. "We are going to roll you onto your back now, Sól. Just let us do everything for you, don't you try . . . that's it . . . good. Good fellow. That's good."

Razi nodded to Embla and Úlfnaor and they sprang forward to join the others kneeling around the bed. Gently, all six of them pressed down on Sólmundr's shoulders, knees and ankles. Sólmundr cried out and his body tried to curl back into a ball, his sinewy muscles trembling with the strain. At his voice, the warhounds, chained on the far side of the camp, began to howl and bay.

Wynter fought hard to keep her hold on the poor man's sweat-soaked ankle.

"Sól," murmured Razi. "Do not be afraid to cry out. There is not a man alive who would not do so under this torment. You cry out, if that is your wish." He nodded to the men and women who were waiting at the door, and they hurried forward with the thick leather straps that were going to hold Sólmundr down. "Keep looking at Ashkr, Sól," he crooned. "Keep looking at him."

Sólmundr had a tremendous grip on Ashkr's hand. Wynter was sure that Ashkr's fingers must simply burst under the pressure, but the blond man just kept smiling down into his friend's face, running his hand through Sólmundr's hair. "*Beidh chuile rud go maith, a chroí,*" he murmured.

The leather straps were pulled tight across Sólmundr's chest, thighs and ankles, and fixed in place by the hammering of long wooden tent pegs into the ground. Finally Ashkr had to unpeel Sólmundr's grip from his hand so that Sólmundr's wrists could be similarly restrained. Sólmundr was clearly terrified now, his mouth compressed into an unsteady line, his breath coming in long, shaky sighs. Ashkr leant over him, keeping eye contact and smiling. He stroked the poor man's hair, murmuring all the time.

"Now, Sól," said Razi, taking a cloth from the bowl of hot water and lathering it with soap. "I must ask Úlfnaor and Embla to leave." He began to wash Sólmundr's torso, cleaning him of sweat and dirt. He crooned sympathetically as Sólmundr tried to curl against the pain. "I know, I know. I am so sorry. Have you anything you wish to do before Úlfnaor leaves? Any prayers or such things you need to complete before I begin? Sólmundr? Have you anything that you wish your Shepherd to do before he leaves?"

Sólmundr, still staring into Ashkr's eyes, tightly shook his head.

Razi nodded and tipped his head to Úlfnaor and Embla. They leant, one at a time, and kissed their friend on his lips and stroked his face. Embla whispered what sounded like a blessing. She hugged her brother. Then they left and it was only the six of them remaining in the tent.

They each took their appointed positions, Wynter and Christopher on Sólmundr's left, a copper bowl of small, silver implements that Razi called "retractors", between them, and a slate and charcoal by Wynter's side. Razi and Hallvor knelt on Sólmundr's right, Hallvor poised with a wicker basket of freshly laundered squares of cloth.

Razi uncorked a little brown bottle and rubbed his hands with a few drops of the contents. The tent filled with the familiar scent of alcohol and lemons. He swabbed Sólmundr's stomach with some of the precious liquid and put the bottle away, then he sat back on his heels and took a deep breath. He looked up through the open top of the tent. New-born sunlight was flooding the fresh sky, and there was plenty of illumination. "And so," he murmured, blinking up into the virgin blue.

Then he calmly began.

He lifted a small sharp knife from the cauldron, raised his eyes to Christopher and nodded. Christopher splayed his left hand against Sólmundr's stomach. The man flinched and gasped with fear, and Razi leant over him, looking into his face. "Sólmundr," he said. "You keep looking at Ashkr, keep looking at him and everything will be over as quickly as I can make it so."

Razi looked down at Christopher's hand. The young

man had his thumb pressed against Sólmundr's hip bone, his little finger just tipping the man's navel. His scarred fingers were spread against the poor man's stomach, pointing straight down towards his groin. Calmly, Razi brought the point of his knife to where the tip of Christopher's index finger rested low on the right side of Sólmundr's stomach. This, he had explained earlier, was the best way of locating the canker that might lurk within Sólmundr's body. Christopher lifted his hand away. Razi wet his lips, released a long, slow breath, and pressed the blade into Sólmundr's quivering flesh.

Blood welled up immediately, and Hallvor mopped at it as Razi made a long, deep incision. His knife was exceptionally sharp, and to Wynter's amazement, Sólmundr had very little reaction to this first cut. Razi laid his knife back into the cauldron with a clink.

"Now, Christopher," he murmured. "I am going to pull back this first layer. I would like to you insert the retractors as we discussed and hold the wound open."

Christopher took two of the metal right angles and held them poised. Razi slid his fingers into the wound, gently pushing the edges apart, and Christopher slipped the silver implements into place. Sólmundr immediately went rigid and began to moan, low and continuous, in the back of his throat. It was a horrible sound, and Wynter couldn't help but glance up at his face. He was bug-eyed and straining, his teeth bared to the gum.

"*Wynter!*" Razi's sharp voice snapped her eyes back to the job. "Pay *attention*."

She fixed her gaze on the awful gaping mouth of the wound and nodded compulsively, her mind blank.

Christopher was translating something for Hallvor who was swabbing blood away from the incision, while Razi put a quick stitch into some area of flesh. Sólmundr was trembling, the blood that ran in bright trails down his stomach shivering with the tremors of his body. Razi's hands were already scarlet to the wrist. Wynter stared without moving.

"Two retractors," said Christopher, his voice coming through faintly, and from a great distance. "Two retractors," he repeated. "Three swabs."

Razi took his knife from the cauldron and cut once more into Sólmundr's body. He sliced down along the same path again, opening another layer of flesh that seemed to lie beneath the first. *My God*, thought Wynter, *we are just like books. Razi is peeling him open one layer at a time, like cutting into the pages of a book.* She watched from miles away as Christopher slid more silver retractors into place.

"Two more retractors. Four swabs."

Hallvor swabbed away the blood again, trying to keep the area clear enough for Razi to see what he was doing. Razi frantically inserted yet more single stitches, and Wynter distantly realised that he was tying off the areas that were bleeding most profusely into the cavity of the wound.

"Iseult!" snapped Christopher suddenly. She jumped and looked up at him, blinking. "Wake *up!*" he said. He was glaring angrily at her, his red hands poised in front of him, his grey eyes spitting fire. Suddenly, the tent snapped back into focus.

Sólmundr was panting in the background, *huh-huh-huh-huh*. Ashkr was crooning to him in soft Merron. Razi's low, deep voice was speaking, murmuring apologies and explanations. Wynter realised she had been sitting there like a stone, doing nothing.

"Do your bloody *job*," snapped Christopher, "or get out!"

She blinked at him, then scrabbled for the slate and charcoal. "Tuh . . . two retractors!" she said, making two marks beneath the R on the slate. "Three, um, three . . ."

"It's *four* retractors. Four retractors, seven swabs." Christopher's voice was softer now. He ducked to catch her eye. "All right?" he said. "*Four* retractors . . . *seven* swabs."

She glanced up at Razi and Hallvor as she made the marks. They were poised over their work, watching her. She forced herself not to look at Sólmundr's tormented face.

"Are you with us now, sis? Can you keep count from here on?" Razi, cool and practical, wanting an honest answer, needing to get on. She nodded. He bent back to his work.

Razi cut down into the successive layers of Sólmundr's muscle, Christopher slipping the silver retractors into place each time. Hallvor worked to keep the area free of blood. Wynter noted every single square of cloth used and then discarded, every single retractor placed into the deepening wound, and she marked them down on her slate.

Sólmundr's frantic moaning grew to fill the tent, a continuous background noise, Ashkr's steady voice its deep underscore. The sun moved overhead, slowly creeping down the walls of the tent, and burnished the top of Razi's curls as the minutes trickled by. Wynter blinked sweat from her eyes – it was going to be another hot day.

Suddenly Razi paused and jerked his knife from the cavity of the incision "I'm through!" he said, his exclamation unusually loud in the ringing silence. At the same time Ashkr whispered something, his voice so quiet that it went unnoticed by them all.

Razi licked his lips and blinked around him, as if amazed he'd got this far. "I . . . I wonder if I may need more light," he said. Wynter, Christopher and Hallvor peered down into the wound, trying to make sense of what they were looking at.

Ashkr reached a shaking hand behind him, his eyes on Sólmundr. "Tabiyb," he said, and suddenly Wynter was aware of how loud their voices were, how still it was. Razi glanced up sharply. Wynter turned to look, and her heart jerked in her chest. Ashkr was staring at them, his tears bright in the streaming sunlight. "Tabiyb," he pleaded. "Sólmundr, he . . . Sól . . ." He looked down at Sólmundr's white, motionless face, and made a helpless sound. "*Sol!*" he cried.

The four of them sat, blank and staring for a moment, unable to process what they were looking at. Wynter looked down at Sólmundr's hand, pinned to the ground just by her left knee. He had ceased his compulsive scrabbling at the ground, and his long, pale fingers lay motionless, the fingernails filthy from clutching at the dirt floor. "Oh," she said.

Razi reached and pressed his bloody fingers to Sólmundr's groin. He tilted his head, his lips parting, as if he was listening to some distant sound. He knelt quietly for a moment, the sun beating down on him from above. Then his eyes slipped back into focus.

"He has lost consciousness," he said, "that is all. Sól is all right, Ashkr. Put your hand on his chest. You feel him breathing?" Ashkr nodded, great tears shivering in his eyes, his attention focused on Razi as if his words and his words alone were keeping Sólmundr alive. "Keep your hand on his chest, Ashkr," said Razi. "You will feel him breathe, you will feel his heart beating, and it will let you know that he is still with us." Ashkr's gaze dropped to the red wound in Sólmundr's side. "*Ashkr!*" The navy eyes shot back to Razi's face. "Keep looking at Sól's face now. Look at Sól's face, that's it. He will revive soon enough, and it is your eyes I want him to see, not your ear." He smiled gently at the distressed man, and Ashkr nodded, turning back to stare at Sólmundr's face.

Razi turned back to his work. "Let us take advantage of this while we may," he murmured. Without any pause, he carefully slid his hand deep into the wound in Sólmundr's side. Christopher watched with calm, emotionless concentration as Razi groped about inside the body cavity. Wynter turned her head away, alarmed at how close she was to retching. "If you are going to be ill," said Razi evenly, "please go outside." Wynter sniffed and gritted her teeth. She was just turning to tell him that she was all right, when she realised that he was talking to Christopher. The young man had turned the most delicate shade of green and was hunched and bug-eyed, trying to control an unexpected bout of nausea. Wynter couldn't help it – she grinned. Christopher turned his eyes to her. Then he ballooned his cheeks in distress and turned his back on the scene, breathing deeply to get himself under control.

Hallvor caught Wynter's eyes and they exchanged a smile.

"Chris," said Razi, "retractor." Christopher swung back, still swallowing repeatedly, and slid two more retractors into place. Wynter noted them on her slate. Razi's face screwed up with concentration. "Shit," he said. "I can't . . ." he growled in frustration. He was rooting about inside Sólmundr, hunting blindly. "Where are you?" he grunted. "Where are you, you whoreson, pox-ridden, bull's pizzle of a misbegotten cur's abortion."

"*Jesu!* Brother!" said Wynter, startled. Even Christopher was given a moment's appreciative pause at Razi's atrocious language.

Razi lifted angry brown eyes to them and hissed impatiently as he felt about in Sólmundr's organs. Slowly his face began to grow desperate. "Curse you," he muttered. "All right then, I shall try the other side of . . . oh! . . . hah!" His face brightened in a moment of pure, childlike delight. "There you are, you scabrous, putrescent . . ." Sólmundr jerked suddenly and Razi froze, his eyes snapping to the man's face. Sólmundr made a grating noise and tried to arch against his tight bonds. "Shit," said Razi. Ashkr briefly met his eyes, then he leaned to peer into his friend's now horribly alert face.

"Hallvor," said Razi, bending once more to his work. "*Hallvor!* I cannot see, God curse it! Good woman, that's it, just keep with me now. We're almost done here. More retractors, Chris."

Sólmundr's hands starfished up against the leather straps and his entire body spasmed. He yelled suddenly, in Hadrish, "*No! Oh, no!*" Then he began to babble in Merron. Wynter did not need to understand his words to know that he was pleading for them to stop.

"Two more swabs, girly," murmured Christopher and Wynter made the note. She forced her eyes back to the operation. Razi's fingers worked quick as a lace-makers, a new urgency to his movements. He took his scissors to some slithering thing in his hand and snipped. Sólmundr bucked, the muscles in his legs and arms straining, and he keened a high animal sound. "All right, friend," murmured Razi, tossing something into a bowl by his side. "All right. We are almost done. Almost done."

Wynter glanced up. Ashkr was leaning over Sólmundr's chest, blocking his view of the operation. He had taken his friend's face between his hands and was forcing him to look into his own, smiling all the time and talking. But Sólmundr had reached the end of his self-control and his face was a rigid mask of terror. Though he kept his eyes set fixedly on Ashkr's face, Wynter doubted that Sólmundr was aware of anything but agony, and his desire that it would stop.

"I am setting your organs back in place now, friend," said Razi, his deep voice warm and soothing. "I must ensure that they are not twisted or . . ." he stopped talking, all his concentration on his work, and he once again slipped his hand into the wound. Sólmundr's hand knotted to a fist by Wynter's knee. His eyes rolled up and he released a scream so agonised that it was nothing more than a long hiss of air. Razi's demeanour did not change. He continued to speak in that same deep tone and feel about inside the man's stomach. Then he withdrew his hand and looked at Hallvor. "Clean water," he said. As he washed his hands, he glanced at Christopher. "Needle and gut, Chris." Christopher bent to prepare the needle. Razi, soaping his hands and rinsing them, glanced at Wynter. "Count those swabs now. Then pay attention and mark off each retractor as it is removed." As soon as his hands were free of slime, Razi took the needle, and, without pause for breath, began the laborious procedure of sewing Sólmundr's successive layers of muscle back together.

An indeterminate amount of time later, Razi snipped the thread on the last stitch and sat back on his heels, his eyes wide. "We . . ." he said. "We are done." He ran his bloody hands through his hair and laughed shakily. "We are done!" he said, and Wynter found herself grinning from ear to ear. Razi looked at Christopher, his grin luminous. "We are done, Chris!"

Christopher nodded, smiling gently.

Razi leant to look down into Sólmundr's chalky face. "We are done, Sólmundr. It is over." Sólmundr rolled bloodshot, swollen eyes to him. "We are *done*, friend, you stuck it out to the end." Razi smiled and put a bloody hand on the man's trembling shoulder. "Such bravery," he said. "I am in awe. I have never seen the like." Sólmundr swallowed and his eyes slid shut.

Hallvor staggered to her feet, groaning and rubbing her calves. She was calling out before she even ducked beneath the tent flap, and whatever she said was greeted with whoops and screams and the frantic baying of hounds. Christopher tilted his head and shut his eyes, weary now, listening to the happy shouting outside. Wynter reached for his hand, and their bloody fingers entwined.

"Can we set loose Sól now, Tabiyb?" asked Ashkr softly. "Can we unbind him and put him in bed?"

Razi watched as Sólmundr's breathing evened out and he

slipped into a deep, exhausted sleep. "Aye," he said. He laid his hand on Sólmundr's steadily breathing chest, and smiled at the feel of his heart beating strong under his palm. "Aye," he said again. "I think that would be just fine."

Squandered Hearts

*R*azi helped Ashkr to remove the leather straps while Christopher and Wynter cleaned Sólmundr's stomach and hands and bandaged his wound. Then, between the four of them, they lifted Sólmundr into the fragrant nest of furs that he shared with Ashkr.

Ashkr, silent now and exhausted, took off his boots and his tunic and crawled up the far side of the bed. Carefully, he fixed the covers up around Sólmundr's chest and took his hand. He looked down on his sleeping friend for a moment, his face tender, then lay down on the furs beside him, watching Sólmundr as he slept. Slowly, Ashkr's eyes slipped closed, and the two men lay peacefully side by side, their lightly clasped hands rising and falling with the motion of Sólmundr's steady breathing.

Razi, standing in the centre of the tent, watched them from the corner of his eye. "Sólmundr will not be fit to travel for quite a while, Ashkr." Ashkr's eyes drifted open and he regarded Razi expressionlessly. "If there is any urgency to your purpose here, I'm afraid it will have to wait at least a fortnight."

The corner of Ashkr's mouth twitched. "Sól and me, we not go no further than here, Tabiyb. You not worry."

Razi frowned in confusion and he traded a worried glance with Wynter. *The Merron were going no further?* Had they misjudged this entire situation?

"You not worry," whispered Ashkr softly, staring at Sólmundr with surprising sadness. He squeezed his friend's slack hand. Then his eyes slid shut and his handsome face relaxed into sleep.

Razi looked questioningly at Christopher. The pale young man was regarding Ashkr with a grim mixture of sympathy and anger. After a moment, he glanced at Razi, shook his head with what looked like despair and resumed tossing the bloody equipment into the cauldron.

A strange, slithering movement overhead caused them to flinch and look up in alarm. The hides were being drawn back into place over the top of the tent. Unseen hands hauled on the guide ropes and, as they watched, the hides closed over the support poles and the sunlight was blotted out.

By the time they had gathered Razi's things and ducked out into the fresh air, exhaustion had, once more, settled on them all. The sunlight and heat was such a shock that it almost sent Wynter staggering. She took a step back and shaded her eyes as people advanced in a rush of sound and colour. Razi's equipment was taken from his numb hands and brought to the fire for boiling. Hallvor came up, drying her arms and talking excitedly to Embla who was translating for her.

"Hallvor wish to speak to you, Tabiyb. She want to

know why not you burn wounds close? She say you sew together, like shirt, the men, Wari and Sól alike. She wonder . . ." Embla tilted her head quizzically, and Wynter saw a tender understanding blossom on her face. She murmured something to Hallvor, who paused in her gesturing and gabbled questions and looked for the first time at Razi. He was oblivious to everything, blinking up at the sun and swaying on his feet, his face a blank and happy mask. The healer smiled, and turned away, gesturing as if to say *later*.

Embla put her hand on Razi's arm, and he started, as if noticing, her for the first time. "Embla," he said, surprised.

"Aye, Tabiyb." Embla gently pushed the curls back from Razi's blood-stained face. "Come." She led him, unresisting, to the table where their wash kits lay and bowls of fresh water steamed gently in the morning light. "We have took your other things from your bags – clothes, cloaks, blankets. We have washed from them the fire smell. They will be dry soon; you and your family can have clean things to wear, yes?"

She glanced back at Wynter, gesturing warmly that she should follow. Wynter nodded and looked around for Christopher. He was staggering away through the crowd, heading for the river. People were patting him on the back and saying things to him, and he was shrugging them off and lifting his hand to deflect their questions with weary irritation. Wynter frowned after him for a moment, then turned back to the others.

Razi stood by the wash table like a lost child, dazed with exhaustion. As Wynter made her way towards him, Embla pushed down on his shoulders until he was sitting on a little folding stool, his elbows on his knees. She took one of the copper bowls of water and began lathering soap onto a cloth. Then she knelt between Razi's splayed legs, took his hand, and began slowly washing his fingers and his palm free of blood. Razi's eyes roamed Embla's face, and Wynter saw the rest of the world fade away for him.

A man approached with a tray of little wooden bowls and laid it on the table. He placed one of the bowls by Razi, and gestured to Wynter to take the others. They were full of porridge, and the smell made her mouth water.

Embla had begun to work the warm, soapy cloth up the length of Razi's blood-stained arm. "I likes this *soap*," she murmured. "It is most pleasing, how it makes this bubbles . . . like foam in sea." As she lathered lazy, caressing circles from his wrist to the crook of his elbow, Embla ran her eyes all the way to Razi's face and back again, taking in every detail of his strong, brown body. The breeze lifted her hair and it drifted around them in the sunlight.

Razi's eyes grew heavy and Embla's smile took on a private depth that made the Merron standing at the wash table smirk at each other and raise their eyebrows. Wynter admired their restraint in not clucking like hens. Quietly, she took Christopher's and her own wash kits from the table and slung them across her arm.

Embla began to wash Razi's chest. Razi inhaled, as if testing her scent, and his eyes wandered to her body, then up again to her face. Embla squeezed the cloth against his collarbone and he sighed as a small tide of shining bubbles cascaded down the knotted half-moon of his scar.

Embla turned her attention to his blood-splattered face, pushing the cloth through his curls, cleaning the blood from his hair. Her movements were not so gentle now, her expression less than tender, and Razi watched her intently from beneath his lashes, his teeth showing white through parted lips.

Wynter, her cheeks pink, took one of the copper bowls of water from the table and placed it on the tray beside the bowls of porridge. She laid two of the squares of folded linen on top and hoisted the whole heavy burden up with a grunt. She turned to tell Razi that she was leaving, but Embla had pulled his head forward to rest against her shoulder, and her face was turned into the damp tangle of his hair. She was murmuring as she soaped the back of his neck, and Razi's hand slowly tightened around her waist as her lips moved against his ear. Wynter smiled knowingly, and without a word, she turned to the river.

Razi's big mare was hobbled on the green along with Ozkar, both of them contentedly munching grass, shoulder to shoulder with the Merron's painted horses. As Wynter passed between the lines of fluttering washing, she looked around for Christopher's chestnut mare. The sturdy little animal was standing apart from the herd, nodding its shaggy head and staring down towards the river. Wynter guessed that this was where she would find Christopher. Carefully, Wynter made her way across the cropped grass, trying not to upset the contents of her tray. To her right, far into the trees, the sounds of sawing and the continuous chopping of hatchets told her that the Merron were hard at work gathering more firewood, or more likely, from the sounds of it, cutting new lodge-poles. Perhaps they were expecting yet more company.

The ground dropped steeply and she watched her footing as she navigated a precipitous little track down to the water. The sounds of the camp died away, muffled by the steep bank of grass and pushed back by the river breeze. Wynter found herself on a pleasant, sandy little shore, sheltered and peaceful, cooled by the proximity of the water. It was a perfect little haven, away from the eyes of the camp.

Christopher sat with his back to her, halfway to the water, his elbows on his drawn-up knees, his arms wrapped loosely around his head. Wynter crunched her way towards him. He had removed his boots and his socks, and his feet were pushed deep into the warm sand. *How delicious*, thought Wynter, her feet itching jealously within the hot confines of her boots.

"Hello, love," she said as she came on level with him. He started slightly, his hands jerking against the nape of his neck, and she chuckled. "Were you asleep?"

Christopher didn't answer, but folded his arms across his knees and rested his head against his forearms, his face hidden from her. He still had his hair bound, and the long wounds on his back and shoulder were particularly angry looking in the bright sunlight. He had not yet washed and his pale body was smeared all over with Sólmundr's blood. With a pang of sympathy, Wynter realised that he was just too tired to care.

Carefully she laid the tray on the ground and sat down to pull off her boots, wincing at the pain in her back. "*Jesu*," she sighed, digging her bare feet into the soft sand. "That feels good." She leaned back, propping herself on her arms and looked up into the blue sky. Exhaustion sang through her veins, a high unending whine, but the sun felt lovely on her bare torso and Wynter closed her eyes for a moment, soaking up its heat. The world instantly spun away in black and red, and Wynter felt herself falling into darkness. She gasped and sat forward, opening her eyes wide and breathing deep. "Oh!" she laughed, blinking spots from her vision. "Oh! It's dangerous to close your eyes!"

Christopher sat wordlessly beside her, a pale, blood-soaked stone in the sunlight. She went to put her hand on his curved back, but there were those awful scratches, so she rested her palm on the nape of his neck instead. He turned his face to her, his cheek resting on his arms. He was spent, the flesh under his eyes swollen into pouches, his narrow face chalky with fatigue. He regarded her without much expression, barely conscious.

"I brought warm water," she said softly, "to wash away the blood." His eyes slid listlessly to the wash kits and basin, then back to her face. "I brought porridge, too." He continued to watch her without expression, his breathing deep and steady like a sleeper's. "Are you awake?" she whispered. He nodded, a barely perceptible movement. "Here," she said and she got to her knees and shuffled around to put the bowl of water and the wash kit between his feet. "You wash yourself; I'll look after your hair."

He lifted his head for a moment to look at the bowl of water, then dropped his forehead back against his arms as Wynter undid his scarf and unpinned his hair. "Oh, Chris!" she admonished softly. "You still haven't brushed it!"

His long hair fell down his back in a scruffy mess of knots and tangles. It was still peppered with the many twigs and leaves and bits of debris from the night the Wolves had attacked. Wynter spread it out against his shoulders like a tatty spider's web, and slowly began picking the rubbish from the worse of its dark snarls. Christopher kept his head down, but at her touch the muscles in his back tensed, and his scarred hands tightened against the tops of his arms, dimpling the bruised flesh.

"Do you think Sólmundr will survive, Christopher?"

He answered in a slow, dull rasp, without lifting his head. "I don't think he wants to," he said.

Wynter nodded in agreement "I can't understand it. He seemed such a strong, vibrant kind of man. I cannot imagine that he would willingly give up on life. You know, I think he only accepted Razi's help because the pain was so intolerable. Otherwise he would gladly have let himself die." She frowned and shook her head. "I cannot fathom it, Christopher."

"In the end," said Christopher quietly, "there is only so much a man can stand to lose. When everything he loves, and everything he is, is broken and burnt like kindling, a man comes to understand that the only thing he has any control over is when and how he dies."

Wynter did not pause in her work. She kept on working her comb through the mess of his hair, but she stared down on his bowed head with wide eyes and she had to force her reply out past an inexplicable lump of fear. "I don't understand that, Christopher," she whispered. "No matter how bad the present, surely every new day is a fresh beginning? Surely every dawn brings the gift of hope?"

Christopher exhaled a little laugh. "I am glad that you do not understand, girly," he said softly. "That makes me glad."

"In any case," she continued. "What of Ashkr?"

Christopher flinched, his fingers digging deep into the flesh of his arms, and Wynter hesitated, worried that she may have misread the love between the two men. "He . . ." she said uncertainly. "Ashkr seems to love Sólmundr very deeply. It seems a crime for Sólmundr to have captured his heart like that and then purposely leave him all alone."

"Aye," whispered Christopher. "It is. It is a God-cursed crime. To squander someone's heart like that. He should never . . ." he shook his head. "It is a God-cursed crime," he whispered. "Poor Sólmundr."

Poor Sólmundr? Wynter frowned. Christopher must be very tired, to have lost track of their conversation so quickly. She had managed to release most of the terrible tangles from his hair, and she ran the comb easily now from scalp to tip, moving in long, soothing strokes, lifting the heavy locks from his back so as not to touch his wounds with the comb.

"We must leave, girly." His voice was distant, muffled within the cradle of his arms. "We cannot stay with these people."

She stopped combing. "But Chris, we need them," she said. Unless . . . do you no longer think that they are headed for Alberon? Ashkr did say that this is as far as they go."

"I have no doubt that they are headed for Alberon," he said dully. "Once they're done here, Úlfnaor and Wari will leave most of the others behind and go on to meet the Prince. Sólmundr would have too, had his health not failed him." Christopher opened his eyes and he stared down at the ground between his feet. "But we cannot stay. Razi. Razi . . . he . . ."

Wynter smiled, thinking she understood. Tenderly, she put her hand on his hair and bent to look at his face. "Christopher," she whispered. "Do not underestimate the depths of Razi's tolerance. The nature of Sólmundr and Ashkr's love is perhaps not so big an issue to him as you might believe. At the palace, it was his fear for *you* that led—"

Christopher squeezed his eyes shut and shook his head. Wynter was distressed to see real anguish in his face. "What is it, love?" she asked. "Do you think they will take vengeance for Wari?"

Christopher abruptly pushed the heels of his hands in under his eyes, pressing hard, his lips drawn back. "We just cannot *stay*, Wynter," he said. "It is not *possible*. Razi will never understand. They would be forced to . . . oh, please," he gasped. "Please, we must leave."

Abruptly he went silent, his body rigid, his blood-stained hands pressed to his eyes. Wynter stroked his arm and his shoulders, alarmed at the quivering strain in his body, the physical tension. When it became obvious that Christopher would say no more, she moved around behind him again and resumed combing. She combed and combed, and gradually Christopher's hair began to regain its lustre, shining black and violet in the glancing sun, flowing through Wynter's fingers like cool, dark water. Still he did not lose his iron rigidity.

"Christopher," said Wynter carefully. "You have seen the maps of the Indirie Valley. You know how wide it is, how long. You know how deeply forested it is. Alberon could have an entire army hidden there and we *still* would never find him. We need these people. We need their knowledge.

Without them, Alberon may move on before we can make contact, or Jonathon could find him before we do and then all will be lost." Wynter looked out across the wide swell of the water, her thoughts running ahead, trying to predict what could not be predicted. "Or Alberon's men may find us," she said quietly, talking to herself now. "They may kill us before we can let them know we mean no harm, or the cavalry may come upon us . . . or the Wolves . . ."

At the mention of the Wolves, Christopher moaned and lifted his arms to cover his head. Wynter shut her eyes to quell the mindless rush of fear that the thought of them brought to her. She did not want to think about those little girls at the Wherry Tavern, she did not want to think about their fate. The fate she would have shared with them, had Christopher not saved her.

"Christopher," she whispered, slipping her arms around his shoulders and leaning into him. "Christopher." He jerked beneath her touch, his muscles as taut as quivering iron. He smelled of blood, and of ashes and of sharp, new sweat. "We're safe here, aren't we?" she whispered "Your people will protect us, won't they? They won't let . . . they'll keep the Wolves away."

Wynter hated the weakness in her voice, hated this sudden wave of helplessness that had risen up and undone her. She had not known, until this moment, how terrified she was of heading out again. Slowly, she bent her head into the crook of Christopher's neck and squeezed her arms tight around his rigid shoulders, ashamed and frightened and overwhelmed.

At first, Christopher remained frozen, as if desperately resisting her embrace. Then, gradually, he uncurled from his defensive crouch and shifted his neck to accommodate Wynter's head on his shoulder. She felt his hand move across to the back of her head. Wynter began to rock gently. Christopher slid his other hand along the top of her arm and let it come to rest in the crook of her elbow. The two of them closed their eyes.

Sunshine warmed them and the peaceful sounds of the river emptied their minds. Gradually, their breathing calmed, their hearts slowed and they relaxed against each other, each of them finding comfort in the other's embrace and in gentle, innocent motion as Wynter rocked them to and fro.

Frith

They made their way up the steep little path, silent and numb, bumping into each other as fatigue made them miss their footing. Wynter's back ached and Christopher limped clumsily along, carrying the copper bowl and towels, his eyes drifting shut even as he walked.

At the top of the path, they staggered blindly onto the grass, heading for the tents. Suddenly, two huge warhounds butted into their space, slobbering and grinning, panting up into their startled faces.

"*Gread leat*," snapped Christopher, jerking to life and pulling Wynter back. "Leave her *be*!" He pushed testily at the dog's blunt heads. They happily ignored him, eager to explore the depths of the porridge bowls. One of them butted Wynter in the stomach. She staggered backwards, upsetting the tray, and that was it for Christopher – he lost his temper.

"*Croch leat!*" he snarled, recklessly punching the dog's huge head with his fist. "*Croch leat, a bhoid clamhach.*"

The dogs growled, and to Wynter's alarm, Christopher lashed out at them with the copper bowl. Any fool could have sensed the huge creatures' rising antagonism, but

Christopher seemed to have lost all common sense, and he raised the bowl again, yelling.

"Christopher," she warned, eyeing the flashing teeth and stiffly raised hackles. "Stop it!"

Christopher pushed her roughly behind him. "Úlfnaor!" he shouted, glaring up towards the camp. "Curb your damned hounds!" It was only then that Wynter noticed the big man walking towards them, his black hair lifting in the breeze, his bracelets flashing as he strode across the grass. "Curb your *hounds*, Aoire!" demanded Christopher in Hadrish. "They are trying my patience!"

Úlfnaor seemed to take no offence at Christopher's tone, his face and posture those of a man with other things on his mind. He whistled as he strode towards them and his hounds broke away immediately, galloping towards him with loose limbed, slavering worship, and falling into place at his heel.

"Coinín," he said, "I was looking for you." He nodded politely to Wynter and she bobbed her head, her eyes sliding to the hounds. Úlfnaor glanced down at them, "*Suigí síos,*" he murmured.

The great dogs sat immediately, and Úlfnaor fondled their ears, his many rings gleaming in the sun. Wynter thought there was an air of heavy sadness to the man, a sense of invisible weight pressing him down. He sighed and turned his attention to Christopher once more, a question on his lips, but then faltered and stared, noticing the young man's ragged state. His dark eyes flicked to take in Wynter's equally frayed condition.

"*Frith an Domhain,*" he said. "You are used up, you both. Why you not rest?"

Christopher clutched the basin and towels to his naked chest, swaying and glaring belligerently from swollen, red-rimmed eyes.

"Thank you for your consideration, Lord Úlfnaor," said Wynter, tearing her eyes from Christopher's grim face. "We are on our way now to lay down for a while in the shade."

"Good," said Úlfnaor, eyeing them both with concern. "Good. Coinín," he said, "the Caoirigh would like you and your family to join them at evening. We dine in Ashkr's tent and—"

"No," snapped Christopher. "We cannot stay."

To Wynter's alarm, Úlfnaor's dark eyes narrowed and his mouth tightened in disapproval. She went to apologise for Christopher's abrupt rejection of the Lord's hospitality, but Christopher cut her off, his voice hard.

"Ashkr has told us that he will go no further than here, Aoire," he said.

Úlfnaor's face cleared in understanding. "Ah," he said.

"It is not possible," continued Christopher, "that we would impose on your time."

"Ah," said Úlfnaor again. "I see." He glanced at Wynter. "There is not understanding for our ways, here, I take it?" he said.

"None," said Christopher, "from any quarter."

Úlfnaor's eyes hardened at that, and he lifted his chin to look Christopher in the face. "Well, Coinín Garron. You are indeed your father's son, *nach ea*?"

Christopher just glared.

Úlfnaor shook his head, as one would to a small, belligerent child. "It just an invitation to dinner, Coinín. Nothing more. In respect for Sólmundr, we do nothing today but declare Frith. At least take tonight to recover your health, eh? Give your family time to rest?" The dark eyes slid to Wynter again. "Your *croí-eile* is much worn, Coinín, *nach bhfuil*? You not want to bring her back into the wilderness so soon."

Christopher glanced at Wynter, standing bruised and exhausted by his side, and all the hard certainty left his eyes. Úlfnaor regarded him carefully.

"Coinín," he said softly, "Wari tell me that Tabiyb, he not wanted to come treat Sól. He tell me that it you who make him agree. I want thank you for this."

Christopher stayed silent, his hair blowing over his face in the breeze.

"I admit, I not wanted Tabiyb come," said Úlfnaor. "I thinked it wrong, not respecting to Sól's choice. But I am glad that Tabiyb take Sól's pain, and now I praise *An Domhan* for his arrival. *An Domhan* has made good choice to bring you here." Úlfnaor looked into Christopher's eyes. "Maybe for both the People *and* for you?"

Christopher's face creased in weary confusion at that and Wynter felt a little prickle of unease.

"Life away from the People has not been kind to you, Coinín," murmured Úlfnaor. He glanced at Christopher's ruined hands, at the claw-marks where his bracelets should be, at his worn face. "Just like it not kind for your father." Christopher raised his chin, his eyes over-bright, his mouth unsteady, and Úlfnaor smiled sympathetically. "We Merron not do well away from our kind," he said.

Wynter frowned, angry at the tension she felt returning to Christopher's body. She slipped her arm around his waist and glared at Úlfnaor. She could not figure out his intentions. He seemed genuinely compassionate, but Christopher was clearly unhappy and Wynter couldn't help wishing that the Aoire would just go away.

"It bad you stolen away, Coinín," continued Úlfnaor gently. "But now, you come home, just like Sól come home. After much years, after much distances, *An Domhan* has bring you back. This is good, that you come to us from nowhere and give us what we needs, when we needs it. This is auspicious." At Christopher's continued silence, Úlfnaor sighed. "The Caoirigh think this is auspicious," he said softly, as if that might mean more to Christopher than just his opinion alone. "And your Tabyb? The Caoirigh think he good luck, a good omen."

"He's not," rasped Christopher suddenly, his bloodshot eyes glittering. "He's not good luck. Don't say that."

Úlfnaor spread his hands. "But the *Caoirigh* say it. You and me, we never know the things they know." He shrugged as if to say *what can you do?* Then he waved the whole thing off with a sigh. "You should to lie down, Coinín. Make your mind clear. I will to see you in Ashkr's tent for dinner." He smiled at Wynter, ignoring her glare. "You rest well, *a luichín,*" he said with genuine tenderness. His eyes flicked to her bound hair. "But," he tapped his head to show what he meant, "you unbind your hair now, yes? And show respect." Then he turned away, his hounds following him, and made his way back across the grass.

Wynter squeezed Christopher's waist and they stood watching as the big man passed amongst the horses and back into the camp. It seemed very quiet in his absence, the sounds of the horses soothing, the breeze from the river sweet.

"I am tired, girly," said Christopher suddenly. "I . . . I'm confused." He blinked around him in bewilderment, finally at the end of his tether.

"Can you make it back to the tent?" she whispered.

Christopher frowned as if not sure, and pushed his hair behind his ear, scanning the horses with unfocused anxiety. Wynter squeezed him tight. "Come on," she said gently. "Let us go lie down."

Embla's hounds were lolling at the door to the tent, and Wynter found herself slowing to a crawl, embarrassed at the thought of what might still be in progress within the painted walls. She had no desire to interrupt Razi and Embla if they were concluding the business they'd started at the wash table.

"Um . . ." she said, eyeing the sprawling dogs. "Christopher. I wonder if . . ."

Thankfully, the tall blonde woman chose that moment to duck from the tent, and Wynter breathed a sigh of relief. Embla noticed them and waved her hand in greeting.

"How do, Lady?" said Wynter, "How does the noon find you?" She released her grip on Christopher's waist and bent to set the tray by the door of the tent. Embla's hounds leapt to their feet, and Wynter skipped warily back as the enormous creatures buffeted each other, vying to snuffle at the empty porridge bowls. Wynter tore her eyes from them just in time to grab for Christopher who was shuffling for the door, completely oblivious to Embla's presence.

"Chris!" cried Wynter, snagging the waist of his britches. "Wait!" He turned a blank face to her, and then looked up at the smiling woman who was blocking his way.

"Well," he breathed, his grey eyes questioning. "What . . .?" A frown grew between Christopher's eyebrows. He looked Embla up and down and flicked a glance into the tent. "What . . .?" he said, narrowing his eyes.

Wynter glanced away, her cheeks burning. Embla was perfectly dressed, her jewellery and hair in place. But her mouth was rubbed and swollen looking, her skin dewy, and there was a richness to her, a languid air of completion, that was hard to misinterpret.

"Coinín is going to lie down for a while, Lady," said Wynter, her eyes averted. "And Úlfnaor has invited us for an evening dinner in Ashkr's tent. Perhaps we shall meet you there?"

Embla touched her gently on her shoulder and Wynter looked up into kind eyes. "Tabiyb sleeps," said the lady, and somehow that simple phrase took all the awkwardness from the situation. Wynter nodded gratefully. To her surprise, Embla reached and pressed her fingers to Wynter's forehead. "You have been hurt, Iseult," she said. Her hand was very cool and soothing against Wynter's bruised skin.

Wynter closed her eyes at the lady's gentle touch and then shook herself. "It's nothing," she said, covering her forehead with her hand. "Chris . . . Coinín saved me before they could do any real harm."

Embla turned to Christopher, who was supporting himself against the side of the tent, watching her with frowning resentment. "Coinín," she said, reaching as if to touch him. He glared, and the pale hand dropped. "You should to sleep now, yes?" she said softly. "You and your *croí-eile*. You should both to sleep." She looked him up and down, her face tender. "You are safe here, Coinín. You not to have worry; the People will to watch over you now."

At her unrelenting kindness, Christopher's resentment crumbled and he just looked at her in unhappy confusion. After a moment, Embla sighed and nodded in understanding. "I see you this evening, yes? For meal? And Tabiyb, he has agreed to declare Frith with us." Christopher closed his eyes in distress at this news, but Embla smiled, looking out over the camp, her face serene. "This make me very glad. You too, Iseult," she said, nodding to Wynter. "You too declare Frith. All of Tabiyb's family. It be very good. Good omen, yes?"

Wynter swallowed nervously and nodded, deeply uncertain. Embla left with a little bow, and Wynter and Christopher ducked out of the sunshine into the tent.

Inside was stifling. It felt steamy and too close; just stepping inside the door was enough to inspire a headache. Christopher stumbled to one of the rear poles. He unhooked something from a keep, and Wynter saw that it was a long, narrow dowel that stretched up into the dim shadows of the roof. Christopher spun the dowel between his hands. Something tightened in the upper reaches of the tent, and, high above them, three little flaps opened outwards, letting in some filtered sunlight and a surprising amount of fresh air.

"Oh, Christopher!" sighed Wynter, turning her face to the gentle draught. "That's lovely!"

Christopher smiled, her delight warming his unhappy face. He hooked the dowel back into position and staggered to their bed. Crawling across the furs, he lay down with a hiss.

Wynter glanced at Embla's bed. Razi was fast asleep, lost amongst the tumbled furs, his face turned to the wall. He was nothing but a long expanse of brown back, gently breathing in the dim shadows.

"Girly?" Christopher asked, suddenly panicked. "Where is Razi?" Wynter smiled at him, not really surprised. He was thoroughly addled with fatigue.

"He is right here, Christopher," she said, gesturing to Embla's bed. "He is asleep."

"Oh," he whispered, dropping his head back. "Oh, that is good."

His eyes slipped closed for a moment, then rolled opened again, roaming the ceiling. "If *she* comes back looking for him," he said, "you tell her he's busy. Raz . . . he wouldn't understand her intentions."

Wynter chuckled. She thought Razi and Embla had a pretty good grasp of each other's *intentions*. "Razi is not a child, Christopher. And I had not thought of you as a prude!"

"He ain't Merron," he said softly. "And Embla is *Caora Beo*. Razi would never understand her."

"You think he will fall too hard," she whispered. "You fear for his heart?" Christopher didn't answer and Wynter crawled across the furs to him. "Razi is a grown man, Christopher. He knows his own mind."

Christopher lay on his back looking up at the ceiling, and Wynter settled onto her side, watching him, her arm beneath her cheek. The air filtering down from the roof was delicious, a cool silk running across their heated bodies, and they lay quietly for the moment, revelling in its touch.

"I never thought I would lie in a *puballmór* again," said

Christopher, inhaling deeply and briefly closing his blood-shot eyes. He put his arms over his head, stretching out against the furs, releasing the scent of pine from the boughs beneath them. "That *smell*," he murmured. "I missed it." He relaxed, his arms curled loosely on either side of his head, his hair fanned out beneath him like black wings. Wynter expected him to drop off to sleep immediately, but he lay awake, his eyes roaming the walls of the tent. There were symbols painted on the outside and they showed up in red silhouette as the sun shone through the hide, moving gently with the breeze. "My father's *puballmór* was painted all over with snakes," he said, lifting his hand to trace the outline of a bear. "The day the tribe adopted me and named me Coinín, he painted a rabbit on each wall, to show that I was one of them." Christopher's eyes glittered and he abruptly splayed his hand against the wall, a dim, misshapen star at the centre of the bear's great chest. "Dad . . ." he whispered.

Wynter reached to stroke the smooth plane of Christopher's stomach. She meant only to comfort him, but at her touch, Christopher snarled and knocked her hand away, his face dark with threat.

Wynter recoiled, and for a moment, Christopher lay frozen, horrified at what he'd done. Then he took her hand. Carefully, he pressed Wynter's palm back down onto his stomach and lay back against the furs, staring blindly at the roof.

They stayed like that for a long moment, Wynter with her arm stretched awkwardly between them, Christopher holding her hand down against his skin. Then he took a deep breath, blinked the shivering brightness from his eyes and said, "You shouldn't startle me, lass. I ain't got much of a grip on myself at the moment."

"Have you a pain?" she whispered. "Do you need Razi?"

Christopher shook his head, his eyes fixed on the roof. "You just startled me," he said.

Wynter gazed down into his rigid, staring face and did not believe him. He had been hurt somewhere, by those men – in his gut perhaps – and he would not tell her. *I will make sure that Razi examines you*, she decided. *Pride or no pride, I will insist that you agree to it.* "Will you not sleep?" she asked softly. Christopher shook his head, his fingers tightening desperately against hers, and she decided to leave it for now.

She subsided beside him, and slowly the tension left Christopher's body. He kept his hand firmly over hers and she did not try and caress him again, just let her hand rest against the warm skin of his stomach, feeling his breathing slowing, watching his face relax. Gradually Christopher's hand loosened its grip.

"Christopher?" Wynter asked softly. "What is Frith? I thought it was your God. But that is not the case, is it?"

He shook his head.

"This ceremony, the ceremony of Frith . . . will it be very bad?"

She had in mind all she'd ever heard about pagans – torture, blood sacrifice, ritual copulation, and it frightened her. She was uncertain what herself and Razi might be expected to do. But, to her surprise, Christopher smiled gently up at the light. He drew her palm to the centre of his chest where she could feel his heart beating. "Oh no, lass," he breathed. "It's a lovely ceremony. I always loved it."

"Oh!" Wynter was amazed, after his reticence with Úlfnaor, to see such wistful pleasure on Christopher's face.

"Frith," he whispered, "Frith is lots of things. Community, common purpose, safety. It's . . . it's hard to explain." Christopher went silent. When he spoke again his voice was heavy and slow, his face solemn. "When we declare a place Frith, we are claiming that place for all the People. We are making it common property, a safe and sacred site for all the tribes. We do it for our shared camp-sites. For our meeting places. For holy ground. Anywhere the People gather without conflict."

Wynter was alarmed to see Christopher's eyes well up. A tear flashed bright and rolled past the slope of his cheek-bone, disappearing into the shadows of his neck. "It lets *An Domhan* know we mean no harm," he whispered. "It means protection. It keeps us safe." He squeezed her hand briefly and closed his eyes.

But that sounds good, thought Wynter. *That sounds beautiful.*

"Why are you crying, Christopher?" she asked, not wanting to shame him, needing to know.

Christopher shook his head vehemently. *No*, his face said, *don't ask me.*

"It sounds lovely, this Frith. It sounds good."

"It is," he said. "Iseult, it really is. You have to believe me."

"Why then, do you want us to leave? When these people can look after us? They would protect us, wouldn't they? They would look after us. If we asked?"

He nodded. *Yes, they would.*

He knows, she thought. *He knows his people have no*

chance of settling here. It distresses him, perhaps, that they are misled, and that we must make use of them to get to Albi. He wants no part of this, playing one loyalty against another. She frowned in sympathy and settled her head against the furs. *But who is to say what the future holds for them?* she thought. *Who can tell what accommodations may be made, once we reach Alberon's camp? There may be room for everyone here, after all?*

The sounds of camp filtered in through the walls of the tent. Peaceful and reassuring. Wynter's eyes drifted shut and without thinking, she ran her thumb comfortingly against the warm skin of Christopher's chest.

Safe, she thought. *Protected. Frith.*

Chess

Someone outside the tent called softly in Merron. At the sound of the voice, Christopher sat up immediately and crawled to the foot of the bed. Wynter surfaced from a heavy doze and rolled onto her back, passing her hand wearily over her eyes. The tent was abruptly filled with golden light as Christopher hooked back the door flap and went outside.

"*Cad é?*" he said quietly. "*Tá siad ina gcnap codlata.*"

Wynter shifted to see out the door. The older musicians from the tavern were standing with little bundles in their hands, smiling and talking softly. Christopher slouched just outside the door, squinting in the sunshine, his thumbs hooked into the waistband of his trousers. The couple offered him the bundles and he took them with a nod of thanks; it was their freshly laundered clothes and blankets, dry now and carefully folded.

He turned to duck back into the tent, and the woman said something to him, her tone that of someone trying to start a conversation. Wynter saw Christopher's shoulders slump and he reluctantly faced them again. He answered in monosyllabic Merron, showing no enthusiasm. But it seemed that the two musicians were unwilling to take the hint and they pressed on. When it became apparent that the conversation could not be cut short, Christopher laid the bundles down and sat back on his haunches in that strange, uncomfortable looking manner that Wynter had only ever seen in the tribal people of the North. The couple did the same and the three of them crouched at the door, talking.

"Has he slept?" murmured Razi.

She startled and peered across at him. He was lying facing her, his head cushioned on his arm, his face grave. She shook her head. "I am not certain. I don't think so."

Razi rolled onto his back with a grimace. "Good God," he said tightly.

"Razi," Wynter was about to ask that Razi examine their friend, was determined that he would not refuse her, when the tent was abruptly filled with shadows again as Christopher came inside and shut the flap.

"Did those two wake you?" he said in quiet Southlandast, laying the clothes at the foot of Razi's bed. They shook their heads. Christopher sat wearily onto Razi's pallet. He hunched, gathering his concentration for a moment, then began pushing off his filthy trousers.

Razi's eyes travelled the length of Christopher's abused back. His jaw tightened, then he turned abruptly away, pushing back the covers and swinging his legs from the bed.

"You don't have to get up yet," said Christopher. "There's plenty of time before dinner."

Razi grunted and reached for his clean things.

Wynter averted her eyes from the men's shameless

nakedness. "Throw me my clothes, will you, Christopher?" she said. In response she got a face full of fragrant, sun-warmed wool and linen. "Well, thank you so much," she said dryly and pulled the blankets over her so that she could change with some decency.

Christopher pulled on fresh trousers and rose to his feet. He shook his hair back and reached behind him, tying his undershirt closed. "I will be back soon," he said without looking at them, and went to step outside.

They glanced up in alarm.

"Christopher!" cried Razi, leaping to his feet, his britches half-laced. "Where are you going?"

Christopher paused. "There's something they want me to do in the forest." He looked from one to the other of them. "You ain't invited," he said. "You're *coimhthíoch*."

"Chris," said Razi carefully. "Will you please step back inside for a minute?"

Christopher hesitated, the light from the door catching the stress in his worn face. He glanced outside; there was a small knot of men and women gathering by the remains of the fire. Christopher tipped his head to catch someone's eye, gestured for them to wait, and then dropped the flap and stepped back into the tent. "What is it?" he said.

"Embla has invited us to a ceremony tonight, I—"

"Yes," said Christopher bluntly. "To declare Frith. Úlfnaor told us you had accepted. You should have *asked* me first, Razi. You should not go accepting invitations to things you do not understand."

Razi looked alarmed. "Oh," he said softly. He glanced at Wynter. "Oh, Christopher," he said, "I accepted for all of us. For Wynter too. Will there be . . . will it . . .?"

"Oh good Frith, it's *fine*," snapped Christopher, unreasonably irritated. "It's *all right*. But you do not know these people. You could have been agreeing to anything, *anything*. You need to be careful." He looked up into Razi's confused face and seemed to come to a decision "We are not staying," he said firmly.

Razi straightened, his eyes hardening. "Now *look*, Christopher—"

"Razi!" At the tone of Christopher's voice, Razi shut up immediately and he looked down at his friend with wide eyes. "We must leave tomorrow," said Christopher softly. "I need you to trust me. We cannot stay."

There was a moment of silent communication between the men.

"Will you not tell me why?" murmured Razi.

Christopher shook his head, his face tight.

"You understand that I need these people, Christopher? I need them to guide me to Alberon."

"We'll find another way. Trust me."

Razi's brown eyes roamed Christopher's face. "Are these people dangerous, Christopher? Are they not to be trusted?"

Christopher looked at Wynter. She smiled, trying to look encouraging. "They ain't bad people," he said softly. He looked back at Razi with a blade-like determination. "But right here and now you cannot be with them, Razi. They are old religion. Very, very old religion and you have met their Caoirigh. There's no taking that back now. You've met the Caoirigh. You will never, *ever* understand them. So we must go."

"Are we not safer here, than out there, where the—?"

"Razi," interrupted Christopher, his eyes widening, his pale face drawing down. "I would rather risk facing the Wolves again than have you and Wynter stay here after tonight."

"*Jesu!*" Wynter exclaimed.

Razi stood frozen for a moment, his eyes wide. "Christopher," he whispered.

"I mean it."

"All right, friend," said Razi. "All right. If it means so much to you. We leave at first light."

Christopher nodded, but Wynter could not help but see the uncertainty and fear in his face now that Razi had agreed to leave. "All right," he said. "Good." He glanced at her, then turned abruptly and left the tent.

Wynter leant forward to get a better view, and Razi hunkered down to watch as their friend approached the crowd. Úlfnaor, Ashkr and Embla had joined the knot of other Merron, and they seemed to be waiting for Christopher. It appeared as though the entire camp had turned out, and everyone had dressed for the occasion. The women wore long shifts of pale green, the men knee-length tunics and trousers of the same colour. All were bare-armed, as usual, their torcs and armbands and rings casting glittering reflections back at the sun.

Christopher limped towards them, an incongruous figure against the background of tall, well-dressed men and women. Everyone turned to him, smiling, and Christopher nodded dully. Ashkr met his eye and gave him a sad smile. Christopher raised his chin, and Wynter was surprised to see him smile in return. Then Úlfnaor lifted his arms, calling out, and Ashkr and Embla fell into place on either side of him. Wari and Christopher stood behind them, their faces set, their backs straight. Úlfnaor set off into the trees and the Merron followed, forming a neat procession behind their lords. Christopher was lost quickly from sight.

"I think Christopher took Sólmundr's place," whispered Razi.

Wynter nodded, not knowing why she felt so disturbed.

Razi got to his feet. "Are you ready, sis?" he asked.

"I would like to clean my teeth," she began, then looked sharply up at him. He was smiling slyly. "Where are we going?"

Razi just lifted his eyebrows and ducked outside.

The camp was deserted, a sunny, unpeopled landscape of breeze-rippled tents and fluttering washing. Wynter stood for a moment looking about her, amazed at how empty it was. There was no noise from the forest. Nothing at all. She scanned the shifting seashadows of the trees, listening for some sign that over twenty people were moving about in there. But there was nothing. This made her very uneasy and she hurried to catch up with Razi, strapping on her short sword as she ran.

"Whose tent is this?" she whispered as Razi ducked furtively through the door. There was no answer. Just scuffling and a muffled curse.

"Razi!" she hissed, pressing herself against the wall and eyeing the tree line. "*Razi!*"

Razi clunked against something. There was silence, then another heartfelt, grunted curse. Wynter glanced into the tent, then back to the trees.

"Whose tent are you ransacking?" she said tightly.

"Úlfnaor's."

"*Jesu Christi!*" Wynter moaned. "Have you lost your reason?"

Razi continued to ignore her. There were soft little clunks as he lifted things and carefully put them down again. Wynter's hand opened and closed on the hilt of her sword. *Come on, come on!* she thought, eyeing the impenetrable trees with growing anxiety.

There was a soft little "ah!" and Razi went still. Wynter crouched to look into the tent. "What?" she hissed, but Razi did not have to reply. She recognised a diplomatic folder when she saw one. Razi met her eyes, then he laid the hardbacked folder on the ground and carefully unlaced its ties.

"Shit," he said, flatly.

"What is it?"

He was staring bleakly at the documents inside the folder. Carefully he lifted one, then another of the thin parchments, his mouth turning down a little more with each one.

"What is it, Razi?"

"The seals are paper thin."

Wynter rolled her eyes in frustration. Thin seals were an absolute bane. There was no way to dislodge them without cracking the wax, not even a heated knife slipped between parchment and seal would work without damaging the crest in some way. "That explains the hardback portfolio rather than the usual leather roll," she whispered. "Someone is being very careful."

"Aye," murmured Razi distractedly.

"Whose seal is it?"

He held a document out to her. What she saw froze her heart.

"Marguerite Shirken?" she whispered.

He nodded.

"Oh good Christ, Razi. What . . .?"

A woman called out down by Ashkr's tent. They were not alone! Another voice answered the first and there was the unmistakable sound of two people conversing as one walked towards the other.

Wynter jerked her head, *Get out of there*, and Razi carefully secured everything before replacing the portfolio and leaving the tent.

Hallvor was crouched in the shade of Ashkr's tent, plaiting cured willow bark into cord and humming quietly to herself. Two other women sat with her, their swords across their knees, playing knuckle bones. The three of them rose to their feet at Razi and Wynter's approach.

"How is Sólmundr?" asked Razi, bowing politely.

The two guardswomen glanced at Hallvor, and she gestured to them to go back to their game. Reluctantly they crouched down into the shade, their eyes on Razi and Wynter. Hallvor led them away from the women, guiding them to the door of the tent. The sun beat down viciously here, the dry ground crackling underfoot.

"Sólmundr?" Razi asked again, looking into the healer's dark eyes.

Hallvor compressed her mouth and her jaw tightened. "*Níl sé go maith*," she said, shaking her head. "*Ní . . . ní . . .*" she stopped talking and sighed in frustration, knowing full well that Razi and Wynter couldn't understand her. She gestured helplessly, looking around as if for inspiration. Wynter shaded her eyes, trying to read her distressed face.

"Sólmundr," Hallvor said. "*Ní . . .*" she cupped her hands and brought them to her mouth, in a drinking gesture. Then she shook her head.

"He will not drink?" asked Razi, repeating her motion with a slurping sound. Hallvor nodded. Razi grimaced."'Tis too damn hot for that," he said. "Can we go inside?" He motioned ducking in under the door, and Hallvor shooed the two of them ahead of her, pushing in after them and closing the door in her wake.

The ventilation flaps had been opened in the roof and the tent was cool and shady. The smoke of a little fire-basin kept away the flies. Sólmundr was propped up in his bed, lying back against a deer shide stuffed with straw. His knees were drawn up under the furs, and his eyes were shut, his white face motionless, his hands lifeless in his lap.

Hallvor crouched down at the foot of the pallet and anxiously scanned Sólmundr's face. Razi and Wynter moved to the head of the bed.

"Hello, Sól," said Razi, kneeling and taking Sólmundr's hand. "I hear you're being a stupid dung-head." The weathered face creased into a smile, and Wynter saw a flash of the good-natured man that they had met at the tavern. She knelt down by Razi's side, as Sólmundr slit his eyes to look at them.

"Tabiyb," he rasped. "You cured my agony. Your hands are gift to the world." Wynter could see Razi's precious opium in the unfocused spread of Sólmundr's pupils. She could smell it on his breath. *We can use this if we are careful,* she thought. *We can take advantage of his confusion to get the information we seek.*

Razi grunted, holding the wiry man's wrist between his

fingers, counting his heartbeats. "Do not insult me with hollow flattery, if your intent is to kill yourself with neglect," he growled mildly. Sólmundr chuffed a tiny laugh and his eyes slipped shut. Razi pushed the covers down and loosened his bandages. "Coinín tells me that you have work to do here," he murmured, lifting the bindings and looking at the wound. "Yet you refuse to get well. You are too lazy to fulfil your duty to your people? Is that it?"

Sólmundr turned his face away, clenching his fists at Razi's touch.

"A pox on my people," he said softly.

Wynter and Razi glanced at him, shocked, but Sólmundr hardly seemed aware of what he was saying. He opened his eyes and stared at the wall of the tent. The painted silhouette of a lamb shivered in the breeze, sleeping peacefully beneath the splayed forepaws of a great bear. "A pox on them," he breathed, "and their ways. Let Úlfnaor deliver that bitch's papers without me. Let *him* dance to beat of her drum. I not go no further."

Wynter and Razi glanced at Hallvor, but her eyes were on Razi, watching as he checked for infection. Razi began to bind the wound again, nodding reassuringly to Hallvor. "Those papers are important, Sólmundr," chanced Razi, glancing at Wynter. "Surely you know this. Surely it matters to you that they get through."

Sólmundr frowned at the little painted lamb. "Nothing matter. Nothing ever mattered except him. Now I useless. Cannot keep even my final promise . . ." He squeezed his eyes shut and covered his face with his hand.

"Well, it did not take him long to replace you," said Wynter with a flash of inspiration. "Christopher has already taken your place at his side. He has accompanied him to the ceremony." She had hoped for jealousy, thought it might spur Sólmundr to anger and jolt him to life, but to her amazement, when Sólmundr whipped back his hand and stared at her, it was hope she saw in his eyes.

"Coinín?" he breathed. "Coinín takes my place?"

Hallvor looked sharply at him. "Sól?" she asked.

"Hally," he said, "*Tógfaidh Coinín m'áitse?*"

Hallvor's eyes welled up and she nodded reluctantly. She murmured something about Ashkr, something that made her hang her head in shame.

Sólmundr laughed. "Oh," he said. He scrubbed at his eyes. His breath hitched. "Oh, they did not tell me! They thought it would to hurt me. Oh, Iseult!" He sat forward suddenly and grabbed Wynter's hand.

"Be *careful*, man!" cried Razi. "You will burst your stitches!"

Sólmundr flopped back against the cushion, dragging Wynter forward as he clutched her hand to his chest, his eyes closed. Then he licked his dry lips and glanced at Hallvor. "*A chroí,*" he whispered. "*Rud éigin le hól.*"

Hallvor's solemn face cracked into a grin and she leapt to her feet. She grabbed Wynter and Razi around their shoulders, squeezing them together with shocking strength. "*Buíochas leat,*" she whispered into Wynter's hair. "*Buíochas, a luichín.*"

Wynter was suddenly reminded of Marni, and the memory of that fierce, gigantic woman brought a momentary lump to her throat. She swallowed down on the unexpected emotion and nodded, patting Hallvor on her sinewy forearm. The dark-haired woman broke away and strode to the door, disappearing for a moment, and returning with a waterskin and three wooden beakers.

Sólmundr accepted the water with obvious thirst, and Hallvor stroked his hair and his strong arms and patted his back as he drank. Eventually he lay back against the cushions, his face weary, hunched slightly with the pain of his wound.

"So," said Razi, eyeing Sólmundr. "I have not wasted my good sutures, my priceless opium and my precious time on a man who is determined to die, then, have I, Sól?"

Sólmundr just smiled in reply. "Coinín will take my place?" he asked. "He will stand by Ashkr?"

Razi glanced at Wynter. "He is in the forest now," she said evasively. "He fulfils your duty as we speak."

Sólmundr shifted carefully in the bed. "I must speak to him," he murmured. "But somehow, I think . . ." He smiled up at the ceiling. "Aye, Coinín is a good man."

"And what of your other duties?" asked Razi. "You will not be fit to travel for at least a fortnight and even then only very slowly. It is vital, surely, that those papers get through? How long do you have before they must be delivered?"

Wynter watched suspicion seep through the drug that was addling Sólmundr's mind. Slowly, his expression hardened as he searched Razi's face. To his credit, Razi didn't turn away and his dark eyes remained steadfastly on Sólmundr's.

"Who are you, Tabiyb?" asked Sólmundr softly. "Why for you ask me this questions about papers?"

"I am your doctor, Sól," answered Razi. "I do not want you getting on a horse and ending up with your guts spilled out across your saddle. Those stitches will not stand up to hard travel. Even if your people were to strap you to a travois I could not—"

"It not your worry," interrupted Sólmundr. "You not speak of it again, *tá go maith?*"

Razi licked his lips and dropped his eyes. Sólmundr glanced at Hallvor who was gesturing innocently to Wynter that she should drink some water. Wynter smiled and accepted, all her attention on the men's low, carefully modulated conversation.

"You know what it is to be blood-eagled, Tabiyb?" asked Sólmundr.

Razi eyelids fluttered at the thought of that terrible torture. He nodded. Wynter stared at Sólmundr. Her throat clicked around the mouthful of water she was trying to swallow. Blood-eagled, good God.

"My people," murmured Sólmundr, "this is what we do with spies, yes? Blood-eagle. I not like see that happen you, Tabiyb." He looked deep into Razi's brown eyes and the light tone of his voice belied the edge of iron in his face. "It not nice way to die," he said.

"I won't mention it again," whispered Razi.

"Good," nodded Sólmundr. "I think that good." There was a moment of uneasy silence, during which Hallvor glanced between the three of them, her dark eyes questioning.

Sólmundr laid his head back against the hide cushion, watching Razi closely. "You play chess, Tabiyb?" he asked. "I suspect you do. I suspect you play very good, yes?" Razi nodded, and Sólmundr's face creased into that charming gap-toothed smile. "But not so good as me, I think," he said. "I think I get Hallvor to fetch my board, yes, Tabiyb? And we play. We play many game together, you and me . . . and your little sister, she stay and watch, yes?"

Sólmundr turned his attention to Wynter. Although he was exhausted, his eyes sliding in and out of focus, she still felt like an insect under glass when he looked at her. "I not think it good idea," he said, "I not think it *safe*, that you two be all alone in this big empty camp. I not like to think that you make mistake. Maybe go in wrong tent, maybe pick up wrong thing. And be accused of spies."

Oh God, thought Wynter, *oh my God.* Razi reached for her hand.

"You not worry, Tabiyb," Sólmundr said. "I keep you out of trouble. Nice and safe, here by my bed. I play with you the chess, till the others come back from forest." He lost his smile for a moment. "Yes, Tabiyb?"

Razi sat rigid and staring, his hand tight on Wynter's. He nodded stiffly. "Yes," he said. "Yes, Sólmundr. Let's play chess."

Seeing

"It is still your move," murmured Razi softly.

Sólmundr rolled his eyes open and licked his lips, peering at the board. They had made less than seven moves in two hours. Still, Sólmundr clung tenaciously to consciousness, shoving his pieces clumsily into place with shaky, sweat-soaked fingers.

Wynter reclined against the furs of Sólmundr's bed, her head supported on a roll of hide, her knees bent to ease the pain in her back. She passed the time watching the painted silhouettes on the tent, and worrying about Christopher. The breeze was quite high, and it snapped and shivered at the hide coverings, making the lodge poles creak.

"You beat me this game, I think," rasped Sólmundr, pushing a rook into place and slumping back against his hide cushion.

Razi grunted and surveyed the board. "Hmm," he said. "And all it took was filling you with opium and removing a portion of your intestines." He hesitated, his hand hovering over the game, then moved his knight and sat back, eyeing Sólmundr with sly amusement. "Your move."

Sólmundr glanced at Razi's face, then frowned suspiciously at the board. It took him a moment, and then he growled and flung up his hand in disgust. "*Cac*," he said. Razi chuckled.

At that moment Hallvor called from outside the tent and the silhouettes of the guardswomen leapt to their feet and rushed off.

Sólmundr curled forward with a grunt, suddenly brisk and dismissive. "Leave now, he gasped sharply, "Ash will need sleep." He reached behind him, groaning with pain at the effort. Razi moved to help, but Sólmundr pushed him away. "No," he said. "Out, out." He pulled a waterskin across his lap and took a little parcel from beside the bed. He began unwrapping it, and Wynter saw that it was a bundle of oat cakes. From outside, the sounds of people talking quietly came drifting across the buffeting air.

"They're back!" cried Wynter, scrambling to her feet.

Razi stood up. Sólmundr glanced at the way he was clutching the hilt of his sword.

"You not worry," he said. "It not danger for your family now." The two men stared at each other. "I swears it, Tabyib." Razi loosened his grip on the sword, pushing it back on his hip. Sólmundr nodded and went back to unwrapping the oat cakes.

"I look after Ash now," he said, laying the food by the side of his bed. "Úlfnaor will take Embla to his *puballmór*." He chuckled at the look this brought to Razi's face. "He and Hallvor take *care* of her," he said reassuringly. Razi reddened and looked away.

Sólmundr grew serious again. He handed Wynter three of the oat cakes. "You mind Coinín now, Iseult," he said.

"What?" said Wynter, gazing at the oat cakes, her eyes wide. Why?" she said, in alarm. "What's wrong with him?"

"He all right in very short time," said Sólmundr, his attention already turning back to his own preparations. "Just need sleep. Let him eat if hungry, and you make sure he drink many water, *tá go maith*?" Sólmundr turned painfully, one hand pressed to his wound, the other turning back the covers on Ashkr's side of the bed. "Out," he grunted. "Now."

Razi spun for the door, his face grim. Long shadows moved against the wall, and before he or Wynter could get out, the flap was dragged back and two men entered the tent. Ashkr was supported limply between them and the men pushed past Razi and Wynter as they helped their lord around to his side of the bed. Sólmundr gazed up at them, questioning them. They eased Ashkr down onto the pallet, pulling off his boots and gently removing his tunic.

Razi and Wynter stood motionless for a moment, frozen by the blond man's condition. Sólmundr was talking softly to him, rubbing his shoulders and his back, anxiously pulling his limp hair from his sweating face, but it wasn't clear whether Ashkr even knew where he was. He was gazing up at the tent walls, his face lax and distressed, his breathing a little too fast.

Razi took in Ashkr's bloodless, clammy skin, the spread of his unfocused pupils, and he growled a curse in Arabic. Sólmundr glared at him. "Out!" he rasped.

Razi ducked under the flap and Wynter followed, the little oat cakes crumbling in her hand. Ashkr's hounds were snuffling about outside the tent. Razi shoved them away with barely a glance. They whined and skipped aside, then went back to sniffing forlornly at the door. Razi and Wynter stood side by side, shading their eyes against the blazing sun, looking around for their friend.

The Merron were milling about, talking softly amongst themselves, and Wynter scanned their ranks for Christopher. Suddenly, she caught sight of his familiar figure through the shifting crowd and she was flooded with relief. He was standing on his own two feet, supporting his own weight, talking to Wari and his woman and the two older musicians from the tavern.

"Razi," she said, gripping his arm. "There he is."

Razi snapped his head around, and Wynter felt him relax as he spotted Christopher. "Good God," he breathed. "I'll kill him. Come on, sis, let us—"

"Tabiyb." Embla's rich voice stopped them in their tracks and they turned to see her break away from Úlfnaor's protective arm and stumble in their direction. The crowd parted respectfully for her, and Úlfnaor and Hallvor followed in her wake, their hands anxiously poised. She came to a swaying halt in front of Razi, her unfocused eyes gravely scanning his face.

"Embla," he said. "What have you done to yourself?" He put his hand to her clammy face. Her eyes were all pupil, the navy irises pushed to the very edge of the blackness, and her skin was shining like wet marble. "Look at you!"

Uncertainly, Embla spread her hands against Razi's chest, and her eyes narrowed. "Tabiyb?"

Razi ran his thumb under Embla's eye and shook his head in disapproval and concern. Wynter flicked a nervous glance at Úlfnaor and Hallvor. They had come up behind the couple, crooning in Merron, laying comforting hands on Embla's shoulders. Gently, Úlfnaor took the tall woman by her elbows and murmured soothingly as he turned her away from Razi. "It all right, Tabiyb," he said kindly. "We take care of her now." Embla went with them placidly enough, but she couldn't take her eyes from Razi, and she continued to strain her neck to keep him in sight as Hallvor and Úlfnaor led her away through the tents.

Wynter took Razi's elbow. "Come on, brother," she whispered. "Let's get Christopher."

Their friend was still standing at the edge of the crowd, chatting. Everything seemed normal, but as they approached, Wynter noticed Wari's *croí-eile* take the big man by the elbow and begin to lead him away. As he turned, Wari stumbled and his woman had to put her hand on his chest to steady him. Wynter felt a little muscle tighten in her jaw. Razi began to push his way forward.

One of the musicians spotted them approaching. She said something, and Christopher turned slowly to look, pushing his hair behind his ear and smiling vaguely.

"What did they give you?" demanded Razi, striding up to the smaller man. "What did they *give* you, Christopher?" He grabbed Christopher's chin, staring into his spreading pupils, and pressed his fingers to his clammy neck.

Wynter came to an anxious halt by their side, clutching Sólmundr's oat cakes to her chest and glowering at the Merron.

"*Tóg go bog é*," said Christopher softly. "*Níl mé ag eitilt . . .*"

"Speak *properly*, Christopher!" snapped Razi. The musicians frowned and stepped forward as one, moving protectively to Christopher's side.

"'S'all right," Christopher pushed them back. "He's just worried." He smiled, pushing them again, and waved them away. "Go on," he said.

The musicians eyed Razi warily. He glared back. The woman handed Wynter a full waterskin, looking into her eyes and clasping Wynter's hands around the neck of it, as if to show Wynter how important it was.

"All right," Wynter nodded, her eyes flicking to Christopher. The woman pointed to Embla's tent. "Yes," snapped Wynter. "Yes. To lie down, I know." The musicians still looked uncertain, but Christopher shooed them away, and they reluctantly left him in the care of his two glaring *coimhthíoch* friends.

"What. Did. They. *Give* you?" demanded Razi again.

"'S'all right, Razi," Christopher licked his lips and looked around vaguely. "I ain't flying, don't worry. I know who I am." He ran a shaking hand over his forehead. "We just held their hands while they flew. Me and Wari, we just held on . . ." He closed his eyes. "Oh . . ." he said. "Very tired."

Suddenly, Razi grabbed him and swivelled him towards the tent, making him gasp and stagger. "Woooo!" said Christopher, fluttering his hands and blinking around him. "Not a good idea!" he warned.

"Razi!" Wynter slapped his hands away from their friend. "Go easy."

Ignoring her, Razi grabbed them both by an arm each and hustled them to the tent. He shoved them inside and dived after them, pulling the flap shut with a *snap*. If it had been a wooden door, Wynter thought that he would have kicked it, he was so enraged.

"What happened, Christopher?" said Wynter, eyeing

Razi, and gently pushing Christopher down onto the bed. The young man was starting to shake now, sweat beading his upper lip and his eyelids, his pale arms slippery. Remembering what Sól had done for Ashkr, Wynter pulled back the covers of their bed. "In," she ordered, pulling off his boots. "Come on, get in. Under the covers."

Christopher crawled into the centre of the bed and curled into a shivering ball. Wynter huddled the covers over him. "Found out . . ." said Christopher. "Merron . . . carrying papers . . . destined for your brother."

Razi crossed quickly to hunker by the edge of the furs, his face questioning.

Christopher grinned at him. "Oh," he laughed, his teeth chattering. "We friends again now?"

"Oh, shush," muttered Razi, "You're a bloody trial to my patience."

"How do you know that they are destined for Albi, love?" Wynter asked gently.

Christopher closed his eyes. "Uh . . ." he said. "Uhhh . . . they, uh, they included him in their bluh . . . bluh . . . blessing. Her too . . ." His voice trailed off into shivering silence.

Wynter grabbed his hands through the blanket. "Chris!" she said in alarm.

"Be over soon," he murmured. "Need sleep."

"Who are the papers from?" asked Razi softly.

Christopher opened his too-black eyes again, staring at them without really seeing. He was almost gone. "Uhh," he said again. "Marguerite . . ." Wynter's hands tightened around his. "Marguerite . . ." he said again urgently, as if afraid they might not have heard him the first time.

"Shirken, Christopher? Marguerite Shirken?"

Christopher nodded. "Aye," he breathed. "Marguerite Shirken. That bloody . . . that bloody . . . witch-hunting bitch." He slipped away, dropping into an unnatural sleep, his lips parting, his eyes rolling back in his head.

Razi pressed his fingers to Christopher's neck. Then he pulled the furs up to the young man's chin and sat back on his heels, his face dazed.

Wynter shook her head. So it was true – the papers *were* destined for Alberon. There could no longer be any doubt in her mind. Marguerite Shirken, daughter and sole heir to King Shirken – the woman whom her father referred to as "that Vile Serpent" – was secretly in communion with the Southlands heir.

"Oh, Razi," she whispered. "What is he *doing*? Our fathers spent the last five years keeping those people out of Southland affairs. Dad gave his health keeping them off Jonathon's back. Between the two of them they sacrificed so much to keep those bloody-handed, evil . . ." She felt herself begin to choke on the words. All the things she had seen up north, all the terrible things, came back to her in a violent burst of sound and smell, and she shut her eyes at the memory of it.

Razi put his hand on her shoulder. Wynter's fists clenched in the furs of the bed and she shook her head again. A terrible sense of betrayal began to burn in her chest. For the first time, for the very first time, Wynter felt herself really begin to *rage* against Alberon. "I'll kill him, Razi," she said. "I'm going to kill him. Everything would be all right if it wasn't for him. Jonathon would not have been pushed to tyranny. You would be safe. Dad . . ."

Razi got abruptly to his feet and stalked to the back of the tent. "I'm going to pack our things," he said. She glanced at him as he hunkered down before their neat piles of tack and saddles and began snapping things into order.

She was just going to help him when shadows moved across the wall. Someone was circling the tent. They came to a halt at the door.

Razi leapt to his feet, his hand on his knife. "Who is there?" he hissed.

"Please, I may to come in?" Ashkr's familiar voice was both a relief and a shock, and they looked at each other in amazement. What was the man doing out of bed? He had been barely conscious the last time they saw him.

Frowning, Razi ducked outside. He let the flap fall back behind him, and his long shadow stretched protectively across the door. "What do you . . .?" he began, then Wynter heard the tone of his voice change utterly as he got a close look at the Merron lord. "Good God!" he said in dismay. "What are you doing on your feet, man? Hallvor? Why have you allowed him out like this?"

Ashkr interrupted him, his voice strained. "Please, Tabiyb, I like come inside. I not have much time before Sól, he wake and catch me gone."

Razi pushed the door flap aside, and Hallvor aided Ashkr across the threshold. Once inside the tent, the tall blond man nodded to the healer and pushed her gently towards the door. She gave him a very concerned look, and then went and crouched outside, waiting.

"I need . . . I need speak to Coinín," gasped Ashkr, stumbling towards the pallet. He came dangerously close to toppling headfirst on top of their sleeping friend, and

Wynter and Razi lurched forward in alarm, helping him to sit on the bed.

"Coinín is sleeping, Ashkr," said Wynter. "He has not slept properly for three nights."

Ashkr looked down at Christopher's twitching face. "He not sleep properly now, *luch bhocht*. Oh . . ." He closed his eyes suddenly and put a shaking hand to his forehead, hunching forward.

Razi laid a hand on his damp arm. "You are icy," he muttered. He flung one of Embla's furs over Ashkr's shoulders, dragging it tight at the man's chin.

Ashkr huddled into the blanket as if it were the depths of winter. "I not stay long," he whispered. "I still sick from the seeing . . . I needs . . ." He blinked as if trying to get his bearings. "Coinín," he said. He leant over Christopher, looking down into his face. "Coinín," called Ashkr softly, his hand hovering over Christopher's shoulder. "It all right. It over."

Christopher moaned, his eyes fluttering rapidly beneath their dewy lids, and his body jerked abruptly under the covers as if he'd been struck.

Razi lifted his hand as if to stop Ashkr. "Be careful," he whispered.

"Coinín," called Ashkr again. Christopher growled long and low in his chest, a frightening, animal sound. Ashkr suddenly dropped his hand to his shoulder and squeezed hard.

"*Wake!*" he said, his voice deep and powerful, and Christopher snapped awake, his eyes wide, his breath stopping in a little grunt.

"Good," crooned Ashkr, releasing Christopher's shoulder immediately. "Good. You come back now. You free."

Christopher's eyes wandered to Ashkr without much comprehension. Then he looked at Wynter. "Iseult," he rasped, "I'm afraid of it."

"Shhhh," she said, gently. His lips were very dry. "Have some water." He drank as though he would never taste water again, leaning up from the bed and gripping the waterskin with frantic desperation. In the end, Wynter had to pull it from him for fear he'd do himself damage. "Enough!" she cried.

To her surprise, when Christopher pulled away, his eyes were focused, though still too black, and his face was attentive. He did not seem at all surprised to see Ashkr sitting beside him on the bed. "Ashkr," he whispered. "It did not go well."

Ashkr compressed his cracked lips and grimaced. "No," he said hoarsely. "No. No . . . it bad. We see only bad things. Bad things in the North, bad things here. Embla, she see blood, she see men dying so fast, one after another like—" He clicked his sweating fingers rapidly, *snap*, *snap*, *snap*, and then hunched into the covers, shivering. "Felled like corn under rain of metal and fire. Úlfnaor, he say it because the People new here. He say, the seeing all mixed up. *An Domhan* not know us yet, he say. When it know us, we be good." Christopher and Ashkr went very quiet at that, looking away from one another, their faces tense.

"Will *An Domhan* know you after you have declared Frith, Ashkr?" ventured Wynter. "Is that what the ceremony is about?" She wanted Ashkr to say yes. She wanted the ceremony of Frith, which Christopher seemed to love so much, to be the only thing necessary. But she knew, somewhere inside her, that there was much more to what Ashkr meant.

Ashkr, his face tender, didn't answer. Instead, he reached across and stroked her cheek with his cold, wet fingers. His eyes slid to Razi, and Christopher spoke sharply, drawing his attention away.

"Your people will never be accepted here, Ashkr," he said. "This is all in vain."

Wynter exchanged a grim frown with Razi. There was so much untold here. It was maddening.

"Go *home*, Ash," continued Christopher. "Tell your people to go *home*. There is no place here for the old ways, and no matter what you give to *An Domhan*, nothing is going to change that fact." He reached and grabbed Ashkr's hand, staring into the man's troubled face. "Ashkr, *please*," he said. "Please take Sólmundr and Embla and go home. Please!"

"But there no place for us there either, Coinín," whispered Ashkr. "Shirken, he push us away and away. He take our Aoirí, he put them to the rack. He destroy our hunting grounds. What are we to do?"

"*Adapt*," said Christopher, his grey eyes wide and urgent. "It's the only way! This world will not always stay the same just to suit you. You must adapt!"

Ashkr chuckled sadly, as if Christopher had made a joke. "Like the Serpent tribe?" he said. "Like the Hawk? That not really work for them, now, has it? Anyway, I not the right person to ask that of, *lucha*. All my life been leading to here, it not in my power to change what *An Domhan* want."

Christopher groaned and turned his head away, but Wynter noticed that he didn't release Ashkr's hand. The two men remained heavily silent for a moment, each deep in thought. Then Ashkr squinted and shook his head, as if clearing his thoughts. "Oh yes," he whispered, "Sól." He shook Christopher's hand. "Coinín, Sól . . ."

Christopher tugged his hand away, his eyes averted. Ashkr smiled humourlessly, "You still think I cruel. You disapprove that I let him love me."

Christopher didn't answer, and Ashkr released a bitter little laugh. He pulled the furs around himself and closed his eyes. "You not know love then," he muttered, "if you think it should to be denied for fear of when it might end."

Ashkr hunched into himself miserably, shivering, and Razi laid a hand on his shoulder. "You should be abed, Ashkr."

The blond man cracked a bloodshot eye at him. "Aye, in moment." He turned to Christopher again and pucked him. "Coinín, your friends tell Sól that you take his place for him. He think you stay."

Christopher's eyes widened. "What?" he cried, pushing unsteadily to his elbows. "What? Are you out of your minds? That poor man! Good Frith! Razi! How could you be so cruel?"

Wynter and Razi drew back in guilt and confusion. Razi hunched his shoulders. "I . . ." he said.

"It good," said Ashkr. "I *want* that you not tell him truth. Sól, he drinks, and he eats a little, and now he sleeps. This good. I want he not stop doing these things. I want you not tell him you leave."

Christopher covered his eyes and lay back down on the bed. "You're cruel." He shook his head. "You're just bloody cruel."

"Today," said Ashkr, laying his trembling fingers against Christopher's chest. "Sól, he will ask you many thing. He will tell you all the thing he wants you to do when . . ." He glanced at Razi and Wynter. "When you . . ."

"I know what you *mean*," snapped Christopher, his hand still over his eyes.

"You agree, Coinín." Ashkr tapped Christopher's chest firmly. Christopher uncovered his face and glared at him. But Ashkr was gazing down at him, his eyes full, and Christopher's expression softened at the desperation in the man's face. "You agree to all that Sól ask? Please? You make him think it all right? Even for just today? Please, Coinín, to you I am begging. Make him this gift, just for today?"

Wynter couldn't help but be moved. She had no idea what it was they were planning to deceive Sólmundr about, but she found herself willing Christopher to agree. Without a word, Christopher jerked his head in consent, and Ashkr took a deep, shuddering breath and pressed his hand to his eyes in relief. "Good," he said softly. "Good." He seemed spent suddenly, all his tenacious energy gone, and he sagged.

"Ashkr," murmured Razi, "will I help you back to your tent?"

Ashkr shook his head, "Hally, she help me." The tent brightened as Razi lifted the door and then flickered with shadows as Hallvor stooped inside and rushed to crouch by Ashkr's knee.

Before he was helped to his feet, the Merron lord laid his hand on Christopher's chest again. Christopher's hands leapt and his mouth tightened in protest, but he said nothing. Ashkr was panting once more, his eyes no more than slits in his pasty face. "Thank you, *lucha*," he said. Then he pressed down hard on Christopher's chest, and his voice became strong for a moment, deeply commanding. "*Sleep*," he said.

To Wynter's astonishment, Christopher went abruptly limp. His eyes slipped closed, his hands relaxed and he tumbled into a deep and mercifully untroubled sleep. "Good," murmured Ashkr, tracing Christopher's face with his finger. "Good."

Hallvor and Razi helped Ashkr to his feet. At the door, Ashkr turned back, his face blotted into darkness, his long hair shivering around him like summer gold. Hallvor supported him, a slim black shape by his side. It was impossible to tell what expression was on their faces.

"I see you at dinner," whispered Ashkr. "Do not forget . . ."

Then Hallvor led him away, and Razi grimly dragged the door across.

Promises Made

"Did I miss aught?"

At Christopher's soft question, Wynter discarded the piece of tack that she was oiling and scurried forward to look in through the door. It took a moment for her eyes to adjust after the sunshine outside, then she peered across the tent at her friend, and he gave her a small, affectionate smile.

"How do, girly," he said.

Wynter sagged with relief. Christopher had pushed back his covers and was sitting on the edge of their pallet, his arms resting loosely across his bent knees. Though his eyes were still strained and pouchy, and his face still drawn, he looked a hundred times younger than he had before.

"You've missed nothing," she said, smiling, "except the Merron's shameless poaching of fish from the King's river, and their continued gathering of unlicensed timber from the King's forest."

Christopher's eyes sparkled. "Bloody Merron," he whispered.

"They are incorrigibly dubious," she agreed, delighted at

his amusement. It seemed as though the scant two hours of drug-induced sleep had refreshed him greatly.

"Where's that stubborn brown bollix we're lumbered with?"

"I am right here," grumbled Razi. "Waiting for my sister to shift her considerable bulk and grant me access to your company." He nudged Wynter with his foot and, without bothering to stand up, she crawled through the door, grinning.

"You look much better," she said, kneeling by Christopher's side.

His dimples flashed. "I hadn't thought it possible to improve on perfection," he smirked, "but I'll take your word for it."

"Let me see you," said Razi gruffly, and he grabbed Christopher's jaw, tilting his head to the light, leaning in close to look into his eyes.

"Stop that!" said Christopher, jerking his head away.

Razi tsked impatiently, and he pulled Christopher forward again, checking his pupils. "Just hold still!"

Christopher slapped his hands away and pushed him violently backwards. "You *stop* that!" he snarled, raising his foot as if to kick out. "Stop *pawing* me! Get *off*!"

Razi pulled back, his hands up. "Christopher," he said, carefully, keeping his distance, his eyes scanning Christopher's face. "You were a God-cursed *mess* when those people brought you back. Your heart. Your *temperature*." He shook his head, his face furious. "And *Ashkr*? The man was practically in *shock*, Christopher! I *cannot* permit that to happen again!" He sliced his hand downwards in imperious command. "I am serious! Whatever it

is you people think you are doing to yourselves, I
cannot—"

"No!" cried Christopher. "You back *off* now, Razi. I
mean it. It ain't none of your concern. Nothing these
people do is any of your concern; you need to stay out of
it." Razi scowled blackly, and for one scalding moment the
two men glared at each other. Then Christopher glanced at
Wynter and to her enormous relief, he winked.

"No bloody manners," he whispered.

"He is very poorly bred," she agreed gently. "Ran terribly wild as a youth."

Razi clamped his teeth against what was most likely a
profanity and turned away, still angry.

"Don't fret, Razi," whispered Christopher. "We're all
right. Embla's all right. The seeing just knocks the feathers
from us for a while, that's all."

Razi sat on the edge of Embla's bed, still looking away.
"So," he said. "We are to leave tomorrow, Christopher?
That is still what you want? I am to lead you and Wynter
out into the wilds. On our own."

Christopher gazed at him for a moment, his grey eyes
solemn. "Oh aye, Raz," he said. "More than ever I'm convinced we've got to get you out of here." Wynter frowned in
alarm at that and Razi looked sharply at their friend. "But
I've been thinking," said Christopher. "You're right, the
Merron *are* your best chance of finding your brother. It's
madness to think that an opportunity like this would ever
come our way again."

"There's no point *telling* me that, Christopher!" cried
Razi. "Their knowledge is useless to me unless we *stay*!"

"In two days' time," continued Christopher. "When

their business here is completed, Úlfnaor and his party will leave and commence their journey to your brother. Here is what I suggest: I suggest that you, me and our girl kiss the Merron goodbye tomorrow and set off on our merry way. We travel, oh . . . half a day, maybe. And we camp out for the duration of . . . of their business. We stay well away. Keep you out of things entirely. Then when they're finished, we come back and we watch from the cover of the woods. Wait for Úlfnaor to take to the trail and . . ." he stopped uncertainly, spreading his scarred hands and looking down. "We follow him," he finished weakly.

Wynter and Razi sat silently for a few minutes.

"Christopher," said Wynter gently. She touched his arm, but he kept his eyes down, focusing on the dirt floor between his bare feet. "You want us to pretend to leave, only to return later and spy on the Merron?" Christopher nodded, his face tight, his cheeks and the tips of his ears pink. Wynter glanced at Razi. "Christopher," she continued. "Sólmundr *told* us what they do to spies. He *warned* Razi. And those dogs . . . if we attempt to hide ourselves nearby, those dogs will sniff us out, they will find us in no time." She ran her hand up and down the top of Christopher's arm. "Would it not be better to stay?" she murmured persuasively. "Could you not try and build on the relationship we already have with them? Perhaps try and convince Úlfnaor that we should go with them? Surely that would be better? Surely that would be *safer* than turning ourselves into spies?"

Christopher looked at her from the corner of his eyes. "We are spies, lass," he said, grabbing her hand and squeezing it. "We're already spies. The only reason we were permitted here at all is because Ashkr wanted Sólmundr to survive, and because Embla has taken a heat for Razi. Úlfnaor would never have brought you here if he were free to choose. He's too noble a man. But the Caoirigh . . ." Christopher huffed bitterly. "The Caoirigh wanted Razi, and what the Caoirigh *want*, the Caoirigh *get*." There was a moment of tense silence as Christopher glared into the corner. "But they never intended for us to go on with them," he said softly. "And now they know you don't support the old ways, well, they would have driven you out tomorrow anyway. Good omen or not, they would never risk you staying for the . . ." he trailed off. Then his grey eyes narrowed as something occurred to him. He glanced at Razi. "What did you say to Sólmundr to get him talking about spies?"

Razi's colour deepened. "I tried to take advantage of his confusion to garner some information about those papers."

Christopher's mouth quirked in amusement. "Oh, aye?" he said. "I bet you got a shock, eh? Bet that warm smile of his dropped a fair measure below freezing when he caught you out."

"Sólmundr said they would blood-eagle him," whispered Wynter. "If they suspected that Razi was a spy, the Merron would blood-eagle him."

Christopher nodded. "I don't doubt it," he said quietly. "Do you know what Sólmundr is, Razi . . . No? That man ain't just Ashkr's *croí-eile*. He is what these kind of people used to call *Fear Fada*. He is a holy warrior, trained from childhood. His sole purpose in life is to keep the Caoirigh safe. If Sólmundr had thought that you meant Ashkr or Embla any harm, he would have slit you from breastbone to groin – both of you – and had you pegged out for the crows to eat your hearts. You're lucky, Razi, you and our girl, you're lucky that Sólmundr is an intelligent man, and not some mindless zealot like most of the *Fadaí*. Otherwise they'd have blood-eagled us long ago and we'd already have had our ribcages cracked, and be wearing our lungs as wings."

"Oh, Christopher," moaned Wynter. "Please don't."

There was a long, tense silence.

"What do you think of my plan?" asked Christopher eventually, staring at Razi.

To Wynter's immense surprise, Razi glanced at her, wordlessly asking her opinion. "I worry about those dogs," she said. "But still, I think it is the best that we can hope for under the circumstances. don't you?"

Razi nodded. "Aye," he said. "I agree. Chris, we leave in the morning, as you have advised. And we will return, as you suggest, in two days. We shall see then where our luck takes us."

Wynter felt Christopher sag with relief. "Oh, thank Frith," he whispered. Sighing, he kissed Wynter's hand and tucked it affectionately under his chin.

Razi looked from their clasped hands to his friend's face. He took a deep breath.

"There are other things we must discuss," he said softly.

Wynter looked at him. Comprehension dawned. "The Wolves?" she said. "Yes, they are still a threat."

Razi glanced at her, then met Christopher's eye again. There was a lot of meaning in that look, and Wynter frowned. "What?" she said.

Christopher pressed his chin down onto Wynter's hand,

clutching her fingers against the soft warm flesh of his throat, as if afraid she'd draw away. He did not take his eyes from Razi's. "Tonight," he said. "My people declare Frith. I want to enjoy it, Razi. I want to dance it with a clean heart. Everything else . . ." Christopher blew sharply into his free hand and fluttered his fingers up into the air as if casting a handful of ash to the wind. He stared at Razi. "I want it forgotten, Razi. That's all. I just want it forgotten."

Razi's dark eyes filled with doubt, and his mouth twisted. "Christopher," he began, his eyes slipping to Wynter.

"Let . . ." interrupted Christopher quickly, holding his hand up. "Let me tell you what the dances mean, shall I? So you can understand a little of what you will see tonight?"

"I think that would be lovely, Christopher," said Wynter, tearing her eyes from Razi and turning to their friend. "I should like that very much!"

Christopher smiled at her. "Would you?" he said. "Will I show you now?"

She nodded and Razi sat back, his face stiff with uncertainty.

"I will show you as much as I can before they come to get us for dinner," said Christopher, limping to the centre of the floor space "You won't have to remember the steps or aught; you won't be expected to dance."

Wynter leant in to Razi. "We can deal with the Wolves, brother," she said softly. "There is no need to make him discuss it."

Razi just frowned, and silently turned his attention to their friend as he began the slow movement of the Merron dance, explaining each gesture as he did.

*

To Wynter's surprise, dinner was not a private affair. When they got to Ashkr's tent, the front of the *puballmór* had been opened outwards and suspended on poles, so that the occupants of the interior could be included in the activities outside. The entire company of Merron was ranged about outside the tent, sitting on mats and blankets, sharing many small cook-fires and chatting. Embla, Úlfnaor, Ashkr and Sólmundr were inside the tent.

Razi came to a halt in front of the awning and bowed. He addressed himself solely to Úlfnaor, and Wynter saw subtle approval brighten the faces of the lords' party. "I regret we come without gifts to such generous company," said Razi formally. "It shames me that I cannot add to your bounty."

Úlfnaor nodded a gracious forgiveness.

Embla, who had been watching Razi as he crossed the camp, rose to her feet with a smile. "Your company is generosity enough, Tabiyb," she said. "It warm us more than any gift."

Ashkr, lounging on the floor by Sólmundr's side of the bed, his attention on a half-played game of chess, clucked like a broody hen and Embla tossed her hair back with tolerant forbearance.

"Forgive my brother," she said with feline composure. "His brains are in his trousers."

Ashkr chuckled and lifted his eyes to smile at the guests. Sólmundr, lying on his side under the furs, one arm cushioning his head, the other draped across Ashkr's lap, laughed quietly.

Úlfnaor shook his head in paternal disapproval at the lords' childish behaviour. He rose to his feet, a small bowl in his hand, and gestured to Christopher and Wynter that they could take his place by Embla's side. They bowed in thanks, and the Aoire edged around them, moving to crouch by the fire with Wari and Hallvor.

To Wynter's immense surprise, the big shepherd began shaping little patties of dough from the bowl in his hand and laying them on the flat irons. He was making griddle cakes! The great and haughty Aoire was making griddle cakes! Wynter shook her head in disbelief. These Merron were incredible. She could not fathom them at all.

At the warm, sweet perfume of freshly baking chestnut dough, Christopher paused on the threshold. He stood looking down at the Aoire, his face wistful.

"*Scòn*," he said softly.

Úlfnaor smiled. "This not be long now. Then we eat."

Christopher went and crouched by the fire, watching the cooking, and Wynter drifted to stand behind him, enjoying the aroma of roasted fish and fowl.

Úlfnaor's dogs lay obediently on the periphery of the fire, following every move of the cook's hands. The rest of the warhounds were within the tent, sprawled casually around their masters, their big brown eyes silently assessing the new arrivals. Sólmundr actually had one of the creatures on the bed beside him, its huge head resting on his hip.

"Tabiyb," Embla extended her hand to Razi, inviting him to her side.

He glanced at Wynter and Christopher. Wynter grinned teasingly at him, while Christopher kept his attention on the cooking Razi hesitated, then he abruptly ducked his head and entered the tent. Embla took Razi's face between her hands and kissed him on the mouth. He shamelessly pressed himself to her kiss, his hand drifting to her hip. They remained locked deeply together for an embarrassing length of time, and pulled away only when Ashkr tutted loudly. Razi broke into a blushing grin. The pale lady licked her lips, grinned in return and pulled her pirate down to sit beside her on her little pallet of rugs. She leant comfortably against him, and he slipped his arm around her waist.

"Who is winning?" he murmured, his eyes on the chess-board.

"I am," she said smugly. "Ashkr hope you distract me. He hope I, too, think only with my trousers!"

Ashkr rolled his eyes, and smoothly made what looked to be a very damaging move. Razi and Embla frowned and leant forward as one, their faces identically absorbed. Sólmundr snorted with mirth, and the dog at his hip opened its eyes briefly and sighed.

"Coinín?" Christopher tore his gaze from Razi. Úlfnaor was holding out a freshly baked cake, his eyes kind. "You look hungry," he said softly.

Christopher took the little cake with a polite smile. He gasped and immediately began tossing it from hand to hand, blowing on his fingers. Wynter laughed, thinking he was being dramatic. Úlfnaor glanced at her. "And you?" he held up another. Wynter took it, squeaked and dupli-cated Christopher's desperate juggling act. The cake was, indeed, much too hot to hold. Úlfnaor must have fingers like stone. The Merron chuckled. Úlfnaor grinned.

"You are wicked!" laughed Wynter, and took a bite. "*Jesu!*" she said, amazed at the smoky deliciousness. "But that is *wonderful*!"

Christopher broke his cake in two, releasing a cloud of

sweet steam. He inhaled deeply, closing his eyes. "Mmmmm," he said.

"Good?" asked Úlfnaor. Christopher nodded, gazing at the cake.

"Coinín." At Sólmundr's soft voice, Wynter felt Christopher tense. He glanced reluctantly into the tent and Sólmundr smiled at him. "Come sit by me?" he invited warmly. "Talk for while? You and me?"

Ashkr briefly lifted his eyes to Christopher, then turned his attention back to the chessboard. Embla kept her gaze fixed on the game, her hands clenched in her lap. Razi frowned unhappily and his eyes slid away.

Christopher looked down for a moment, his face blank. Then he carefully laid his uneaten *scòn* on the fire stones and got to his feet. "It would be my pleasure," he said.

As Christopher ducked into the tent, Sólmundr shifted painfully, trying to push the hound from his hip, and hoisted himself up against the stuffed deer hide at his back. Ashkr and Razi leapt to aid him.

"*Amach leat, Boro!*" said Ashkr, pushing the unwilling hound from the bed. It ducked its shaggy head in a futile attempt to make itself invisible, and wormed its way back to Sólmundr's side.

Sólmundr chuckled breathlessly and scrubbed between the dog's sharp ears The dog butted its head up into his caress, licking his toughened fingers and scarred wrists. "Stupid fellow," murmured Sólmundr. "I can tie him, if you want?" He waved his hand, indicating a pair of posts that were embedded in the ground behind the bed. Wynter had assumed they acted as a support for the cushions, but now she saw that there was a hoop-and-pin at the top of each where the hound's chain could be secured.

Christopher shook his head. "I ain't scared of him," he said.

Carefully, Sólmundr manoeuvred himself to face away from the others. He settled heavily into the deer hide cushion and patted the blankets. Christopher crawled across the bed and sat down beside him. The warhound placed one massive paw on Christopher's lap, and, with a gusty sigh, laid its head back against Sólmundr's stomach. "What do you want to talk to me about?" said Christopher quietly. Sólmundr leaned in, and their soft conversation was lost to hearing as Ashkr suddenly disputed a move and Embla took noisy exception.

"Úlfnaor," said Wynter quietly, watching as the Merron finished their cooking. "I have no desire to cause offence . . ." she let her voice trail off, waiting for Úlfnaor to give his consent for her to continue. At court, this sentence was a signal that you were offering what might be unwanted advice or information. Everything hinged on the response. If the reply was "*Then do nothing to offend*" you had been told that your advice was not wanted. If the reply was along the lines of, "*Good intentions are never an insult*", then you had been given an invitation to proceed. Wynter crouched uncertainly by the fire and squinted through the smoke.s

"I not offended, *lucha*," assured Úlfnaor. "You good."

Wynter hesitated, knowing that he hadn't understood. Razi was, as usual, paying attention to everything, and without looking up from the chessboard, he said, "My sister would like to discuss something, Úlfnaor. But she does not wish to cause offence in the asking."

Úlfnaor smiled in wry amusement. "You ask me what you need, *lucha*. I promise, I not set my dogs on you."

"This food you have trapped and caught?" Wynter waved her hand at the meal. Úlfnaor looked at her, suddenly alert. "And this wood that you have gathered to cook it on? It is not legal. If the cavalry came upon you they would—"

"We need licence?" he asked softly, his face sad.

Wynter nodded.

"Even here?" he asked, waving at the deeply forested land around them.

Wynter nodded again. Úlfnaor sat back. He looked around the camp, his dark eyes resigned. "Even here," he said.

"Úlfnaor," asked Wynter. "Has it got very bad? Up North? Have things got worse?" He nodded, and she shook her head in despair. "But when I left, about four or five months ago, Shirken had . . . well, things had settled down quite a bit. There had been talk of a treaty for your people, and of rights of way, licences to hunt and gather in perpetuity . . ."

The Aoire snorted. "Yes," he said. "There had been *talk*."

"But had a treaty not been signed?"

"When the Red Hawk left, all that withered away," said Úlfnaor. "Shirken, his hatred, it come back to his heart again and he rage once more against his own. Then his hatred, it begin again to hiss, hiss, hiss against the People." The big man shook his head. "The Red Hawk," he said wistfully. "My people say he excellent good man. But he called away too soon, and now . . ." he spread his hands, his many rings flashing. "All good things fall away before they are ready. And my people, they suffer."

The Red Hawk. The Protector Lord Lorcan Moorehawke. Wynter had almost forgotten this Northlands nickname, given to her father due to his mass of dark red hair. She lowered her head at this unexpected mention of him, her eyes suddenly and uncontrollably full. Lorcan. He had worked so hard, he had given so much, and most of the good he'd done seemed to have already slipped away, as temporary as a barricade of snow. Could good never prevail? Was it always to be just that? A barricade of snow? Wynter swiped furiously at her eyes and looked off into the camp.

"It all right, little mouse," Úlfnaor's voice was gentle, his large hand patted her shoulder. "We see what we can do here, eh? If maybe the place that send us the Red Hawk will open its arms to the People? We see how our luck goes, once *An Domhan* knows we here."

He shook her knee to get her to look at him and his eyes narrowed with concern. "What they do here?" he asked. "If you not have licence for hunt and gather? What the soldiers do to us if they come?"

Wynter sniffed and wiped her face. "For places like this," she gestured toward the deep woods. "Where there are no guild bonds. Well, usually there is a fine. You understand? Money? And, of course, they make you buy one – a licence, that is."

Úlfnaor was squinting at her, as if trying to figure out a hidden meaning to her words. "They just ask for *money*?" he said.

Wynter nodded.

"Then they *gives* you licence?" he asked, carefully scanning her eyes to make sure.

Wynter nodded again. To her surprise Úlfnaor's pale face broke into a disbelieving grin. He waited, as though expecting a punchline, then he squeezed her knee and bent double, thoroughly overcome with laughter.

Wynter glanced around the tent in confusion. Ashkr and Embla were equally tickled; Ashkr, his face bright with good humour, chuckled, and Embla laughed through splayed fingers. her eyes sparkling. The non-Hadrish speakers were looking between Wynter and their Aoire, grinning in bemusement as the black-haired man's laughter continued. Only Sólmundr and Christopher, focused entirely on their own conversation, did not look up. Wynter glanced their way, just in time to see Sólmundr swipe discreetly at his eyes. With a start, Wynter realised that both men were crying.

"Oh, mouse!" cried Úlfnaor, slapping her knee, and gasping for breath. "Oh, there nothing more better than good laugh!"

A Gentle Night

"We lift our arms." Christopher slowly rose from a crouch, lifting his bent arms out from his body. He leaned to the side and shuffled in a rhythmic circle, sweeping his arms up like the spreading wings of a hawk. "This shows how we fly above hatred, and soar above our petty differences like a bird, circling high."

Úlfnaor crooned low in his throat, his deep voice the throbbing heartbeat of the Merron song. His people hummed, their harmonies drifting in and around Úlfnaor's voice. There were no words, only sound, and the *shuffle, shuffle, stamp* of the Merron's stately dancing. Slowly, the Merron spread their arms and tilted their bodies. They had become circling hawks, moving slowly around the ceremonial fire.

"We push our hands out." Christopher brought his hands to his shoulders, palms outwards, and pushed, spiralling downwards as he did, until his arms were outstretched before him, his knees bent. He stamped, his head down, and paused for a silent beat before rising. His arms drifted elegantly behind him. "*To show that we reject conflict, past and future. It has no part of us here.*"

The Merron stamped as one, and paused, pale dust rising from their soft boots. The firelight shone through their curtains of hair and illuminated the bracelets on their out-stretched arms. There was a moment of suspension, then they rose upwards in perfect unity, their arms drifting behind them.

Through the flames, Wynter watched Christopher, his dark hair swinging as he spun in place. He stepped to the side and turned away from the fire, his arms coming upwards, his face lifting to the sky in the gesture that symbolised the greeting of the dawn of friendship. He had his back to her, so she could not see his face, only the outline of his slim body, so slight next to his lofty companions.

"You like our dance, Iseult?"

Wynter turned and smiled into Embla's face. The lady had leant forward to murmur in her ear, and even this close she was beautiful. She smiled at Wynter affectionately, kindness radiating from her.

"I like it very much, Embla. I think it is very beautiful."

They were seated on the edge of the activities. Embla, Razi and Ashkr sitting on a freshly sawn log; Wynter and Sólmundr comfortably nestled in heaps of furs at their feet, their backs against the log. The six warhounds were ranged placidly about them, snoring. Boro, as ever, lay by Sólmundr's side, his great head in the wiry man's lap. Dusk had gathered rapidly and the fire was just beginning to blind them to the surrounding forest. If Wynter looked overhead and let her eyes adjust, the sky was a navy bowl, brightly encrusted with stars.

Razi, his eyes on the dancing, absently ran his hand up the arch of Embla's back and rubbed her shoulders. Embla had her arm looped across his knee, her soft white hand casually stroking the inside of his thigh.

"You know what these mean?" she asked Wynter. "These steps?"

Wynter nodded. "Christopher told us," she said. "He seems to love this ceremony very much."

"So he should," said Embla wistfully. "It means so much good things. It is . . . it is *gentle*? Is that correct? Gentle?"

Wynter nodded. *Gentle*, yes, an excellent word.

"You do not dance this ceremony of Frith, Embla? You and Ashkr and Sólmundr?"

Embla smiled. "No," she said. "We do not. Sól would, if he in health, but me and Ash? No. Me and Ash, we outside of Frith." The fire flickered in her eyes, and for a moment Embla's face was solemn.

Wynter glanced at Sólmundr, propped against the other end of the log. Ashkr had leaned forward, his arms clasped around his friend's shoulders, his chin resting on the top of Sólmundr's head, and the two men were watching the dancing with what could only be described as sorrow.

Ashkr murmured something in Merron, and Razi glanced at him. "Pardon?" he said softly.

"Coinín, he cry as he dance."

Both Razi and Wynter glanced sharply across the flames, looking for their friend. Sólmundr reached up and took Ashkr's hand.

"Úlfnaor too," he said.

Wynter snapped her attention to the Aoire. Sure enough, the big man's face caught the light as he spun, and bright tracks of firelight reflected from his cheeks and sparkled in his eyes.

"Poor Úlfnaor," murmured Embla. "He not think this time ever come."

"He not able to face it, I think," said Sólmundr, tightening his grip on Ashkr's hand.

"I not think it ever come either," said Ashkr. "I—" he bit his lip, cutting himself short. He looked across at Embla, turning his cheek to rest against Sólmundr's wavy hair. "You think it ever come, Embla? You ready?"

Embla turned to face her brother, and her bright hair swung forward, blotting her expression from Wynter's sight. "I always know it," she said. "I never lose sight."

Ashkr lowered his eyes. Then he turned to look out at the dancers again, his chin resting on Sólmundr's head. Sólmundr brought his friend's fingers to his lips and kissed them. "You not worry," he said softly.

Suddenly Embla turned away from the dance and buried her face in Razi's neck, pulling his arms tightly around her again. Razi held her close, his dark hand moving to caress the back of her head. His eyes met Wynter's for a moment, and they stared at each other, alarmed. The dancers revolved, their gentle song rising above the crack and hiss of the fire, dust lifting from their rhythmically tramping feet. At their head, Úlfnaor spun, raising his arms high above his head, his face alive with tears, the fire burning in his eyes.

The ceremonial dance ended with a long, suspended silence, then a single upwards clap of the dancers' hands.

There was a ripple of laughter, hair was pushed back, grins were exchanged and, as seemed to be their way, the Merron dissolved into immediate, happy informality. The musicians rushed to grab their instruments and suddenly the gathering was a party. People began swinging each other around in exuberant sets, dancing for the sheer fun of it. Suspicious-looking waterskins began to pass from hand to hand.

Embla leapt from Razi's embrace and pulled him up by his hands "We will dance now, Tabiyb! Show me how high you can leap."

Razi, dazed at her sudden change of mood, allowed himself to be dragged into the heaving crowd and they whirled away into the sets. Wynter leaned forward, looking for Christopher. Where had he got to?

Embla and Razi came spinning around from behind the fire. Wynter saw that Razi, even as he swung his lady round and round, was searching the shadows, anxiously looking for Christopher. Then Razi's face brightened, and he grinned and lifted his chin in greeting. His eyes were fixed on a point just over Wynter's head and she relaxed, smiling. Sure enough, within moments, a pair of hard, slim arms slipped around her shoulders and that lilting Northland accent murmured in her ear.

"How do, girly? Did you like our dance?"

Christopher sat down on the log and pulled her in so that she was sitting between the warm sprawl of his legs. She leaned her head back against his chest, his arms closed around her and she was at once safe and protected, surrounded in the warm, spicy scent that was uniquely his.

"I loved it," she said. "It was very beautiful." She tilted her head so that she was smiling up at him and he pulled back slightly to gaze down into her face.

"I'm glad," he whispered.

"Ashkr said something odd while we were watching the dance," she said. "He said that Úlfnaor never really believed this day would come. Embla said she had always known it would, but Ashkr said he had never really believed it either. They all seemed so sad, Christopher, and Úlfnaor was actually . . ." she hesitated for a moment, not wanting to shame Christopher by letting him know she'd seen them both crying. "Úlfnaor," she said, "seemed very upset when he was dancing."

Christopher lowered his chin, looking out at the dancers. The fire leapt and flared in his pupils, the shadows of the dancers flickering across his face. He said nothing.

Wynter felt a question rise in her throat and lodge there, like a dark stone. She spat it out before she lost her nerve. "Why are Embla and Ashkr outside of Frith, Christopher? Why are they not included in that lovely dance?"

Christopher's grey eyes followed Razi and Embla as they, once again, crossed in front of them. Razi was smiling as they spun, and Embla's hair fanned out behind her, her face illuminated with joy. "They just ain't," he said.

Wynter frowned and pulled away, turning to see him better. "Christopher Garron," she said flatly. "You are asking us to risk our lives leaving here. At least *try* to explain why."

Christopher glanced down at her. His dark eyebrows drew together in distress. He shuddered. "I *can't* explain, lass, it's too complicated. I need you to trust me, that's all.

I need you to trust me when I say there ain't nothing I can do but get Razi away from Embla." He tilted his head unhappily, his eyes bright. "Please, lass," he begged. "Please. I need you to trust me."

Wynter held his eyes for a moment, but she could not stay angry with him. His distress was too deep. The conflict within him too obvious. She put her hand on his cheek. "I trust you, Chris," she said softly. She rested her forehead against his shoulder, running her hand gently up and down his arm. Christopher settled his smooth cheek against hers. She felt the butterfly touch of his eyelashes on her cheekbone as he blinked, and she slipped her arm around his waist.

"I trust you," she whispered.

Christopher pulled back a little to see her face, and Wynter turned her head against his arm. Slowly, she closed her fingers around the twisted band of wool that Christopher still wore on his wrist. "Would you like to go back to the tent?"

They gathered their weapons from behind their seat and walked, hand in hand, through the trees and down into the dusky shapes of the Merron tents. The party was a good way behind them now, a bright, noisy background to the gathering darkness. They passed Ashkr's *puballmór*, dark and silent, its walls closed up.

Tomorrow felt years away and, right now, Wynter felt no fear of any kind. She was not nervous of the dark, nor of Christopher, nor of the comfort that they intended to give each other. Everything about this moment felt good, everything felt right. Up above them the sky was a bright, moonless expanse of stars, so deep and thick that she could have reached up and run her fingers through their glittering multitudes. She walked with Christopher's hand clasped lightly in her own, her head dropped back, and watched the sky, utterly entranced.

Christopher, equally enchanted it seemed, walked slower and slower until he was lagging behind, his arm extended as if she were pulling him unwillingly along. At their tent, Wynter turned to him, smiling, expecting to find him looking up at the stars. But he was staring at her, his eyes dark with unhappiness, his face tense.

"Wynter . . ." he said. *Wynter*, not *Iseult*, and she knew at once that he was looking for a way to break free.

Wynter felt her eyes fill with tears and all her calm certainty tumbled down around her, her happiness draining away. She pressed her lips into a tight line and waited for Christopher to extract his fingers from her grip.

"Wynter," he whispered again. He made no move to pull away, but Wynter saw unmistakable desperation in his face. His eyes slid from hers and his breath quickened, like someone in the grip of a rising panic.

Deliberately, and with firm resolve, Wynter released his fingers. Christopher staggered backwards a step, as though her grip had been the only thing holding him up, and he pushed his shaking hand through his hair, looking around him like a hunted fox. "I . . . I just realised that I am not tired," he whispered. "We . . . perhaps we . . ."

"It is all right, Christopher," she said, trying to keep the hurt from her voice, trying very hard not to quaver. "I understand." She dug her fingers under the stupid twist of wool at her wrist and pulled hard. "I am not a child," she said, sounding calmer than she felt. "I am not cruel enough to try and hold you to what was nothing more than a moment of kindness on your part." She tugged at the stubborn wool. "I've been unbearably foolish. I only hope that—"

Christopher slammed into her, almost knocking her from her feet. His arms clenched around her and she was reminded of just how strong he really was. He clutched her violently to him and she was filled with fear as her breath was crushed from her. "No," moaned Christopher. "No. No."

"Christopher!" she choked, staggering backwards a little under the force of his weight. "Chris!"

Wynter flexed her own not inconsiderable muscles, and loosened Christopher's grip enough to get some air, freeing her arms from their prison against his chest. He continued to cling to her and to moan into her neck. *No. No.*

"Christopher," she whispered, stunned. She lifted her hands. Uncertainly, then gently laid them against his back. He shook his head. "Christopher," she whispered again. "What's wrong?"

He shook his head, burrowing his face against her, his arms tightening.

"Christopher. You know I *want* to be here? This is something that I want."

"Can't," he whispered. "Can't . . . I can't trust my . . . I don't know . . ." he ground his teeth and vehemently shook his head again.

Wynter blinked out at the night, hurt, confused and mostly scared, lost for a moment for what to do or say. "Perhaps . . ." she said, "perhaps we can just go inside? We could lie on the furs and close our eyes. We do not have to sleep. We do not have to talk, or do anything at all. We can just lie together, on the furs, and rest."

They stayed clenched together for a moment without speaking, Christopher's fists knotted in her tunic, Wynter rubbing unhurried circles on his back. Then she broke away from him, and he let her take his hand. She didn't look at his face, just led him by the hand into the tent and over to their bed. She took off her tunic and removed her boots while he stood, a silent, motionless shadow dimly outlined against the faintly illuminated walls. "Come on," she said softly, sitting on the edge of their bed. "Come on, Christopher."

She saw him bend and heard him remove his boots. She heard the rustle as he unlaced and discarded his undershirt. His shadow disappeared for a moment, then she felt him crawl up the furs on the inside of the bed and lie down in the dark. She felt her way across the covers and found him. "Give me your hand," she said and he did. She lay down close to him, feeling the heat of his skin, and held on to the scarred, gap-fingered anchor of his hand. She shifted a little closer.

He tensed.

"I'm only going to kiss you good night," she said softly. "Is that all right?"

She felt him nod.

Her lips found his bare shoulder and she kissed it gently. "Good night, Christopher," she said.

"Iseult?"

She waited, her mind racing, but Christopher didn't say anything more, just closed his hand a little tighter around hers. They lay together for a long time with their hands clasped, breathing quietly into the dark and saying nothing.

After a while, light footsteps ran towards their tent and the two of them sat forward, quietly reaching for their weapons. Another set of footsteps caught up with the first and they came to a halt just outside the tent. Embla's voice, laughing and hushed, came through to them on the still air.

"What for you worry?" she whispered. "They make sport is all, and sleep. Come on, Tabiyb. Come back with me . . ."

"Wait." Razi's voice, low and anxious. "I just want—" He was cut short and there was a moment of breathlessness, a kind of shuffling quiet. Razi released a faint, breathy grunt. "Uh . . ." he said. "W . . . wait just a moment, sweetheart. I want to be certain . . ." Embla chuckled. Razi's tall shadow fell against the door. Christopher sank back onto the furs and Wynter lay down beside him, closing her eyes. The tent flap was drawn back and there was a long, searching silence.

"You see?" whispered Embla. "They safe, two little mice in their bed. You not always need worry."

Wynter listened as Razi stood quietly in the doorway, looking at them as they pretended to sleep. After a while he sighed. "Embla?" he said.

Embla's voice was husky when she answered, and slightly muffled Wynter figured she must be standing very close to Razi, holding him perhaps, as he looked into the tent. "Aye, Tabiyb, what is it?"

"When . . ." he said hoarsely. "When I have finished what I have to do . . . Stop. Embla." He turned away and the tent flap fell back into place. "Embla," he said gently. "Stop. Listen, when I have finished my business and I am free to return to you, do you think . . .? Would you consider . . .?

Embla, is it possible that we could be together? You and I? Is that something you think you might like?"

Christopher tensed beside Wynter, his hand clamping down on hers. There was a very brief moment of silence from outside the tent, then Embla said softly, "I should like that very much, Tabiyb . . . that we be together."

Christopher lurched forward, hoisting himself onto his elbow, staring at the door.

Razi laughed. "Then I shall make it my business to find you, Embla. When this is all over. I shall . . ." His words were cut short and he grunted softly. There was a series of subtle noises, shifting and sighs. Then Embla whispered huskily for Razi to *come on*, and they moved away into the night.

"Christopher," said Wynter. "Are you all right?"

"That bitch," whispered Christopher, shocking her. He flung himself back against the covers and she felt him put his arm over his face. "Oh God," he hissed. "That bitch."

Temptation

The next morning, Embla, Hallvor and Úlfnaor made their way through the shadowy, sleeping tents and helped the three of them carry their stuff down to the grassy plains. Ashkr's *puballmór* stayed dark and silent. The blond lord had said his goodbyes the night before, explaining that he wanted Sólmundr to sleep as long as possible before waking up to the truth about Christopher's departure.

In deference to his wishes they worked in silence, stepping around each other like thieves in the misty pre-dawn gloom, wordlessly emptying the tent of their belongings. On the last trip, Wynter emerged with her final piece of kit, to find Christopher standing motionless in the shadows, staring down towards Ashkr's tent, his face grave.

"Hey," she hissed. "Hey." She came up behind him and nudged him with her elbow. "Come on, we are almost done."

Embla's quiet voice drifted through the mist and they both turned to watch as the lady walked down to the plains with Razi. Her dogs ran ahead of them and the tall couple followed on, their heads down, murmuring to each other.

Razi had his saddle over one shoulder and Embla carried his backpack in her hand. She had her arm around Razi's waist, and her silhouette blended into his as their cloaks swung behind them. Christopher watched them with hard eyes. He had been trying to get Embla's attention all morning, but she had been purposely avoiding him, quite blatantly deflecting Christopher's every attempt to approach her.

"Come on," murmured Wynter. "The sooner we leave, the sooner he will be free of her."

On the grassy plains, Ozkar came to Wynter immediately and she greeted him with an affectionate tug of his fringe. "Good boy," she said, glancing at Úlfnaor and Hallvor who were setting the last of the things down by Razi's saddlebags.

Beside her, Christopher murmured in Hadrish as he tended to his little chestnut mare, but all of his attention was focused on Embla, and he glared at her as he spoke. Wynter felt herself grow tense. Christopher's temper was an unknown quantity at the moment and Wynter was surprised to find herself worrying about what he might do.

Embla stood a little apart from the activity, her cloak pulled tight, watching as Razi tacked up his mare. He kept smiling over at her, his eyes shining, and Embla eyed his body with open, wistful appreciation. Hallvor, her work done, drifted across to her. Úlfnaor handed Razi his bedroll and stepped back, brushing off his hands. He raised his eyebrows, looking around for stray equipment. They were done.

Abruptly, Christopher stepped away from his horse, his hands opening and closing in nervous anticipation, his eyes on Embla. Wynter reached and took his mare's reins. She glanced meaningfully at him. If he wanted to speak to Embla, he was going to have to press the issue now.

Úlfnaor picked up Razi's matchlock, meaning to hand it to him. At the last minute he turned it over in his hands, his dark eyes thoughtful. "What you think of this things, Tabiyb?" he said. "Me, I think they very clumsy. It not good, depending all the time on this black powder. What for you do when no black powder left?"

"I agree with you," said Razi, tugging the stirrups into place. "But it's the future, I'm afraid. There is nothing can be done about it. Here, if I may?" He ducked under his horse's neck and took the weapon from Úlfnaor. "Let me show you something." The two men bent their heads over the weapon.

As soon as the men had turned away, Christopher darted forward and grabbed Embla by her arm. "I need to talk to you," he murmured, staring into her face. The lady sighed, not looking at him, and Wynter saw Christopher's fingers clamp down. "*Now*," he hissed.

Embla grew very still. She turned her head to stare coldly into Christopher's hard, grey eyes. Hallvor frowned, and the warhounds turned their heads, their ears pricking forward. There was a moment of breathless suspension, Hallvor, Embla and Christopher poised on the brink of something, the dogs bristling. Wynter's hand dropped to the hilt of her sword.

Then Embla laughed in false good humour and waved her hand in dismissal. She glanced at Hallvor, took Christopher's arm, and purposely moved him away from the wary healer. Christopher guided her across the dewy grass and brought her to a halt by Wynter's side.

Wynter glanced furtively at Razi. He and Úlfnaor were still utterly engrossed in the gun. Razi pointed at the river, and Úlfnaor swung the weapon to his shoulder, sighting down the barrel at the dark and foggy water.

"Embla," whispered Christopher, "before Tabiyb goes, you need to tell him that you can't be together. You need to tell him that he's not to come back and find you."

Embla frowned, and Christopher pulled her closer, his fingers digging into her arm. "You *tell* him, Embla. I don't care what you say. Tell him he's too young for you. Tell him you were only making sport. Tell him you're *wed* . . . anything. Just convince him not to come back for you."

Embla tugged her arm free, drawing herself to her full height. "I not want to!" she hissed. "Why *for* I not have this? Why *for* I not get this for me? Ashkr, he—"

"Ashkr is *different* Embla, you know that, because *Sólmundr* is different. It's cruel and Ashkr should never have let it happen, but at least Sólmundr understands, at least it's been his choice. Tabiyb will *never* understand!"

"*Stop* it, Coinín. Stop! It not fair you say this things! Why you be cruel? Why you make me not happy on this my *seachtain deireanach*."

"You are misleading him," said Christopher. "You are knowingly offering things you cannot give."

Embla gazed at him for a moment, then her face changed and she leant her head close to his, gently persuasive now. "Coinín," she whispered. "You know Tabiyb not ever mean to come back. I just woman he make sport with, that all. He leave now, and he go back to his life. He become wrapped in his business, and he forget all about the promise he make to me." Embla laid her hand beseechingly on Christopher's arm. "But Coinín," she whispered. "You know what I like to believe? I like to believe Tabiyb maybe will think of me sometime, and he maybe will smile. I like that, Coinín. I like that I will live in his heart, and now and again I will make someone like Tabiyb smile."

Something in Embla's face twisted Wynter's heart when she said that, some hopeless yearning. The pale lady put her hand over her own heart and said, "I will carry this thought with me, Coinín. It will get me through much things."

She stopped talking and held Christopher's eyes with her own.

To Wynter's immense surprise, Christopher's expression softened. "Listen to me," he said. "You don't know Tabiyb like I do. *He always keeps his promises.* He *will* come looking for you, Embla. He *will* come, and then what will happen?"

Embla studied Christopher's face, her eyes wide.

"When he finds out, he won't understand," said Christopher. "He'll lose his head, Embla. He'll kill Úlfnaor, he might even get to kill Sólmundr, and in the end the People will have to kill *him*. And it will be because you have misled him. Is that what you want? You want Tabiyb to die because of you? Because you misled him?"

Christopher gazed up into Embla's face, his eyes filled with compassion. There was a brief moment of silent communication between the two of them. Then Embla abruptly turned and walked stiffly to Hallvor's side. Hallvor saw her lady's unhappiness and she glared at Christopher. Wynter stepped to his side, glaring back.

Embla's hounds ran up to her, whining. They butted the lady's hands and licked her fingers in an attempt to rouse her from her sudden despondence. She pushed them sharply away and they milled about for a moment before trotting over to join the other dogs who were ranged in a tense line, staring into the trees. Hallvor murmured something soothing, but Embla turned, pulling her cloak tightly around her, and regarded Razi with troubled eyes. He was taking the matchlock from Úlfnaor. Still chatting quietly away, he slid it into the holster on his saddle and tied the keep.

Wynter took Christopher's hand, and they stood watching as Embla decided what to do.

"Well," said Úlfnaor. "Time for goodbyes." Razi nodded, smiling. "The People never able thank you enough, Tabiyb," said Úlfnaor. "For what it is you do for Sól."

"It was my pleasure," said Razi. "I only hope that I have left enough instructions for Hallvor to see Sólmundr through to full health." His eyes flicked back to Embla as he spoke. She lifted her chin and smiled at him, slow and warm, and Wynter's heart sank as Razi's face was suffused with happiness. He grinned, his eyes shining, then he turned his full attention back to Úlfnaor who was offering him his hand. Razi accepted the big man's handshake with warmth. "We will meet again, Úlfnaor, I am certain of it."

Úlfnaor faltered, frowning. He went to speak, then seemed to think better of it and smiled instead, nodding. "Perhaps we will, Tabiyb. Who can know the will of *An Domhan*?"

Razi turned away and led his horse to the healer. "Goodbye, Hallvor," he said taking her hand. "It was a pleasure to work with you."

Hallvor smiled warmly at him, understanding the tone,

if not the words, and pumped his hand in a two-fisted grip that could have crushed stones. She said something wry. Embla murmured a translation and Razi laughed.

"Coinín?" said Úlfnaor quietly, walking to Christopher's side. "You really go with the *coimhthíoch*? You not stay with the People?"

Wynter glowered, and pointedly took Christopher's hand.

"They are my *family*, Aoire," said Christopher.

Úlfnaor sucked his teeth, as if Christopher had made a bad joke.

"Sometimes desperation makes poor choices, *a chroí*," he said. Christopher huffed and looked away, and Úlfnaor leant in, speaking kindly. "Listen to what I tell you now, *Coinín mac Aidan*. You are Merron. Merron! It not right you out alone. I tell you now, the Bear tribe be happy to take you in. We adopt you, Coinín. We see you safe."

"Thank you, Aoire," said Christopher, his grip on Wynter's hand tightening. "But the Bear's breast is too savage for my comfort. I cannot accept."

Úlfnaor nodded regretfully and shrugged. "Goodbye then, Coinín, may *An Domhan* know you always." Christopher bowed slightly and the Aoire put his hand on the top of his head, murmuring something. "And you, *lucha rua*." He turned to Wynter who regarded him with narrow-eyed suspicion. Úlfnaor laughed. "I think," he said, chucking her fondly under her chin, "our *Coinín beag* trades one fierce breast for another, *nach ea*? You should be Merron, *lucha*, it good to see such spirit in such small things."

"Goodbye, Úlfnaor," she said coldly, "I wish you and your people joy."

Úlfnaor smiled tolerantly at her but she turned away and gathered Ozkar's reins. "Let's go," she said to Christopher. "It is . . ." The rest of her comment died on her lips and the three of them watched as Razi gathered Embla into his arms and kissed her with lingering tenderness. Úlfnaor sighed unhappily and Wynter bit her lip, but Christopher lowered his head and growled. The couple ended their kiss with a sigh, and stood in each other's arms, their foreheads touching.

Úlfnaor stared at them, some glimmer of understanding dawning in his face. "You take him away now, Coinín," he said firmly. "Take him away and never let him look back."

The two men exchanged a tight glance. Christopher snatched his reins from Wynter and leapt into the saddle. "Come on, Tabiyb!" he snapped, urging his horse forwards. "'Tis almost daybreak!"

Razi and Embla skipped apart as Christopher danced his mare too close.

"Chris!" exclaimed Razi.

Christopher glared down at him. "We have work to do," he said in Southlandast. "Or have you forgotten? Put it back in your trousers, man, and let us get to our business."

Suddenly a long, agonised shriek split the morning air. Everyone ducked, reaching for their weapons, staring all around. The forest exploded in a frenzy of snarls and angry barking, and deep in the trees a horse screamed. The sound made Ozkar leap and side step, his eyes rolling, and Razi's horse danced in fear.

The warhounds, somewhere out of sight in the forest, began to howl.

Christopher's mare threw her head and he growled at

her, tugging her into a tight, dancing circle to stop her bolting. He drew his katar and edged his mare sideways, putting himself between Wynter and the thrashing shadows. Wynter drew her short sword, peering into the dark. A man was screaming out there, high and rhythmic, the sound of someone caught in a snare, and that poor horse still shrieked its agony out into the dark. Growls and snarls underscored the shrill sounds of pain.

Behind Wynter, the camp erupted with panicked activity. People were ducking from tents, half-dressed and dishevelled, swords in hand. The horses were milling about on the grass, crying out and fighting their hobbles, infected with fear. Úlfnaor bolted past, dashing into the shadows without a word. Hallvor darted after him. One after another Merron warriors ran past, and the three friends hesitated as the fierce tide of men and women rushed into the trees. Then Razi secured his reins to the pommel of his saddle, slapped his horse away and ran into the forest. Christopher and Wynter followed suit, heading towards the baying hounds and the terrible screaming.

Protection

They ran deep into the trees, following the noise. Wynter could hear Úlfnaor yelling at his hounds. Then Embla and, unmistakably, Ashkr snapping orders and whistling.

Razi, dashing furiously ahead, came to a sudden halt. The awful, pained shrieking of the horse was right in front of them now, and Razi took an involuntary step back from the sound. Wynter ran up to him, pushing through the bushes to get past, and he flung his arm out to keep her back. "No," he said.

Christopher came to a sliding stop, staring past Razi, his face appalled.

Impatiently, Wynter batted Razi's arm from her path and stepped forward. Three Merron warriors were standing in a frozen semicircle around the horse, and Wynter stepped between them, her sword dangling uselessly by her side.

It was a fine chestnut cob, at least fifteen hands and deep-chested, a handsome, sturdy mount. The hounds had gutted it and torn at its throat, then left it while they pursued its rider. Its entrails were tangled in its feet and it was on its knees, moaning now, in a high, inhuman kind of way. As Wynter watched, the horse lowered its forehead to the ground as if in prayer. There was blood on its lips and in its nostrils, and its breath came in snorting, agonised gusts. Its ornate tack jingled lightly with each shuddering breath.

Razi knocked against Wynter's shoulder as he pushed by, heading for the sounds of human suffering further on. Christopher came to her side, his face blank, his eyes on the snarling wolfskin that decorated the horse's rump.

"*Jesu,*" breathed Wynter, staring as the poor horse tried to rise to its feet. Its hoof slipped, pulling its own guts further from its torn belly, the long intestinal loops steaming in the morning air. The horse exhaled a weak, agonised whinny. "*Jesu Christi,*" Wynter whispered again, her gorge rising. "*Salva nos.*" The horse blew another gusty breath and shuddered. Slowly it toppled to its side, its legs spasming helplessly.

At that, everyone seemed to step forward at once. Wynter stooped with the Merron as they huddled round the poor creature. She helped two of the men take the bridle and heaved on the horse's head so that its neck was stretched taut. Then a woman stepped over it and slit its throat in one quick, deep slice.

The horse's blood sluiced out onto the forest floor, spreading quickly across the matted leaves. Almost immediately the painful tension left the horse's body and it relaxed, its strong legs curling inwards, its final breaths bubbling from its gaping throat like swamp gas. Wynter stepped back, but the Merron did not release their grip on the bridle. The men kept the wound stretched taut, allowing the blood to flow freely, and the woman stroked the creature's quivering neck as its life ebbed from it.

Wynter looked at Christopher across the growing scarlet tide. He had stepped forward, gore splattering his boots, and was staring at the wolf-head. It glared at him, its silver teeth glistening in the new light.

Loups-Garous, thought Wynter. She took in the horse's tack. *Travelling light, no saddlebags, no bedrolls, no camping equipment.* She looked out into the trees, settling her sword in her hand. *That means they can't be more than a day's ride from their companions.* Scouts then, spiralling out from a central camp. Looking for something. Spies. Wynter glanced back at the brutalised animal. Spies. *Just as we had intended to be*, she thought with a shudder. *This could have been us.*

The sounds up ahead were calmer now, men and women calling to each other in unhurried commands. The man had stopped screaming. Christopher met her eyes across the heads of the crouched Merron. Gesturing at him to follow, Wynter stalked after Razi.

They followed a wide trail of broken brush that cut a blood-stained path through the trees. After a few yards they came to another horse, mercifully dead this time, its throat ripped cleanly out, a quick kill. The Merron were stripping it of its fine tack, grimly pulling the saddle from its back, undoing the buckles of its harness. The wolfskin was casually flung onto the growing pile of Loups-Garous' equipment. Its jewelled eyes seemed to follow Christopher and Wynter as they padded slowly by.

The horse's rider was sprawled in the trees a yard or so further on. Hallvor was crouched over the body, her back to

them. Úlfnaor's dogs were standing by, panting happily,
their tails wagging. As Christopher and Wynter came up
the trail, the hounds looked up in unison, grinning, their
long tongues lolling. They were painted in gore, their wiry
fur matted with blood. There was a sudden, brutal, cracking sound, and Hallvor began sawing at something with
her knife. The dogs whined in excitement, bowing and
snuffling.

As Wynter and Christopher slid past, Hallvor, her arms
elbow-deep in blood, sat back on her haunches, revealing
the man's body. Wynter saw that he had been raggedly
decapitated. There was no sign of his head. Hallvor had
cracked open his rib cage and was now calling to the eager
dogs, offering the man's heart to the warhounds that had
killed him. She had split the organ into two, and Wynter
watched in sick fascination as the huge creatures stepped
forward and delicately took a half each from Hallvor's dripping fingers.

"*Maith sibh a chúnna,*" murmured the healer, wiping
her arms on the dead man's shirt. Two other Merron came
down the trail, and Hallvor motioned them to help her
strip the Loup-Garou of his finery. Christopher pulled
Wynter along by her elbow, and they moved on.

They followed the sounds of people moving through
the trees and found themselves back on the edge of the
grass plains. Razi stood with his back to them, his falchion
sword still in his hand. He was watching as a group of
Merron gathered around Úlfnaor and Wari. They seemed
to be looking at something that lay on the ground at their
feet.

As Wynter and Christopher stepped from the trees,

Ashkr pushed his way through the ranks of the Merron, his dogs at his heels. He was carrying something in his hand. It took Wynter's numbed brain a few seconds to realise that it was a dripping human head. Once the Merron saw who was shoving them aside, they parted ranks and let Ashkr through to the centre of the circle, stepping back to give him room. His dogs immediately tried to get past him, baying and snarling. At the sight of the dogs the shape on the ground cried out in fear.

My God, thought Wynter, *it's a man.*

Ashkr roared at the dogs, an unusually vicious sound from the Merron lord, and the warhounds backed down at once, dropping to their bellies in the dirt. The man on the ground made an awful, spasming, uncoordinated attempt to crawl away, and Wari kicked him. The man howled and then abruptly lurched upwards, shrieking a string of vile curses in Hadrish.

At the sound of the Wolf's voice, Christopher flinched, and Wynter felt him draw away. She placed a reassuring hand on his back, her eyes on Razi.

Stepping between the Merron warriors, Razi admitted himself to the inner circle, then stalked around the man on the ground. He came to a halt beside Ashkr, and the two men stood side by side, dark and light, both gazing coldly down at the Wolf. Wynter thought that Razi looked oddly detached and speculative, like a trader in a mart, sizing up a substandard horse. She slipped, unheeded, through the warriors and into the inner circle. Christopher drifted in her wake, but once he was within the ring of Merron he came to a halt on the edge of things, motionless and silent, his head down.

Embla stood by Úlfnaor, her sword in her hand, her warhounds flanking her. To Wynter's amazement, Sólmundr was also there. The lady had her free arm around his waist, holding him up. Wynter moved round to stand by their side, and so got her first good look at one of David Le Garou's Wolves.

He was young, mid-twenties at most, and clean-shaven, with shoulder-length brown hair. Wynter's eyes were drawn inexorably to the chewed mess of his legs and the way he was holding his exposed guts into his belly with both hands. She fought down a hot surge of vomit and pulled her attention back to the angry contortion of his expression He was staring at Wari, his eyes a vivid blue in the chalky white of his face.

"You God-cursed savages," he spat in choked Hadrish. "You whoreson vagabonds. David will eat your pox-riddled hearts, you hear me? He'll burn your eyes! You—"

Ashkr crouched abruptly by his side and leant forward to make eye contact. The Wolf flinched away in momentary fear, but quickly gathered himself and snarled defiantly once more. "Stand back, you cur. I have no wish to share your fleas."

Ashkr nodded. "See your friend?" he said. He placed the severed head on the ground. It had been chewed and savaged by the hounds as they tore it from its owner's body, but the features were still recognisable. Ashkr turned the head to face the now silent Wolf. Gently, he pulled the clinging hair from its lifeless forehead, tucking it neatly behind the bloodied ears. He lifted his eyes to those of the Wolf. "See your friend?" he repeated. He tapped the dead cheek. "He the lucky one," he whispered.

The Wolf stared at the slack-lipped, waxy face of his dead companion, then drew back and gobbed a long, bloody spit at Ashkr. Wynter jumped, her sword jerking upwards, but Ashkr just sighed and wiped his face with the hem of his shirt.

"That very silly," he said, his voice just as soft as before. "I the only person here who might have kill you before you too broken up to care." He sucked his teeth and spread his hands. "Ah well," he said and stood up, smiling down at the man. "Ah well."

The Wolf fell back, his knees drawing up to his torn belly. His eyes scanned the ring of faces that glowered down at him, and Wynter saw Christopher shrink back against the surrounding Merron, his eyelids fluttering, his face turned away in fear. But pain overtook the Wolf before he could find Christopher, and he gasped, rolling to his side, and locked eyes with Razi instead.

They knew each other well; Wynter saw it in the shock that froze the Wolf's face, and in the slow, cold satisfaction that spread itself into Razi's smile.

"*Sabah alkhair*, Reinier," said Razi quietly, wishing the man "good morning" in Arabic

The man lurched slightly, as if he would have been jumping to his feet if not so hideously wounded. He stared at Razi, then his lip curved into a knowing sneer and his eyes hardened. Razi grinned at him. The Merron frowned. There was a suddenly wary reappraisal of Razi, and their eyes dropped to the wicked blade that gleamed in his fist. Wynter tensed and tightened her grip on her own weapon as a subtle shift of focus rippled around the surrounding warriors.

The Wolf muttered something in Arabic, then gurgled a clogged laugh, his lips splattered red. "It *is* you," he choked in Hadrish. Razi bowed, spreading his arms sarcastically. "David knew it!" hissed the Wolf. "He *knew* it! Gérard said you were dead, but David knew, as soon as the boys brought those bracelets back to camp . . ." He shifted painfully, his eyes roaming the crowd, searching. "He knew 'twas your little mongrel. And where the mongrel is, the master ain't never . . . hah!" He had found Christopher at last. Razi stepped forward, his sword jerking convulsively upwards.

The Wolf laughed again, contorting his body around to see the pale young man. Christopher flicked him the briefest of glances, slid a look at Wynter, then dropped his gaze. His face was perfectly blank, his body utterly still.

The Wolf twisted his head in the dust and grinned up at Razi once more. "David is looking for you, al-*Sayyid*." He drawled Razi's title, giving the words a contemptuous emphasis. "He will find you soon. You haven't a hope."

Smiling, Razi sheathed his falchion and dropped to a crouch. He rested his elbows on his knees. "These people are going to blóod-eagle you, Reinier," he murmured. The Wolf's eyes grew wide and Razi drew the word out for him. "*Blood-eagle*," he said. "You will die screaming. I shall enjoy the sound."

There was a long moment of silence, Razi and the Wolf looking into each other's eyes, the severed head on the ground between them. Then the Wolf purposely rolled to his side, all the better to face Razi. He released only the smallest whimper of pain, though the movement must have been excruciating, and laid his head in the dust for only a moment before raising it once again. He flicked a glance to Ashkr, to Úlfnaor, to Embla and Sólmundr.

"We all speak Hadrish, do we?" he said. Then he smiled. "Yes, I can see it in your eyes. You four, at least, understand me." The Wolf raised himself onto his elbow, clenching his scarlet fist in the dust. "All right, al-Sayyid," he said, staring Razi in the eye. "I will die screaming, if that is what you wish." He grinned, blood in his teeth. "I shall scream very loud, shall I? Tell these sheep what a rabid little cur your mongrel is? What a dangerous piece of work you've brought in amongst them?"

Razi's face went pale, and he jerked back slightly. The Loup-Garou laughed.

"You should have seen him, when the boys took his trinkets. You should have seen him change! Know what we call his kind?" he gurgled. "*Slywolf . . . Feeblewolf . . .* pathetic, slithering fools who try and deny their nature and run with the sheep." He spat on the ground.

Wynter stared at him, disbelieving. "Do you mean Christopher?" she whispered.

The Wolf turned to his attention to her, and Christopher moaned, twisting his head away. Understanding brightened the Wolf's blood-stained face and he leaned towards her. "You want to be careful, bitch," he rasped. "You better take care. His kind can only hold themselves in check for so long, and then—"

The Wolf jerked forward suddenly, his mouth all fang, his eyes yellow. Everyone skittered back at the inhumanity of his face. He laughed at their fear, and fell back, just a man again, scrabbling with bloody fingers in the dust. But there were claw-marks in the dirt now, deep and long, a permanent testament to the moment when his scarlet fingers had gouged into the impossibly hard ground. He grinned at Wynter. "He didn't tell you, did he?" he gasped. "You stupid bint. He didn't tell you that you were bedding a Wolf?"

Razi surged to his feet. "Shut up," he cried, "shut your filthy mouth."

The Wolf laughed again as Razi loomed over him. "Oh," he gasped. "You reckless bastard. He'll turn! They always do. His kind can't help it. They *always* bite the hand that feeds them." He leered at Wynter. "Or eat the bitch that fu—" With a roar, Razi lifted his foot and stamped his heel down onto the Wolf's temple.

The Wolf's head changed shape in a sickening way, and Wynter slapped her hand over her mouth, her stomach rebelling. Razi lifted his foot again and Wynter turned away, everything combining at once to finally bring her stomach into her mouth. She heard the ripe, flat smack of Razi's heel connecting with the Wolf's head, and the circle of Merron skipped back as Wynter vomited hot bile onto the ground at their feet. Once she started, she couldn't seem to stop and she heaved and gagged for what seemed like an eternity as things continued to happen around her.

Her first coherent thought was *Christopher*, and she straightened, wiping her mouth with the back of her arm, and looked anxiously to where he had been standing. He was gone, his katar abandoned in the dust, and Wynter stared at the discarded weapon, her spine creeping with cold fear. Then she realised that the Merron were all standing in wary silence, watching as something transpired behind her. The subtle, metallic scrape of a sword being drawn from its scabbard froze her in place for a moment, then she turned slowly and followed the Merron's gaze.

Razi had drawn his falchion again and was standing facing Úlfnaor, his arms hanging by his sides, his face unreadable. The Merron lords were ranged in a pale row, their swords loosely ready in their hands, their expressions wary. Behind them, and all around her, the watchful ranks of the People stood, weapons at the ready, postures tense. Wynter tightened her grip on her own sword, her eyes darting around the crowd.

Razi took his knife from the sheath on his thigh. Slowly, his eyes on Úlfnaor, he twisted knife and sword so that the blades of each rested along his forearms, then he held them out, offering the weapons, handle first. He lifted his chin and spoke in his deep, clear voice.

"I am al-Sayyid Razi ibn-Jon Malik al-fadl," he said.

Wynter stared anxiously at Úlfnaor, but Razi's name and title did not seem to register with the big man, and after a pause, Razi went on.

"I am a messenger for the Good King Jonathon," he said. "I am dispatched by his Majesty to find the Royal Prince Alberon in hopes of conveying to him his father's desire for reconciliation, and as an opening for negotiations for peace." Razi dropped to one knee, his weapons held out for Úlfnaor to take from him. He bowed his head in submission. "But these Loups-Garous will see me dead before I can fulfil my duty, Aoire. I can no longer expose my companions to the danger of travelling alone. I throw myself on your mercy, in the hope that you will understand that what is good for this kingdom will ultimately be good

for your people. I beg your protection. Aoire. I beg your
protection in my journey to the Prince."

Wynter flung herself onto her knees by Razi, her eyes
flicking up to take in Úlfnaor's uncertain face. "Razi!" she
hissed, putting her hand on his outstretched arm. "Razi,
stop. You can't." Razi didn't look at her, just continued to
hold his weapons out in supplication, his head bowed.
Wynter tugged at his arm, begging him in Southlandast.
"They will kill you, Razi! Christopher says . . ."

"It matters not."

"*Razi!* Did you hear me? They will—"

"It matters *not*, Wyn. I will not bring you back out there
alone."

Wynter turned to Embla. "Tell him! Tell him what
Christopher said to you. Tell him!"

Embla's eyes were wide with panic, and she stepped
back, her hand to her mouth, not knowing what to do.
"Oh Lady, *please!*" begged Wynter. She dashed her hands
under her eyes, wiping the tears from her cheeks. "Lady,
please!" she insisted firmly. "*Please!* Tell him that he cannot
stay!"

Embla remained silent, and Wynter looked around for
Christopher, or Ashkr, or Sólmundr, anyone who might
support her, but they were nowhere to be found.

Úlfnaor reached down and placed his hand on the hilt of
Razi's knife. Wynter looked up into the man's dark eyes.
"Don't, Aoire," she whispered. "I beg you." Úlfnaor glanced
at her, his expression hard, then he took Razi's weapons
from him and handed them to Wari.

Wynter got slowly to her feet, expecting that at any
minute the Aoire would demand her sword from her.

Úlfnaor watched her carefully, but made no move to disarm her. Razi allowed his empty hands to drop to his sides, his eyes still on the ground. Embla continued to stare at him, her hand pressed to her mouth.

Wynter backed slowly away. She knocked against something with her heel. It rolled away in the dust, and she knew without looking that it was the severed head. Her foot nudged against the Wolf's body and she sidled her way past it, her eyes fixed on Razi and the heavily armed warriors standing over him. Úlfnaor's dark eyes followed her as she backed through the surrounding Merron. The crowd parted and soon Wynter found herself on the outside of the circle, staring through the silent ranks of warriors as Razi continued to kneel, vulnerable and defenceless, in their midst. She got one last glimpse of his kneeling figure, then the wall of Merron closed against her and Razi disappeared from her sight.

Wynter ran towards the river, instinct taking her to the little beach where she had last found Christopher. Sure enough, there were footprints leading across the sand, and in the shadows of the willow trees, at the far end of the beach, she saw his slim silhouette.

"Christopher!" she screamed, running towards him. "Christopher!"

The hunted look on his face brought her to a halt a few yards from him. He glanced at her, then away, for all the world like someone waiting for a stone to be flung at him. The Wolf's horrible words fell between them like a dark wall, and for a moment Wynter faltered. Then she lowered her chin and did the only thing she could think of.

"Christopher!" She shot forward and grabbed his arm, startling him. "Razi has thrown us under Úlfnaor's protection! I told him not to! I told him that they would kill him, and he did it anyway! Úlfnaor has taken his weapons, Chris. Razi has told him that he works for the King! What are we to do?"

Christopher stared blankly at her, and Wynter shook his arm, desperate. "Chris! Help me! What do we do?"

He looked around him for a moment, utterly lost. Then he closed his eyes and twisted his arm from her grip. "Get Sól," he whispered.

"*What?*"

"Sól." He pushed her gently away.

"Chris . . ." she staggered back a few steps, panic rising in an uncontrollable tide. "Chris," she lifted her hands. "What . . .?"

"Get *Sól!*" His unexpected shriek made her leap and cry out. "*I want Sól.*" He howled this last word, and Wynter skittered back even further. Christopher moaned and staggered out into the shallow water, his fists clenched at his temples.

A long shadow fell across them, and Wynter spun with a cry. Ashkr was standing on the edge of the sunlight, staring at Christopher. Wynter instinctively put herself between them, her sword half-drawn. *Get back!* Ashkr stepped forward, his eyes locked with hers. Gently he closed his hand over Wynter's and pushed down until her sword was once again sheathed in its scabbard. Then he strode past her, wading out into the shallows to stand by Christopher.

"Coinín," he said.

Christopher gasped out another long, desolate moan and bent almost double.

Wynter took three or four splashing steps towards them, and he cried out, twisting away. "No," he moaned. "Not her. Tell her to *go*. Get me Sól, Ashkr, I want Sól."

Wynter came to a wounded halt, staring.

Gradually, without any force, Ashkr pulled Christopher up and around so that the young man's bowed head was resting against his chest. Christopher pressed in, and Ashkr's eyes met Wynter's across the top of his head. Wynter stood with her hands pressed to her mouth, tears rolling down her face. She didn't know what to do. Ashkr, his face unreadable, slowly tightened his arms and pulled Christopher close.

Spoken

They took Wynter's sword and her dagger and brought her to Embla's tent. Razi was already inside, and he surged to his feet as she ducked in the doorway, his fists up, ready to fight.

"It's me!" she hissed, holding her hands out.

He strode forward and grabbed her shoulders, looking behind her. "Where is Christopher?"

Angrily, she shrugged free of his grip. "They took him! He would not see me! He would only see Ashkr and Sólmundr, and they took him!"

Razi covered his face with his hand and groaned. He spun away and stalked to the opposite end of the *puballmór* where he stood in the shadows, his head in his hands.

"You should have told me!" she hissed, and Razi shook his head. "How *dare* you not tell me?"

The tent flap was lifted and a tall, dark shape filled the door. Razi leapt forward, grabbing Wynter and pulling her back. Then the door fell back into place and they saw that it was Ashkr, grave and staring, his eyes moving between the two of them.

"Tabiyb," he said. "Coinín say you always know this about him, but you never will to talk."

Colour flared to Razi's cheeks and he averted his eyes.

Ashkr looked him up and down. "So Coinín tell truth," he said softly. "You shamed of him."

"No," cried Razi. "No, of course not . . ."

"*Yes*," insisted Ashkr. "*Yes!* You *shamed*, Tabiyb You hide Coinín's nature. You make him hide even from his *croí-eile*."

"No," cried Razi desperately. "That was Christopher's choice. He has always suppressed this part of himself! He has never wanted—"

Ashkr stepped forward, his face close to Razi's. "Come now, then," he demanded. You come talk. You let Coinín know he good."

Razi's arms dropped to his sides, and Wynter saw guilt and helplessness rise up in his dark face. He spread his hands and whispered, "I do not know what to say. I . . . I have never known what to say."

Ashkr softened instantly. He put his hand on Razi's neck. "You just be his friend, Tabiyb. That all Coinín need from you, to know you his friend." He smiled and pushed Razi's hair back from his face in a strangely paternal gesture. "It be good," he said, then he turned to Wynter. "Iseult," he said. "I will talk with you."

Razi gripped Ashkr's arm, panicked. "No!" he said. "Christopher would not want us to—"

Ashkr gently removed Razi's hand from his arm. He turned again to Wynter and she glared at him, her anger at Christopher and at Razi suffusing everything. Unfazed, Ashkr held up his wrist and tapped the plaited copper and silver bangle he wore there. "You know what this mean?"

"It is a token of fidelity," she answered tightly. "It means you have pledged yourself, heart and body, to Sólmundr."

He nodded. "From time I know what it is to love, I know I love Sól, and he, too, always feel this way for me. For long time I try to pretend I not feel this – because of who I is and *what* I is . . . *Caora Beo*. But, true in my heart, Iseult, Sól the only person I ever feel this way for. He make me happy. I like think I make him happy too. So . . ." Ashkr trailed to silence and closed his fingers around his bracelet.

Suddenly his face drew down, and Wynter knew he was remembering something terrible. Something that brought him great anger and pain. Against her wishes, she felt her anger subside.

"Then those pirate come," whispered Ashkr, "and my Sól, he is gone. I eighteen when this happen, and I understand with perfect clearness that I have lost only good thing in my *thóin caca* of life. Three long year he gone, and my heart it bleed every day . . . then here he is! I not believe it! My Sól! Walking from out the trees! It like dream. I look at the scars on his body. I see his poor neck and—"

Ashkr gritted his teeth and bit down on his emotions. He took Wynter's hands in his own, looking down at the tokens they both wore on their wrists. "This what I need tell you," he said. "I sorry I go on and on. This really what I need you to know . . ." He seemed uncertain suddenly, as if not sure he should be saying this. Wynter squeezed his hands. She nodded encouragingly.

Ashkr's voice lowered. "Sól, he go through many thing when he slave," he said darkly. "He suffer many hurts. He . . . he made feel shame, Iseult. You understand?"

Wynter swallowed, her eyes full. She nodded.

"Sól, he think that if he tells to me this things, then that be all I will ever see. He think I will look at him and not see him no more, but only what it is was done to him. He think it better to keep all this things inside him. Not said." Ashkr leaned in close to Wynter, willing her to understand. "Shame make Sól not speak. This thing that keep him silent to me. This thing that keep Coinín silent to you. It shame. They fear the truth will make us turn away, Iseult. This why they hide from us this very important things. You understand?"

Wynter nodded again, and Ashkr searched her glittering eyes.

"Good," he whispered. "That good. Now!" He abruptly dropped her hands and turned to Razi. "Now, Tabiyb. Come tend this wounds on Coinín's back. Give to him reason to tell you what he feels."

Razi remained pressed against the wall, his face frozen, and Ashkr dipped his chin. "It all right, Tabiyb," he said gently. "Be strong now, like good man you are, and go be friend to Coinín."

For a very brief moment Wynter thought Razi was going to refuse. Then he lurched for the back of the tent, plucked his doctor's bag from the shadows and ducked through the door. She went to dash after him, but Ashkr stopped her.

"Your chance come next, *lucha*. We take our time getting there, *tá go maith*?"

Wynter nodded. "All right," she said.

The sound of Christopher weeping brought her to an uncertain halt by Ashkr's tent. It was a muffled, keening sound, underlaid with the deep murmur of Razi's voice. Wynter rested her hand on the wall of the tent and listened.

"But I can *feel* it!" said Christopher, his voice rising in panic. "I've let it out, Razi. After all these years – after everything that's happened me – *now* I let it out! And I can't control it! Any bit of anger at all! Any bit of desire, and it leaps up in me! I'm bad, Razi! I'm *dangerous!*"

Wynter bowed her head. She glanced back at Ashkr and Sólmundr, sitting in the shade of the trees, watching her tensely. Sólmundr gestured her to go inside.

Razi mumbled something, and Christopher interrupted him sharply. "*You know I will! You've seen what I'm like!*"

"Christopher," said Razi, his tone very clear and measured, "that was years ago, and you were out of your mind. You were crazed with fever."

"I could have *killed* you! You could have *died.*" Christopher broke into sobs again, and Wynter could take no more. She stumbled her way around the side of the tent and pushed through the door.

The two men jumped at her abrupt entrance, and Christopher wailed in horror.

"No!" he cried. "No! Iseult! No!"

The sight of him almost drove Wynter from the tent in fear. His swollen, blotchy face, his frantic desperation. *He is a Wolf,* she thought. *A Wolf.* At her expression, Christopher hid his face, and Wynter cringed with shame. *Oh, you fool,* she thought, *he is Christopher. That is all. That is everything.* Clenching her hands against her own cowardice, Wynter stepped in and let the door drop behind her.

Razi had been kneeling by Ashkr's bed, holding Christopher in his arms, but at her approach Christopher snatched himself away and retreated to the middle of the pallet, his head in his hands, his knees drawn up. He was barefoot and bare-chested, dressed only in his trousers, and Wynter figured that he had finally allowed Razi tend to the cuts on his back.

"Christopher," she said softly. He moaned and shook his head. Wynter moved closer to the bed. At her approach, Christopher pressed his face harder into his knees.

Razi shifted uncomfortably. "Sis," he whispered, his face pleading. *Don't. Please. Don't say anything.*

Wynter hesitated. Then she stooped and, without thinking, removed her boots. She took off her tunic. Then she crawled across the furs of Ashkr's bed and knelt beside Christopher. She put her hand on his back. Razi took a shaky breath, staring at her. She leant close and whispered in Christopher's ear.

"Those Wolves. They would have hurt me."

Christopher dragged a sob through his nose, his face hidden. "Nuh . . ." he said. "Sh . . . shhhhhh."

"You would not let them," she said softly. "They would have hurt me, and you would not let them." She put her arms around him and, without hesitation, he turned into her embrace. "I will always remember that," she whispered, holding him tight. "I will always, *always* remember that, Christopher. That you saved me from them." She felt his arms creep around her waist and his fists knot in the fabric of her undershirt.

"You are not like them," she whispered.

For a brief moment Christopher wept with frightening

intensity, his entire body shuddering, his face pressed hard against Wynter's shoulder, then he clenched his arms around her and held his breath until he was able to stop. She felt him swallow hard. He drew a deep breath and released it. Wynter put her hand on the back of his head, clutching the fine wool scarf that still bound his hair in place.

"I will not let you go," she whispered, her lips pressed to his ear. Christopher pulled her closer, turning his forehead to rest against her neck. "Will you promise me the same, Christopher? Will you promise? Not to let me go?" After a moment she felt him nod, and she closed her eyes in relief and rested her cheek against his hair.

Razi got quietly to his feet. She glanced up at him and he held a finger to his lips. "I will just go see that Sólmundr is all right," he said. "He should not be out of bed."

Wynter nodded, smiling. Then the sudden alarm in her face stopped Razi cold, and he dropped back down by her side. "What?" he said.

Christopher had become a dead weight in her arms. As she stared at Razi, Christopher's fists abruptly relaxed their grip on her shirt and slithered down her back. He was completely unconscious. Razi frowned and dug his fingers into his friend's neck, checking for a pulse. Then he relaxed, his eyes closing in relief. "He's asleep, darling, that's all. Here, let me . . . that's it." Between the two of them, they laid Christopher back onto the furs of Ashkr's bed. He opened his eyes briefly, gazed at them, then curled onto his side, tucked his hand under his cheek and fell back asleep.

Razi looked at him for a moment, his face carefully schooled.

"It's about time," said Wynter.

"I . . . I should go and check on Sólmundr."

Despite his contained expression, Razi's voice was horribly shaky, and Wynter reached over before he could pull away and dragged him into a fierce hug. Just for a moment he submitted, his chin dropping briefly to her shoulder, his arms closing around her. Then he pushed away. "I won't be long," he said.

Half an hour or so later, Wynter saw Razi's long shadow as he came around the tent. She was lying by Christopher's side, holding his hand and listening to the peaceful sound of his breathing. He had not stirred since Razi's departure, his mind finally allowing his body to succumb to the exhaustion of the last few days. Wynter had no doubt that Sólmundr would allow him the use of his bed for as long as he needed, and did not stir as Razi's shadow dipped to pull back the flap.

"He's still asleep," she began, but it was not Razi at all, it was Ashkr, and the look on his face stole Wynter's smile. She sat up, her hand moving protectively to Christopher's shoulder. "He's *sleeping*, Ashkr," she said.

Ashkr had their hats in his hand, and he came across and handed them to her. "It grow hot outside," he said. Wynter took them grimly, knowing that Christopher would get no more rest.

"Where is Razi?" she asked.

Ignoring her, Ashkr hunkered down by the bed and shook Christopher.

"Coinín," he whispered, "wake up."

Christopher snapped awake with a snort. "*Cad é?*" he

rasped. He ran his hand down his face and licked his lips.

Ashkr reached behind him and uncorked a waterskin, offering it silently. Christopher rolled to his elbow to quench his thirst, and as he drank, Wynter saw the memory of where he was and what had happened seep into his pale face. He lowered the waterskin and stared at her. For a moment, she thought he was going to repeat his previous rejection of her, then he smiled uncertainly. There was a hesitant silence, neither of them knowing where to start.

"Are you all right?" she whispered finally.

He nodded.

"And . . ." she looked down at the token on her wrist, afraid to ask. "Are we . . .? Christopher, are we still all right?"

He stared at her, his eyes wide. Wynter thought he seemed frighteningly unsure of himself. Then he nodded again. She tilted her chin. "Then what is my name, Freeman?" she demanded. "You seem to have been forgetting it recently."

Christopher's lips twitched, his grey eyes glittering even as they creased up into his old amusement. "Your name," he said, taking her hand, "is Iseult Ní Moorhawke Uí Garron, and you are my *croí-eile*."

They smiled shakily at each other, and Wynter ran her thumb along the twist of wool at his wrist. "Good," she said softly. "Good." Then she clamped down hard on his hand, purposely squashing his fingers so that he yelped. "Don't you forget it," she said.

"Ow!" Christopher wriggled his fingers. "A bloody shrew," he groaned. "I've shackled myself to a bloody shrew! My life is ruined." He glanced at Ashkr and the laughter died in his face. "Ash," he said.

The two men regarded each other, their expressions heavy with an unspoken understanding. Ashkr seemed to hesitate, then he straightened his back and cleared his throat. "I want to call for Council," he said.

Christopher's eyes widened. "Council . . . why?"

Ashkr looked away. "What it is you tell me yesterday . . . about there being no place here?" The blond lord glanced fleetingly at him. "I wish you to press this case. I want to hear proper. I want others to hear proper. So we can make choice."

Wynter saw excitement grow in Christopher's tired face. "Will they grant Council?" he said. "I can't imagine . . . it's very late, Ashkr, I can't imagine they would agree."

"Yes," agreed Ashkr. "It very late. Already our business here delayed by Sól be sick." He looked up at the walls of the tent, his eyes tracing the bear and the lamb. "But, Úlfnaor, I think he will agree. He falter, I think, in his duty, and he welcome delay. Sól too, if it not take too long and make us suffer in the wait. But my sister . . ." He trailed off, his face darkening. "Embla, she maybe not want to listen. She tired, I think, of wait." He looked at Christopher's pale and worn face. "But still, Coinín, if it happen. If I make it that they agree . . . will you to speak? What you say to me before? Will you make case?"

Christopher stared at Ashkr. "Aye," he said. "I will."

"Chris?" asked Wynter cautiously.

"You let me handle this now, lass," he said, speaking in quiet Southlandast. "You just make sure that Razi don't give any promises, all right?" Before Wynter could reply, Christopher turned to Ashkr and said, "Come on, my Lord. Let us go press for Council."

Council

*O*n arriving back at the plains, Wynter was gently taken by the arm and escorted to Razi's side. Though the Merron had returned Christopher's weapons, they left Razi and Wynter unarmed and the two of them were placed sitting on a log in the shade, thoroughly excluded from the activity. Two warriors hunkered in the dust a few feet away, guarding them and silently following the proceedings from afar.

There was an air of tense dissatisfaction amongst the milling ranks of warriors, and they huddled around Ashkr as he furiously pressed his case. There were raised voices and sharp gestures. Everyone seemed to have an opinion and everyone seemed determined to be heard. Now and again, one or another of the Merron would glance across at Wynter and Razi, their looks filled with confusion, pity or just plain animosity. Embla and Úlfnaor were silent, their faces tight. Sólmundr sat hunched against a tree, listening gravely to the babble.

Razi, taut as a bowstring, switched his attention from Christopher to Embla, to Úlfnaor and back. Wynter kept her eyes on Christopher. He was standing by Ashkr's side, listening quietly as the Merron lord argued with his people.

Neither Wynter nor Razi bothered with conversation. Everything that might happen now was out of their control, their future depending on the decisions of others.

Abruptly, Úlfnaor clapped his hands and yelled a firm command. All the urgent chatter came to a halt and the Merron grudgingly moved into a rough semicircle and hunkered in the dust. Christopher joined them. Ashkr, Wari and Úlfnaor went to stand by Sólmundr. Embla dithered for a moment, her face grim, then she flung her hands up in surrender and took her place by her brother. Sólmundr's position against the tree had become the equivalent of the royal table at a banquet, and the row of Merron lords stood flanking their seated friend, their arms folded.

It was full light now, and a clear blue sky burned above the trees. Wynter squinted across the growing heat shimmer, watching as the Merron got settled. It was difficult to believe that only three hours earlier they had taken to their horses, planning to ride out of camp.

Úlfnaor stepped forward and looked around, his face expectant. One of the warriors raised her hand and, at Úlfnaor's nod, stood to say her piece. Everyone listened in polite silence as she gave a short, earnest little speech. With a jolt, Wynter realised that this was the Council. Ashkr had got his wish and, without fuss or circumstance, the debate was already underway.

Razi spoke quietly by her side, his eyes on the lords. "Do you know anything about these meetings, Wyn? Are they anything like Father's council?"

Wynter ran her eyes around the circle of crouching men and women, and couldn't help but smile at the thought of Jonathon's po-faced councilmen squatting in the dust. She lost the smile quickly; Jonathon's councilmen might be a bunch of brittle old twigs, but with one stroke of a pen they could destroy this whole camp. They could destroy this whole nation.

Sadly, Wynter surveyed the ring of grimly attentive warriors and their casually imposing row of lords. *They haven't a hope*, she thought. *They will never fit in here. It would be madness for Jonathon even to let them try.* These were a people rapidly running out of time, a nation lost to time.

She glowered and leaned forward, resting her elbows on her knees in an unconscious mirror of Razi's pose. She hadn't bothered to answer Razi's question and he didn't seem to mind. He just sat frowning across at the Council, anxiously rubbing his fingers against his palms in that old, unconscious gesture. After a while, his agitated fretting grated on Wynter's nerves and she reached across and clamped down on his hand.

"Stop it," she hissed. He stiffened and sat upright, his hands clenching, and she was instantly sorry. She patted his arm. "Sorry," she whispered.

"I will not bring you back out there alone," he said tightly. "I cannot. I cannot. I won't. If Christopher is about to try and persuade them . . ." He shook his head.

Wynter looked at him, his rigid posture, his determined face. "Razi," she said, "Christopher is convinced that if you stay, these people will see you dead. He seems to think that you will object violently to their practices.

He is . . ." She hesitated to comment on Razi's relationship with Embla. "He is worried that you will force them to do you harm."

"He underestimates me," said Razi, "if he thinks I cannot extend my tolerance to some dubious pagan rituals. He, of all people, should know that I have been forced to tolerate far worse in my time."

"I believe," said Wynter carefully, "that – as Christopher sees it – the problem may lie with Embla's involvement in things. Pagan practices are quite . . . are supposed to be . . ." She bit her lip, unwilling to detail the types of *practices* in which pagans were reputed to indulge.

Razi swallowed. "Embla is a grown woman. I cannot control what she does. If her religion involves . . ." He resumed the anxious fretting of his hands. "It does not matter to me," he said softly. "It is not the sum of what she is to me."

Wynter put her hand on his arm and squeezed gently. Glancing up at the Merron, Razi's eyes widened and he shot to his feet. Wynter followed his gaze, and rose slowly to stand by his side.

Christopher had raised his hand and was waiting to be recognised. At a nod from Úlfnaor, he pushed himself to his feet and stepped forward. There were some cries of protest as he began to speak, some attempts to shout him down, but the objectors were shushed quickly and decisively, and Christopher was allowed to continue.

At first, Sólmundr listened without reaction. But as Christopher's quiet voice went on, the warrior slowly turned his head to stare at Ashkr. Wynter could see a barely contained hope rise up in Sólmundr's weathered face, a spark of excitement that he could not quite conceal. Ashkr glanced at him only once, then looked away.

By the time Christopher finished speaking, Embla's face was incandescent with fury, Úlfnaor's blank with shock.

Christopher bowed and returned to his place within the circle of warriors. He crouched in the dust, his eyes down. There was a moment's stunned silence, then many arms shot upwards, asking for permission to speak. Úlfnaor looked blankly around. He did not seem to know what to do. When he remained silent, Embla stepped into the ring and swept her arm up, yelling. The Merron slowly lowered their arms, shocked at having been denied their right to speak.

For a moment, Embla stood, fuming, in the centre of the circle. Then she took a deep breath, straightened her back and turned to address her people. She spoke formally and forcefully and at length. A speech, a rousing speech. The Merron listened carefully, and Wynter saw her win them over.

During this speech, Úlfnaor glanced unhappily between Embla and Christopher, and once again there was the sense of a man with an invisible weight pressing down on him. When Embla was finished, she turned back to him and glared. The big Aoire regarded her with sad eyes, then his mouth tightened in agreement and he bowed. Embla returned to his side, her back straight, her shoulders stiff with tension. Wynter saw her glance once at Razi, then look away.

Úlfnaor looked around the circle once more – there were no more hands raised. He glanced at Ashkr. The blond man was staring blindly at the ground. He seemed miles away. Úlfnaor nodded. He raised his hands and seemed about to make a statement, but then Ashkr, his head still down, muttered something, and the Aoire stepped back.

Ashkr stood for a moment, staring at the ground. Then, to the obvious shock of his people, he swept a hand upwards, snapped a command, and strode from the circle, heading straight for Wynter and Razi. Úlfnaor called after him and Ashkr shouted back over his shoulder something that Wynter took to mean *wait*. He stalked across the dusty sunshine and came to a glowering halt in the shade before the two *coimhthíoch*.

Everyone but Christopher turned to watch.

Ashkr looked so fierce that Wynter stepped back a pace. Razi, however, was collected enough to manage a stiff little bow. Ashkr bowed impatiently in return, and then motioned that they sit. He crouched in the dust at their feet, looking Razi grimly in the eye. "I still call you Tabiyb?" he asked.

Razi coloured and nodded. "It is the title I prefer to all others," he said. "So yes, please, continue to—"

"You listen what I tell you now, Tabiyb. You not tell me no lies now, you agree? You not twist truth or hold nothing into your heart for me now, when I ask of you this questions?"

Razi's hands clenched on his knees. He nodded again.

"Coinín, he say there no hope here for us. He say we misled by . . . by people. They make promise they not ever keep. He say we not ever be allowed to settle in this place, that there nothing here for the People or for any of the tribes. He say . . ." Ashkr lost some of his fierceness and his eyes opened a fraction wider. "Coinín, he say that nothing we do change this, that we can to forget this wakening a new land to *An Domhan*. Our . . . our . . . we not need . . ." Ashkr looked over his shoulder. His people were watching him, Sólmundr in particular, painfully anxious. Christopher, his head in his hands, was the only person not looking in their direction. Ashkr glanced at Embla and his face hardened. "My sister, she say that Coinín only tell this because he not of the Religion. She say Coinín willing tell anything, any untruths because of this." Ashkr turned enquiring eyes to Razi. "Is this true, Tabiyb? Coinín, he say this things just because he not of the Religion? He lie because of this?"

Razi stared at Ashkr uncertainly, and Wynter cursed Christopher for having kept so much from them. Who could tell what the consequences of one misplaced word might be? If Razi confirmed what Christopher had said, the Merron might simply go home and leave them stranded here without a guide to Alberon's camp. On the other hand, what might these people do to Christopher, if they came to believe that he had tried to deceive them? Unwilling to risk a comment either way, Razi glanced silently to where their friend crouched in the dust.

Ashkr slapped his palm into the ground. "Tabiyb!" he cried. "Does Coinín lie?"

"Christopher is a deeply honourable man, Ashkr. I doubt very much that . . . I assure you that Christopher would not lie simply in order to get his own way. If he has told you something, then it is because he believes it to be the truth."

Ashkr searched Razi's eyes. Wynter was not sure what it

was she saw in the blond man's face now. Was it hope? Fear? Grief? She could not read him.

"Then . . . what *you* say, Tabiyb?" he asked softly. "You think there hope here for the People? You think it worth for us to go on?"

Wynter thought of the Loups-Garous. She thought of the long trek to Alberon's camp, and of the many nights that they would face, alone in the dark, just the three of them, with David Le Garou and his Wolves searching the shadows for them. She gazed into Ashkr's questioning face and thought, *Tell him "yes" Razi. Lie to him. Promise him anything; just make sure these people get us to Alberon.* She stole a glance at Razi. He was scanning Ashkr's face, no doubt trying, and failing, to read the man. *Tell him "yes"!* she thought.

"Ashkr," he said. "I have no idea what it is that Christopher so objects to in your plans. But I can assure you that if you grant my companions and me safe progress to the Royal Prince, if you offer us your protection and do your best to fulfil that duty, then I shall exert every *ounce* of my considerable influence to ensure that you are granted haven in this kingdom."

Ashkr frowned. "You able make this kind of promise, Tabiyb? You this kind of man? You have such power?"

Razi snorted. Wynter heard the bitterness in his voice when he said, "Yes, Ashkr. I most certainly have."

"Even . . ." Ashkr hesitated, his eyes dropped to Razi's hands. He touched Razi's dark skin. "Even though you man of colour?"

Razi's jaw tightened. "Yes, Ashkr. Even though I am a man of colour."

"I would think it bode very well for the People," said Ashkr softly. "That man of colour be permitted have such influence here."

Ashkr looked across at his people again. Wynter saw him find Sólmundr. The wiry man was hunched forward expectantly, his eyes glued to his friend.

"I believe you, Tabiyb," murmured Ashkr, still gazing across the sun-filled camp at Sólmundr. "I believe you do your best for us, and the People maybe really find a home here."

Wynter saw Sólmundr scan his friend's face, saw the hope in his eyes as he tried to read Ashkr's expression. Ashkr's mouth tightened. He held Sólmundr's gaze for a moment, then he shook his head. Sólmundr's hope instantly drained away and Wynter's heart clenched in anxiety and guilt at the grief in his face. For the briefest of moments the two men stared desolately at each other. Then Sólmundr nodded curtly and sat back. Ashkr's face hardened, his brows drew down, he set his jaw.

"My sister is right," he said, rising to his feet. "We will move fast now. We fulfil our duty." He glanced down at Razi. "And we get you to the prince, Tabiyb, that you may fulfil *your* duty. Thank you." He reached forward, smiling, and Razi numbly accepted his handshake. Thank you for truth," he said, then turned and strode away.

As he entered the circle, Ashkr lifted his arms and yelled in Merron. The warriors all lurched to their feet in joyful relief and the tall man was momentarily engulfed in their noisy ranks as he made a loud and resolute proclamation. Christopher and Sólmundr remained seated, their faces blank.

Razi got to his feet, rubbing his hands on his thighs. Wynter stepped to his side, her heart itchy with the conviction that somehow, something huge had just slipped irretrievably from their grasp.

"You under our protection now, Tabiyb," said Úlfnaor, handing Razi his sword and knife. "We take you the rest of the way. We keep you as safe as we can."

Razi bowed absently. Wynter took her weapons from the Aoire and leaned to peer around him, trying to keep Christopher in her sight. Úlfnaor turned to follow her gaze.

Christopher was helping to get Sólmundr to his feet. He looked angry and upset, and when Wynter and Razi tried to catch his eye he pointedly turned away, shoved his shoulder under Sólmundr's arm and helped Ashkr lead him off between the tents and out of sight.

"Give him time," said Úlfnaor. "He rage that you go against him, but sometimes it hard to see there is two sides to one truth, *nach ea*?" He slapped Razi on the shoulder. "Come," he said. "We put you to work, eh? You help tidy up this Loups-Garous mess. It take your mind off things."

Wari took Razi into the forest to dig the Wolves' graves, and Wynter was commandeered to construct the drying frames necessary for the meat and hides that the Merron were harvesting from the Wolves' dead horses. The work was obviously designed to keep the two of them separated and out of mischief, and Wynter spent the morning under the watchful eye of a small group of men and women, while the majority of the Merron occupied themselves in some secret industry, deep in the forest.

Christopher and the lords retreated to Ashkr's *puballmór*

and remained there. Over the course of the day, Wynter found herself staring across the rippling heat haze, wondering what was going on within the silent, sun-blasted walls of the tent.

A small pile of Loups-Garous' belongings was deposited in the centre of camp, and the Merron came and went, helping themselves. Wynter didn't even bother looking; she had no desire to own anything tainted with the smell of Wolf. But when Razi returned from the forest to collect the second body, she was surprised to see him stride over and crouch to root in the pile, his back to her. He seemed to be looking for something in particular, and after a moment Wynter saw him draw his dagger and set to worrying at something hidden from her sight.

Just as she was rising to her feet, Razi straightened and thrust his find into the ammunition pouch on his belt. He stood staring down at the pile of rich tack and finery, and something in the furious set of his shoulders stopped Wynter from crossing to his side. He glowered once in the direction of Ashkr's tent. Then he spun on his heel, strode back to Wari, heaved the remaining body across his strong shoulders and stalked into the shadows of the trees.

Wynter went back to her work.

Quite early in the evening, the Merron began to trickle back through the trees, and Wynter found herself no longer needed at the drying frames. For a long, indecisive moment, she stood gazing at Ashkr's resolutely quiet tent. Then she turned and wandered through the murmuring activity of camp, looking for Razi.

She caught sight of him, hunkered by one of the tents, deeply engrossed in a pantomime conversation with Wari and another man. Razi had something in his hands and they were all hunched over it, frowning. Razi handed it to the man. As Wynter approached, things seemed to come to a conclusion, and Razi stood and shook the man's hand with the decisiveness of a bargain sealed.

Wynter waved to catch his eye and he wandered over. His eyes widened as he took in her work-sullied clothing. "Good God, sis. What have you been doing, rolling in a trough of offal? You'll breed flies!"

"You're hardly fit for court yourself, Razi Kingsson!"

Razi looked down at himself. Stripped to the waist, he was filthy from digging the graves, his skin and trousers covered in mud and gore. "Oh!" he said, absurdly surprised. "Oh my." He held up his grimy hands as if trying to fathom how they had come to be that way. "I'm foul!"

Wynter took him by the elbow. "Come along," she said. "Let us go wash."

As if on cue, the two of them paused and glanced back in the direction of Ashkr's tent, hidden from them now by the rest of camp. Suddenly Wynter felt overwhelmingly exhausted and unbearably hot. Glancing up at Razi's dirty face, she saw the same weariness in him. She slipped her hand into the crook of his arm and shook him gently. He glanced down at her. "Would you like a swim?" she asked.

He nodded. Behind them, a steady gentle tapping started up, the sound of a small hammer striking metal. Wynter looked back. The man with whom Razi had been speaking was hunched near the door of his *puballmór*, beating some small piece of silver into shape.

"Is he a smith, Razi? Have you commissioned some work?"

"Aye," he sighed. "But, I must confess, I am not certain I shall go through with the idea. I'm afraid it may, in fact, be tasteless and crass." He grimaced at her. "I would like to think about it for a while, if I may, before discussing it?"

Wynter studied his weary face. "All right, Razi," she said gently.

Smiling, Razi pushed back her hat, found a clean piece of skin and kissed her forehead. "Let us go swim."

An Lá Deireanach

A couple of hours later they were strolling back across the plains, sun-dried and river-scoured, tired, hungry and refreshed, when Razi stiffened and came to an awkward halt. Wynter looked up to see Christopher striding across the grass, his hair flying.

"Where have you been?" he yelled. "I've been looking for you!"

He was carefully groomed, dressed in his cleanest clothes, the sleeves of his undershirt rolled to the shoulder. To Wynter's amazement the tops of his arms were glittering with silver. He came to a halt in front of them and she stared at the bear emblems decorating the bracelets at the tops of his arms.

"Christopher," she said. "Where . . .?"

"We've been invited to dinner," he said curtly. "It ain't nothing formal. Just put on clean clothes."

"But Chris," she said again, reaching for the bracelets.

He shifted his arm from her touch. "Sól and Ash gave them to me. They're a gift." Wynter met his eye. Merron bracelets were much more than a simple gift. They were a pact. They were a promise. They meant you belonged. Christopher averted his gaze. "Dinner is in Ashkr's tent," he murmured. "Don't be long." He began to turn away.

"Chris," said Razi.

Christopher came to a halt.

"Don't be angry," said Razi.

Christopher's shoulders slumped, but he didn't turn back. "Go change your clothes," he said. "I'll see you at dinner." And he strode off, heading down through the smoky camp to Ashkr's tent.

Razi went to run after him. Wynter caught his arm. "Razi," she said, "the smith is calling you." He turned to see the man waving at him from the door of his tent. "Go on, Razi," urged Wynter gently. "Go conclude your business. I shall change my clothes. You can meet me at the tent when you are done. Go on, brother. Chris just needs some time."

"You would like more drink, Iseult?"

Embla leant across to fill Wynter's beaker, and Wynter was once again struck by the richness of the beautiful woman's clothes. *Nothing formal, my foot!* she thought, tugging at her travel-worn shirt and straightening her britches. *Curse you, Christopher Garron. Had I known the lords would deck themselves out like sultans, I might at least have polished my boots.*

Razi chuckled at something Ashkr was saying, and Wynter smiled, glancing his way. He was resting back against a cushion, his arm curled loosely around Embla's waist, his long legs splayed perilously close to the remains of the dinner things. Wynter had to admit, this meal had been a wonderful idea. Strange at first, and stilted, it had not taken long for the Merron's easy good humour, Razi's smooth diplomacy, and the rather liberal distribution of wine, to ease the tension.

You understand, Razi had said when they entered the tent. *I have no intention of standing in the way of your duty, Embla? I do not presume to come into your life and tell you how to live. Whatever it is you must do, I shall respect it, as I respect you, totally and without question.* Embla had kissed him, Ashkr had poured him a drink, and all had gone smoothly from there.

This one night, thought Wynter, *that's all we need get through. One more night of their odd formalities, and then we shall be on our way, safer than ever. And within one week we shall be in Alberon's camp.*

One week. It was hard to believe they were so close.

Razi laughed again, bringing her attention back to Ashkr's amusing story.

Sólmundr, reclining against Ashkr on the far side of the tent, shook his head. "You never remembers that right, Ash! It was Úlfnaor, and not Wari, who the licence men throw in the river. But it was Wari what was so ill after. You remember? It was this that open his eyes to Soma? Till then he dangerous in heat with that crazy village woman who want for him to kill her father."

"Oh, *Frith an Domhain!*" exclaimed Embla, sitting back from filling Wynter's beaker, her eyes wide. "I forget all about that woman! She mad in the head! What it was that Wari see in her?"

Ashkr grinned slyly and held a hand out in front of him to symbolise huge breasts. Razi spluttered his drink, coughing. "Ashkr!" he admonished.

Sólmundr tutted. "You to have no heart, Ash. Embla right, you always thinks with your trousers."

Embla made a dismissive noise. "He right about that woman, though. I tell you now, it not Wari's heart she capture."

"Stop that!" cried Sólmundr, laughing despite himself. "He in *love* with her!"

"He in love with *something*," said Ashkr slyly. "But I think it hid beneath her skirt."

Wynter blazed red and snorted with laughter. She twisted her head against Christopher's shoulder, looking up at him. He was very quiet, the only one of them who had yet to thaw. "Are you all right?" she whispered. He smiled tightly at her and nodded.

The Merron subsided into chuckles. Sólmundr leaned stiffly forward to help himself to a drink, and Ashkr rested back against his cushion, sighing happily. He ran his hand up his friend's back, his eyes roaming the walls of the tent. Gradually some of the joy left his face. "It get late," he said softly.

There was a moment of heavy silence as the Merron noblemen regarded the growing shadows on the walls of the tent. Sólmundr sat back, his face grave, and Ashkr draped his arm around the wiry man's shoulder.

"Coinín," said Embla, leaning forward to see him. "You light the fire-basins now."

"It's not that dark yet," murmured Christopher.

Razi glanced at his friend, disapproving of his sullen tone.

Sólmundr glared. "You light the fire-basins now," he commanded.

Christopher got silently to his feet and lit a candle from Ashkr's tinder box. He moved around the periphery of the tent with it, lighting the four fire-basins that the lords had waiting, and the *puballmór* was instantly filled with warmly dancing light. When he had lit the last basin, Christopher snuffed the candle and stood for a moment, his shadow thrown long against the wall. Wynter glanced at him, but he just continued to stand there, gazing down at the neat pile of weapons they'd left by the door.

Behind her, Ashkr teasingly challenged Razi to another game of chess. Sólmundr objected, claiming he should have first right to challenge, now that his body was free of Razi's opium. Razi dryly offered to take them both on, playing two boards at once, and there was a loud chorus of approval from the Merron lords.

"My man has balls," crowed Embla.

"Oh?" countered Ashkr. "Still? I surprised you not wear them away yet. I amazed he can still to walk!"

"Good *God*," gasped Razi, mortified, "*Ashkr!*"

Wynter laughed and looked once again at Christopher. He was still staring absently at the weapons. "Chris," she called softly. "Are you all right?"

He glanced quickly at her, placed the candle in Ashkr's tinderbox, and crossed back to the company. But to Wynter's surprise he did not return to her side, just ran his hand over her hair as he passed by, and edged around the dinner things to go sit between Razi and Sólmundr. "I'd like to see this game," he said, smiling at his friend.

Razi grinned, delighted at Christopher's sudden warmth. He straightened expectantly, waiting for someone to offer a board.

Embla was staring at him. "Tabiyb," she whispered. "I want . . ."

"We will play the game now!" said Ashkr loudly. Embla's eyes darted to him. "We play chess, Sól and me. We beat the trousers off your man and then we see who has the biggest balls! We drink to it," said Ashkr. "Yes? We drink to beating your man in chess."

"Aye," whispered Embla. "Aye, Ash, we drink to that."

"Coinín," said Sólmundr flatly. "You get drinks now."

Wynter caught Christopher's eye as he rose to his feet. He was desperately unhappy. She tried to question him with her eyes but he turned away, rubbing his hands on his trousers, scanning the shadows at the back of the tent.

"You drink, *a chroí?*" murmured Embla, running her hand along Razi's face. "Drink to victory?"

Razi nodded uncertainly.

"Come help me, Embla," said Christopher. "I don't know where everything is."

As Embla rose to help Christopher, Razi looked across at Wynter. His dark eyes were troubled. Like Wynter, he felt this odd charge between the Merron. Outside, the dogs shifted, their chains clinking in the empty silence of the camp, Wynter turned to listen to the quiet sound. Ashkr's soft voice drew her attention back to the company.

"Tell me what you do this winter, Sól."

"I not want tell that now," said Sólmundr, pulling his head away from Ashkr's caressing touch. His friend drew him close, whispered *please*. Sólmundr closed his eyes. "I not want to, Ash," he whispered.

Embla and Christopher were coming around the edge of things now, a tray of six tiny silver beakers and a jug carried between them. Embla glanced at Sólmundr as she picked her way across the mats. "You tell it now, Sól," she said. "Make Ash happy." She knelt on one side of Razi, and Christopher knelt on the other. Between them, they began to set out the little beakers.

Sólmundr laid his head back against Ashkr's shoulder and stared up at the smoky ceiling. Ashkr kissed the side of his neck. "Tell me what you do this winter, Sól," he murmured again. "Tell me where you go."

"I go with the tribe to the winter hunting ground," began Sólmundr softly.

Ashkr smiled and sat back against the cushion, his eyes closed. "Yes," he said. He pulled Sól closer. "Then what you do?"

"Then I leave the tribe in the valley," continued Sólmundr, "and I go to our lodge on the mountain."

"Yes," murmured Ashkr.

Christopher uncorked the jug and began to fill the little beakers with thick, amber coloured liquid. Embla placed them, one at a time, before each member of the company.

Sólmundr's eyes were very bright now, gazing at the ceiling. His hoarse voice was as soft as the gentle hiss of the fire-basins. "I hunt the little red deer," he whispered. "I hunt good and I get much food for the winter. Much hide. I maybe hunt also the bear, and make for me a black fur coat." Ashkr nodded. "And there not be any licence men, not either any cavalry, to harry us and spoil our winter rest."

"Ash," said Embla softly, leaning forward and offering her brother his drink. Sólmundr and Ashkr straightened, took their beakers, held them solemnly, waiting. Embla lifted hers. Wynter and Razi glanced at Christopher. When he took his, and, without looking up, raised it, they followed suit. Wynter looked down at her drink. It was very heady, smelling strongly of resinous honey.

"*Croí an Domhain*," toasted Ashkr. "*Ar fad do Chroí an Domhain!*"

The Merron and Christopher downed their drinks, emptying their cups in one swallow. Razi and Wynter hesitated. They glanced at Christopher. He nodded, and they downed the drinks.

Wynter gasped as honeyed fire burned its way to her stomach. *Jesu*, she thought, *that is unbearably sweet!*

"Gah!" spluttered Razi, "that is bitter!" Wynter stared at him. He tried valiantly to hide his disgust and couldn't. One eye closed and his entire face puckered in reaction. "Gah!" he said again, laughing. "Woman! Are you trying to kill me?"

Embla laughed shakily. Christopher took the beaker from Razi's hand, carefully laying it behind him on the floor.

Ashkr pulled Sólmundr back against him. "Finish the story, *a chroí*," he murmured, wrapping his arms around his friend. "What you do, in our lodge, all the long winter, when firelight paint the walls and the snow pile heavy on the door?"

Razi gasped, working his tongue around his mouth to rid himself of the bitter taste. "Oh, Embla!" he said, "I . . . I think I need some water."

Christopher rose to his knees and placed a hand on his friend's shoulder.

Ashkr glanced at him, then murmured once again to

Sólmundr, "Tell me what you do, Sól, this winter in the lodge."

Sólmundr closed his eyes. Two bright tears made an unexpected trail down his cheeks. "I . . ." he said, "I . . ."

"You be happy," insisted Ashkr, squeezing tightly. "Say it, you be happy."

"I . . . be happy."

"And you have beautiful blond man to warm your bed."

Sólmundr sobbed, shaking his head.

"Yes," insisted Ashkr. "Yes. Beautiful man. As many as you wish."

"No," whispered Sólmundr. "No, Ash. No."

"But who warm your heart, *a chrot*? While that man warm your bed?" Ashkr wrapped himself around Sólmundr and buried his face in his friend's neck. "You tell me," he moaned, "tell me, who warm your heart?"

"You," sobbed Sólmundr. "You. Always you. Never anyone but you."

Wynter stared at the two men, shocked by their sudden distress.

"Embla!" The alarm in Razi's voice snapped Wynter's attention back to him. At the sight of him she lurched to her knees, her eyes wide. He was bent forward, clutching his chest. "Christopher," he gasped. "Chris . . . what . . .?"

"Shhhh," soothed Christopher, rubbing his back. He glanced at Wynter and she hunched warily, her hands closing to fists.

"Christopher?" she snarled.

"Shhhh," he said again. "It will be all right."

Razi stared around him with unfocused fear. He tried to rise, and Christopher and Embla leapt to catch him, supporting his head and shoulders as he collapsed backwards. Razi cried out and gasped, his arm flying out in aimless self-defence.

"It's all right!" said Christopher, his voice breaking in a sob. "It's all right, Razi . . . please . . ."

"You've poisoned him!"

"No! No, Iseult! Trust me!"

But Wynter was already flinging herself backwards, rolling across the furs, and scrambling for the pile of weapons they had left by the door. She scrabbled around in blind panic for a moment, before realising that the weapons were gone. She came to a despairing halt, feeling the air pour through the narrow gap where someone had reached in under the hide wall and drawn their weapons outside.

Behind her, Razi kicked out and sent the tray of little beakers flying. Christopher was trying to soothe him, repeating that it was all right, everything was all right. Razi lashed at him in rage and fear. Wynter remained hunched by the door, staring in horror through the gap under the wall. The tent was surrounded by Merron, all silently waiting in the rapidly encroaching dusk. Her stomach shrank to a cold walnut at the realisation that this was what Christopher had been doing, that time he had stood here, his shadow thrown against the wall. He had been showing the others where the weapons were, letting them know what part of the wall to lift.

She turned on him, snarling through furious tears. "God curse you for a traitor, Christopher Garron," she hissed. "God curse you! What are they going to do with him?"

"No," he moaned, shaking his head. "No, lass. Please. It's to keep him safe. That's all. I promise you, it's the only way."

Razi weakly lifted his arm, then let it fall. His head and shoulders were supported across Christopher's lap and he was trying in vain to push the young man away. His eyes rolled beneath heavy lids, closed briefly, opened again. Gasping, he made one last attempt to grab the front of Christopher's shirt. He succeeded only in batting at his friend's chest, and then his arm slithered down to fall slackly between them and his body went limp in Christopher's arms. Wynter cried out in despair.

Ashkr called out something and bright light flared across the hide walls as a ring of torches roared to violent life outside the tent.

"You come take care of Tabiyb, Iseult," said Embla. She was helping Christopher lay Razi down onto the furs, rolling him gently onto his side, propping him into position with cushions at his back. "This herbs very strong. They may to make him sick, and if you not careful, he can to choke."

Wynter watched, frozen, as Christopher passed his hand over Razi's curls. He glanced at her. "Come on, lass," he said softly. "Come take care of our lad."

Behind her, Ashkr whispered to Sólmundr, "Let me go now, *a chroí*. You know I got to go." He still spoke Hadrish, and Wynter wondered if it were so that the Merron outside would not understand.

"*Iseult*," said Christopher urgently. "Come *here*. Please."

"We got no time," said Embla. "Come *here*."

Wynter scrambled across the mats and pushed Embla to one side. "Razi!" she cried, shaking him and peering into his slack face. "Wake up!"

Christopher grabbed her arm and she jerked away from

him with a cry. He grabbed her again and pulled her up to face him.

"There's no *time*!" he yelled. Wynter snarled at him, and his fingers dug into the tops of her arms. "I want you to look after Razi," he hissed urgently. "Don't leave him on his own." He pulled her closer. "And don't leave Sól on his own. I don't trust what he told Ash, I don't think he *does* intend going on. Don't let him out of your sight."

Wynter blinked at him in frantic confusion. She could feel her anger draining from her, leaving only fear.

Embla had crossed to the others, and when she spoke, her voice was soft and persuasive. "Ash," she said. "Let him go. *Ash*, let Sól go. He not part of this no more."

She guided her brother to his feet, but Ashkr kept hold of Sólmundr's hand, stretching his friend's arm up as he stood. The men were not looking at each other, their faces curiously vacant, but their hands remained joined as if welded.

"Let go," murmured Embla, prising their fingers loose. "Let him go, *a chroí*."

Christopher got to his feet and Wynter was too stunned to do anything but watch as he crossed the tent and crouched to look into Sól's face. "Let go now, Sól," he said. "You're out of time."

Abruptly Sólmundr shook Ashkr's hand away. Ashkr stumbled backwards, his face despairing, then he seemed to gather himself, and, with a deep breath, straightened and stiffly turned to face the door. Embla joined him. Outside the tent there was no sound but the gutter and flare of torches and the soft clink of the warhounds' chains. After a moment, Embla reached out and took her brother's hand.

Christopher stayed crouched by Sólmundr, gazing into his eyes.

"You not have to keep your promise," whispered Sólmundr, his empty fist clenched to his chest. "I know it too much to ask."

"I shall fulfil my promise, Sólmundr. I swear it."

Sólmundr's face softened in desperate gratitude. "You not let them see you, Coinín," he warned. "You know what they do if they catch you. Úlfnaor, he will not be able save you from it."

Christopher nodded.

Wynter rose to her knees. "Chris . . ." she whispered, very frightened for him suddenly. She understood now that Christopher meant to join the Caoirigh. He intended to leave with them and to hand himself over to that silently waiting throng.

There was a murmur from outside. Embla looked back. "We need to go, Coinín."

"Christopher!" cried Wynter, surging upwards.

Christopher lurched to his feet and dashed across the tent to her. He grabbed her and she clenched her arms around him, pulling him in. "Don't go!"

He whispered into her hair, speaking only for her. "Stay in the tent, girly," he whispered. "You'll be safe in the tent." He pulled back, glaring into her eyes. "Listen, no matter what happens . . . no matter . . . no matter *what* happens, these people will look after you now. I promise you that. I want you to promise me that you will *accept* their protection. Promise me that you'll force Razi to accept it."

"Oh God, Christopher! What are they going to do to you?"

He shook his head, his eyes full. "Promise, Iseult! *Please!* Tell me you'll accept their protection, no matter what. Even if . . . Iseult, just promise me you won't fall prey to the mastery of the Wolves!"

Wynter gripped Christopher by the tops of his arms, the silver of his bear-bracelets cold beneath her hands. "Stay!" she hissed. "What could they do to you if you stay?"

He shook his head.

"Stay! *Please*, they can't make you go."

Christopher gently shrugged free of her grip. He kissed her fingers. "They ain't *making* me do aught, lass. It's my choice. Once we decided to stay, I couldn't just stand by and . . . I can't let him down, lass. If you knew, you wouldn't either." He glanced down at Razi. "You'll tell him I'm sorry, all right? Tell him it was all I could think of to keep him safe."

"Tell him your*self*!" cried Wynter. "Where are you *going* that you can't tell him yourself?"

"Coinín," Ashkr's whisper made them both turn. A dark shadow had fallen across the door. Embla glanced back at Razi, she looked at Wynter, then turned away. Ashkr did not look back at all. Sólmundr stared expressionlessly at the dancing flames of the fire-basins, his hand still clenched over his heart.

Ashkr bowed his head. His hand tightened briefly on Embla's and they parted. The pale lady stooped, lifted the door flap and ducked outside. As soon as Embla and Ashkr had stepped out into the flaring light, Christopher turned and walked after them.

Wynter didn't try and stop him, she didn't reach for him or speak in any way. She was simply too numbed by confusion and fear. So Christopher ducked through the door and passed outside and Wynter silently watched him go. He took his place beside the twins. For a moment he was outlined darkly against the torches and the waiting Merron. Then a figure stepped in from the side, the tent flap was dropped, and he was gone.

A Promise Kept

Wynter sank to her knees beside Razi, her eyes on the door. Outside, there was the unmistakable noise of many people shifting quietly about. Wynter listened, trying to make out voices. There was nothing. She flicked a glance at Sólmundr, who was leaning back against one of the tether poles, staring blankly at the walls. He looked like a man who had been hollowed out and left an empty shell.

"Sól," whispered Wynter, "what will become of them?"

He didn't reply.

Suddenly Razi gasped and drew up his knees, startling her. He curled desperately and groaned. Wynter was certain he was about to vomit, but as quickly as it had hit, his distress drained away and he relaxed again into sleep. She pushed the cushions tighter around him and took his hand. Outside the tent, a man spoke, and a shadow passed rapidly across the wall. The torches bobbed about for a moment and then the light began to fade as they were carried away.

No! Wynter scrambled forward. *Christopher!* Peering through the gap, she was alarmed to see the crowd padding away into the darkness. Already the torches were nearly out of sight. Soon the Merron would disappear into the forest and that would be it. She would have to sit here and wait, not knowing.

Wynter laid her hand on the door. She glanced across at Sólmundr. The warrior just continued to gaze at nothing, not caring whether she stayed or went. Behind them, Razi moaned in renewed discomfort. He drew up his knees, clenched his fists again, then slowly relaxed once more. Wynter waited, listening as Razi's breathing evened out. She shouldn't leave him. Christopher had begged her not to leave him. *Christopher.* Gritting her teeth, Wynter ducked under the door flap and ran into the gathering darkness.

The warhounds rose to their feet, and Wynter felt them rush forward as she ran past. There was a sharp, metallic click as they reached the ends of their chains. She glanced back. There were only three of them, and they stood in a row watching her, their heads cocked in canine curiosity, blessedly silent. *Good dogs*, she thought, *stay quiet.* Then she rounded a tent and they were lost from sight.

Sliding to a halt, she crouched in the shadows at the edge of camp. The Merron were at the tree line already, just a bobbing line of orange torches. Before she could even catch her breath, the forest sucked the torchlight into itself and she lost sight of the procession.

She dithered for a moment, frozen by fear of discovery. Then she stumbled to her feet and dashed across the open ground, her heart in her mouth. What if someone was watching? What if there were pickets? The words *blood-eagle* scrabbled across her mind. Then she was amongst the trees and swamped in inky blackness, running blindly forward, though she had no idea which way to go.

She ran for several aimless minutes, then jerked to a halt, listening in the dark. The forest around her was as silent as a grave, and she could hear nothing to indicate that she was on the right track. She began to push forward again, moving as quietly as she could through the thick undergrowth.

The trees ahead were abruptly silhouetted against a flare of light, and Wynter crouched, staring, as, one after another, a series of torches were lit around the perimeter of a huge clearing. Soon the forest ahead was ablaze with light, a flaming heart at the centre of the darkness. Somewhere within that blinding radiance a great bass drum began to throb, its rhythm slow and deliberate.

The trees above Wynter's head came alive as unseen things began to call harshly in the rustling branches. Wide-eyed, Wynter peered up into the darkness. With a cry, something huge launched itself into the air above her. A chorus of croaking, angry caws followed as the occupants of the treetops fought amongst themselves. Ravens! The trees were full of ravens, woken from their sleep and set to quarrelling by the unexpected light. Wynter ducked her head, cursing, as twigs and bits of debris rained down on her. She blinked her eyes clear of dust, and began to creep forward as the enormous birds jostled and argued overhead.

It was difficult to focus against the light, and for a moment the Merron were nothing but black figures moving against a backdrop of fire. Then Wynter's eyes adjusted and she saw clearly. Ashkr and Embla stood side by side a short distance away, their backs turned to Wynter. At Ashkr's right hand was Christopher, at Embla's left, Wari, and all four stood to stiff attention, watching the ceremonies. Wynter peered beyond them, trying to take everything in.

At the centre of the clearing loomed an enormous, horseshoe-shaped structure of neatly stacked logs and bundles of twigs. A great, dark shape, it brooded in the flickering light of the torches. The space encircled by its arms cradled a deep, unyielding mass of shadow, against which the Caoirigh were illuminated like icons.

It is a pyre, realised Wynter suddenly. *They have constructed a pyre*. She shrank back, her fists closing against the loose leaf-mould, her mind trying to retreat *They have constructed a pyre*. For whom?

More torches flared to life, and they revealed another structure, towering behind the squat body of the pyre. At first Wynter thought it was a marble pillar, then she saw that it was the trunk of some enormous tree, severed from its roots and held upright by wedges and ropes. It had been trimmed of its branches and shaved of its bark. Sap wept from the pale wood, oozing in long, glowing rivers down its length.

Halfway up this pillar, perhaps twenty feet from the ground, a deep niche had been carved into the wood. Etched in shadow like the heart of the pyre, this space was just big enough for one person to stand within. Wynter stared at this wavering, man-sized patch of darkness, and the lump of terror in her throat grew so big that she could not breathe.

The Merron began to chant, and dark figures came forward, advancing on the twins. As they approached, Ashkr and Embla lifted their arms from their sides and held them out in identical poses of acceptance. Ashkr's hands were shaking.

Hallvor came from behind the pyre and stood to one side, her head bowed. Her bare arms were looped with coils of willow-bark cord. She looked as though she were wrapped all around with thin, dark snakes. Slowly, she lifted her arms to shoulder height, and Wynter saw that the ropes were decorated with many small medicine bags and crow feathers. The medicine bags swayed like small, black malignant growths.

Úlfnaor stepped from the shadows. His dark hair was loose as usual and flowing around his shoulders, but he had dressed it with black crow feathers; they twirled and fluttered as he strode past Hallvor and came to stand before the Caoirigh. Solemnly, the Aoire kissed each twin on the cheek, and at each kiss, the surrounding people chanted something low.

Christopher and Wari crouched to pick something from the ground. There was a warm flash of firelight on copper as each man lifted a shallow metal bowl and turned to face the Caoirigh. Christopher's face was briefly outlined in fire. Wynter saw him glance at Ashkr, then he bowed his head and his expression was lost in shadow.

The drums and the Merron chant stopped dead. In the heavy, crackling silence Úlfnaor drew his knife and slowly cut into Ashkr's outstretched forearm. Ashkr jerked slightly and his hands clenched, but that was all. To Wynter's horror, Christopher calmly lifted his bowl and caught the stream of blood that poured from Ashkr's wound. Úlfnaor repeated the ritual with Embla. The pale lady flinched as the knife cut her flesh, but then, like her brother, she stood perfectly still as her blood drained brightly into Wari's bowl. The sound of liquid trickling against copper was horribly loud.

This is not real, thought Wynter, *this cannot be real.* She tried to see Christopher's face, but it was turned from her.

The blood kept flowing, Embla and Ashkr standing patiently as it poured into the upraised bowls. Úlfnaor, his face cast into shadow, waited with his arms at his sides, his head angled downward. The sound of blood spattering onto metal, the harsh crackle of the torches, and overhead, the rustle of unseen wings were all that was to be heard for what felt like two lifetimes. Then the bright stream of liquid slowed, became a trickle, broke into an unsteady procession of heavy drops. Then stopped.

The drums beat out once more.

Embla swayed slightly, and Ashkr had lost some of the rigidity in his spine, but other than that they remained noble and aloof. Christopher and Wari turned and held out the bowls of blood. Once again, Wynter caught a brief glimpse of Christopher's face. It was blank and as empty of emotion as a death mask.

Not real, she thought again. *Not real.* She scanned the semicircle of darkly watchful faces, took in their intense solemnity, and brought her loam-stained hands to her mouth. *Not real.*

Úlfnaor dipped his hand into Christopher's bowl, turned, and with fingers of dripping scarlet smeared a line of blood down the centre of Hallvor's forehead. She smiled and closed her eyes. Úlfnaor murmured a question. Hallvor nodded her consent, and the Aoire painted her mouth.

With a murmured prayer, Hallvor licked the glistening colour from her lips.

Úlfnaor dipped his fingers again, and this time he marked Christopher's forehead, painting a shining red stripe from Christopher's hairline to just between his dark eyebrows. The Aoire paused, his dripping finger poised over Christopher's lips. Again, he murmured the question. There was the slightest moment of hesitation, a minute tightening of Christopher's mouth. Then he nodded, and Wynter moaned in revulsion as Úlfnaor painted Christopher's lips with Ashkr's blood.

Úlfnaor turned to perform the ritual on Wari, and Wynter stared at Christopher. His lips were trembling, his mouth gleaming scarlet in the torchlight. As Wynter watched, a large drop of blood formed on Christopher's lower lip, shivered and fell.

The Merron began to line up for their turn, and Úlfnaor's shadow once again darkened Christopher's pale face as the Aoire dipped his fingers into the copper basin. Just before he turned away again, Úlfnaor lifted his dark eyes. Wynter saw the shock on his face as he took in Christopher's still dripping mouth. Christopher met his eye. Úlfnaor paused for only a fraction of a second. Then, his body shielding Christopher from the others, the big man lifted his hand and with the ball of his thumb discreetly wiped the young man's mouth clean.

Christopher's eyes fluttered shut in relief, and Wynter had to rest her forehead against the ground for a moment as she fought the churning in her stomach.

One after another the Merron came forward, and each took the blood of the Caoirigh onto their brow and onto their tongue. Ashkr, Embla, Wari and Christopher stood unmoving, torchlight crawling across their faces. Hallvor stood to the side, the dark coils of rope looped in silent promise along her arms.

When all the Merron had been anointed, the healer took the empty basin from Christopher's hands and carried it into the black depths of the pyre. Úlfnaor took the basin of Embla's blood and led his people around the clearing. He dipped his hand as he went, casting dark, shining droplets before him, anointing the ground, as he had the people, with the life's blood of their most precious, their most beloved *Caoirigh Beo*.

Immediately, Christopher and Wari turned their attention to the twins. Wari took a cloth from his belt, pressing it to Embla's arm. He murmured to her and she nodded, her face turning so that Wynter caught a sliver of that perfect cheekbone, a brief glimpse of Embla's mouth. Christopher bent Ashkr's arm against a similar pad of cloth. He glanced up into the tall man's face, but they did not speak.

The procession came back around. Úlfnaor still casting bright drops of blood left and right. The drums throbbed their slow, unhurried beat. Solemnly, the Merron arranged themselves on either side of the pyre, and Úlfnaor, the bowl in his hands, disappeared into its waiting shadows.

In the ensuing quiet, Ashkr said something, very softly. Christopher looked up at him, his eyes full, and Embla reached across and took her brother's hand. Abruptly, the drums ceased, and the Merron turned to face the Caoirigh, their eyes writhing pits of shadow. There was an overwhelming sense of *now*. Feverishly, Wynter groped about in the leaves until she found a branch. She pulled it against her thigh, staring at Christopher, waiting for him to move.

The Merron spoke, their voices as flat and sonorous as the worshippers in a Midlander's Mass. From the darkness of the pyre came Hallvor, her arms outstretched, her ropes writhing hungrily in the light breeze. The drums began to beat again, very loudly.

Hallvor strode up to Embla. Smiling gently, she said something.

Embla took an involuntary step back, and Ashkr's hand tightened against hers, halting her retreat. He smiled at her, and whispered. Embla's eyes overflowed as she stared into his loving face, and Ashkr leant in so that their foreheads were touching. He whispered again in brotherly reassurance. Then Hallvor reached between them and took Embla's hand. Ever so gently, she turned Embla away from her brother. For a brief moment the twins remained in contact, their foreheads touching, then Embla was forced around to face the crowd.

The lady faltered for only a moment, then she straightened and flung out her arms.

"*Ar Fad do Chroí an Domhain,*" she said, her voice cracking. And then, louder and with real strength and conviction, she cried, "*Ar fad do Chroí an Domhain!*" The congregation roared its joy.

Still smiling, Hallvor took Embla's outstretched arms and brought the lady's hands together in an attitude of prayer. Deftly, she tied Embla's joined hands with twists of black rope. The drums grew louder and the Merron crooned low. Some of them began to sway, their eyes drifting shut.

Hallvor quickly looped the rope around Embla's body, binding the pale lady's arms against her chest. She cast a loop around Embla's neck and down around her bound wrists, then yanked the rope tight. Then, holding the free

end in her hands like some form of lead, the healer turned
to her people, her arms outstretched in triumph.

"*Féach!*" she cried, "*Féach! Caora an Domhain!*"

The Merron whooped, lifting their arms over their heads
in a single rising clap.

Suddenly all the women of the group rushed forward,
hands out, and they crowded around Embla, petting her
and kissing her cheek. Tenderly, they patted Embla's back
and touched her hair, supported her with hands on her
elbows and arms around her waist. Hallvor led them
around the back of the pyre. Embla walked calmly amongst
them, her head down, her face turned from Wynter's view.
Wari followed discreetly in her wake.

Wynter stared, wide-eyed, as the women disappeared
from view, then she desperately switched her attention to
Christopher. Surely he must act soon? Surely he could not
allow the Merron to split the twins apart?

The blood on Christopher's forehead had trickled down
each side of his nose and run in scarlet tracks under his
eyes. His mouth was smeared with red. As Wynter
crouched in the shadows, clutching her pathetic branch
and willing him to act, he stood motionless by Ashkr's side,
his face blank, and did nothing.

The women led Embla to the back of the clearing. The
men stayed behind, staring at Ashkr whose breathing was
very shallow and fast. Within the shadows of the pyre, the
patch of waiting darkness that was Úlfnaor shifted slightly
and the torches glittered in his eyes. There was a long,
patient stillness.

Suddenly, Ashkr took a step back, and Christopher
straightened in surprise. For the first time, Wynter saw his

blank mask fall aside and that familiar, blade-like determination rise up in his face. He tilted his head, gazing up at Ashkr, his eyes questioning.

Wynter lifted her branch, ready to leap forward. She had no plan of action. Like herself, Christopher had no sword, no shield, no knife. *No hope*, she thought desperately, hoisting the branch. *We have no hope.*

Ashkr lifted his beautiful hands, as if trying to form words with them. He spoke quietly, his eyes huge and liquid. At his words, all the urgency left Christopher's posture, and resignation and sorrow numbed his face once more. He did not speak, just nodded, squeezed the tall man's arm and patted his shoulder reassuringly.

Across the clearing, the women had gathered at the foot of the big pillar. They were helping Embla onto some kind of platform. Wari, his face twisted with the agony of his wounded shoulder, began hauling a rope, hand over hand, and slowly Embla was hoisted from the ground. Gradually she rose higher and higher against the surface of the pillar until she reached the man-sized patch of darkness that had been carved into the body of the trunk. Wari ceased his steady hauling and secured the end of the rope, leaving the platform suspended, fifteen, maybe twenty feet off the ground, holding Embla on level with that wavering, black hollow in its surface.

Wynter stared up at the pale lady – out of reach, now, completely beyond saving – and her eyes filled and overflowed with tears. There was no plan, she realised. There would be no rescue. Numbly, she lowered the branch to the ground and sank into the leaves.

Embla stood on the suspended shelf of her platform,

gazing serenely down on Ashkr. The crow feathers on the rope around her neck rose and fell against her white skin, a medicine pouch nestled against her breast like a black toad. Ashkr took a deep breath, straightened his back, and bowed. His sister tilted her head fondly, then without further hesitation, stepped backward into the shadow of the niche.

Still Ashkr hesitated. Looking down at his wrist, he slowly closed his fingers on the plaited band of silver and copper there. Suddenly he turned, grabbed Christopher on either side of his face, and pulled him forward, kissing him on the mouth. Wynter leapt in shock. Christopher's hands clenched and his spine stiffened, but he did not pull free. The kiss lingered, gentle, heartfelt, desperate, then Ashkr broke away, and, without looking back, strode purposefully towards the pyre.

As Ashkr approached, a torch flared to life within the darkness. The interior was revealed, and the sight of it filled Wynter with despair. Úlfnaor stood waiting, the flaring torch in his hand. Behind him, an eight-foot stake threw unsteady shadows against the log walls. On either side of him, the corpses of the twins' beautiful stallions knelt as if in prayer. Their massive heads were bowed, their foreheads touching the ground at their bent knees. It seemed for all the world as if they were paying obeisance to the tall, blond man who now strode through the ranks of his people and into the heart of his funeral pyre.

As Ashkr passed amongst the Merron men, they reverently touched his hair, his shoulder, the bracelets on his arms. He accepted this without any reaction. Three of the warhounds lay dead on the ground near the entrance to the pyre. Ashkr stepped across their bodies and walked between the hunched forms of the horses and past Úlfnaor. He came to a halt at the stake. Laying his palm against the smooth wood, he looked beyond it to the stars. For a moment he contemplated the sky. Then he turned, leaned his weight against the stake, lay back his head, and shut his eyes.

The women by the pillar began to sing, their voices sweet and high.

Hallvor came swiftly around the corner of the pyre. Wynter could hardly see now through her tears, but she watched as Hallvor bound Ashkr to the stake and Úlfnaor piled birch bundles around Ashkr's feet and up to his chest. The men fetched more tinder from behind the pyre and piled it around the bodies of the horses and around the warhounds, up and up until the interior of the pyre was stacked with brittle kindling. Hallvor took a large pitcher and slowly poured oil onto the branches at Ashkr's feet, singing as she did so. Then, smiling, she kissed Ashkr and left.

Alone now, Úlfnaor stood at the foot of the stake and gazed up at the man he'd protected for so long. Ashkr was watching the stars, his head pressed back against the wood. Úlfnaor's eyes abruptly overflowed. He shook his head. He spoke. Ashkr glanced down, and at the sight of the Aoire's tear-stained face, he smiled reassuringly. *It's all right*, that smile said, *I'm all right*. Gesturing with his chin, he indicated that Úlfnaor should leave. Úlfnaor faltered for just a moment longer, then he bowed and walked stiffly between the stacks of kindling until he was outside the pyre. Ashkr turned his attention back to the sky.

High above him, Embla stood in her little altar of shadows and she, too, was watching the stars. Wynter could see her chest rising and falling rapidly, the medicine pouch swaying between her bound wrists. The song of the women drifted up to her, as bright and as clear as the stars themselves. Behind the pillar, Wari stood poised, his sword resting lightly on the taut line of a rope that rose up from him into the darkness and out of Wynter's sight.

At the pyre, Úlfnaor ordered the men aside and they lined up neatly on either side of him, gazing at Ashkr. The Aoire held the blazing torch aloft, as if to show it to his people, and turned slowly in place. As he turned, Wynter saw Úlfnaor search the tree line. He found Christopher and deliberately locked eyes with him. Still turning, Úlfnaor maintained eye contact, until finally, Christopher, his mouth twisted in bitter despair, nodded. Then the Aoire dropped his head, and completed his slow turn until he was, once again, facing the pyre.

Christopher stepped backwards into the trees.

Silently, Úlfnaor raised the torch above his head. His people roared. Úlfnaor hesitated only a moment, then Wynter saw his shoulder jerk, his arm whip forward, and he threw the torch. It flew through the air, flaring and sparking, tumbling end over end, and landed irretrievably in the tinder at Ashkr's feet. The oil-soaked wood roared to life, and Wynter leapt recklessly to her feet, the branch dropping from her hand. She wailed, but her voice was drowned by the Merron's roar as the fire raced its way towards Ashkr's body.

The blond lord cried out in fear, throwing back his head as the flames flared around him. At his voice, Embla snapped her head around. She saw the rising smoke and she howled, pressing herself back into the shadows, turning her face away. Christopher froze in the darkness of the undergrowth, his eyes fixed on the now crackling heart of the pyre.

Suddenly Ashkr began to scream – high and uncontrollable. His voice seemed to break a spell and Christopher spun with a cry, diving behind a tree. Wynter leapt to fly after him, thinking he was trying to escape. But, instead of running, Christopher fell to his knees, scrabbling at the base of the tree. He almost fell over as he surged back to his feet. He had something in his hands. He was struggling with it. Wynter saw that it was his crossbow. Suddenly everything fell into place for her.

Oh hurry, she thought, pushing her way through the bushes towards him. *Christopher, hurry!*

The drums still beat out their violent rhythm, but Ashkr's screams seemed to have shocked the men into stillness, and they stood, motionless and staring, as he thrashed against his bonds. The women, too, had stopped singing and they stood, wide-eyed, their faces turned to the pyre. High above the drums and Ashkr's agony and the vast rush of the flames, Embla could be heard howling and weeping in torment at her brother's pain.

Christopher, hidden in the trees, fumbled the lever on his crossbow. His hands were shaking so badly that he almost dropped it, but, as Wynter pushed towards him, he finally engaged the bolt. He jerked the bow to his shoulder. He took aim. Then his eyes overflowed, obscuring his vision, and he had to lower the bow again and dash his arm across his face.

Abruptly, Ashkr's screaming turned to shrieks and Wynter had to clap her hands to her ears. Within the pyre, the flames had eaten their way up Ashkr's body. His tunic and his beautiful hair were alight. With a cry of revulsion, Christopher slapped the crossbow to his shoulder and fired.

Wynter understood now why Úlfnaor had shooed his people to either side of the pyre. He had been leaving a space for Christopher to fire through, a clear path straight to the heart of the flames. Wynter saw the bolt's dark shadow speed between the ranks of men. There was a hard thud, and Ashkr's cries ceased. The sound of drums and fire rushed in to fill the void.

There was a moment of stunned stillness amongst the Merron. Wynter crouched, terrified, expecting them to see the bolt sticking from their Caora's chest, expecting them to turn as one and fix their eyes on Christopher. *You know what they do. You know what they do if they catch you.* But Ashkr was hidden by a sudden wall of fire as the kindling to the front of the pyre began to burn in earnest, and the Merron just stood in silence, listening to the flames rush upwards to heaven.

Christopher staggered backwards, the crossbow dropping to his side. High above, Embla still howled her anguish to the stars, mourning her brother and everything else she'd lost. But even as Wynter began to push her way through the bushes and crawl towards Christopher, the Merron began to sing, and the lady's grief was muffled beneath their voices and the incessant drums. Numbly now, almost without thought, Christopher reloaded the bow, took staring aim, and fired. The high thread of Embla's despair cut off in mid-wail.

Before Wynter could reach him, Christopher staggered away into the darkness, muttering and sobbing. All his numb restraint, all his tenacious self-control seemed to have fled, and his progress through the undergrowth was clumsy and carelessly loud.

Wynter, equally careless, flung herself after him. "Wait!" she sobbed, rushing blindly forward, her eyes unaccustomed to the darkness. "Wait!"

She staggered into him unexpectedly, and the two of them almost fell. Christopher spun and flung a punch. He was not anticipating so small a target, and he missed. His fist whistled through the air just above her head, and Wynter ducked. Thank God she was short! Christopher's punches were swift and fiercely directed. Had Wynter been taller, she would no doubt have had the bones of her nose smashed up into her brain. Christopher's momentum toppled him into her, bringing them both to the forest floor, and he raised the butt of the crossbow, intending to smash her across the head with it.

"It's me!" she cried. "It's Wynter!"

He went limp and they lay tangled for a moment, their hearts thundering in the darkness. Behind them, the Merron shouted in unison, a long rising "*HaaaaaAH!*" There was a monstrous *crack*, and a pained creak, like a big door opening. Wynter turned to look, but the clearing was no more than a patch of flame in the darkness. There was a loud, yawning groan, then the ground leapt beneath them as a huge *boom* shook the forest floor. Ravens surged from the trees above, cawing in alarm.

"Embla," moaned Christopher. Wynter pushed herself from him and crawled forward, staring through the trees. He curled immediately into a tight ball, muttering.

They would have done that to her, thought Wynter numbly. *What an awful way to die.* She thought of that rushing plummet downwards, and the great smacking pressure; tons of wood crushing you into the mud, and she thanked God for Christopher, and his recklessness and his bravery in saving Embla from such a death.

There was silence from the Merron, and for a moment only the harsh calls of the ravens cut above the angry noise of the fire. Smoke and the pleasant smell of roasted meat drifted through the darkness. Wynter knew the smell would become awful soon, as all human burnings did. The smoke would turn oily, carrying a wretched stink that would not leave the nostrils for days. It was a stench she had hoped never to endure again. *They will smell of it,* she thought. *When we travel with them. They will stink of Ashkr's death.*

Christopher moaned again. Wynter could hear him scrabbling softly in the dirt as he crawled through the bushes. Then another sound rose up through the flame-roar – the Merron, yipping and whooping, breaking from their shock and coming to life, celebrating the final, the most precious sacrifice of their *Caoirigh an Domhain.*

Christopher staggered to his feet and Wynter turned to find him dimly outlined in firelight, leaning against a tree. "Women go to the earth," he rasped. "Men to the fire." His eyes flashed as he turned his head to stare at her. "Despite what they say, it ain't what we do. I ain't never seen it before . . . only . . ." He shook his head, his face creased in pain. When he spoke again, his voice was too harsh, too loud as if to counteract his tears. "Only the old Religion still worship this way, and only when they are desperate, and frightened."

He sobbed and covered his mouth to hold back his distress. The light subsided a little, and Wynter crouched in the darkness, staring at him in the dimness. Only the flaring outlines of his cheekbones, the glitter of his eyes and the bright tracks of his tears were visible. "She chose them specially, didn't she? To support everything she says about my people. She chose them, knowing they'd never be understood."

Behind Wynter, figures moved against the flames and music was rising, joyful and wild. These people, who had been so kind to her and so generous, were dancing now and singing as they celebrated the murder of their own. Wynter nodded, and scrubbed her wet cheeks. Yes, Christopher was absolutely right. These people confirmed every malicious thing the Shirkens had ever claimed about people of difference. Their vicious campaign against the pagan Merron would be very difficult to argue against after this, and with them, all the others – the Jews, the dissenters, the Musulmen, the reformists – all would burn in the same fires.

"Razi will never understand," she whispered. Embla once again rose to her mind, all that beauty and all that kindness wilfully slapped down into darkness. Wynter put her hand to her mouth, the firelight trebling and doubling as her eyes filled again.

"She spared Razi," whispered Christopher. "He, too, was destined for the pyre. Everything they love . . . everything they love should go with them to *An Domhan*. Sólmundr and Boro – and Razi – should have burned." He closed his eyes. "All the Caoirigh had to do was ask, but they didn't. They spared them. Razi will never understand,

Iseult! He'll—" Christopher turned abruptly, shoving his way through the dark undergrowth, disappearing into the blackness of the trees. Wynter turned back for a moment to the firelight and the singing. Then she stumbled to her feet and pushed after him, following the sound of his clumsy progress until she caught up. She slipped her arm around his waist, and they staggered together through the darkness, heading for the tent.

The dogs were howling. Wynter could hear them scrabbling and running to and fro, their barks coughing to abrupt silence as they hurled themselves to the ends of their chains. Christopher dropped to a crouch in the shadows at the tree line, and Wynter hunkered by his side, silently scanning the empty camp. There was no sign of intruders. After a moment of wary surveillance, they darted across the moonlit space between forest and tents, then slunk around the shadows until they could observe without being seen.

The warhounds were in a frenzy of distress, all their attention focused on Ashkr's tent. As Wynter watched, Boro flung himself to the end of his chain and scrabbled desperately against the earth in a futile attempt to reach the door. Christopher rose to his feet and lowered his crossbow, listening. From within the tent, barely audible above the noise of the hounds, came sounds of a muted struggle. Something clattered softly and there was a faint cry, choked off almost immediately. Boro howled and flung himself once again at the tent.

Wynter and Christopher took off in a run, heading straight for the door. Sliding to a halt, they pushed their way through. Christopher dived left, Wynter dived right, and both came to a frozen halt – in similar attitudes of shock and despair.

"No!" shouted Wynter, rolling to her hands and knees and shooting forward.

With a choked cry, Christopher flung his bow aside and scuttled forward to join her. "You *bastard*," he screamed. "You bloody . . ." His words were lost as he shoved his arms under Sólmundr's shoulders and heaved upwards, taking the warrior's weight. Wynter scurried around behind the tether pole and struggled to free the belt by which Sólmundr was attempting to hang himself. It wasn't hard to do, the pole was only about four feet high, and once Christopher had shoved Sólmundr upwards and supported him against the wood, Wynter found it easy to slip the tether pin free of the belt and let the loose end slip back through the tether ring.

She staggered back, and Christopher and Sólmundr slithered down, coming to rest in a tangled heap at the base of the pole. Christopher scrabbled at the man's neck, digging his fingers underneath the tight leather, and worked the buckle free so that Sólmundr could breath. Sólmundr gasped and heaved air into his lungs, howling in despair.

Flinging the belt to one side, Christopher spun back around, his face scarlet with rage. "You *bastard*!" he screamed again. "Don't you *dare*!" The warrior slid to his side on the scattered cushions, sobbing, his arms coming up over his head, and Christopher instantly curled around him. He knotted his scarred hands in the rich fabric of Sólmundr's tunic and in the tangled waves of his sandy hair. "You *owe* me!" he sobbed. "You *owe* me."

Wynter's legs started to shake and she let go, sliding her weight down the tether pole until she was kneeling on the cushions, her forehead resting against the smooth wood. She closed her eyes and listened to the men weep. Then she turned and crawled across the mats and the furs until she got to Razi.

Still unconscious, and untroubled now by his former discomfort, Razi slept innocently on. Wynter laid her forehead against his temple, trying not to think about the morning, and about what they would tell him when he woke. After a while, she pushed the cushions to one side and lay behind him, her head resting between his shoulder-blades, her hand on his neck. His pulse thudded steadily beneath her fingers. She closed her eyes and for the rest of the night she just lay there and listened to him breathe.

Cold Morning

"Get your hands *off* him!" snarled Wynter. The look on her face must have been unmistakable, because Hallvor stepped back immediately and moved aside so that Wynter and Christopher could help Razi to his feet.

At the door, a warrior stared in, her eyes wide with curiosity, and Christopher snarled at her, "*Croch leat! Agus ná bí ag stánadh.*"

Razi, startled at Christopher's sharp tone, turned to blink uncertainly at him. Christopher glanced up into his shocked face and adjusted his grip on Razi's waist. "It's all right," he murmured. "We've got you."

"What happened to me?" slurred Razi, his voice thick.

Christopher looked away. "It's all right," he said again, miserably. He glanced across at Wynter who was supporting Razi from the other side. She nodded and the three of them began to make their way to the door.

Razi stumbled and groaned, overcome again with nausea. He had remained unconscious for the entire night, and when dawn began to break and they still could not rouse him, Wynter and Christopher had reluctantly called for Hallvor's aid. To Wynter's dismay, the healer had administered yet more drugs to counteract Embla's initial dosage. Even then, it had taken Razi an alarming amount of time to regain his senses, and he had been confused and distressingly vulnerable ever since.

"Wynter?" he groaned as they pushed his head down and helped him to duck through the door. "What has happened to me?" Wynter hated the shaky uncertainty in his voice, and she looked away, furious and miserable.

"Shhh," she said. "It's . . . shhh, you will be all right."

Outside the tent, the frigid air hit them like a slap, and Razi straightened with a gasp, squinting in the dim early light. After a few steps, he pulled Wynter and Christopher to a halt, his arms tightening on their shoulders as he got his bearings.

Mist was rising, slow and white from the grass, and the dew was just beginning to glitter in the first shimmer of morning. High above the trees, a thick pall of smoke dirtied the clarity of the rosy sky. Blearily, Razi took all this in, then he noticed the small band of Merron horsemen and women waiting by the forest, and his frown deepened at the sight of his own mare, and Wynter's and Christopher's horses, all tacked up and ready to go. His dark eyes widened as he picked Sólmundr from the row of waiting horsemen, Boro lying miserably at his horse's feet.

Wynter saw memory seep into Razi's face.

"Darling," she whispered. "Listen . . ."

"Wait . . ." he said, his voice deepening. "Wait a moment." He began to shrug free of her grip. "Wait a moment," he said again, looking around him. "What?"

"Listen, Razi . . ." But he was pushing away from her, and stumbling backwards, staring at Christopher.

"What did you *do*?" he cried.

The warrior by the tent stepped protectively to Christopher's side, her face wary. Hallvor ducked through the door and joined her. The healer had Razi's cloak in one hand and his backpack in the other. She looked Razi up and down and said something soothing, but Christopher did not translate for her. Instead, he just stood, flanked by the tall, well-armed women, silently watching his friend.

"Razi," said Wynter, stepping forward, her hand up. Razi glanced at her, then he spun away and stumbled down the track between the tents, tripping and only barely keeping his feet as he tried to run. Wynter strode after him, her heart clenching as she realised where he was heading. "Razi!" she called, breaking into a trot. "Don't!"

She caught up, easily outstripping his uncoordinated pace, and grabbed hold of him. "Listen!" she pleaded, slipping around to face him, putting her hands on his chest. "Razi, please!"

He stared past her and she saw the shock and dawning horror in his face as he took in the circle of beaten ground where Embla's tent used to stand. With a cry he pushed Wynter aside and staggered across to stand in the centre of the bare earth. He stared at the ground. "Where . . .?" he said. "Wynter? Where . . .?"

Wynter's eyes filled with tears and she shook her head, her hands spread helplessly before her. She did not want to say it. Someone moved quietly behind her and Wynter turned to find Christopher standing in the shadows, watching. He had Razi's cloak in his hand.

The jingle of tack and the soft thud of hooves came drifting through the tents. The Merron were walking their horses along the tree line, shadowing Razi's progress through the camp. They came into view and brought their mounts to a halt, their watchful faces pale in the shadow of the forest. Hallvor had joined them; she pulled her mare up beside Úlfnaor's horse and waited in patient silence.

Razi lifted his eyes to the pall of black smoke that stained the sunrise. He inhaled deeply and Wynter knew that he was registering the dark, bitter scent of the pyre that lay beneath the fresh morning air. "No," he whispered. "Oh no."

"Listen," said Wynter again, but she did not know what to say to him and so trailed into useless silence. Razi lurched suddenly towards the forest. She darted across and knotted her fists in his tunic. Oblivious to her presence, Razi jerked forward, three shambling steps, and Wynter had to stagger with him, clinging to his tunic to prevent herself from being flung to the ground. "There is nothing to *see*, Razi! Believe me!" she wailed. "There is nothing!" Heedless, Razi continued to wade forward, and Wynter clung to him in panic, trying in vain to stop him.

"Embla is dead," said Christopher, his flat voice hitting them like a randomly thrown stone.

"Oh, Christopher!" gasped Wynter, appalled at his bluntness.

Razi froze, his eyes widening, and slowly he turned to stare at their expressionless friend.

Christopher dipped his chin, his eyes locked on Razi's. "We drugged you," he said, his voice hard and toneless.

"Embla and I put it in your drink. That's why you feel so ill. That's why you can't remember. Then Embla and Ashkr went into the forest and they allowed their priests to murder them. They believed that this was their honour and their duty, and that it was necessary for the survival of their people."

Wynter felt Razi begin to shake. He clenched his fists, his eyes overflowing, and took a step towards Christopher. Wynter tightened her hands in his tunic. "Stop, Razi," she said. "Stop, *now*."

"There ain't nothing you could have done to prevent Embla's death," said Christopher. "Nothing. And you could never have talked Embla out of it. Never. No one alive could have."

Razi took another convulsive step forward and Wynter pushed on his chest, frightened by his rage. Had he wanted to, Razi could have flung her aside like a kitten, but he hardly seemed to notice her presence, so concentrated was he on Christopher.

Christopher went on. "Don't tell yourself that you could have fought them either – stolen her away somehow, and saved her that way. Embla would have killed you herself, Razi, rather than desert her duty to *An Domhan*." He stepped close suddenly and Razi loomed over him with rage-black eyes. Christopher gazed up with fearless calm. "There was nothing you could ever have done to stop this," he said. "You meant nothing to Embla when compared to her duty. Do you understand? You could *never* have come between Embla and *An Domhan*."

"They killed her," grated Razi, his voice coming harsh and rusty from between viciously gritted teeth.

"Hush," said Wynter, spreading her fingers against his chest. "Razi, hush now. Think—"

"They *killed* her!"

Christopher nodded. "And Ashkr too. It was—"

Razi cut him short with a hiss. "I will *destroy* them."

Christopher stared unflinchingly into Razi's furious eyes. "Do you recall," he said softly, "what you told me that time in Algiers, when I came to you with my plan to rescue my girls?"

Razi's muscles leapt under Wynter's hands. For a moment he gaped at Christopher, his mouth open, his eyes wide. Then he threw himself backward and spun clumsily away, staggering once more towards the trees.

"Wait!" Wynter ran after him and Christopher followed suit, the two of them striding along on either side of Razi as he stumbled towards the forest. "Razi!" she begged, appalled that he might run into the trees, terrified that he would witness the contents of that still burning pyre. That he would see that terrible fallen tree "Please!" she cried. "There is nothing to see there! I swear it to you!"

But Razi wasn't listening to her. He was desperately trying to block out what Christopher was saying. "Marcello was so angry at you," said Christopher. "He was so angry that he threw a chair through the rosewood screen, do you remember?"

"Stop! Stop it!" Razi flung his hands up to cover his ears.

Christopher overtook him and dodged in front, walking backwards, trying to catch Razi's eye. "He was angry because he thought I'd be destroyed, Razi. But I wasn't. I understood. In the end, I honestly understood."

Razi came to a halt, his face desperate. He turned right and then left, trying to avoid Christopher, and then he just stood still and closed his eyes. Slowly he hunched his long body forward and brought his hands to his head. "Oh, don't, Chris," he whispered. "Please don't do that to me."

Christopher stepped in close, his head bowed, his forehead almost on Razi's shoulder. "I understood," he said, "because I knew you meant every word of it. You weren't just saying those things to shut me up. It wasn't just a clever way to let things go. You really meant it. Do you remember?"

Wynter put her hand on Razi's back. He shook his head. "Don't," he whispered again. "Please." Wynter rubbed his shoulder, staring at Christopher. He had yet to break from his calm, flat composure, his eyes fixed on Razi's averted face.

"I remember every word," whispered Christopher. "I remember it as if it were yesterday. You said, 'To my eternal shame, the sufferings of those that you love can be nothing to me when weighed against the future of my father's kingdom, because in my father's kingdom the freedom of thousands like them hangs in the balance.' I remember that, Razi, because sometimes it's the only thing that lets me sleep at night. It's the only thing that helps me live with the fact that we let so much go unavenged."

Wynter's eyes overflowed and Razi moaned, clutching his head. Christopher kept staring at him, saying nothing more. After a moment Razi looked up and met his gaze, his own eyes full. "I do not understand why these people have spared us, Razi," Christopher said. "After what we have witnessed, God knows they'd be much better off had they slit our throats and left us in a ditch. But they have spared us, and they seem determined to aid you in fulfilling your duty to your father's kingdom." He lifted Razi's cloak and held it out to him. Razi looked from his friend's face to the cloak and back again.

Christopher's expression softened and his grey eyes filled with sympathy and tenderness and love. "You have business to do, al-Sayyid," he whispered and he spread the cloak, like a master-of-the-robe preparing to dress his lord.

As Christopher reached up and settled the fabric around his shoulders, Razi's eyes drifted to the dark smoke that smudged the sky above the trees. Christopher pinned the cloak into place, and then, without looking at Razi's face, gestured to someone behind them. As if from nowhere, two Merron warriors advanced from the shadows. They had all the confiscated weapons laid across their out-stretched arms, and as they approached, they held them out, their heads respectfully bowed.

Razi remained motionless as Wynter and Christopher strapped on their swords and knives and slipped their buck-lers onto their belts. Even after Christopher had taken his last dagger and slipped it into his boot, Razi still had not moved. The warriors remained patiently at attention, his weapons held out across their arms. Without another word, Christopher walked away, heading for the horses. Wynter turned to their still motionless friend.

"Razi," she said softly. He made no acknowledgement of her, his eyes unbreakably focused on the rising smoke. Wynter clasped his slack hand in hers, squeezing gently. "There was nothing else he could have done, Razi."

Slowly, painfully, Razi's hand tightened on hers.

"If it is of comfort, Embla did not suffer in the end. It was very quick."

Razi's brows drew down and he dragged his eyes at last from the smoke and turned his attention to the Merron waiting by the trees. Christopher had just reached his horse and Razi watched as he took to the saddle, then he switched his gaze to Úlfnaor.

"Razi," said Wynter, alarmed at the cold murder that she saw rising in his eyes. Without glancing at her, Razi suddenly shook free of her grasp and reached for his weapons. "Razi!" she insisted. "We have a long way to go. Can you do this?" Razi jammed his knife into his thigh sheath and buckled on his sword-belt. Snatching his falchion from the warrior's arms, he slammed it into the scabbard on his hip. He lifted his eyes once more to the Merron, and, glaring at Úlfnaor, he snapped the sword keep in place. The Aoire watched him calmly across the rapidly brightening air.

"Razi," hissed Wynter, and he turned at last to stare at her. She laid her hand on his arm. "Brother," she said softly. "Can you do this?"

For a moment Razi's eyes grew dangerously wide, and Wynter thought perhaps he would speak. But he snatched his arm free instead, and swung away, striding across the misty grass to the waiting horses. Wynter watched him for a moment, then she jogged after him.

Razi was already pulling his mare's head around to face the trail as Wynter reached the horses. As if on cue, the Merron turned their mounts in unison with him, and as Wynter hopped the stirrup, the whole group began to move past her, travelling along the tree line, heading for the dense forest to the north of camp.

Only Christopher hung back, holding his horse in place and waiting as Wynter settled into the saddle. He met her eye as she pulled Ozkar around and the two of them exchanged a look of weariness and grief. Razi, and those others at the head of the line, had already disappeared into the trees, the rest of the group following rapidly behind them, and so Wynter and Christopher were alone when the Loups-Garous howled.

Wynter grabbed for her sword, her eyes darting to the forest.

"*Jesu!*" she yelled. "Where are they?"

The howls came swooping down again, like a bird of prey through the dark smell of the pyre.

"Where are they, Chris?" she yelled, Ozkar dancing anxiously beneath her. "They sound so close! Are they here?"

Up ahead, the Merron pulled to a halt and stared into the trees.

The Wolves howled once more, so close, and Wynter spun to Christopher, another oath poised on her lips. At the sight of his face, she straightened in the saddle, staring, and then she reached across the gap between their horses.

"Christopher," she whispered. "Chris . . . it's all right." She took his hand, prying the clenched fingers from the pommel. "It's all right," she whispered again.

At the far end of the line Razi plunged from the forest, his eyes wide with concern. He scanned the Merron, and Wynter raised her free hand to let him know where she was. Razi pulled his mare to a halt, staring at Christopher. Wynter kept her hand raised and dipped her chin meaningfully. *It's all right. I have him.* Razi's mare turned and snorted beneath him, as Razi's eyes hopped between

Wynter and the rigid, staring man beside her. Wynter nodded. *It is all right.* And, with one last look at Christopher, Razi pulled his horse's head around and trotted to the head of the line again, calling to Úlfnaor as he did. "They are about a mile away," he yelled. "We must travel fast, and leave that bloody fire behind! Before they follow the smoke right to us."

Úlfnaor hesitated, no doubt thinking of the ten or more men and women he was leaving behind, then he nodded, and gestured his people forward once again. Wynter squeezed Christopher's hand and looked behind her. The tents remained silent, grey and still in the misty air, the camp as lifeless as a town of ghosts. Christopher's fingers moved in hers and she turned to find him gazing at her.

"Are you all right?" she whispered.

He nodded stiffly. His fingers tightened momentarily on hers before he let her go and gathered the reins to him, pulling his horse back onto the trail. "Come on, lass," he said.

Side by side they followed the Merron into the forest. Up ahead, Razi forged onwards, his eyes cold, his face set. By his side, Úlfnaor pushed his painted stallion through the undergrowth, keeping pace.

As Wynter and Christopher crossed over into the shadows, the Wolves called out once more. This time, neither of them flinched and they didn't look back.

Four Days Later: Diplomacy

Wynter finished securing the edge of her bivouac and looked across the clearing to where Úlfnaor's people were setting up their shelters. Christopher had wandered across to the Merron side of camp, and Wynter sat back on her heels and wiped her hands, watching as he came to a halt at Sólmundr's side.

The Merron had left all their luxurious tents and bedding back at their main camp, trading comfort for stealth and speed as they made up for lost time. Wynter had no doubt that as diplomatic envoys representing Marguerite Shirken, one of the kingdom's most powerful neighbours, they would be made very comfortable on their arrival at Alberon's camp. Until then, however, poor Sólmundr was sleeping on hard ground with nothing but a bivouac for shelter, and it was taking its toll.

The warrior was slumped against a tree, his eyes closed, and he did not seem to notice Christopher looking down at him. Boro, however, grinned sloppily and writhed onto his back, offering his belly. The *whump whump whump* of his tail rang out on the quiet evening air. Murmuring nonsense,

Christopher hunkered down and scrubbed the warhound behind his ears. Boro's tongue unfurled like a happy flag, and Sólmundr's weathered face momentarily creased into that charming, gap-toothed grin.

"Hello, Coinín," he murmured.

The dimples at the corners of Christopher's mouth made a brief appearance.

For a while, the two men watched in silence as the Merron went about their work, then Christopher sighed, patted Boro on his head and got to his feet. He said something, his head tilted, his thumbs hooked into the waistband of his trousers, and Sólmundr smiled in response, waving his hand as if to say, *later.* Christopher nodded uncertainly and walked away. Sólmundr shut his eyes once again and turned his head against the trunk of the tree.

Christopher did not look in Wynter's direction as he crossed to their side of camp. He kept his eyes down as he crouched by their fire, filled the copper basin from the cauldron, laid out his wash kit, and prepared to scrub himself clean of the last four days of sweat and grime. It was the same each time Christopher went to speak to Sól; he would not look at herself and Razi on his return, and Wynter suspected that he kept his eyes down for fear of the disapproval he might see in Razi's face.

Across the clearing, Hallvor crouched by Sólmundr. She whispered a question, but Sól turned away without answering. He kept his eyes shut, and, after a moment, the healer got to her feet and left him alone, his back turned to his people, his face creased in pain.

Wynter gazed at Sólmundr, sitting there alone with his

dog sprawled miserably at his feet. She glanced at Christopher, silently pulling his tunic over his head, then she turned to look at Razi. He was at their highline, tending his horse, his every movement tight with irritation, his dark face grim. Everything about him screamed *stay away*, and Wynter hesitated for a moment, uncertain. Then she took a deep breath and crossed to him.

As she approached, he glanced at her, unsmiling, and went on with his work.

"Razi," she said. "I want you to examine Sólmundr."

Razi jerked the saddle-blanket from his horse and flung it across a bush. "He has his own healer," he said.

"I think that he needs *you*."

Without replying, he crouched by his pile of tack and began to tug his saddlebags free of their straps. Wynter ducked under the horse's neck and drew closer.

"He is in great pain," she murmured. "Surely this hasn't escaped your attention?" Again, he did not reply, and Wynter gazed down at the top of his head, willing him to look at her. "I cannot believe," she said softly, "that you would exact your revenge on a wounded man."

Razi froze. Slowly he turned his head and Wynter's heart bumped in her chest at the expression on his face. Over the course of the past four days Razi had been lost in brooding silence or occupied with orders and plans – distant, glowering, removed. Now he glared at her with unfiltered rage, and Wynter couldn't help but recoil.

"Do you *dare* to imply that Sólmundr would not have participated in their deaths?" he hissed. "Do you *stand there* and *tell me* that he did not send them to the grave?"

"No, Razi," she whispered, "I do not."

Razi went back to fussing with the equipment. Wynter watched as he fumbled awkwardly with the straps, his usually nimble hands rendered clumsy by rage. She crouched by his side.

"Razi," she ventured "I have no desire to defend the Merron. What they did . . . it is beyond my comprehension But you are a *good* man. You are a *doctor*. Sólmundr needs you, Razi. This neglect is beneath you."

Razi sneered "Protector Lady, you have no *concept* of what is beneath me. I have come to think that *nothing* perhaps is beneath me. Were I a proper man, were I any kind of a man at all, I would . . . but I am not a man, am I? I am a hollow machine! I am a clockwork puppet of *state*, and so I do *nothing* when I should act and I habitually allow those who—"

Suddenly Razi unlatched his saddlebags and began a feverish search for his grooming brushes. He threw the contents of the bag about, hardly seeming to see or feel them, and with a stab of panic, Wynter realised his self-control might finally be unravelling. She moved closer and carefully laid her hand on his forearm. Razi's powerful muscles jerked under her palm as if he had only barely stopped himself from flinging her aside, then he froze to an absolute stillness, staring at the brushes in his hands without seeing them at all.

As Protector Lady, Wynter knew that there were many things she should say to Lord Razi now. She should remind him that they needed these people, and that he could not allow his personal rage to come between him and those who would help him fulfil his duty to the future of his father's kingdom. She should tell him to don his mask, hide his pain and school himself to rigid diplomacy as they had all been raised to do. As the Protector Lady, Wynter should tell the Lord Razi to stop lashing out like a reckless apprentice boy, to straighten up and to behave himself, like the prince he was.

"Razi," she said firmly, her fingers tightening on his arm.

Razi's brown eyes flicked to hers, then away again. He waited, his dark face tight, his mouth compressed. He knew what she was about to say, and Wynter knew at once that she couldn't say it. She couldn't be anything more, or anything less than simply Razi's friend.

"Razi," she said again, gently now. She went to push his too-long curls from his face, but Razi jerked his head from her touch, and she let her hand drop. "I am so sorry," she whispered. "Truly, Razi. I am so very sorry."

There was a moment of silence between them, Wynter looking gently into Razi's face, Razi staring at nothing. Then he turned away. Wynter said no more, just remained crouched by his side, gazing at him in useless sympathy. When it became clear that he would not look at her, she patted his arm, got to her feet and walked back to the fire. After a long moment of inactivity, Razi slowly gathered his grooming tools together and began to brush his horse.

Christopher had just finished washing himself and was standing by the fire, naked as a babe, towelling himself dry. Wynter blushed and dropped her eyes. She still was not quite used to his utter shamelessness. *You had better get used to it*, she thought, *you having pledged yourself to him for ever.* She glanced shyly at him and crouched by the fire, laying out her own wash kit. *For ever*, she thought. *My Hadrish boy*.

Truth be told, she was a little jealous of Christopher's complete lack of self-consciousness. She suspected that the Merron would hardly blink an eye should she discard all her clothes and saunter brazenly amongst them. However, a lifetime of conditioning was not so easily overcome, and she would just have to make do with stripping to her undershirt and britches, and giving herself as good a wash as that would allow.

She glanced at the fires. A terrible risk with the Wolves lurking. Christopher had been appalled at Úlfnaor's sudden insistence on them. Razi had simply been angry. They were, he said, a terrible waste of his time. Wearily, she sat back on her heels and closed her eyes. Every inch of her ached. Wolves or no Wolves, waste of time or not, it would be sweet to wash and to drink hot tea. It would be a blessing just to sit still.

Sighing, Wynter pressed her hand to the base of her belly and let the heat of her palm ease the cramping there. Her woman's time had come upon her the day they had left camp and had just finished its final day, thank Christ. She hated dealing with that particular complication when she was travelling.

Soft footsteps approached, and Wynter glanced up to find Hallvor gazing down with her usual grave composure. A vivid memory blazed unbidden to Wynter's mind – the tall, dark-haired woman outlined in fire, Ashkr writhing behind her, his screams turning to shrieks as the flames set his hair alight. With an effort, Wynter pushed this memory down and straightened, her face schooled to polite enquiry.

Christopher was just finished lacing his britches, and he glanced warily at the healer. Wynter was aware of Razi slipping around from behind his horse and glaring across the distance between them, his grooming brushes in his hand. Hallvor bowed towards him, but her politeness went unacknowledged.

Wynter got to her feet, deliberately drawing the woman's attention from her glowering friend. "Good evening, Hallvor," she said.

Smiling, the woman bowed again. She said something questioning and kindly. Out of habit, Wynter glanced to Christopher, waiting for him to translate. He was frozen in the act of pulling on his undershirt, and Wynter was stunned to see his face blaze to scarlet.

Oh, good Christ! she thought, immediately on alert, *what now?* If the subject was bad enough to make her shameless Hadrish boy blush to the roots of his hair, Wynter was fairly certain that she simply wouldn't want to hear it.

Hallvor nodded encouragingly to Christopher. He dropped his eyes as he tied his shirt, and the expression of helpless embarrassment on his face almost made Wynter laugh. He held his tongue for a moment, and took his time rolling his sleeves to his shoulders. Then, without looking at either woman, he mumbled something inaudible, his chin buried in his chest, his face half-turned away.

"Pardon?" asked Wynter, leaning forward slightly, amused, despite her wariness, at his unaccustomed reticence. "I can't hear you."

Christopher's colour deepened and he tutted, his discomfort slipping into irritation. Hallvor said something and Christopher waved his hand impatiently, as if to say *I know, I know, don't go on.* He hesitated. Then he sighed, squared his shoulders, and looked stoically out into the trees.

"Hallvor says that she knows it is late," he said, "and she is sorry that she did not offer before. But she would like to offer you now some blackberry leaf tea to ease your woman's pains."

Wynter snapped upright and snatched her hand from her belly.

"*Christopher!*" she cried, mortified to feel her face blazing.

"What?" he said belligerently.

"For Godsake! That's just not . . . a man doesn't . . ."

Christopher compressed his mouth "It's just blackberry leaf tea, lass. To ease your woman's—"

"Christopher! I will *not* speak to a man about such things! It's not *right*!"

"I ain't just any *man*!" he said indignantly, but his face and neck were mottled red, and his eyes were anywhere but on Wynter. Confused, Hallvor murmured something diffident, and Wynter leapt in, cutting Christopher off before he could translate anything more.

"Tell her I do not *need* her tea!" she cried, sounding, even to herself, like a petulant shrew. "Tell her that it is not *proper* to speak of such things to a man!"

Hallvor, standing awkwardly between them, began to look very uncertain of herself. Christopher stared at Wynter, his back rigid, his face stiff. She could tell that he was shocked at her unprecedented lack of diplomacy, and when his eyes darted to Razi, she realised, with a pang, how this must feel for him. For the last four days they had been united in keeping Razi's temper in check, and now she could almost hear Christopher thinking, *oh no, not her too*.

Christopher spoke quietly in Southlandast, his eyes on Wynter. "Hallvor is just being nice," he said. "You ain't got no idea how strange you are to her, Iseult, and she's just being nice. It ain't her fault that you don't speak Merron."

"Leave her be," warned Razi, his deep voice carrying low and dangerous across the evening air. "She doesn't want that woman's concoctions."

Wynter was surprised to see a steely resentment rise up in Christopher's face. "How long do you think these people will keep on trying before they reckon you just ain't worth their time?" he said. "How long do you think it will be before you wake up one morning and they're gone? *Then* where would you be? Alone in a forest with Wolves after you, *that's* where you'd be." He turned to Hallvor, his face apologetic.

"Christopher," Wynter hesitated for a moment, her eyes on the leaves at his feet. "Would you tell Hallvor that I do not have need of her tea." She lifted her eyes briefly and dropped them again. "But there are things I would like to rinse out at the river, and I would love to bathe. Could you ask . . . ?" She stopped. *Wait a moment*, she told herself, *Dad taught you better than this*. Taking a deep breath, Wynter straightened and looked Hallvor in the eye, addressing her directly.

"Hallvor," she said respectfully, "I thank you very much for the offer of your tea." She bowed, and Hallvor bowed graciously in response. "I apologise for my childish reaction. Where I come from, women are very . . . very private. I am not accustomed to such openness. I have no need of your tea, Hallvor, but thank you so much for your kindness. I should, however, like to go down to the river and wash out my supplies. Should the women be heading that way, I would very much like to accompany them. I could help you in gathering food and you could provide me with company and protection."

Christopher translated softly. Hallvor nodded, her eyes on Wynter, her grave face warm with understanding. Wynter suddenly realised that this was exactly how her father would have behaved in a situation where there was no shared language. The way Hallvor maintained eye contact with Wynter, and not the translator; the way she had opened communications through the finding of common ground; her patience – all these things Wynter had seen before, as Lorcan went about his diplomatic work in the North. It occurred to Wynter that this stringy woman, grimy and sweat soaked, her bare arms smudged with dirt, was far more refined and subtle a diplomat than she would ever have given her credit for.

Once Christopher had finished translating, Hallvor bowed again and, speaking directly to Wynter, told her that she intended to leave for the river within a few moments. Wynter nodded, and the healer crossed back to her own people, patting Christopher on the shoulder as she left.

Christopher watched her leave, then wearily dragged his hands across his narrow face. Wynter regarded him evenly from beneath the shadow of her hat. His pale body was still dappled with bruises, his eyes swollen with lack of sleep. She thought gratefully of Úlfnaor's insistence on lighting fires. Tonight, it would be good for Christopher to sit within the comfort of flickering light and, please God, go to bed with a belly full of hot food.

As if sensing her stare, Christopher glanced around at her.

"How do," she said softly.

He eyed her. "We friends again?" he asked.

She shrugged. "I suppose," she said. "For want of anyone better."

He rolled his eyes and Wynter grinned, the whole thing suddenly amusing to her. "You're a bloody menace, woman," he said, smiling despite himself. "I never have a clue what's in that red-headed noggin of yours." Wynter looked past him to the Merron and he followed her gaze. The men had slung their longbows across their shoulders and were tying back their hair. "I had best go," he said, stooping to gather up his crossbow and quiver. "I'm to join the hunt."

Wynter bent to retrieve her wash kit and linen. "And I'll go and be nice to our murderous sisters." She looked squarely at him as she straightened and he nodded, understanding that nothing was forgotten.

Christopher slung his quiver on his back and shouldered his bow, warily eyeing Razi as he did. Wynter expected Razi to protest their being separated and she turned to him, ready to argue the point of showing their trust in the Merron. But Razi just stared silently from his position by the horses, his grooming brushes held loosely in his hand, his face unreadable.

"Úlfnaor is having a hard time with his people," said Christopher quietly. "They don't think you can be trusted, Razi. They think you'll slit our throats as soon as you get the chance, steal Shirken's papers and then leg off. They think you'll betray them to the cavalry and then have Úlfnaor tortured into giving up the Prince."

Razi's dark eyes narrowed slightly and his generous mouth curled at the corner. Wynter swallowed at the glint in his eye. She suspected that the Merron weren't far wrong in their assessment of his intentions. When Razi's use for them was over, Wynter suspected that the Merron would quickly discover the true depths of Kingsson wrath. Christopher was no fool, he could not possibly be unaware of this; still he carried on speaking, his eyes fixed on Razi's face. "Úlfnaor is leaving you here alone with Sólmundr and the papers as a measure of trust, to prove to the others that he hasn't misjudged you."

"He is leaving me alone, but taking my family with him," said Razi quietly. "That is no great test."

"I betrayed you," Christopher said. "And Iseult is my *croí-eile*. These people think they are protecting *us* from *you*." He paused, waiting for Razi to speak. But Razi just lifted his eyes to regard the Merron, his lip still curved into that knowing half-smile, and, after a moment, Christopher walked away without looking back.

"I'm going, Razi," whispered Wynter. His expression did not change, and after a while she nodded uncertainly and settled the wash kit on her shoulder. "All right then," she said, "I will see you soon."

Wynter turned away, her stomach knotted, her heart heavy with misgivings.

As she passed him, Sólmundr waved a tired farewell.

Ceap Milleáin

This late in the season and this high in the mountains, the heat leached quickly from the air and the day slid very rapidly into night. As Wynter hurried back from the river, she could not help but fear the swiftly growing shadows. The Wolves had not howled for two days. Razi maintained that they had turned back in search of their lost men. He insisted that they were far behind. Still, Wynter pulled the hood of her cloak tighter and quickened her pace to keep up with the other women.

They moved quietly around her, their steps light and confident. It would not be easy for anyone to catch them unawares, and Wynter once again found herself in grudging admiration of them. They were unlike any women she had ever met, except perhaps Marni, and she found herself more comfortable in their fierce, independent company than she cared to admit.

Hallvor pushed through the dark branches of the trail and Wynter jogged along behind her, keeping close. The healer had a dozen fish hanging from a pole on her shoulder and they gleamed in the dappled light of the new-risen moon. A knapsack filled with hazelnuts and water-root bounced on her narrow back, her long, dark hair tangled in its straps. She had been very kind to Wynter at the river. Despite their having no shared language, she had conveyed a warm, maternal protectiveness.

She is a murderess, thought Wynter, *a religious fanatic.*

Hallvor glanced back and smiled encouragingly.

Culland, one of Úlfnaor's warhounds, loped silently alongside her, his tongue lolling, and Wynter took comfort in his massive presence. Somewhere to her left, Soma and the other warrior, Frangok, were speaking softly to each other, their progress through the undergrowth a whispering shush in the gathering dark. Wynter also felt protected by them. They too had been kind.

They protected Embla, too, she reminded herself. *They were kind to Ashkr.*

She pushed onwards, miserable and conflicted.

Soon the scent of wood smoke came drifting through the trees and Wynter's chest knotted in renewed tension. They were nearing the camp. *Razi,* she thought, peering through the gloom, *please do not have done anything you'll regret.*

The glow of the camp-fires became visible, glimmering softly through the shifting leaves. The women paused, listening for conversation. There was nothing. Wynter strained for sounds. Silence.

Hallvor gestured to the hound and he shot ahead. The women drew their swords and darted after him. Breaking into the flickering light of the clearing, their faces hardened at the sight of an empty camp.

Wynter looked around in confusion. She was surprised

to see both camp-fires blazing merrily, neat little stacks of wood at their sides. She had fully expected Razi to neglect the Merron fire in favour of their own, but it was obvious that he had been carefully tending to both. Nonetheless, Sólmundr was gone, his cloak tossed aside at the base of his tree, and there was no sign of Razi in the quiet, crackling gloom.

Frangok spat on the ground and snapped something angry at Hallvor. Wynter took a wary step away from her, her hand on her sword. *Oh, Razi*, she thought in despair. *No!* What were she and Christopher to do now? And then, even worse, she thought, *what if the Wolves have him?*

Hallvor lifted her sword to indicate the highline on the far side of camp.

"*Féach*," she said softly.

Wynter looked in the direction indicated and nearly sobbed with relief. Razi's big mare was still there, dozing in line with the other horses.

Hallvor released a low whistle and called warily into the darkness beyond camp. "Sól? *An bhfuil tú ansin?*"

Something moved in the shadows and all the women crouched, their swords raised, but they straightened almost immediately when they saw that it was Culland, with Boro at his side. Culland jogged across to the women, but Boro stayed on the edge of the trees, the firelight shining in his eyes. A low whistle sounded behind him, and the big hound turned immediately and slunk away into the darkness.

"Sól?" called Hallvor, more confident now.

Sólmundr's familiar rasp came drifting hoarsely through the trees. "*Fan noiméad . . . Bhí orm mo chac a dhéanamh . . .*"

Hallvor relaxed. Whatever Sólmundr had said, the Merron women sheathed their swords, shaking their heads dryly at each other. The sense of relief was palpable.

Boro came trotting into the clearing again, Razi and Sólmundr on his heels. Razi, his dark eyes shuttered, was supporting Sólmundr with an arm around his waist. Sólmundr was labouring along, his mouth crooked into a pained smile, his hand pressed to his stomach. He rasped something at the women, which made Soma and Hallvor laugh, and then he grinned at Wynter.

"I had need for to relieve myself," he panted. "Tabiyb, he help me." He tightened the arm he had draped across Razi's shoulders, squeezing his neck in rough good humour. "He very kind to me, this one," he said, adding teasingly, "though he make too much talk. Is that not right, Tabiyb? Talk, talk, talk, till almost I tell to him . . . 'shut up, Tabiyb, you too noisy for my brain'."

Wynter half smiled, torn between delight at Razi's irrepressible kindness and anxiety at his cold, ill-tempered expression.

"Here," said Razi, pushing Sólmundr into Hallvor's arms. "Take him." He turned away immediately, heading for his side of the clearing.

Sólmundr slung his arm across Hallvor's shoulders and called after him. "Thank you so much, friend. I very grateful." Razi ignored him, striding angrily away.

"You good man!" called Sólmundr.

But as soon as Razi had turned his back, the wicked fun drained from Sólmundr's face. Grimacing in pain, the wiry man turned his forehead into the crook of the healer's neck and his hand knotted in the tunic at her shoulder.

"*Ó, a mhuirnín,*" Hallvor whispered, turning her cheek into the sandy waves of Sólmundr's hair. She murmured comfortingly to him and Soma came forward to help get him settled against the base of the tree.

Frangok began to unload the newly gathered supplies. Wynter was tempted to help, but after a moment's hesitation, she crossed instead and sat opposite Razi, who was crouched by their fire. He did not speak and they sat in tense silence, staring into the flames as Hallvor's whispered conversation came drifting across the crackling stillness of the camp.

The healer was undoing Sólmundr's bandages, trying to get a good look at his stitches. As she pulled back the lower bindings, he cried out in sudden pain, his voice instantly muffled by his hand against his mouth, and Wynter saw Razi's clasped hands tighten against each other, his nails digging into the flesh. At the sight of the wound, Hallvor said something sharp and appalled, and Razi leapt instantly to his feet, staring across the clearing.

Wynter gazed up at him. *Go!* she thought. *Go to him.* But at that moment, the rest of the men chose to return, a doe slung between them, their faces glowing in triumph, and Razi turned away, his expression shuttered once more.

Christopher, a brace of hare dangling from his hand, met Wynter's eyes as he emerged from the shadows. Wynter glanced over at Razi, tightened her mouth and shook her head. *No change.* Christopher grimaced and crossed to hunker by the Merron fire. Grimly, he proceeded to skin his catch. Drawing her knife, Wynter went to crouch with the Merron. She held out her hand and Christopher gave her the still warm body of the other hare.

As she worked, Wynter watched from the corner of her eye as Úlfnaor deposited his bow by the bivouacs and went to check on Sólmundr. The warrior lifted his chin in greeting as his old friend approached, and Úlfnaor squatted by his side, his face tender. He asked a question. Sól nodded, and gasped a reply through gritted teeth, his hands clenching as Hallvor tended his wound. Úlfnaor glanced at Razi, and Wynter saw a moment of grave pleasure cross the Aoire's face. It was the kind of look a father might give a son who has lived up to his expectations.

"Úlfnaor would like to speak with you."

Razi grunted and threw the scraps of his meal onto the fire. "We have already planned tomorrow's journey," he said, wiping out his bowl. "There's nothing left to discuss."

"Úlfnaor has *formally* requested permission to speak with you," said Christopher. "Are you asking me to go back to the Merron and tell their leader that you are snubbing him?"

Razi gazed at him, and Christopher held his eye. There was a moment of belligerent silence, then Razi broke eye contact and Wynter relaxed, knowing that he would acquiesce. She returned her attention to cleaning out her bowl and did not look up again, not even when Razi said, "Very well," and Christopher walked away from their side of camp.

She was just putting away the cooking things when Christopher returned, two beakers of hot tea in his hands. "Thanks," she said, accepting one of the beakers.

Christopher nodded and sat down. Úlfnaor had come over and was standing on the opposite side of the fire, his eyes on Razi. Their friend kept his seat, gazing wordlessly up at the Merron leader, his face cold.

"What does he want, Chris?" murmured Wynter.

Christopher shook his head. He didn't know.

Úlfnaor gestured to the ground, *may I sit?* Razi gave no indication of consent, but after a moment, the big man took a seat anyway. Ceremoniously laying his sword on the ground behind him, he turned to Razi. "I thank you for your kindness to Sólmundr," he began. "You a good man, I very grateful."

Razi did not acknowledge Úlfnaor's words. Úlfnaor continued, "My people thought that you would maybe to hurt Sól . . . out of need to venge yourself for what you believe we done wrong. But I know you would not to do this . . . not yet." Razi frowned at that and Úlfnaor smiled in understanding. "The Merron understand the importance of vengeance to honourable person, Tabiyb. We respect it. In order to survive, a good man must kill his enemies, or he die instead. The strong crush the weak. It the way of the world. We know that true justice only come when you feel the blood of your enemy on your own two hands, *nach ea?*" He held out his hands, palms up, as if to show the blood on them. "We understand," he repeated softly. "It the way of the world."

Razi lifted his gaze from Úlfnaor's outstretched hands and met his eye. There was a moment of laden silence.

"I understand you love Embla," whispered Úlfnaor. "You had *hopes* for her." Razi's eyes narrowed and he straightened slowly. This was not a subject he was willing to discuss. "But I must explain to you, you not *see* Embla the way we see her, the way she see herself. She and Ash, they warriors destined for honourable death, holy warriors. They the bridge between the People and *An Domhan*. They die in this new land, so to wake *An Domhan* to our life here, so to ensure that others *not* to die, so that—"

"It is a man's duty to *protect* the ones he loves," interrupted Razi quietly, "not to spill their blood in the hope that their deaths will make his life easier."

Úlfnaor flinched. He stared at Razi for a moment as if looking into an unexpected abyss, then his face hardened and he went on. "Fine words, Tabiyb," he snapped. "Words worthy of a perfect world. But I think perhaps that a man like you, a man of duty . . . I think perhaps you understand what it is to sacrifice a friend to bigger things." His eyes flicked to Christopher, dropped to his mutilated hands.

"What?" cried Christopher, appalled. "I never . . .! Razi, I never said . . ."

Razi rose slowly to his feet. "Your time to speak is over, Úlfnaor. We are finished."

Úlfnaor glared up at him, but Wynter had seen it briefly in the big man's eyes: the comment about Christopher had been a guess, a wild stab in the dark, and the Aoire was shocked at its impact. She put her hand on Christopher's arm and he turned to her, his eyes huge.

"Iseult! I never . . . I wouldn't . . ."

"Shhh," she said, looking into his eyes, squeezing his arm. "Shhh. I know."

"I am in earnest, Úlfnaor," snarled Razi. "You will not use my failings to justify your cowardly, murderous nature. Leave me now, before I do something I will regret."

"I not try justify nothing to you," said Úlfnaor. "I try explain that I understand what you *feel*. How it is you must burn to avenge the death of she who might one day be your *croí-eile*."

Razi continued to stand at rigid attention, the light of the fire wreathing his face with living anger. "I care not a jot for your understanding," he hissed, "I care not a jot for *you*, Úlfnaor. You are a murderer. A superstitious coward, and were it not for the fact that I *need* you, I would cut your beating heart from your chest and stamp it into the dust beneath my feet. I advise you to leave me be. I advise you leave me *now*, as I am very close to acting on my feelings."

Úlfnaor seemed to hesitate, his black eyes reflecting the firelight. Then he abruptly shrugged his cloak behind his shoulder and reached to the small of his back. In a flash, Wynter drew her knife, Christopher's black dagger was in his hand, and the two of them were surging to their feet. But instead of a weapon, Úlfnaor took a familiar package from his belt and held it up for Razi to see. Wynter let herself sink back to the ground.

It was the diplomatic folder.

Razi put his hand out to Christopher. "Sit down," he said softly.

At the sight of Wynter and Christopher's weapons, the Merron had drawn their swords, but Hallvor waved her hand and murmured for them to stand down. The warriors subsided into cautious watchfulness. Úlfnaor's hounds stayed by the healer's side, as obedient to her as they were to their master. Sólmundr made no attempt to move, just looked at Úlfnaor from his position at the base of the tree, no trace of surprise in his face.

Úlfnaor laid the folder on the stones ringing the fire. "When my people come and say that the Princess Shirken ask me to carry her messages, I think to myself, *why*? Why should it be that this woman, this . . ." He paused, looking down at the package, distaste rising in his face. Wynter had no doubt that there were many words that would best describe Marguerite Shirken running through his head. She could think of a few: *lunatic,* for example, *zealot, blood-soaked murderer. Tyrant.*

Úlfnaor tore his eyes from the package and looked up at Razi. "She who has decorated the trees of our homeland with the heads of the People, why she ask for us to do this very important thing? And not only she ask for *Merron* to carry her message . . . she ask for *Bear* Merron, Tabiyb. She ask for *me*." He frowned, searching Razi's face for signs that he understood.

Razi looked the big man up and down, lifted his eyes to the ring of watchful men and women across the clearing, and then resumed his seat, his face coldly attentive.

"Marguerite Shirken is many things," said Úlfnaor. "Many, many very *bad* things. But she is excellent good soldier, and she know always her enemy. She know the Merron," he said quietly, "and she want us gone. We an offence to her just by being alive." The big man's eyes widened suddenly at the memory, and he nodded to himself. "So she asked for me," he whispered. "And I know at once that I to be the instrument of my people's downfall. I say to the other Aoirí, '*No!*' I say to them, '*send someone else, one of the other tribes . . . Hawk, Snake, even Panther*'." He chopped his hand down, as if once again addressing the other Merron leaders. "*Send someone else . . .*" he hissed.

"What difference would that have made?" asked Wynter,

"to have sent another in your place? Why did she want only you?"

Úlfnaor wiped the heel of his hand under his eye and shook his head silently.

"Because you are of the old Religion," said Christopher.

Úlfnaor nodded, his eyes still bright, and Christopher's face tightened in bitterness. "Shirken knew that you'd have to make the Bridge," he said. "Your people would never allow you to bring them into a new land without first waking *An Domhan* to their presence. Shirken knew this, and so she forced your hand. Am I right? She made the other Aoirí send you, knowing that you'd have to sacrifice your Caoirigh, as the old People always must do when crossing to a new place."

"Also, I think . . ." said Úlfnaor, "I think that, secret in their hearts, the other Aoirí want this to happen. In their hearts . . ." He looked up at Christopher, greatly upset.

"They hoped the blood sacrifice would make things better," whispered the young man.

Úlfnaor's face creased up and he nodded.

"So you sit there and tell me that you had no choice? Is that it?" Razi's words were hissed and low, his voice barely cutting above the sound of the fire. "No choice but to murder two of your own?" He sneered bitterly and shook his head, then he spat into the fire, a sudden, compulsive gesture of contempt.

Úlfnaor took a moment, then drew a deep breath and sat up straight. "I not know how she will manage it," he said evenly. "But I believe Shirken will somehow make it known to Royal Prince Alberon what it is I must do when we come here. She will use this as excuse to finish her war against the People and when she does . . . *paf*!" He slapped his hands together. "We will to be caught, Shirken on one side, the armies of Royal Prince Alberon on the other, and in the middle . . ." he dusted his hands, as if wiping away a crushed insect. "The Merron. Destroyed in one final sweep. An entire peoples gone."

Wynter knew he was right. Beside her Christopher sat leaning forward, his elbows on his knees, staring quietly at the big man. Razi's expression did not change, and Wynter thought perhaps he didn't think it such a bad idea that the Merron be swept away, that he might even think it a good thing.

"You could have told her 'no'," said Razi. "You could have stayed at home."

Úlfnaor took in his unyielding expression, and went on. "There was a man," he said. "He work for your King, as you do. Maybe you to know him? He a good man, he try to do much for the Panther Merron." Úlfnaor lifted his hand to his head, indicating his hair. "My people called him the Red Hawk."

This unexpected mention of Lorcan knocked Wynter back, grief stabbing through her chest.

"I told he a big man?" continued Úlfnaor, still trying to describe Lorcan. "Almost big as Merron. He have wide shoulder, much . . ."

"I knew the Protector Lord Moorehawke," snapped Razi sharply. "You are not worthy to speak his name."

Úlfnaor stared at him, then at Wynter, who averted her glittering eyes. Christopher looked down at his hands, distress evident in his face, and understanding dawned in the big man.

"Oh," he whispered sadly, "what befell him?"

No one answered. Wynter because she could not; Razi because he would not.

Úlfnaor sighed and nodded. "I sorry that he gone. He good ma—"

"Do *not* . . ." hissed Razi. "Do *not* use Lorcan's name to curry favour with me. I will not tolerate it."

Úlfnaor looked Razi hard in the face. "The Red Hawk tell my people that in this kingdom here, justice not only about the strong crushing the weak. He say, that in this kingdom here, even the weak and even the very low, they can to have justice because the King here, the Good King Jonathon, he make what he call a *Charter of Rights*. Is this the truth?"

When it became clear that Razi would not answer, Wynter spoke in his stead. "Yes, it is true," she said. "King Jonathon established a Charter of Rights and a system of justice whereby even the lowest of persons can argue their case in law against even the highest."

Úlfnaor stared at her as if this were more than he could ever have hoped for. "The Red Hawk, he say that all this laws wrote down, permanent and unchanging." Úlfnaor scribbled his fingers across his palm, as if writing. "That any man who can to read, can go see this laws, to know them for himself and so it always easy to understand what is law and what is outlaw?"

Wynter nodded. "That's right," she said. "There are copies in every town hall, free and available for any man to read and copy at will."

"Any man who can to read," whispered Úlfnaor. He glanced across at Christopher. "Your father teach you to read, Coinín?"

"He did," said Christopher evenly, his mouth twisting into a knowing little smile.

"Yes," said Úlfnaor. "*An filid* Garron always much concerned that the Merron learn to read."

"He was indeed."

"Your father very strong in this desire," said Úlfnaor, "He all the time say we never will control our own history until the day we able to write it down. It make him much trouble with the council." Christopher regarded him silently, that bitter little smile still in place. After a moment Úlfnaor nodded. "Your father was right," he said softly.

"I know he was," said Christopher.

"This charter?" said Úlfnaor, turning his attention to Wynter again. "It apply to all?"

"Even the King himself."

"*Even the King himself?*" repeated Úlfnaor in disbelief. Wynter nodded.

"It not a trick?" he said. "The King, he not one day say 'this is law' and then next day say 'this is outlaw' so that you never to know where you stand?"

Wynter exchanged the briefest of looks with Razi. *Not until recently*, she thought. "It is a very new system of governance," she said, "and so is still finding its feet, but the King is determined to make it work. And so he shall, if things are not disrupted beyond repair by this misunderstanding with his heir."

"So this what you work for, Tabiyb," said Úlfnaor. "You work to save this charter." It was a statement, not a question. Úlfnaor tapped his finger against the folder. "While I maybe work to kill it."

Razi stared at Úlfnaor, his eyes a little wider. This strange turn in the conversation had unexpectedly swept him from his black thoughts of vengeance, placing him right back into the political and diplomatic heart of things. Wynter could see in his eyes that he was thrown by this, and did not know how to react.

Úlfnaor went on, "I think you very important man, Tabiyb much more than simple messenger. I am wrong?"

Razi did not respond, and Úlfnaor nodded in approval. "If so, I tell you now that *this*," he poked the diplomatic folder with his finger, "this will be poison to your King's vision of the future. The future that the Red Hawk so proud of." He met Razi's eye. "You tell the Royal Prince that, Tabiyb Razi. You tell your Royal Prince that whatever this *bitch* promise him, whatever it is she ask him for in return, it will to rot him. *Tá go maith?*"

"Why not tell him this yourself?" whispered Razi.

Úlfnaor laughed and shook his head. "I cannot to take the risk. I not know what way the wind it blow today or tomorrow. I only know that my peoples must to depend on goodwill of these peoples." He tapped the folder again. "I not to risk pissing them off, because they may hold the life of my peoples in their fist . . . but Tabiyb," he leant forward, urgent now, imploring, "Tabiyb, in my heart, I hope it you that hold the Merron in your hands. I hope it *you*, and your Good King Jonathon. Because otherwise . . ." Úlfnaor hesitated, afraid to articulate his fears, and when he spoke again his words were so soft as to be almost inaudible. "Otherwise, I think all is lost for us. All is lost for everyone."

"What do these papers contain?" Razi demanded

abruptly, indicating the folder. Wynter winced. Razi was asking the Aoire to betray Shirken's trust, to violate his duty and break the oath he must have sworn when he undertook it.

Úlfnaor frowned, his lips compressed in disapproval. "Even if I knew this," he said, "I would not tell you."

Razi tutted reflexively and sat back, but Wynter knew that he had not really expected Úlfnaor to give him the information.

Úlfnaor gazed down at the folder once more, running his work-roughened fingers across the embossing on the cover.

"In many way I the perfect instrument to carry these papers," he said softly. "I strong in pride and so will see my oath through to end. I faithful to my own kind and so ask for nothing but chance to negotiate for them. I followed by many loyal warriors who will to die for me if I needs it. And also I *ignorant savage* what cannot to even read my own name." Úlfnaor slapped his hand down on the folder, his lips drawing back bitterly from his teeth. "Even if I open this folder and break all the pretty little seals within, what could they tell me about the future of my people? Nothing!" He spat the word. "Nothing! I not have the skill to understand them." He whisked his hand over the folder as if tempted to throw it into the fire.

"Since always my peoples have provided for themselves with these," he held his hands out to Razi, his beautifully crafted rings flashing in the firelight, his palms ingrained with a lifetime's work. "And this," he reached behind him and savagely jerked his sword free of its scabbard, holding it out for Razi to see. "Since *An Domhan* first split itself into man and beasts and trees, these have been the only things we have needed for to survive. The Merron are strong, Tabiyb Razi, we clever, we brave! We needs no one but *ourselfs*!" Úlfnaor shook the sword in his two hands, his frustration and anger breaking from him in a low cry. Then he flung the gleaming blade to the ground at his feet. "But no more," he said, "not any more."

He looked over his shoulder at his people. "The world has changed on us," he murmured. "Our lifes no longer in our own hands.

Úlfnaor turned to look Razi in the eye and his next words chilled Wynter to the bone. "I could to kill you here, Tabiyb. In this clearing, in the middle of this forest I could with no problem crush you. You would be dead, my people would be safe from you. I could do this easy, I know it. But I know also that outside this clearing, when we in camp of Rebel Prince, *you* will to be the stronger man. There, *you* can to crush *me*, and my peoples with me."

He got to his feet. "By leaving you alive, I put my peoples' life in your hands, Tabiyb Razi. And so I offer myself to you, instead, as *ceap milleáin*. If you want it. I ask only that I get to finish my work first."

He waited for a reaction, his face expectant. Wynter regarded the Aoire in confusion. What was *ceap milleáin*? Christopher was tense and quiet by her side, and she did not betray her ignorance by glancing at him.

Razi's expression did not change and he continued to sit, staring across the flames, his dark eyes hooded, his hands resting loosely between his knees. When he made no move to further the conversation, the big man nodded, sheathed his sword, and gathered up the folder.

"Think about it, Tabiyb Razi," he said. "My *Fadaí* will support me in this, and so my people will accept it." He stood for a moment, gazing down at Razi who did not look up to meet his eye. "I understand you hesitate," said Úlfnaor softly. "I not mean to try and control your need for revenge. I not mean to . . . limit you. But in my heart hope you accept." Then the Aoire bowed, an unprecedented move on his part, and crossed in silence to his people.

Christopher released a long shaky breath and scrubbed his hand across his mouth. "Good Frith," he whispered. "*Ceap milleáin . . .*"

"What does this mean?" said Razi, his eyes on Úlfnaor. "What is he offering me?"

Christopher hesitated, and Wynter realised that he was nervous of what Razi might do with the information.

"He is offering *himself*," said Christopher at last. "Úlfnaor is offering himself as *ceap milleáin . . .* as . . ." he searched for the words. "As . . . appointed blame? Um . . . appointed guilt?"

"Scapegoat?" she whispered and Christopher nodded.

"Aye," he said. "As scapegoat. I've never heard of an Aoire offered as *ceap milleáin*," he said. "It's huge. It's powerful, Razi. I . . ." He glanced at the Merron. Nervously, he rubbed his hands on his trousers. He looked frightened. "It's huge," he whispered again.

Razi's face remained hard, his eyes on Úlfnaor. "What does that mean to these people?" he said. "In what way does it affect our situation?"

"It means . . ." Christopher trailed off. He licked his lips, his eyes travelling the knot of glowering warriors across the camp. "They must accept it," he assured himself. "When you wreak your vengeance on Úlfnaor for Embla's death, they *must* accept it and wash their hands of any retaliation." He looked at Razi suddenly, his face sharp. "But the rest are exempt from punishment for her death, Razi! You understand? Everyone is exempt. Only Úlfnaor takes the blame. It's how the tribes halt feuds that have gone too far. And you *must* let him finish his business," he warned. "It's law. You must let Úlfnaor deliver those papers and complete his negotiations for his people and then let the others go home. It's law, Razi! You *must!*"

"Must I?" said Razi softly. "Really? I *must*?" Wynter turned to stare at him. "And what if I refuse?" he said, his words low, his eyes darkly flickering in the firelight. "What if I refuse his offer, what then?"

Christopher looked shocked. "Then . . ." he trailed to a halt, utterly lost for words. It apparently had not occurred to him that Razi would refuse. "Then," he said. "I suppose . . . you . . ." He shook his head. "I don't know," he whispered.

"Why would you refuse, Razi?" asked Wynter carefully. "What would it gain?"

Razi stared at the Merron from hooded eyes and she knew why. Razi did not want his revenge meted out like a dose of physic, controlled and curtailed. Razi wanted blood. He wanted *blood*. And only *he* would decide whose blood and how much.

"Razi . . ." she whispered.

"*Razi*," interrupted Christopher. "This is the equivalent of your father kneeling at an enemy's feet and handing him his crown. You cannot possibly understand how significant this is to these people."

Razi stared at him for a long moment, then looked down into the fire and would speak no more.

Return

*C*hristopher sat at the camp-fire with the Wolves and played his guitar. He had, as usual, lost himself in the piece, and his eyes were closed, his pale face rapt as his long fingers moved in nimble precision against the strings. Wynter, chained with the rest of the slaves in the shadows and the cold, sighed, never wanting the music to stop.

The big, blond Wolf by Christopher's side faltered in his attempts to follow the tune on his own guitar, and Christopher stopped playing. Without looking up, he reached across, and gently repositioned the Wolf's fingers. The Wolf tried the chord again and Christopher nodded, his eyes down. He resumed playing, slower now, pausing between each chord so that the Wolf could follow. Beside him, Christopher's father sat, stone-faced and unmoving, his mandolin on his knee, waiting for David Le Garou to tire of the lesson and order proper music to start.

Bells tinkled softly in the darkness behind the slave line, and Wynter tensed. They had not prowled the slave lines like this for months, but Jean, in a fit of Wolfish temper, had done away with the last boy. And the girl? Who knew? One morning she just wasn't there. Now the Wolves' *boys* were once again seeking fresh entertainment for their masters, the bells at their ankles and wrists chiming as they stalked down the line.

Wynter shut her eyes. *Do not let it be me,* she thought.

A familiar voice spoke in her ear. "That's all right, sis. You're not one of them." Alberon smiled down at her. "Come on. You're in the wrong seat."

She grinned into his sunny face and allowed him help her to her feet. Behind her, the bells moved down the line and Wynter heard one of the others groan in fear.

David Le Garou bowed courteously as Alberon led her around the fire.

"My Lady," he murmured.

"Monsieur Le Garou," she said, favouring him with a gracious tilt of her head.

By the fire, Christopher whispered, "Dad? What's wrong with my hands?"

"Would you like to lie down in my tent, sis?" asked Alberon, putting his arm around her shoulders. "Have some wine?"

Wynter grinned and said that she would, and some roast beef too, if it was available. She glanced across the clearing to where Razi was standing.

Alberon chuckled at how absorbed he was in the proceedings at the fire.

"Brother!" he called. "Come along. We've no time for that! There's work to do."

Razi turned, his face uncertain. "But . . ."

"No buts, brother. We have business! Come along."

Alberon extended his hand. "Come *along*," he demanded, his voice deepening.

By the fire Christopher whispered "*Dad?*"

Wynter wanted to go to him, but a voice inside her head, as loud and clear as her father's voice, said, *he is not so important.* And she hesitated, trying to remember what it was she needed to do.

Alberon's arm tightened around her shoulders and she shivered at how cold he felt. "These things happen all the time," he insisted. "We have bigger things to consider."

"No," whispered Razi, his eyes on the fire. "No. I am not that kind of a man."

"Oh?" said Alberon. "Really? Then who am I?"

Razi spun to look at him.

Wynter had never heard Razi scream before. The sound was terrible. She pressed against Alberon, terrified, and Razi backed away from them.

"Who am I?" gurgled Alberon. Wynter suddenly knew who it was that stood with his arm around her, and she jerked and cried out, trying in vain to pull away.

Don't look! she told herself. *Don't look!* But even as she thought it, her head was turning and she looked up.

It was Isaac, the man Alberon had sent to kill Razi. The man Razi had allowed be tortured so horribly, before the palace ghosts released him from his pain. Isaac's eyeless sockets welled and overflowed, clotted tears rolling down his cheeks. His terrible mouth, only inches from her face, worked against its shattered teeth, that cultured voice coming, impossibly clear, from those ragged lips.

"Mary?" he said. "Don't you know me?"

Wynter screamed, and across the clearing, Razi's scream echoed her own.

Embla had stepped from the shadows by his side, dirt in her hair and in her eyes.

"What have you done?" she asked. "Tabiyb, what have you *done?*"

"I've done nothing!" A confession, a shameful admission of guilt.

"Nothing!" agreed Embla. "You have done *nothing*."

Isaac sank to his knees, pulling Wynter with him, so the two of them knelt in the mud. "Mary," he whispered. "*Ora pro me . . . ora pro me . . .*"

Pray for me. Pray for me.

By the fire, Christopher, at last, began to wail.

Wynter took a deep breath and opened her eyes wide.

Pray for me, she thought. *Pray for me!* But she couldn't remember why she wanted the prayers or why her heart was slamming against her ribs like a rat in a cage.

The camp-fire was still burning, and she lay perfectly still for a moment, listening to the loud hiss of the flames and watching the moonlight slide and shiver on the trees at the edge of the clearing.

Christopher had slipped down from their pillow of saddlebags, and he lay facing her, his shoulders hunched, his chin tucked into his chest. He was moaning in his sleep and there were tears leaking steadily from beneath his dark eyelashes. Wynter felt around beneath the cloaks until she found his hand. She clasped it gently and pulled it close to her heart, unconsciously running her thumb across the gap where his middle finger used to be.

She shut her eyes again and let the hissing of the flames fill her head. For a moment, the sound relaxed her. Then it seemed to intrude upon her peace of mind and she realised that it was very loud, much too loud, and it was moving. Wynter opened her eyes again. She listened, staring out into the darkness. Then she slowly lifted her head to look over Christopher's shoulder.

The Merron were sleeping. Úlfnaor and Hallvor lay protectively on either side of Sólmundr, lost in the dark bundles of their cloaks and blankets, Úlfnaor's dogs fast asleep at their feet.

Only Boro was awake, his head resting on Sólmundr's knee. He was watching intently as something crossed the clearing towards him. Wynter could clearly make out the movement of his eyes as he followed its progress across the forest floor. His tail thumped against the ground and he whined softly. Wynter scanned the area. She could see nothing, no floating light, no shadow, but she felt it in the air, that hair-prickle tension that presaged an apparition. Carefully, she lifted herself onto her elbow and waited.

Boro settled his chin against Sólmundr's limp hand and his eyes followed the invisible presence as it tracked a path across the clearing and up to his master's side. The big dog whined softly again, and his tail thumped in melancholy greeting.

Slowly the clearing filled with the roar and crackle of an enormous fire. Then Wynter heard it, soft and almost inaudible, Ashkr's voice whispering gently through the sound of flames.

"Sól . . . Sól, *a chroí* . . ."

Sólmundr stirred, sighed, and opened his eyes. His

attention wandered for a moment, then his eyes fixed on a point very close to him and he smiled. "Ashkr." He lifted his hand, as if to touch the air, and suddenly Ashkr was there, kneeling by his side.

He was all flaring brightness, white and shimmering, flickering like a thousand moonlit flames, but perfect in every detail, right down to his pale eyelashes. His handsome face was filled with tenderness, and his mouth curved into a gentle smile as he gazed into Sólmundr's face. "*Mo mhuirnín*," he whispered.

Sólmundr traced the empty air where his beloved's face should have been. "Ash," he breathed. Ashkr's smile deepened and he nodded as if to say of course. Sólmundr gazed at him, his fingers poised against Ashkr's translucent cheek. "*Fan liom*," he said. "*Táim beagnach in éineacht leat . . .*"

Ashkr's face fell. He looked Sólmundr up and down, as if unable to believe his eyes. *No.* He vehemently shook his head. *No.*

Sólmundr smiled and nodded. "*Sea . . .*" he insisted softly. "*Fan liom*, Ash. *Fan.*" His eyes grew heavy and slipped shut. Slowly, his hand drifted to his chest as if the strength was fading from his arm.

Ashkr bent urgently over him, his hands hovering. It was obvious that he was longing to touch Sól's face, longing to wake him. For the briefest of moments, his shimmering fingers brushed his friend's cheek, and at the contact, Sólmundr moaned and shuddered with pain. Ashkr drew back in despair, and then he was gone.

"Wait!" Razi's urgent voice drew Wynter's attention to him. He was lying on his back, staring up at the moonlit canopy, his eyes bright with tears. "Wait!" he cried. There was a sudden, bright movement above him, like a sheet being snatched up and away, and Razi closed his hand on empty air as if to catch it.

"Please," he whispered.

Wynter tried to follow the flicker of light, tried to see if it had been Embla. But it was gone.

The clearing shivered into focus. The air snapped back into place. The sound of the fires abruptly dropped into reality. Wynter took a deep, convulsive lungful of air and subsided limply against her saddle. Beside her, Christopher growled in his sleep, his face darkening.

Razi sat upright. He stayed absolutely still for a moment, staring ahead of him, his eyes wide, then he pushed his covers back and scrambled to his feet.

"Razi!" hissed Wynter, rising to her elbow. "What are you doing?" Ignoring her, Razi stumbled to their pile of tack and rooted frantically about until he found his doctor's bag. He rose, the bag clutched in his hand, and looked about him as if uncertain of what he was doing. Then he swung around and crossed rapidly to the Merron side of camp.

"Sól," Razi dropped to his knees by the sleeping man. "Wake up."

At his clumsy intrusion, Hallvor and Úlfnaor jerked awake, startled. The warhounds growled in irritation, but they did not rise to their feet. Úlfnaor pushed himself onto his elbow, frowning. "What you doing?" he asked sharply.

Across the fire, the others shot to hands and knees, calling out and groping blindly for their swords. "*Cad e?*" cried Wari. "*Aoire?*"

Gesturing them to silence, Hallvor pushed her sleep-tangled hair from her face and sat forward. "Tabiyb," she whispered, staring at Razi questioningly.

Razi did not acknowledge her.

"Sólmundr!" he said again. "Wake up."

The warriors began to rise, swords in hand. Úlfnaor murmured soothingly, "*Bígí ar bhur suaimhneas*," gesturing that they should sit back down, and they subsided warily.

Wynter pushed back her covers and got to her feet. She slid her knife into its scabbard and watched as Razi patted Sólmundr's cheek and called his name. The warrior sighed and weakly shoved Razi's hands away.

Hallvor reached across and took Sól's hands, gently holding them still.

Razi gazed up at her. "He is terribly hot," he whispered. "I should like to examine him, if I may? I . . . I should like to offer him my assistance."

Úlfnaor translated, and Hallvor's face softened in understanding. Sadly, she shook her head. She was telling Razi that there was nothing he could do.

"Please," insisted Razi, and the healer sighed, nodded and bent forward to help him.

Wynter glanced at Christopher. Weighted down by his exhaustion, he slept on. Wynter hesitated only a moment, then she turned her back on him and picked her way across the camp to stand in the shadows by Razi's side.

Úlfnaor pulled Boro to one side, allowing Razi to push Sólmundr's covers back and lift his shirt. The bandages were clean and neat, and it was obvious that Hallvor had been doing an excellent job of taking care of her friend. Sólmundr lay quietly against his saddle now, his eyes half open, his breathing slow and heavy through slack lips. He hardly seemed to notice as Razi unbound his wound, but Hallvor continued to hold his hands against his chest and after a moment, his eyes slid to her and he smiled, as if seeing her for the first time.

"Hally," he breathed, pleased and surprised.

Hallvor murmured something and squeezed his hand.

"Hally," he whispered confidentially, smiling, "*bhí Ashkr anseo.*"

Hallvor and Úlfnaor exchanged a startled look. Úlfnaor glanced sharply at his people. They gazed silently back across the flames, their eyes gleaming as brightly as the weapons they held in their hands.

"Shhh," soothed Hallvor, leaning over Sólmundr, her eyes on the others. "Shhh, *a chroí.*"

Heedless of her anxiety, Sólmundr smiled. "Ashkr," he repeated.

"Shhhh," said Hallvor sharply. "Sól! *Shush.*"

Suddenly Razi drew back, and Wynter's stomach clenched at the sight of the putrid yellow stain soaking through the bottom layers of the bandages. She became aware of a terrible smell, and her heart sank.

Oh, she thought in dismay. *Oh no.*

Sólmundr jerked and moaned weakly as the final bandage came loose, and Razi sat back on his heels, his face blank.

All around the wound, the flesh of Sólmundr's stomach was swollen tight, red and heated looking. The skin around the stitches was a suppurating mess. Wynter put her hand to her mouth, distressed at the sight and at the obvious hopelessness of the poor man's condition. She raised glittering eyes to Razi's face. He gazed at the wound for a moment, then he gently pressed his fingers down against one of the stitches. Pus oozed thickly from around the knotted thread, and Sólmundr moaned again in pain.

Razi withdrew his hand. Hallvor said something soft and kind.

"Hally, say not to mind," whispered Úlfnaor. "She say you did everything that within your power, Tabiyb. You could not to have done more."

Razi shook his head once in disagreement.

Frangok's voice cut across them, hard and flat. "*Is maoin do Chroí an Domhain Sólmundr,*" she said.

Whatever this meant, it did not make Úlfnaor nor Hallvor happy and Wynter saw their expressions draw down in disapproval. Wari and Soma hung their heads, uncomfortable at Frangok's tone, but the remaining warriors, Surtr and Thoar, seemed to be on Frangok's side, and they nodded their support as the warrior pressed her point.

"*Tá Ashkr ag fanacht le Sól,*" she insisted, jabbing her sword in Sólmundr's direction.

"Aye . . ." echoed Sólmundr dreamily, "Ashkr."

The Merron looked sharply at him.

"*Agus Embla?*" asked Frangok, leaning forward to see Sól's face.

Every one of the Merron seemed to hold their breath, waiting to hear Sólmundr's reply, but the poor man seemed oblivious to all but his own smiling thoughts.

"Sól?" demanded Frangok. "*Embla.*"

"Embla," sighed Sólmundr dreamily. "Embla."

"Ahhhh," sighed Frangok, as if suddenly aware of a huge truth.

The warriors instantly snapped their attention to Razi. Something in their faces chilled Wynter. She moved so that she was standing between them and the still oblivious Razi. Her hand tightened on the hilt of her knife, and there was an unmistakable rising of hackles amongst the warriors.

Úlfnaor's deep voice cut across the tension like a slap with an open palm.

"*Níl Tabiyb ach ina coimhthíoch,*" he rumbled dismissively.

The red-headed brothers turned their eyes to him, their faces hard, and Úlfnaor tutted, as if they should know better. He slid a disparaging look at Razi, and Wynter was shocked and enraged at the obvious disrespect in his face.

"*Giota. Spóirt. Choimhthígh,*" he sneered, contempt for Razi palpable in every emphasised syllable.

There was a brief moment of hesitation. Then Surtr and Thoar nodded and sat back. Úlfnaor spread his hands to the still uncertain Frangok, and tilted his head. *Come on*, that gesture said, *you know I'm right*. The frowning woman paused, then, sighing in resignation, she rammed her sword into its scabbard and pulled closer to the fire, her eyes on Sól.

Wari yawned suddenly, rubbing at his tired face, and dragged his cloak up to his chin, murmuring in the manner of someone complaining about the cold. Soma began to root about in their things. She pulled a blackened pot from their kit and it soon became obvious that she was preparing to make some tea.

Wynter stood uncertainly, her hand still on her weapon, her eyes skipping from one warrior to the next. The Merron seemed to be settling themselves down for a vigil, all their tension gone in the blink of an eye, and she found herself, as usual, thrown by their mercurial twists of mood. Hallvor's soft voice drew her attention back to Razi. The healer was patting his arm and calling him, trying to wake him from the reverie he seemed to have fallen into.

"There is nothing I can do," he said. His gaze wandered up to meet Wynter's. "Sis," he said. "There is nothing . . . I have no sulphur. I have no . . . I have not even a brace of mouldy biscuits to lay against the suppuration." He looked back down at Sól. "I have left it too late," he said. "I have left it far too late. I have neglected him and now there is nothing I can do."

"Did any of the others see the ghost?"

Wynter glanced sideways at Christopher and pulled her cloak tight. "I do not believe so," she whispered.

"Think," he hissed. "Think hard. Did they see Ashkr's ghost?"

Wynter shifted uncomfortably and looked back across the camp to where the Merron sat around the fire, keeping vigil over Sólmundr. "I think that Sól . . . I am certain that Sól told them of it," she whispered.

"Oh, God *curse* him," said Christopher.

Wynter anxiously shushed him, but it was simply a reflex. No one was listening. They may as well have been invisible, sitting there side by side on their blanket rolls, dimly lit by the glowing embers of their own fire. Even Razi, alone and brooding in the shadows at the edge of the clearing, paid them no heed.

"What way did they react to the news?" hissed Christopher. "Were they alarmed?"

Wynter scanned the Merrons' patient, waiting faces and shrugged. "I cannot say that they were alarmed, exactly. Though they seemed to have some differences of opinion on the matter. All in all, they seemed to take it very well." She gestured to the warriors. "They have been like this ever since."

Once the warriors had settled down, Hallvor and Razi had wrapped Sólmundr's wound in clean bindings, changed his sweat-soaked shirt and made him as comfortable as possible. Then Razi had removed himself from the company and retreated away from everyone. He had been silent ever since, seated at the base of a tree, wrapped in his cloak, staring at Sól.

For a while, the Merron had occupied themselves with quiet prayers. Then Úlfnaor and Hallvor had placed a fire-basin of smouldering herbs at Sólmundr's feet, and taken a seat on either side of their friend. Since then, the Merron had simply sat in calm silence, waiting for their friend to die.

Boro lay with his head on his master's lap, his eyes fixed on Sól's face. The warrior was wrapped loosely in his blankets and his cloak, sweating and shivering, glassy-eyed with fever. Thankfully, he seemed to have drifted far from his pain, and as the smoke from the fire-basin twined slowly around his body, Sólmundr lay placidly staring through the gaps in the canopy of the trees, his eyes roaming the stars that trembled overhead.

"I fear that he has not much time left," murmured Wynter, glancing again at Christopher. He had yet to cross the camp and pay his respects. This surprised Wynter. In the short time they'd known each other, she had thought the two men had become very close, and Christopher's distanced reaction to Sól's decline worried her.

Christopher gazed at Sólmundr, then at Úlfnaor, but said nothing.

Frangok crossed from the Merron fire and knelt at Sólmundr's side, a beaker in her hand. Hallvor tilted his head forward, to make it easier for him to drink, but he did not even try, and the liquid dribbled from his slack lips, running down his neck and staining his shirt. Sighing, Frangok carefully dried his face and returned to the fire with the beaker still full of tea.

"That is the first time I have seen that woman pay any attention to Sólmundr," observed Wynter. "Until now, she and those brothers have been consistent in their disregard for the poor man."

"That is because they are superstitious *chards*," said Christopher. The venom in his voice took Wynter by surprise and she turned to stare at him. "This is all Ashkr's *fault!*" he cried softly. "What did he expect these people to *do* after he was gone? Did he think that they would forget what Sólmundr *was*? Did he think they would simply throw their arms about the poor fellow and cry, 'Ah well, come back home!' Good *Frith*. If Ashkr had only *once* stopped to consider that poor man instead of himself, but no . . . not the bloody *Caora*. Not the bloody anointed of God!"

Christopher turned to Wynter in wide-eyed frustration, all set to continue his hissing tirade, but at the confusion in her face, he paused. The anger drained from him at the realisation that she did not understand, and he turned wearily back to face the clearing, his voice dull.

"Sólmundr should have died when Ashkr died, lass. Those people don't care that it was Ashkr's wish to spare him." Christopher stared at Frangok, his face dark with bitterness. "*Tá Sólmundr ina 'Neamh-bheo' dhóibh anois,*" he sneered, apparently unaware that he had spoken Merron. "Walking Dead. Very bad luck. They will only be truly content once Sól is dead and everything is as it should be. They believe that Ashkr cannot make the journey to *An Domhan* without his *croí-eile*. They believe he has come back to claim Sól and take him with him as his own." His eyes went to Boro. "No doubt they'll cut the poor hound's throat too in the end. He was Ashkr's property, after all."

Christopher flicked an anxious glance at Razi, and Wynter's stomach went cold with horrible understanding. She remembered Christopher standing in the flame-licked shadows as Ashkr burned and Embla lay crushed beneath that tree. She remembered him telling her, his voice choked with tears, how Razi too should have died; how Embla had spared him, just as Ashkr had spared Sólmundr.

"Christopher," she whispered. "They spoke of Embla. I heard them say her name." Christopher turned slowly and they looked each other in the eye. "Frangok asked Sól had he seen Embla. I am certain of it . . ."

"What did Sólmundr say?" whispered Christopher, his lips almost too numb to form the words.

Wynter shook her head. "He did not answer, he was too far gone . . . but I think I understand now, why Úlfnaor was so terribly insulting to Razi afterwards. He was sneering, and slyly scornful of him. He called him . . ." she frowned, trying to recall the words.

"*Coimhthíoch?*" whispered Christopher, and Wynter

hissed in negation, holding up her hand to shush him, still trying to recall the words.

"Guttah . . ." she tried. "Guttah sport quivheeg . . ." She looked questioningly to him. "Guttah sport quivheeg?"

"*Giota spóirt coimhthigh*," repeated Christopher softly. "A bit of foreign sport." He glanced at Razi, sitting all alone by his tree, weaponless and distant. "How did the others take that?"

"It seemed to calm them. What . . .?"

"Úlfnaor fears for Razi's life," murmured Christopher. "He must have been trying to convince them that Razi was naught but a heat to Embla. Naught but a bit of sport. Nothing worth returning for."

"But, Christopher," she whispered. "I think Embla *did* return. I think I saw her. I think I heard Razi speak to her." Christopher jerked, as if to get to his feet, and Wynter clamped down on his arm, holding him in place. "No one else saw," she hissed. "I think even Razi believes it was a dream." She dipped her chin, staring into his eyes. "We will say nothing," she said firmly, "and hope that . . ."

There was a flurry of movement on the Merron side of camp. Hallvor called out in alarm, and Úlfnaor echoed her, distressed. Wynter and Christopher leapt to their feet. In the shadows, Razi pushed himself up and stepped forward.

Sólmundr's breathing had become suddenly laboured, each breath coming in a long, sawing rasp. Boro stood over him, barking, and Hallvor directed Úlfnaor to pull the huge dog away. She began to move Sólmundr down, preparing to lay him flat on his back.

"No," cried Razi, his hand out. "Don't lie him down."

The Merron turned as one and glared at him. Razi faltered, then continued softly. "If you prop him up a little more," he said, "his breathing will come easier and he . . . his passing will be that much more comfortable."

Úlfnaor translated, and everyone looked to Hallvor. She stared at Razi for a moment, then nodded. The Merron leapt to comply, and soon Sólmundr was sitting against the tree, a small pile of blankets and saddlebags at his back, his breathing a little easier than before.

Boro pulled free of Úlfnaor's grip and ran once more to Sólmundr's side. Whining, his tail between his legs, the giant hound nudged at his master's limp fingers, but the warrior did not respond. Instead, he sank against his support, his head lolling back, his eyes fixed on the stars. His face was slack, and his chest heaved laboriously with every breath.

"It is nearly over," whispered Razi.

Christopher took a step forward.

"Won't you go to him, Chris?" asked Wynter gently.

Christopher's gaze dropped to Boro, and he watched as the warhound snuffled desperately at his master's unresponsive hands.

"Chris? Won't you go to him?"

Christopher shook his head. He stepped back and took Wynter's hand, and together they stood and watched, waiting helplessly as Sólmundr struggled towards his end.

"*Féach* . . ." Frangok's soft whisper drew everyone's attention, and the tall woman got slowly to her feet, her eyes fixed on the darkness beyond the firelight. "*Féach*," she said again raising her hand to point into the shadows. "Ashkr . . ."

Caora Nua

The roar of flames grew to fill the clearing, and the company rose to their feet and watched as a pale column of flickering light approached through the trees.

"He is here," whispered Christopher, clenching Wynter's hand. "Good Frith. He is really here."

Regal and shimmering, a flaring brightness against the dark, Ashkr's ghost paused at the edge of the clearing. His handsome face was filled with tenderness as he regarded his dying friend. Úlfnaor whispered something and the Merron stepped away from Sól.

Sólmundr, oblivious to everything, continued to gaze up at the stars, his breath labouring slowly in and out, his body limp. Boro prowled in front of him, whining, his eyes on Ashkr. He barked uncertainly. Ashkr glanced at him, then tilted his head and gestured, *stand down*. The enormous warhound hesitated, then he dropped by Sólmundr and flattened himself into the earth, gazing at Ashkr's ghost with confusion and dismay. The other hounds had already slunk into the trees, their tails down, and Wynter saw their eyes gleaming in the darkness as they hovered in the shadows.

Hallvor backed slowly to stand with the others. Her eyes switched between Úlfnaor and Ashkr's ghost. "Aoire," she urged, her hand out as if to draw Úlfnaor to her side. "Aoire . . ."

Úlfnaor stayed crouched by Sólmundr, gazing into his friend's lax face. "Sól?" he whispered.

Sólmundr did not seem to hear him and, after a moment, Úlfnaor sighed in resignation. He laid his hand on Sól's labouring chest. "*Slán go fóil, a dhlúthchara. Fear maith a bhí ionat i gcónaí. Fear láidir, agus fear saor go deo . . .*"

Christopher's breath caught for a moment, then he coughed. "He is saying goodbye . . ." he whispered hoarsely. "He's telling Sól that he was always a great man, strong and . . . and for ever free."

Úlfnaor pressed his forehead to Sólmundr's, then he rose abruptly and crossed to stand with the others, his head down.

Smiling, Ashkr's ghost drifted forward. His eyes never left Sólmundr's face, and Wynter understood that no one else here mattered to him, no one else even existed. In death, as in life, Sólmundr was all there was for Ashkr.

Ashkr passed Razi and for a moment the young man was illuminated by spectre light. His eyes were wide as he watched the spirit pass, his cloak clenched tightly around him, as if to protect himself against the supernatural. Then the ghost moved on, and Razi was thrown into shadow once more.

Ashkr came to a halt at his friend's side. "Sól," he whispered. His voice was gentle through the violent roaring of the flames, and it wrung Wynter's heart to hear the love in it. She moved closer to Christopher, held his hand a little tighter.

Ashkr leant down. "Sólmundr," he insisted.

Sólmundr tore his attention from the ragged stars above and focused on the face that he had loved so well. He twitched a weary smile and whispered something too dry and low to hear. Ashkr regarded him gravely and sank to his knees by his side. "Sól," he said. "*Mo mhuirnín bocht . . .*"

Sól's lips tugged up at the corners. His eyes slipped shut and struggled opened again as he fought to stay awake. He whispered again, and Ashkr nodded, reaching almost to touch Sól's hair.

How unjust, thought Wynter, *how unutterably sad that they should have been parted.* Her mother and father rose unexpectedly to her mind, and the brief pittance of time that they had enjoyed together before death tore them apart. She hoped that they were together now. She fervently hoped that her father's ghost did not wander the palace, a thin shadow of his vibrant self, doomed to become nothing but a single-minded shade. She glanced toward Razi – a shadow among shadows, raw and burning still at the loss of Embla – and she squeezed Christopher's hand, overcome with dread that they might lose each other.

Wynter glanced up into Christopher's face, about to whisper his name. But, to her surprise, he was not looking at Ashkr and Sólmundr. He was staring into the trees, and even as Wynter turned to him, he snapped to attention, his eyes widening in anger and in fear. She spun to follow his gaze.

A second pillar of light was travelling smoothly towards them through the darkness of the forest. Ashkr glanced in its direction and smiled. He turned to look at Razi. "Tabiyb," he said, "Embla is coming for you."

"NO!" howled Christopher. There was a flurry of movement, a sudden, yelling rush of men and women, and Christopher dithered, momentarily torn between leaping backward for his sword and leaping forward to protect Razi.

Wynter drew her knife and dashed forward, followed by Christopher, who stooped and snatched his dagger from his boot as he ran. There was a series of shouts. Frangok's voice rang out, then Hallvor's. Úlfnaor yelled. There was a clang of metal on metal, and Wynter ducked instinctively.

Out of the corner of her eye, Wynter saw Thoar dive for his sword. She swerved in his direction, but to her amazement, Hallvor leapt on him, knocking him to the ground. The red-headed warrior exclaimed in shock, and the two Merron rolled into the bushes, grappling for the sword. With a yell, Wari dived to Hallvor's aid.

Frangok surged forward, her knife in hand, her eyes on Razi. Wynter veered for her with a cry. But almost immediately Úlfnaor flung out his massive arm and hit Frangok hard across the throat. The blow stopped the tall woman in her tracks, and she dropped at Úlfnaor's feet, gagging and writhing, clutching at her paralysed throat.

Surtr was halfway across the clearing, advancing on Razi, his face set. But Christopher was already heading for him, running full tilt. Even as Wynter spun towards them, Christopher leapt into the air and flung his legs forward in one of his spectacular flying kicks. He caught the warrior on the shoulder, his soft boots impacting the man's muscular body with a meaty *thud*, and the two of them flew sideways, slamming to the ground in a flurry of leaves.

They slid to a halt near Sólmundr's feet, instantly rolling apart. Surtr whipped his knife around and Christopher curved his body into an abrupt arc, barely avoiding the slim blade. Wynter saw the tip of the knife catch the cloth of Christopher's dark tunic and her heart skipped a beat at how close he'd come.

Christopher rolled and Surtr rolled, and both came to their knees, snarling at each other, their knives poised. Úlfnaor came forward, a massive, dark shape striding between the two men, and he knocked Surtr's weapon from his hand. Wynter had just time to see the shock in Surtr's eyes before Úlfnaor kicked him in the chest and sent him into the dirt. Surtr sprawled onto his back and Úlfnaor stood over him, his face sharp with threat, his sword pressed to Surtr's neck. The red-headed warrior stared up at his leader, stunned and hurt, all his fight gone.

Wynter skidded to a crouching halt, breathless.

There was a moment of bewildered stillness.

On the opposite side of the fire, Wari stood over Thoar, his foot on the dazed man's weapon hand, his sword at his neck. Hallvor, kneeling by Frangok's side, spoke urgently to her and massaged her throat.

Shakily, Wynter took all this in. She began to straighten, and Christopher, still on his knees, relaxed slowly, his hands dropping to his side. He looked about with the same dazed confusion as Wynter. Their eyes met. Then Christopher's attention slipped past her and Wynter saw his face slacken in shock. She spun on her heel, following the direction of his gaze.

Soma was striding towards Razi, a knife in her hand, and Razi, trapped by the unwavering attention of his lover's ghost, was oblivious to the danger. Embla stepped from the trees, staring into his eyes. She placed a shimmering hand on his chest. Razi gasped and jerked his arm upwards, as if trying to push her away.

"Nuh . . ." he said. "Don't . . ."

Soma raised her knife.

"Razi!" screamed Wynter. "Razi."

At her voice, Embla tilted her head and looked past Razi to Soma.

"*Ar fad do Chroí an Domhain*," whispered Soma, staring at the ghost, her eyes wide with fear. "*Ar fad do Chroí an Domhain.*"

She drew back for the fatal blow.

Dreamily, almost slowly, Embla lifted her hand, and Soma jerked to a frozen halt. Her mouth dropped open, her eyes bugging in distress.

"Soma an Fada, daughter of Sorcha an Fada," murmured Embla, her lips curving fondly. "You are released from your duty."

Embla spread her fingers and the knife dropped from Soma's hand and tumbled to the leaves by her side. Embla glanced at the weapon and it shot away through the leaf-mould, slithering out of Soma's reach, coming to rest against the fire-stones. Soma dropped to her knees with a moan and clutched her knife-hand, rocking as if in great pain.

Embla smiled at Wari. "Wari an Fada, son of Sven an Fada, come forward and tend your other-heart."

Wynter gaped at the beautiful apparition, unable to

comprehend the difference in her speech. All the fractured hesitance had gone from Embla's voice, and she was speaking with an unprecedented fluency, no trace of her drawling accent remaining. Wynter was certain that Embla had spoken Southlandast, a language that Wari did not understand. But the huge man was already striding forward, his face twisted in concern for his wife, and Wynter understood at once – Embla wasn't speaking Southlandast. She wasn't speaking Merron. Embla was speaking some other language, at once strange yet familiar, unknown and yet known to them all.

Wari helped Soma to her feet and she retreated into the sanctuary of his arms, cradling her hand and whimpering. Cautiously, his eyes fixed on Embla's ghost, Wari led his wife back to the others.

"Rise up," murmured Embla, gesturing to the Merron. "Rise up now, and cease this struggling against one another."

The warriors did as they were told, the former combatants helping each other to their feet, and Embla once again focused her attention on Razi. She smiled her slow, heated smile, her eyes roaming his face. He seemed suspended by the shimmering hand she had pressed over his heart, and his body was vibrating slightly out of his control. He still had his hand up, the fingers spread, as if to ward Embla off, and he stared at her, wide-eyed, his face twitching in distress.

Christopher came to Wynter's side. "Let him go, *Caora*," he said softly. "He ain't yours."

Wynter raised her knife, though she knew it was useless against this kind of threat. "Let him go, Lady," she whispered. "Please."

Embla ignored them both. Only Razi mattered to her

and she gazed at him with yearning tenderness. "Tabiyb," she breathed. "My good man."

At her voice, all Razi's pain seemed to leave him and his body relaxed against her supportive hand. He blinked at her as if seeing her anew. "Embla . . ." he whispered, amazed. He reached as if to touch her translucent face. "Em . . ." he said. His dark eyes shone suddenly brighter, filled with the broken reflections of Embla's pale light. "I would have taken care of you," he whispered. "Why would you not trust me to take care of you?"

Embla half-closed her eyes and sighed, as if Razi's words were the sun and she were basking in their heat. Dreamily, she ran her hand up his chest, leaving shimmering ghost-fire in the wake of her trailing fingers, and she cupped Razi's cheek in her palm. At the touch of ghost-flesh, Razi's lips parted over gritted teeth, and he moaned in pain, even as he pressed his cheek further into her hand.

"My good man," sighed Embla again, watching him through lowered lids. "My good omen. What a blessing you were to me."

She ran her thumb over his lips, and Razi shuddered, wisps of ether rising from his warm skin. His eyes rolled back under their heavy lids, his face grew blank, and his long body began a slow tilt forwards.

"Embla!" cried Wynter. "Release him!"

Embla withdrew her hand in quick alarm, and Razi staggered, his eyes flying open. She put her hands on his chest to steady him, and he gaped at her, his mouth open, his face vacant.

Embla stared at Razi in sad understanding. He was lost to her, and she to him.

For a moment she watched as he tried to collect his fuddled wits, then her face hardened. She took a deep breath. She drew herself up. When next she spoke, her voice was deep and rich with command, all her cool nobility brought to bear on the dazed man before her.

"Listen to me, Lord Razi Kingsson, Most Favoured Son of Jonathon the King. I would speak with you." Embla waited until Razi was able to focus on her, then she stared into his eyes. "This world is dark," she said. "You fear that soon you will drown in its darkness." She lifted her hand, but did not touch his face. "You must not drown," she commanded. "It is your duty not to drown."

Razi gazed desperately at her, his eyes glittering.

Embla nodded, as if to seal a bargain, then her eyes slipped past Razi and came to rest on Úlfnaor. "There is to be no more blood," she said. "This is a new beginning."

Frowning, Úlfnaor shook his head – he did not understand.

"No more blood," insisted Embla. "Ashkr and I. We are to be the last."

Hallvor cried out in Merron, very distressed, and Embla looked kindly at her. "Do not despair, Hallvor an Fada, Healer, daughter of Ingrid an Fada. The Bridge is strong here. It has always been strong. We were foolish to think otherwise, and arrogant. Here, as everywhere, the People walk as one with the World's Heart, and the Bridge needed no blood to open its gates. Its gates were always open, its path free to all." Embla turned once more to Úlfnaor. "This is *your* duty Úlfnaor, Shepherd of the World. You understand? There shall be no more blood. You must teach this. This is your duty."

Úlfnaor nodded, his eyes wide. Embla looked pointedly from one to the other of the warriors that surrounded him. One by one they dropped to their knees and bowed their heads as if taking an oath, and Embla smiled in approval. She put her hand on Razi's shoulder. "Behold," she said to the kneeling men and women. "Your new Caora."

Christopher hissed in a breath.

"Christopher?" whispered Wynter, her heart hammering. "Did she just . . .?"

"Shhhh!" he hissed sharply, his eyes on Embla. "Shush."

Embla looked from Merron to disbelieving Merron. "*Caora Nua,*" she said. She stared at Úlfnaor and he stared back at her, his face shocked.

"Embla," Ashkr's quiet voice drew his sister's attention to him. He was kneeling by Sólmundr's side, his face grave. "You must go now. You have done your duty." Embla frowned sadly and he smiled. "It is all right, my heart. Say your goodbyes, free your man from his loss."

"No," whispered Razi. "Stay." He once again lifted his hand to Embla's face, and she tilted her cheek to his touch. Her shining hair drifted up and clung to Razi's fingers, twining like glowing weed around his arm. Razi bent his head to her, his dark face outlined by Embla's pallid light, his eyes filled with her glowing reflection. For a moment, their lips almost touched. Then Embla frowned, turned her head and stepped away. Razi . . . was left alone in darkness, his fingers touching cold air.

Christopher froze and gasped in shock as Embla passed too close, and Wynter jerked him backward, pulling him free of the ghost's chilly shadow.

"Good Fr . . . Frith!" he hissed, his teeth chattering.

Wynter rubbed his back, her eye on Razi. He stumbled a few steps, his hand to his forehead, as if unsure of where he was. *Caora Nua*, she thought, her heart filled with dread.

Embla's voice drew her attention.

The pale lady was leaning over Sólmundr, peering into his unconscious face. "He has not much time, brother." She glanced at Ashkr. "You sincerely wish to do this?" He tutted and gave her a reproving look.

Embla sighed and straightened. Ashkr rose to his feet, and they stood side by side, gazing down at their dying friend. Sólmundr, bathed in the combined aura of the two powerful spirits, grimaced and shifted uncomfortably, his fingers jerking in distress.

"I will miss you, Ash," said Embla softly.

Ashkr smiled again, his eyes fixed on Sólmundr. "You will have the comfort of the World to keep you, my heart."

Wynter was astonished to see tears well up in Embla's eyes. They shimmered for a moment on her ghostly lashes, then overflowed in phosphorescent trails down her face. "You shall be no more," she whispered. "How am I to bear that? The knowledge that you shall be no more? How . . .? Ashkr, how shall *Sól* bear it? That he shall have no hope of ever seeing you again?"

Ashkr tutted gently. "Do not cry, Emmy."

Embla shook her head and buried her face in her hands.

"Oh, Embla," sighed Ashkr, throwing up his hands in fond exasperation. He pulled his sister to him and squeezed her tight. Their embrace sent a flare of ghost-light high into the tree above them. Threads of ghost-fire shimmered in the bark of the trunk behind them, and pale phosphorescence writhed to momentary life along the branches over their heads.

"Do not cry!" laughed Ashkr, pushing his sister to arm's length. He grinned in his usual teasing way. "This is what I *want*. Understand? You and Sól must just learn to live with it."

Embla swiped her face clear of tears. "All right, Ash," she said. "All right, my heart. I understand." She broke free of his arms and took a deep breath. "All right," she said.

Embla smiled at her brother and put her hand on her heart. "Goodbye, Ashkr, Son of the World. You have been my best friend and my rock. My life would have been empty without your smiling presence. My heart will be broken at your loss." Despite her set face, Embla's voice cracked on these last words and it took her a moment to go on. Then she straightened to her full regal height, tightened her hand to a fist and lifted her chin. "*Ar fad do Chroí an Domhain*," she said. "As always, all for the Heart of the World." And with those words, she was gone.

Ashkr watched his sister's light fade away. Just as the last shimmering glow was going from the air, he reached as if to touch her once again. "Not for the World, Embla," he whispered. He glanced sharply at Úlfnaor. "Not for the World, Shepherd," he commanded, "But for Love. You remember that. You teach it. *Ar son an Ghrá*." Then he turned abruptly, knelt at Sól's side and, with shocking roughness, shook his friend awake.

"Sólmundr," he said. "Sól!"

Sólmundr jerked and opened his eyes with a grunt. He immediately registered the feeling of ghost hands clenched on his shoulders and he gasped hoarsely with the pain of it.

Ashkr glared down into his face, and Sólmundr stared up at him, confused and alarmed by Ashkr's fierceness.

"*A chroí*," he breathed.

Ashkr shifted his grip to the back of Sólmundr's scarred neck, and Sól cried out, his body arching like a bow, as ghost fingers clamped down on his bare flesh. Ashkr slid his free hand down to the site of Sólmundr's terrible wound and pressed his palm hard against the bandages there. Wynter heard a sound like a branding iron hitting flesh, and Sólmundr's fingers dug into the bedding on either side of him, his hands closing into agonised fists. He cried out again, and the Merron stepped towards him, then stopped, uncertain what to do.

Christopher lurched forward, but Wynter gripped his arm, pulling him to a halt. She stared at Ashkr's luminously determined face. "Wait," she whispered. Christopher hesitated. Wynter squeezed his arm and he stayed uncertainly by her side.

Ashkr bowed his head, grinding his teeth as if in pain. Both he and Sólmundr were shaking now, as ripples of ghost-fire radiated from Ashkr's splayed hand and spread across Sól's body.

Hissing and popping, tendrils of green light writhed across Sólmundr's chest, flowing up his arms and entwining his neck until he was wound all around with thick ropes of crackling power. Sparks cracked hotly across his lips and teeth and eyelashes, and he sobbed and arched as Ashkr pressed down harder and harder against his wound. Gradually the light from the two men became almost too bright to watch.

A desperate, agonised groan filled the clearing, and Wynter, squinting now against the brightness, was shocked to realise that the sound was coming, not from Sólmundr, but from Ashkr. As the light intensified, so too did the ghost's pain, and soon Ashkr was doubled over, eyes opened wide, teeth bared in agony.

"Stop!" pleaded Sólmundr. "Stop!"

Suddenly Ashkr screamed and the ghost light expanded to an unbearable level.

There was a flare of white.

Sólmundr yelled out, "Ash!"

Then the light collapsed and was abruptly gone.

Wynter stumbled backward in the sudden darkness, her ears ringing with the aftershock of nothing. She brought her hands instinctively to her head and moaned. It felt as though a gunpowder barrel had just exploded soundlessly in her face, and she reeled drunkenly about, unable to get her balance. Someone to her left said something too loudly in Merron, and someone behind her coughed harshly as if to clear their lungs of smoke. She heard someone say her name, but it was far away and muffled.

Then a voice came through clearly – brokenhearted and sobbing; just the one word, repeated over and over. "No . . . No . . . No . . ."

Wynter lifted her head and squinted in the direction of the voice, stung by the sorrow and the loss in that one repeated syllable.

Sólmundr was kneeling at the base of his tree, one arm wrapped around his stomach, the other supporting himself against the wide trunk. He was looking desolately out into the darkness, crooning his one word litany over and over.

Someone stumbled to her side, bumping into her, and Wynter clung to them without thinking. She glanced up to find Razi's face looming above her. He was staring at Sólmundr, stunned. "Good God," he said.

He let go of her and went to step forward, but someone grabbed his shoulder, pulling him back. Both Wynter and Razi spun, their arms flashing upwards. Úlfnaor stepped back immediately and spread his hands to show he meant no harm. He jerked his chin in Sólmundr's direction and they turned to find that Christopher was already at the man's side. The other Merron moved forward but Úlfnaor halted them with a gesture, silently motioning them back.

"Sólmundr?" Christopher crouched down, laying his hand on Sól's shoulder. "Sól . . .?"

"*Tá sé caillte . . . tá sé caillte . . .*" keened Sólmundr, shaking his head and rocking to and fro. "*Ó, a chroí.*"

"Sól," Christopher leant forward, peering under Sólmundr's arm, trying to see his wound. "Can you just . . ." he pushed the man's strong shoulder and turned him so that his back was against the tree. Sólmundr slid down until he was sitting on the now tangled heap of bedding. "Let me see." Gently Christopher pulled Sólmundr's arm away and lifted the bandages. "Good Frith!"

Sólmundr raised his hands to cover his face and Christopher took the opportunity to push his shirt higher, tugging the bandages aside. Wynter stepped forward, Razi and Úlfnaor by her side. She heard Hallvor exclaim in awe, and a murmur of wonder rippled from Merron to Merron.

Christopher ran his fingers across Sólmundr's stomach. There was no sign of the wound, no infection, not even the slightest mark remaining. Only the old, tangled network of scars and lash marks from Sólmundr's years as a slave now marred the man's pale skin.

Christopher spread his scarred fingers against the site of Sólmundr's operation.

"He has saved you," he said.

Sólmundr dropped his hands and thumped his head against the tree, staring desolately into the branches above him. Christopher gazed up at him.

"He has saved you," he said again. Sólmundr shook his head in despair and Christopher shook him by the shoulder until the warrior slid his eyes to him. "You're going to live, Sól," he said, grinning luminously into Sólmundr's tear-stained face. "Ashkr *saved* you. You're going to live."

A New Departure

"I not hungry."

"You owe me," said Christopher cheerfully, "and so must do as I say. I command you to eat."

Sólmundr slid Christopher a withering look. He snapped the leathery ribbon of venison from the younger man's hand and turned back to painting his horse. "I knowed man like you before," he muttered darkly, sticking the dried meat into the corner of his mouth and dipping a brush into a bowl of blue dye. "He used stand at head of galley with whip in his hand."

Christopher, already walking back to his side of camp, grinned and waved dismissively over his shoulder.

"I crushed his head with my shackle-chains!" called Sólmundr, carefully refreshing the outline of the bear that snarled across his horse's flank.

"Yes, yes," laughed Christopher. "You are a fiery and dangerous brute. My blood runs cold with fear."

Wynter smiled as Christopher came up behind her. She finished cinching the girth on Ozkar's saddle just as

Christopher slid his arms around her waist and dipped his face to her neck.

"What about you, Protector Lady?" he murmured, slyly nipping at her ear. "Are you hungry?"

"Unhand me," she said. "You are a lecherous cur."

"Mmhmm," he agreed. "Amazing how two nights of good sleep will restore a man's appetite." He pulled her close, his lips moving against her neck.

Wynter elbowed him in the ribs and Christopher broke away with a grin, slipping around to her side, his arm looped around her waist. He followed her gaze and the two of them surveyed the clearing.

"I fear we are a touch underdressed," said Wynter.

Indeed, the Merron were washed and brushed and polished as never before, dressed in formal pale green, every movement of hand or arm bright with the glitter of silver jewellery. The tall warriors had also adorned their horses, renewing the painted decorations on their hides and polishing their ornate tack until it shone. Even the rangy warhounds were decked out in silver ornaments, their collars and braceleted front legs gleaming in the sun.

Christopher nodded to where Razi had just finished consulting with Úlfnaor. "Behold our dusky pearl," he said. "I think we will have to recommence calling him your Highness."

Wynter eyed their friend as he approached them. Lost in thought and unaware of their scrutiny, Razi was folding his maps back into their case as he walked. His boots shone like mirrors and he had changed from his simple, dark, travelling tunic into a well-tailored coat of deepest scarlet. He was clean shaven for the first time in weeks, and without his curling, piratical beard Wynter thought he looked at once much younger and infinitely more lordly than before.

"If we do call him your Highness," she observed softly, "it could well be the death of him."

Christopher's arm tightened around her. "Don't, girly," he said. "Don't say that. He is safe now." He lifted his chin, smiling with dark pride. "He is *An Caora Nua*. These people would die before they let Alberon do him harm."

Wynter tightened her jaw and bit back her doubts. She could not forget so easily what these people had done to their last Caoirigh, and she could not bring herself to trust that they would not do the same to Razi. As for Razi himself, though he seemed to have mastered his temper in the two days since the ghosts' dramatic visitation, Wynter was not too certain that his feelings had changed. She doubted that he would be so quick to relinquish his revenge.

The man in question glanced up and caught his friends staring. Whatever expression was on their faces, it made him falter, his eyes skipping between them.

"Well, then . . ." he said. "It is time."

Wynter nodded gravely.

Razi studiously occupied himself with fixing the map case to his saddle. "Úlfnaor is certain that we will meet with a contact today. Should all go as planned, we will be in Alberon's camp by nightfall." He paused. "By nightfall. It is difficult to believe."

"What is the plan?" asked Wynter.

Razi glanced at Úlfnaor. "We will allow the Merron make first introductions. Úlfnaor wants to judge Alberon's intentions towards his people and does not want my presence to skew their reception. I think he is wise. My addition to their party can only serve to complicate what seems an already tangled set of negotiations."

"And you hope we will pass unnoticed?" said Christopher dryly. "No offence, Razi, but you're a touch of coal amidst the snowdrops here, ain't you? And Iseult and I, while pale enough, are like a couple of circus midgets next to this lot. We can hardly expect to remain inconspicuous for long."

Razi glanced sideways at his friend. "We can only do what we can do," he said, gathering his reins and preparing to mount. "Even the first few minutes of Alberon's greeting should give Úlfnaor a fair measure of his feelings towards him. That is something at least." He hopped the stirrup and rose fluidly into the saddle. "Perhaps we will get lucky," he said, eyeing their richly dressed companions, "and the flare of sunlight on silver will blind all to our presence."

Wynter gazed up at him and made no effort to hide the concern on her face.

"Are you ready, sis?" he asked. She nodded and he crooked a brief smile. "Then let us go, we have no more time to waste." He kicked his mare forward and trotted across to where Úlfnaor was just mounting his own horse.

"Well, lass," said Christopher, "tonight will tell us much."

He smiled at her, his grey eyes clear as ever. His arms were permanently bared to the shoulder now, exposing the silver spirals of the tribal bracelets that he wore in place of his own. With his long, loose hair and his borrowed, pale-green cloak, Wynter thought he looked very much the Merron, despite his relative lack of height.

"You look entirely at home," she said, and even to herself, her tone was hard to fathom.

The smile slid from Christopher's eyes, and Wynter instantly regretted its loss; it had been too long gone as it was. He straightened from his easy slouch, his hand shot to the bracelet at the top of his left arm, and he glanced uncertainly around.

"I . . ." he said. "Iseult. I ain't taken sides against . . ."

"Oh, Chris, stop!" She held up her hand, disgusted with herself. "I'm sorry."

She looked across the clearing to where Razi was speaking to Úlfnaor and ran her hand across her mouth. Christopher stood in silent discomfort by her side.

"I am sorry," she said again. "It is just, Razi changes his coat and shaves his face, and he is once again my Lord Razi. You," she gestured to Christopher's clothes. "You are once again a Merron. To tell the truth, I am envious, Christopher. I have no such armour, and the thought of riding into Albi's camp, naught but a ragged woman in dusty clothes, makes me feel vulnerable and alone."

Christopher held her gaze, searching. He lifted a hand to touch the heavy coil of hair pinned to her head. "Let loose your hair, Iseult, roll your sleeves to the shoulder." Solemnly, he ran his thumb across her cheekbone. "I will give you one of my bracelets, and, as my *croí-eile*, none would challenge your right to wear it."

Wynter closed her eyes and leant for a moment into his touch. Then she straightened. "Thank you," she said. "But those things would be nothing more than a disguise, Christopher. I am not Merron, and I never will be."

There was a moment of shock in Christopher's face, and

Wynter firmly held his gaze, her chin lifting. Then his expression hardened into acceptance and he nodded.

"You are Iseult Moorehawke," he said grimly. "The Protector Lady. You need no armour to make you thus." He reached behind her and handed her the reins of her horse. "Mount up, Protector Lady, and let us go."

He walked from her, his pale cloak swinging behind him, and Wynter turned away before he had even reached his horse. Once mounted, she breathed deeply and took a moment to survey the men and women around her. Then she sat straighter and schooled her features into the aloof detachment of her courtly mask.

I am the Protector Lady, she thought. *I have work to do.* She clucked Ozkar around and kicked forward.

When she came to a halt at Razi's side, Úlfnaor glanced absently her way. His eyes went to slide past, but almost immediately he frowned and looked back at her. Wynter held his eye without expression. For a moment, the Merron leader searched her face, uncertain. Then he bowed, dipping his head low so that his long hair fell forward over his shoulders. Wynter saw the shock in his people's faces and they stared up at her, their eyes wide. She surveyed them without a change of expression.

When Úlfnaor straightened from his bow, Wynter returned his graciousness with a regal tilting of her head. Christopher danced his horse to her side.

"Are we ready?" he asked, his voice hard.

Razi and Úlfnaor exchanged a look. Razi nodded, and together the two leaders wheeled their horses around and led their people onto the trail that would lead to Alberon's camp.

Glossary

The language used by the Merron in this book is equivalent to modern day Irish. The most commonly used words and phrases are translated here, except for any that are already translated in the text.

Note: Apparent inconsistencies in the spelling of some words, like "Domhan" and "Domhain", relate to the rules of Irish grammar.

abair leo a gcuid airm a chaitheamh uathu – tell them to throw down their arms
ach – but
a chroí – my dear
a dhuine uasail – honoured person
agus – and
amach leat – out with you! Get out!
a mhuirnín – beloved/sweetheart/darling
an bhfuil drochghoile ort aris? – have you a pain in your gut again?
an bhfuil tú ansin? – are you there?
An Domhan – the World (the Merron's version of God)
an Lá Deireanach – the Last Day

anois – now

anseo – here

ar son an Ghrá – for Love

bhféidir go n-inseofa dóibh go bhfuil *xxx* anseo – perhaps you would tell them that *xxx* is here

bhí Ashkr anseo – Ashkr was here

bhí orm mo chac a dhéanarmh – I had to take a shit

bígí ar bhur suaimhneas – relax, be calm

buíochas leat – thank you

cé hé sin? – who is that?

ce hiad na ceoltoirí – who are the musicians?

cén fáth an teanga coimhthíoch – why the foreign tongue?

cé thú féin? – who are you?

conas atá tú? – how are you?

croch leat! Agus ná bí ag stánadh – push off! And don't be staring

croí-eile – other-heart

dhá luch beaga – two small mice

fan liom – wait for me

fan nóiméad – wait for a moment

féach – look

fear saor – free man (*Is fear saor mise freisin* – I am a free man too)

filid – ancient noble and hereditary title. A filid would be responsible for preserving the history of his people in oral form and then teaching it to the next generation. The preservation of history in its oral form was very much the traditional role, and any moves to write history down would have been frowned upon. The modern version of this word, *file*, has come to mean simply "poet".

gabh mo leithscéal – excuse me

gread leat – shove off! Beat it!

iníon – daughter/daughter of

le meas – with respect

luch – mouse

lucha rua – red mouse

luichín – little mouse

mac – son/son of

maith sibh a chúnna – good dogs!

mura mhiste leat – if you don't mind

nach bhfuil?/nach ea? – isn't it/he/she?

nach Merron thú – are you not Merron?

níl mé ag eitilt – I am not flying

níl sé réidh – he isn't ready

níl sé go maith – he isn't well

níl Tabiyb ach ina coimhthíoch – Tabiyb is only a foreigner

puballmór – the words "puball mór" literally mean "big tent". Here the word "puballmór" signifies the Merron's distinctive conical tents

rua 'gus dubh – red and black

rud éigin le hól – something to drink

sea – yes

seachtain deireanach – last week

scéal? – a shortened version of "aon scéal?": what's the story? Any news?

suigí síos – sit down (plural)

tá an Domhan do m'iarraidh – the World is calling me

tá Ashkr ag fanacht le Sól – Ashkr is waiting for Sól

tabhair nóimead dúinn – give us a minute

táim beagnach in éineacht leat – I am nearly with you

tá go maith? – all right?

tá mo chac orm – I have to shit

tá m'uain tagtha – it is my time/my time has come

tarraing siar/tarraingígí siar – pull back (singular and plural)

tá sé beagnach ina mhaidin – it's nearly morning

tá sé caillte – he is lost

tá siad ina gcnap codlata – they are fast asleep

tá teanga na Hadran acu – they speak the Hadrish tongue

thóin caca – shit arse

tógfaidh Coinín m'áitse? – Coinín will take my place?

extras

www.orbitbooks.net

about the author

Born and raised in Dublin, Ireland, **Celine Kiernan** has spent the majority of her working life in the film business, and her career as a classical feature animator spanned over seventeen years. Celine wrote her first novel at the age of eleven, and hasn't stopped writing or drawing since. She also has a peculiar weakness for graphic novels as, like animation, they combine the two things she loves to do the most: drawing and storytelling. Now, having spent most of her time working between Germany, Ireland and the USA, Celine is married and the bemused mother of two entertaining teens. She lives a peaceful life in the blissful countryside of Cavan, Ireland.

Find out more about Celine Kiernan and other Orbit authors by registering for the free monthly newsletter at www.orbitbooks.net

Merron Religion, Ritual and Hierarchy

The Merron are a fiercely proud and independent nation, self-reliant and bowing their knee to no royalty but their own. For centuries they have followed the seasons as pastoral nomads, living off their tribal lands, and trading their famous crafts with the settled communities they call "village folk" or "foreigners" (*coimhthíoch*). However, their lives are rapidly changing for the worse. Under the violent and repressive rule of King Gunther Shirken and his heir the Royal Princess Marguerite, the Merron no longer have freedom of movement to travel with the seasons, nor the right to follow their ancient way of life. They find themselves gradually squeezed further and further into confined territories of the Northland mountains, far from the grass plains they need to maintain their herds of horses, and far from the way of life which has provided for them for generation after generation. They see their people persecuted and their religious leaders tortured and killed as part of the Shirkens' unrelenting effort to control all aspects of life in the Northland kingdom.

The Merron have become a desperate people, fast running out of time and options.

Each Merron clan has its own territory and, except for the annual gathering (*an aonach*) where the four tribes gather for a month-long fair, the clans rarely travel beyond the long established borders of their ancestral homes. To encroach on another clan's territory would be a terrible crime against Merron civil and religious law. Should a clan be forced to make such a move, even against their will, it would be expected that they make great reparation to both their God and their fellow clans or else find themselves outcast from the nation. To travel to a land where no tribe has ever dwelled is to move far from the sight of God (*An Domhan*). Should a clan find itself the first Merron in a new land, they would need to "make a bridge" between themselves and *An Domhan* and so awaken God to their presence. Failure to do so would condemn them to an existence separated from *An Domhan* and outside the natural order of things.

There are four tribes of Merron: Snake, Hawk, Bear and Panther. Though each tribe originates from a different area of the Northern Europes, and each has slightly differing traditions and cultures, all consider themselves Merron and all speak the Merron tongue. The noble-folk we meet in this book are envoys chosen by a council of all four tribes to negotiate on their behalf in the Southlands, and are religious and military leaders from the Panther and Bear tribes. Panther and Bear Merron would consider themselves the most traditional of the tribes, still following closely the fundamental principles of the Merron's ancient religion. Bear and Panther Merron often refer to themselves as the People (in reference to their being those most closely linked to *An Domhan*) but any followers of *An Domhan* are entitled to be considered one of the People.

The People practice an extreme and fundamental form of pantheism. To them, God is everything and everything that exists is but a manifestation of God. So to the Merron a human being is the same as a tree, a tree is the same as a rock, a rock is the same as a dog – because all of them are God in its many forms. God's most pure expression – its consciousness or its soul, if you like – is referred to as *Croi an Domhain* (the Heart of the World) and when a Merron dies he or she may walk with or within this consciousness as an honoured and beloved manifestation of God's heart, at once one with God but retaining their own individual personality and thoughts.

An Domhan's most treasured representatives amongst the living are those people called the *Caoirigh* (pl.). They are considered to be the closest of all living creatures to *Croi an Domhain* and as such are worshipped as the purest manifestation of *An Domhan*. They usually live long and honoured lives amongst the Merron, during which they lead Merron religious ceremonies, offer their blood as sacrifice to *An Domhan* and take "vision quests" in order to divine the future or communicate with *An Domhan*. As with all Merron ranks and higher professions, the title of *Caora* is hereditary, so the children of *Caoirigh* will inevitably grow up to be the next generation of *Caoirigh*. Sometimes it is an *Aoire* who will father or bear the child of a *Caora* but mostly *Caora* of one clan will reproduce with those of another. In general there can only be one

Caora per clan, but for a *Caora* to have a multiple birth (twins, triplets, etc.) would be considered fantastically auspicious and those children would be particularly honoured by the clan into whose care they were eventually given.

The *Caoirigh* are protected by a group of warriors known as *na (fir/mná) Fada* (the Long (Men/Women) Born into their titles, *na Fadaí* (pl.) are sent to special camps where they are trained from childhood to defend the Merron faith. In ancient times they would have been the enforcers of religious law. Their duties would have included punishing dissenters and ensuring strict adherence to the religion's rules. In *The Crowded Shadows, na Fadaí* that accompany Úlfnaor are there as much to ensure he fulfils his duty as they are there to protect him.

As *An Domhan*'s most honoured representatives amongst the living, the *Caoirigh* are the highest authority in Merron religious matters. Their word is final when it comes to religious law. However, most *Caoirigh* are happy to leave everything to their *Aoire* (Shepherd) and it is the *Aoirí* (pl.) who truly wield all the power and carry all the responsibility for religious and political matters amongst the Merron people. They are the Merron's royalty, their politicians and their decision makers.

The future of the Merron people is in their hands.

The Merron are very keen on openness and overt shows of honesty and trust. They openly wear the symbols of their tribal affiliations on their arms and in painted symbols on their horses and homes. They take offence at the slightest implication that they may be untrustworthy or criminally inclined and make a show of offering the same trust to visiting members of other tribes or clans.

Names are extremely important since a Merron name tells that person's family lineage, their profession, their hereditary titles and sometimes (as with the name Garron) the place where that person was born. The exchange of names is a sign of trust and acceptance. You must be invited to introduce yourself to a Merron – especially a Merron nobleperson. Just to walk up and offer your name is a huge social faux pas that would be accepted with resignation from a *coimhthíoch* but severely frowned upon from another Merron.

The wearing of long hair is a symbol of tribal affiliation. Up until a certain age (nine or ten) children of both sexes wear their hair cropped close to their head, only being allowed to grow it long once they have been accepted as adult members of their tribe. Around this time they will also receive their tribal bracelets. For an adult Merron to have their hair shorn, or to shear their own hair, is symbolic of them having been cast from or breaking their affiliation with their tribe. In *The Crowded Shadows* Sólmundr and Ashkr give Christopher a set of Bear bracelets to symbolise Christopher's adoption into the Bear tribe. In reality, Christopher's adoption would first have to be approved by an *Aoire*. Then he would need to be publicly "named" by his adopting parent (in this case Sólmundr) who would cut and burn Christopher's hair as a symbolic casting aside of Christopher's allegiance to the Snake Merron and his starting anew as a child of the Bear. Due to the circumstances of *The Crowded Shadows*, Christopher's adoption would certainly have been accepted by the Merron travel party, but as soon as is possible (probably at the next *aonach*) Sól and he will need to go through the full adoption ceremony – including the shearing of Christopher's hair and Sólmundr's publicly naming him as his son.

This adoption would be a bittersweet acceptance for Christopher who has witnessed his "first father", the *filid* Aidan Garron, struggle against his superiors in order to improve the lot of the Merron people. Aidan Garron understood that the Merron way of life was no longer sustainable, and he fought to preserve Merron tradition while trying to move his people forward as a nation. He knew that in order to survive the changes around them, the Merron needed to adapt. But in the end, the struggle to change the Merron mindset proved too difficult, and Aidan Garron chose a life apart from the tribes rather then continue the fight to save them.

Christopher understands that in everything they do and say the Merron are upholding a code which outsiders find difficult to understand, and it is this which often leaves them open to misinterpretation. For example, though they are skilled diplomats and fluent in several Northland languages, the Merron in *The Crowded Shadows* insist on communicating via Hadrish, a language they barely know. To them this is a point of pride and personal honour, a gesture of respect to their guests. To outsiders it can make them appear ignorant, even brutish. In this, as in many aspects of their behaviour, the Merron stand in their own way. By refusing to bend to circumstance and adapt to their surroundings they are perpetuating the misunderstandings and miscommunication which may well be the undoing of their nation. For it is this vulnerability which Marguerite Shirken hopes to exploit to her own end, and so it may be that the pride and tradition which has kept the Merron strong for centuries may be the very thing which aids in their ultimate destruction.

if you enjoyed
THE CROWDED SHADOWS

look out for

LORD OF THE
CHANGING WINDS

by

Rachel Neumeier

Chapter 1

The griffins came to Feierabiand with the early summer warmth, riding the wind out of the heights down to the tender green pastures of the foothills. The wind they brought with them was a hard, hot wind, with nothing of the gentle Feierabiand summer about it. It tasted of red dust and hot brass.

Kes, gathering herbs in the high pastures above the village of Minas Ford, saw them come: great bronze wings shining in the sun, tawny pelts like molten gold, sunlight striking harshly off beaks and talons. One was a hard shining white, one red as the coals at the heart of a fire. The griffins rode their wind like soaring eagles, wings outstretched and still. The sky took on a fierce metallic tone as they passed. They turned around the shoulder of the mountain and disappeared, one and then another and another, until they had all passed out of sight. Behind them, the sky softened slowly to its accustomed gentle blue.

Kes stood in hills above the high pastures, barefoot, her hair tangled, her hands full of fresh-picked angelica, and watched until the last of the griffins slid out of view. They were the most beautiful creatures she had ever seen. She almost followed them, running around the curve of the mountain's shoulder, leaving her angelica and elecampane and goldenseal to wilt in the sun; she even took a step after them before she thought better of the idea.

But Tesme hated it when Kes did not come home by dusk; she hated it worse when her sister did not come home before dawn. So Kes hesitated one moment and then another, knowing that if she followed the griffins she would forget time and her sister's expectations. There would be noise and fuss, and then it would be days before Tesme once again gave reluctant leave for Kes to go up into the hills. So she stayed where she was on the mountainside, only shading her eyes with her hand as she tried to follow the griffins with her eyes and imagination around the curve of the mountain.

Griffins, she thought. *Griffins . . .* She walked slowly down from the hills, crossed the stream to the highest of the pastures, and went on downhill, her eyes filled with blazing wings and sunlight. She climbed stone walls without really noticing them, one after another: high pasture to hill pasture. hill pasture down to the midlands pasture. And then the low pasture, nearest the barns and the house: the fence here was rail instead of stone. This meant Kes had no convenient flat-topped wall on which to put her basket while climbing over. She balanced it awkwardly against her hip and clambered over the fence with one hand.

Her sister, Tesme, spotted Kes as she walked past the nearest barn and hurried to meet her. The griffins, it was plain, had not come down so far as the house; Tesme's eyes held nothing of fire and splendor. They were filled instead with thoughts of heavy mares and staggering foals. And with worry. Kes saw that. It pulled her back toward the ordinary concerns of home and horse breeding.

"Kes!" said her sister. "Where have you been?" She glanced at the basket of herbs and went on quickly, "At least, I see where you've been; all right, fine, did you happen to get milk thistle while you were in the hills?"

Kes, blinking away images of shining wings, shook her head and made a questioning gesture toward the foaling stable.

"It's River," Tesme said tensely. "I think she's going to have a difficult time. I should never have bred her to that Delta stud. He was too big for her, I knew he was, but oh, I want this foal!"

Kes nodded, taking a step toward the house.

"I got your things out for you – they're in the barn – along with your shoes," Tesme added, her gaze dropping to Kes's bare feet. But her tone was more worried than tart, the foaling mare distracting her from her sister's lack of civilized manners. "You just want your ordinary kit, don't you? Don't worry about those herbs – somebody can take them to the house for you." Tesme took Kes by the shoulder and hurried her toward the barn.

In the foaling barn, Kes absently handed her basket to one of the boys and waved him off toward the house. Tesme hovered anxiously. Kes saw that she could not tell Tesme about the griffins; not now. She tried to make herself focus on the mare. Indeed, once she saw her, it became less of an effort to forget sunlit magnificence and concentrate instead on normal life. River, a stocky bay mare with bulging sides, was clearly uncomfortable. And certainly very large. She looked to have doubled her width since Kes had last looked at her, and that had only been a handful of days ago.

"Do you think she could be carrying twins?" Tesme asked apprehensively. She was actually wringing her hands.

"From the look of her, she could be carrying triplets," Meris commented, swinging through the wide barn doors. "I've been waiting for her to explode for the past month, and now look at her. Kes, glad to see you. Tesme, just how big was that stud?"

"Huge," Tesme said unhappily. "But I wanted size. River's not *that* small. I thought it would be a safe cross."

Kes shrugged. Usually crossing horses of different sizes worked all right, but sometimes it didn't. No one knew why. She looked at her kit, then back at the mare.

"Mugwort," she suggested. "Partridge berry."

"Good idea," said Meris. "Partridge berry to calm her down and help her labor at the beginning – mugwort later, I suppose, in case we need to help the strength of her contractions. I have water boiling. Want me to make the decoctions?"

Kes nodded.

Meris was a quick-moving little sparrow of a woman, plain and sensible and good-humored, equally at home with a foaling mare or a birthing woman. Kes was far more comfortable with her than with most other people; Meris never tried to draw Kes out or make her talk; when Kes did talk, Meris never seemed surprised at what she said. Meris was willing, as so few people seemed to be, to simply let a person or an animal be what it was. No wonder Tesme had sent for Meris. Even if River had no difficulty with her foal, just having Meris around would calm everyone's nerves. That would be good. Kes gave the older woman the packets of herbs and slipped into the stall to touch River's neck. The mare bent her neck around and snuffled down Kes's shirt. She was sweating, pawing at the stall floor nervously. Kes patted her again.

"What do you think?" Tesme asked, seeming almost as distressed as the mare. "Is she going to be all right, do you think?"

Kes shrugged. "Jos?" If they had to pull this foal, she wanted someone with the muscle to do it. Jos had been a drifter. Tesme had hired him for the season six years past, and he had just never seemed inclined to drift away again. He was very strong. And the horses liked him. Kes liked him too. He didn't *talk* at you all the time, or expect you to talk back.

"I'll get him," Tesme agreed, and hurried out.

Kes frowned at the mare, patting her in absent reassurance. River twitched her ears back and walked in a circle, dropping her head and shifting her weight. She was thinking of lying down but was too uncomfortable to do so: Tesme, with her affinity for horses, could have made the mare lie down. Kes neither held an affinity for any animal nor possessed any other special gift – if one did not count an unusual desire to abandon shoes and sister and walk up alone into the quiet of the hills. She did not usually envy Tesme her gift, but she would have liked to be able to make River lie down. She could only coax the mare down with a touch and a murmur.

Fortunately, that was enough. Kes stepped hastily out of the way when the mare folded up her legs and collapsed awkwardly onto the straw.

"How is she?" Tesme wanted to know, finally returning with Jos. Kes gave her sister a shrug and Jos a nod. He nodded back wordlessly and came to lean on the stall gate next to her.

Foals came fast, usually. There was normally no fuss about them. If there was trouble, it was likely to be serious trouble. But it would not help, in either case, to flutter around like so many broken-winged birds and disturb the mare further. Kes watched River, timing the contractions that rippled down the mare's sides, and thought there was not yet any need to do anything but wait.

Waiting, Kes found her mind drifting toward a hard pale sky, toward the memory of harsh light striking off fierce curved beaks and golden feathers. Tesme did not notice her bemusement. But Jos said, "Kes?"

Kes blinked at him, startled. The cool dimness of the foaling barn seemed strange to her, as though the fierce sun the griffins had brought with them had somehow become more real to her than the gentle summer of Minas Ford.

"Are you well?" Jos was frowning at her, curious. Even concerned. Did she seem so distracted? Kes nodded to him and made a dismissive "it's *nothing*" kind of gesture. He did not seem fully convinced.

Then Tesme called Kes's name sharply, and, pulling her attention back to the mare, Kes went back to lay a hand on River's flank and judge how she was progressing.

The foal *was* very big. But Kes found that, after all, once the birth began, there was not much trouble about the foaling. It had its front feet in the birth canal and its nose positioned properly forward. She nodded reassuringly at her sister and at Jos.

Tesme gave back a little relieved nod of her own, but it was Jos who was the happiest. The last time a foaling had gone badly, the foal had been turned the wrong way round, both front legs hung up on the mare's pelvis. Jos had not been able to push the foal back in enough to straighten the legs; he had had to break them to get the foal out. It had been born dead, which was as well. That had been a grim job that none of them had any desire to repeat, and the memory of it was probably what had wound Tesme up in nervous worry.

This time, Kes waited until the mare was well into labor. Then she simply tied a cord around each of the foal's front hooves, and while Tesme stood at the mare's head and soothed her, she and Jos added a smooth pull to the mare's next contraction. The foal slid right out, wet and dark with birthing liquids.

'A filly!" said Meris, bending to check.

"Wonderful," Tesme said fervently. "Wonderful. Good *girl*, River!"

The mare tipped her ears forward at Tesme, heaved herself to her feet, turned around in the straw, and nosed the baby, which thrashed itself to its feet and tottered. Jos steadied it when it would have fallen. It was sucking strongly only minutes later.

After that, it was only natural to go to the village inn to celebrate. Tesme changed into a clean skirt and braided her hair and gave Kes a string of polished wooden beads to braid into hers. Tesme was happy. She had her foal from the Delta stud – a filly – and all was right with the world. Jos stayed at the farm, keeping an eye on the baby foal; he rarely went to the village during the day, though he visited the inn nearly every evening to listen to the news that travelers brought and to have a mug of ale and a game of pian stones with the other men.

Kes was not so happy. She would as soon have stayed at the farm with Jos and had bread and cheese quietly. But Tesme would have been unhappy if she had refused to go. She was never happy when Kes seemed too solitary. She said Kes was more like a silent, wild creature of the hills than a girl, and when she said such things, she worried. Sometimes she worried for days, and that was hard on them both. So Kes made no objection to the beads or the shoes or the visit to the inn.

They walked. The road was dry and firm at the verge, and Tesme – oddly, for a woman who raised horses –

liked to walk. Kes put one properly shod foot in front of another and thought about griffins. Bronze feathers caught by the sun, tawny flanks like gold. Beaks that gleamed like metal. Her steps slowed.

"Come on," Tesme said, and impatiently, "There's nothing to be afraid of, Kes!"

Kes blinked, recalled back to the ordinary road and the empty sky. She didn't say that she was not afraid, exactly. I had been a long time since she'd tried to explain to Tesme her feelings about people, about crowds, about the hard press of their expectations. From the time she had been little, everyone else had seemed to see the world from a different slant than Kes. To understand, without even trying, unspoken codes and rules that only baffled her. Talking to people, trying to shape herself into what they expected, was not exactly frightening. But it was exhausting and confusing and, in a way, the confusion itself was frightening. But Tesme did not seem able to understand any of this. Kes had long since given up trying to explain herself to her sister.

Nor did Kes mention griffins. There seemed no place for them in Tesme's eyes. Kes tried to forget the vision of heat and beauty, to see only the ordinary countryside that surrounded them. To please her sister, she walked a little more quickly.

But Tesme, who had been walking quickly and impatiently with her hands shoved into the pockets of her skirt, slowed in her turn. She said, "Kes—"

Kes looked at her inquiringly. The light of the sun slid across Tesme's face, revealing the small lines that had come into her face and set themselves permanently between her eyes and at the corners of her generous mouth. Her wheaten hair, braided with a strand of polished wooden beads and tucked up in a coil, held the first strands of gray.

She looked, Kes thought, startled, like the few faint memories she had of their mother. Left at nineteen to hold their father's farm and raise her much younger sister, married twice and twice quickly widowed, Tesme had never yet showed much sign of care or worry or even the passage of time. But she showed it now. Kes looked down again, ashamed to have worried her.

"Are you all right?" Tesme asked gently. She usually seemed a little distracted when she spoke to her sister, when she spoke to anyone; she was always thinking about a dozen different things – mostly practical things, things having to do with raising horses and running the farm.

But Kes thought she was paying attention now. That was uncomfortable: Kes preferred to slip gently around the edges of everyone else's awareness – even Tesme's. Close attention made her feel exposed. Worse than exposed: at risk. As though she stood in the shadows at the edge of brilliant, dangerous light, light that would burn her to ash if it fell on her. Kes always found it difficult to speak; she never knew what anyone expected her to say. But when pinned by the glare of close attention, the uncertainty she felt was much worse. She managed, in a voice that even to her own ears sounded faltering and unpersuasive. "I – I'm all right. I'm fine."

"You seem preoccupied, somehow."

Since Tesme frequently noted aloud that her sister seemed preoccupied, even when she was paying quite close attention, Kes did not know how to answer this.

"There's something . . . *Is* there something wrong?"

Kes could find no words to describe the magnificence of bronze wings in the sun. She would have tried, for Tesme. But the mere thought of trying to explain the griffins, the hard heat they had brought with them, the strange look of the sky when they crossed it in their brilliant flight . . . She shook her head, mute.

Tesme frowned at her. "No one has been, well, bothering you, have they?"

For a long moment, Kes didn't understand what her sister meant. Then, taken aback, she blushed fiercely and shook her head again.

Tesme had come to a full halt. She reached out as though to touch Kes on the arm, but then her hand fell. "Some of the boys can be, well, boys. And you're so quiet. Sometimes that can encourage them. And besides the boys . . ." She hesitated. Then she said, "I like Jos, and he's a wonderful help around the farm, but Kes, if he bothers you, you surely know I'll send him away immediately."

Kes said, startled, "Jos?"

"I know you wouldn't encourage him, Kes, but lately I've thought sometimes that he might be, well, watching you."

"*Jos* doesn't bother me," Kes said, and was startled by the vehemence of her tone. She moderated it. "I like Jos. He wouldn't . . . he isn't . . . and he's too old, anyway!"

"Oh, well, Kes! He's not *that* old, and he's not blind, and you're growing up and getting pretty, and if he notices you too much, there are other places he could get work." But Tesme looked somewhat reassured. She started walking again, if not as quickly.

Kes hurried the few steps necessary to catch up. "I like Jos," she said again. She did, she realized. His quiet, his calm, the competent way he handled the horses. The way he never pressed her to speak, or seemed to expect her to fit into some unexplained pattern of behavior she couldn't even recognize. He was comfortable to be around, as so few people were. He had been at the farm for . . . nearly half her life, Kes thought. She could not imagine it without him. 'He doesn't bother me, Tesme. Really, he doesn't. Don't send him away."

"All right . . ." Tesme said doubtfully, and began to walk a little more quickly. "But let me know if you change your mind."

It was easier to nod than protest again.

They walked a little farther. But then Tesme gave Kes a sideways look and added, "Now, if there's a boy you *do* like, you'd let me know, Kes, wouldn't you? I remember what I was like at your age, and shy as you are, you *are* getting to be pretty. You know you don't need to slip off silently to meet somebody, don't you? If you want to walk out with Kanne or Sef or somebody, that's different, but you would tell me, wouldn't you? There's a world of trouble for a girl who's too secretive, believe me."

Kes felt her face heat. "I don't like anyone!" she protested.

"That changes," Tesme said, her tone wry. "If it changes for you, Kes . . ."

"I'll tell you. I'll tell you," Kes said hastily, hoping to sound so firmly reassuring that Tesme would let the subject die. It was true anyway. Kanne? She suppressed an urge to roll her eyes, not wanting her sister to reopen the subject – but *Kanne?* Kanne was a baby, and too interested in himself to even notice a girl. Sef was almost as bad, all but welded to the smithy where he was apprenticed. Kes couldn't imagine either of them, or any other of the village boys, ever choosing to simply walk out across the hills and listen to the wind and the silence.

"All right . . ." Tesme said. She did sound somewhat reassured. "It's true you're not much like I was. On the whole, that's probably just as well." She glanced at Kes, half smiling and half worried.

Kes had no idea what to say to this, and so said nothing.

"You're yourself, that's all," Tesme concluded at last, smiling. She patted Kes on the shoulder and lengthened her stride once more.

The inn, set by the road near the river, right at the edge of the village, was all white stone and dark wooden beams. It had a dozen pretty little tables in its wide, walled courtyard, across from its stables, which were screened from the inn by small trees and beds of flowers. Jerreid and his wife, Edlin, and their daughters ran the inn, which was widely acknowledged to be the best of all the little country inns along the western river road that ran from Niambe Lake all the way down to Terabiand. The inn was not overlarge, but it was pleasant and very clean, and every window looked out onto one flower garden or another. And the food was good.

Many ordinary folk and even nobles broke their journey in Minas Ford as they traveled from the little jewel-pretty cities of the high north to the sprawling coastal town of Terabiand in the south – the Ford of the town's name had long ago been replaced by the best bridge anywhere along the river – and, as the saying went, everyone and everything passed along the coast at some time. And so a good proportion of everyone and every-thing traveled up from Terabiand and through Minas Ford eventually, and since Minas Ford was conveniently a long day's journey from Bered to the south and an easy day's journey from Riamne to the north, many travelers looked forward to a stay at Jerreid's pretty little inn.

Every upstairs room had a window, shutters open in this fine weather; every table, outdoors or in, was graced by a slender vase of flowers. Edlin made the vases of fine white clay, glazing them with translucent glazes in blue and pink and white. She made them to keep cut flowers, and she had the gift of making in her hands: It was common knowledge that flowers stayed fresh in one of Edlin's vases twice as long as they lasted in an old cracked mug.

Edlin also made tableware that was both pretty and very hard to break. She sold bowls and plates and platters from a shop behind the inn, leaving the running of the inn almost entirely to her husband and their three daugh-ters. Edlin grew the flowers herself, though, and picked them fresh every week to arrange in the vases. That was, famously, as close to the work of the inn as she would come. Jerreid, fortunately, seemed perfectly happy to leave his wife to her dishes and glazes and gardens.

"Tesme!" Jerreid said, as they came into the yard. He was a big, bluff, genial man with a talent for making his inn feel homey and all his visitors feel welcome. He'd been leaning against one of the outdoor tables, chatting with what looked like half the folk of the village – a big crowd for the middle of the day. There were no travelers present at the moment, although some would probably stop later in the day. But Chiad and his wife had torn themselves away from their farm to visit the inn, along with a dozen children and cousins and nephews. And Heste had abandoned her bakery for the moment – well, the morning bread was long out of the ovens, and perhaps she had a little time before she would start the pies and honey cakes for the evening. But Nehoen was also present, which was less usual. His big house with its sprawling lands lay well outside the village, and he did not usually come to the inn except on market day. And Caris had for some reason left her weaving to visit the inn, as well as Kanes and his apprentice Sef the smithy.

Kes looked at them all nervously, wondering nervously whether she might guess what had drawn them all away from their ordinary business. She hoped she did not blush when she glanced at Kanne or Set. How could Tesme possibly think—? Was Kanne even fourteen yet? And Sef! She looked hastily away from the smith's apprentice, aware that she probably *was* blushing, now.

"You seem happy," Jerreid was saying to Tesme. His smile, at least, seemed ordinarily cheerful. "How is your mare? River, wasn't it? She must have done well by you, yes?"

"Yes, yes, yes!" Tesme came across the yard, leaving Kes to follow more slowly. She took Jerreid's hands in hers and smiled at him. "A filly, healthy and big, and River's fine. We're celebrating. Have you any blackberry wine left, or did you drink it all yourself?"

"We've plenty—"

"But you might want to hold off on the celebrations." said Chiad. Dark as the earth he worked, serious by nature and not given to celebrations at even the best of times, he looked at the moment even more somber than usual. He slapped the table with one broad hand for emphasis as he spoke.

"Give the woman a chance to catch her breath!" exclaimed Jerreid, shaking his head in mild disapproval.

Chiad gave him a blink of incomprehension and instantly transferred his attention back to Tesme. "You've got your young foals down by the house, haven't you, Tesme? Do you know what Kanne saw this morning?" Kanne was Chiad's son, and he now sat up straight in his chair and looked important.

Kes knew. She heard it in Chiad's voice. She saw it in Kanne's eyes.

Tesme arched her eyebrows, still smiling, if a little less certainly. "If it wasn't someone underselling me with Delta-bred stock for cheap, I don't think I'll mind, whatever it was."

"You will," said Chiad, heavily, with a somber shake of his head. "Tell her, boy."

Kanne laid his hands down flat on the table and sat up even straighter, looking proud and important. "Griffins!" he said.

This had not been what Tesme expected, and she looked blank.

"Griffins!" Chiad said. He slapped the table, shaking his head again in heavy disapproval. "Of all things! Half lion, half eagle, and all killer! My barley is likely safe enough, but you'd best look after your stock, Tesme!"

Tesme still looked blank. She said after a moment, "Kanne, are you sure they weren't just eagles?"

"Now, that's what I said," Jerreid agreed, nodding.

"Sure, I'm sure," Kanne said importantly. "I *am* sure! I know what eagles look like, Jerreid! These weren't eagles or vultures or any bird!"

"Griffins never leave their desert," said Heste, frowning. Her attitude suggested that she had said this before, repeatedly.

"They do," said Nehoen, so patiently it was clear he'd said this before as well. "Griffins in the spring mean a hard summer." Nehoen was not sitting at the table. He had gotten to his feet when Tesme and Kes had entered the courtyard. Now he moved restlessly, leaning his hip against one of the tables and crossing his arms over his chest. He was old, nearly fifty, but he was one of the few gentlemen of the village and thus showed his age far less than a farmer or smith.

"What?" said Tesme, blinking at him.

Nehoen smiled at her. He owned all the land out on the west side of the village near the river, and he could not only read, but owned far more books than all the rest of Minas Ford put together. His grandmother had been an educated woman of the Delta, and had put great store by books and written learning. He explained now, "Griffins in the fall mean an easy winter, griffins in the spring a hard summer. They say that in Casmantium. There wouldn't be a saying about it if the griffins never left their country of fire to come into the country of earth."

"But why would they?" Tesme asked. "And why come

so far? Not just so far south, either, but all the way across the mountains into Feierabiand?"

"Well, that I don't know. The mages of Casmantium keep them out of Casmantian lands—that's what their cold mages are for, isn't it?—so maybe if the griffins wanted to move, they had to cross the mountains. But why they left their own desert in the first place?" Nehoen shrugged. "Who can guess why such creatures do anything?"

"Griffins are bad for fire," said Kanes. The smith's deep voice rumbled, and everyone hushed to listen to him. "That's what I know. They're made of fire, and fire falls from the wind their wings stirs up. That's what smiths say. They're bad creatures to have about."

Smiths knew fire. Everyone was silent for a moment, thinking about that.

"Griffins," said Jerreid at last, shaking his head.

"Griffins," agreed Nehoen. He began a rough sketch on a sheet of paper somebody had given him.

Chiad's wife said, practically, as she was always practical, "Saying Kanne is right, as I think he is, then what? Fire and hard summers, maybe—and then maybe not. But it stands to reason a creature with eagle talons and lion claws will hunt."

"Surely—" Tesme began, and stopped, looking worried. "You don't think they would eat our horses, really?"

"Nellis stops wolves from eating livestock," said Chiad, laying a broad hand on his wife's hand.

She nodded to him and went on herself, "Jenned stops mountain cats. Perren stops hawks from coming after chicks." Perren was a falconer as well as a farmer, and gentled hawks and falcons for the hunt. Chiad's wife added, "I can keep foxes off the hens, and my little Seb stops weasels and stoats. But I don't know who's going to stop griffins eating your foals or my sheep, if that's what they want. What we need is a cold mage. I wonder why our mages in Feierabiand never thought to train up a youngster or two in cold magic?"

"We've never needed cold magecraft before," Chiad answered his wife, but not as though he found this argument persuasive.

His wife lifted her shoulders in a scornful shrug. "Well, and we don't need ice cellars until the summer heat, or a second lot of seed grain until a wet spring rots the first sowing; that's why we plan ahead, isn't it? They should have thought ahead, up there in Tihannad—"

"Now, now." Jerreid shook his head at Chiad's wife in mild reproof. "Summer we have every year, and wet springs often enough, but if griffins have ever come across the mountains before, it was so long ago none of our fathers or grandfathers remember it. Be fair, Nellis."

"Whoever thought or didn't think, it's my horses that are going to be eaten by griffins," said Tesme, sitting down rather abruptly at the table in the chair Nehoen had abandoned.

"They wouldn't eat them," Nehoen said, patting her shoulder. "Griffins don't eat. They may look part eagle and part lion, but they're wholly creatures of fire. They hunt to kill, but they don't eat what they bring down."

"That's even worse!" Tesme exclaimed, and rubbed her forehead.

Kes watched her sister work through the idea of griffins

coming down on her horses. It clearly took her a moment. She wasn't used to thinking of the danger a big predator might pose if no one in the village could speak to it or control it.

In every country there were folk with each of the three common gifts. But just as Casmantian folk were famously dark and big-boned and stocky, Casmantian makers and builders were famously the best. There were makers everywhere, but more and better makers in Casmantium; to find makers with the strongest gifts and the deepest dedication lo their craft, to find builders who could construct the strongest walls and best roads and tallest palaces, one went to Casmantium.

In the same way, one could recognize Linularinan people because they commonly had hair the color of light ale and narrow, secretive eyes, but also because they were clever and loved poetry. Everyone in Linularinum could write, they said, so probably it wasn't surprising that Linularinum had the cleverest legists. There were legists in Feierabiand, at least in the cities, but if you wanted a really unbreakable contract that would do exactly what you wanted, you hired a Linularinan legist to write it for you.

But everyone knew that if you needed someone with a really *strong* affinity for a particular sort of animal, you came to Feierabiand. As Tesme held an affinity to horses, others held affinities to crows or mice or deer or dogs. In Feierabiand, every town and village and tiny hamlet had one or two people who could call wolves and mountain cats—and more important, send them away. But griffins were creatures of fire, not earth. No matter how dangerous or destructive they might prove, no one, even in Feierabiand, would be able send the griffins back across the mountains.

Tesme was looking more and more unhappy. "Maybe you and Edlin would let us borrow the use of your lower pasture for a while?" she said to Jerreid. "Mine isn't big enough for all the horses. Will I have to move all the horses, do you think? How big are griffins'? How many did you see, Kanne?"

"Dozens," the boy said. He sounded pleased about it. "Big."

Nehoen silently held out a sketch he'd drawn. It showed an animal with a savage look: a creature half feathered and half furred, with the cruel hooked beak and talons of an eagle and the haunches of a cat. Everyone crowded forward to look. Kes, peering over Kanes's shoulder, winced a little. The monster in the drawing was a crude misshapen thing, neither bird nor beast; it looked clumsy and vicious.